I0600966

Winter's Mother 2

Winter's Magic Part 4

L. STARLA

Disclaimer: This is a work of fiction. Names, characters, businesses, places, events, locales, and incidents are either the products of the author's imagination or used in a fictitious manner. Any resemblance to actual persons, living or dead, or actual events is purely coincidental.

WINTER'S MOTHER 2 Copyright © 2023 Laelia Starla.
All rights reserved. No part of this publication may be reproduced, distributed, or transmitted in any form or by any means, including photocopying, recording, or other electronic or mechanical methods, without the prior written permission of the publisher, except in the case of brief quotations embodied in critical reviews and certain other non-commercial uses permitted by copyright law.

To request permission, contact the author:
laelia@starlaarts.com

Cover illustration © Jana Hoffmann
Graphics & book design by L. Starla
Editing by Felix Staica

First edition 2023.

ISBN-13 (Paperback) 978-0-6452783-7-8
ISBN-13 (eBook) 978-0-6452783-6-1

Note from the Author

This book contains coarse language, and scorching hot sex scenes, including steamy m/m/f and m/f/f romance, that may upset or offend some readers.

Dedication

—This one is for Angel the cat who has kept my lap warm during long writing sessions, and whose antics inspired the character, Luna.

Epigraph

"Fairy tales are more than true: not because they tell us that dragons exist, but because they tell us that dragons can be beaten."
—Neil Gaiman

Playlist

"Everything is Burning" IAMX
"The Way We Were" Stateside
"Reach" The Butterfly Effects
"Losing Hold" Esterly; Austin Jenckes
"Bloody City" Sam Tinnesz
"Love and War" Fleurie
"Deep Water" American Authors
"Forever & Ever More" Nothing But Thieves
"Goliath" Karnivool
"Every Step That I Take" Tom Morello; Portugal, The Man;
Whethan
"Fever Pitch" Grey Hearts Red
"Stardust" IAMX
'Red Stars" The Birthday Massacre
"The Parting Glass" Ronan Keating
"Fire In Me" Julia Stone
"Novocaine For The Soul" Eels
"Warrior" Anilah
"Radioactive" Imagine Dragons
"Fire Breather" Laurel
"Burn" 2WEI, Edda Hayes

Playlist available on Spotify.

The Cast of Characters

The Council of Mages, Fleurieu District

High Magus: Kieran Lane, Monique's father (Mayor)
Seat of Aether Mana: Alannah Winters (Conjurer, Dress Maker)
Seat of Elemental Mana: Liam Winters (Warlock, Police Officer)
Seat of Organic Mana: Ross Winters (Abjurer, Doctor)
Seat of Emotional Mana: Nora Winters, née Maher (Shaman, Vet)
Seat of Energy Mana: Steve Maher (Alchemist, Pharmacist)
Seat of Names Mana: Monique Lane (Alchemist, Council's Secretary)
Seat of Cosmic Mana: Lucas Ó Máille (Clairvoyant, Lawyer)
Seat of Physical Forces Mana: Matthew Ryan (Warlock, Police Officer)
Seat of Matter Mana: Mr. Duncan Sheridan (Alchemist, Pharmacist)
Seat of Senses Mana: Mr. James Maher (Illusionist)

Adult Pure Blood Mages

Brendan Winters, (Enchanter, Dark Syndicate Boss)
Alvar Elofsson (Seelie Noble), Married to Estelar
Danny Erling (Warlock, Police Officer), from Mount Gambier
Johnathan Ryan (Warlock, Limestone Coast District Leader, Mayor), from Mount Gambier
Jaxon Hayes (Warlock, Police Officer), from New South Wales
High Magus O'Grady (Mayor), from New South Wales
Jessica Ó Máille (Clairvoyant)
Chester Rowan (Conjurer)

Teenage Mages

Neve Winters, daughter of Alannah & Brendan Winters
Jasper Rowan, son of Chester Rowan
Caitlin Maher, daughter of Monique Lane & Steve Maher
Fiona Ryan, daughter of Jessica Ó Máille & Matthew Ryan
Lorcán Ó Máille, son of Lucas Ó Máille
Kane Sheridan, grandson of Duncan Sheridan
Rónán Doyle, son of Danielle Sheridan

Other Magicals

Cara Hughes (Half-mage Shaman, Conservationist)
Jacob Bennett (Boggart, Dark Syndicate Spymaster)
Caleb Hawthorn (Fae- Endarkened, Unemployed)
Bridey Hawthorn (Fae- Endarkened), Caleb's older sister
Estelar (Elven Princess of the Seelie Court)
Erik & Elna Alvarsson, (Fae- Enlightened), twin children of
Alvar & Estelar
Saoirse (Mermage Warrior)
Tyler Quirke (Half-mage Warlock, Police Officer), from New
South Wales
Nick Patterson (Orc, Orchardist)
Ben Sanders (Weredingo, Vet Assistant)
Connor Foley (Half-mage Abjurer, Marine Biologist)
Bailey Dougherty (Half-mage Warlock, Bartender)
Bianca Oakley (Fae- Wood Nymph, Cabaret Singer)
Amy Smith (Dwarf, Metallurgist & Council Blacksmith)
Luna (Alannah's cat, not technically magical).

Chapter One

Everything beyond the mystic perimeter was burning. Fire rained in apocalyptic torrents from the mouths of three gargantuan beasts in the sky. Liam crossed the garden toward the Mount Gambier Council Chambers. Jerking his head towards the sound of his name, he spotted Bailey Dougherty beside the pub across the carpark. *Figures he'd gravitate towards his natural habitat.* He started striding toward Bailey but stopped when the warlock punk shook his head and pointed down the street. Lava continued to flow from the Blue Lake, although the recently erected wards kept the magma from reaching the Council Chambers and surrounding buildings.

Bailey jogged up to him. 'On the horizon, look!' He gestured to the distant shadows flying directly for Mount Gambier. 'Looks like more of their friends are coming.'

'Shit! They must be from the southern seamounts.' He wished he could channel senses mana or get his hands on a pair of binoculars so he could see the dragons clearly. 'We need to hurry and evacuate the rest of this area before they get here. Have you cleared out your sector?'

'Yeah, Naracoorte's empty. Cara and I have been helping with this place.'

'Thanks, man. I better let the mayor know what's going on. Keep your eye on the sky and get me on the radio if you have any issues.'

With a nod, Bailey took off toward Cara Hughes, his girlfriend. Liam had paired them on purpose because their relationship gave them additional incentive to protect one another. A pang of jealousy tightened his chest as he watched them work together and for the umpteenth time that day; he wanted his wife by his side. Powerful as she was, Alannah had more hope defeating the dragons than anyone else there. He also worried about Brendan worming his way back into her broken soul while they sought refuge at Cailleach Estate together. He disliked High Magus Kieran's decision to keep her in the reserves—supporting the war effort with her conjuration expertise—but he respected the need to protect her.

He turned away from the devastation and went back inside the Council Chambers where he found Councillor Johnathan Ryan—the town's mayor—talking to a local mage.

Councillor Ryan glanced at him with a furrowed brow. 'I'm glad you found Danny—err, Warlock Erling—alive. It saddens me that the rest of Warlock Grant's team perished.'

'What about Doran?' asked Liam.

Ryan's eyes narrowed. 'Who?'

'Hugh Doran. The man who helped us get Warlock Erling back here. Tall blond guy with a British accent.'

'Hm. I have no idea who that man is. Might be worth asking the High Magus to do a background check on him. Internet is down across town so I can't exactly look up his file on *my* computer.'

He tensed. 'Will do. The last thing we need to worry about right now is a potential traitor in our midst.' He moved closer to Ryan and whispered, 'Can I speak to you in private?'

The mayor led him into a boardroom and shut the door. 'What's the situation out there?'

'Not good. Three dragons have taken to the skies above us and there's another thunder of them heading this way from the south. I'm not sure how many—they are too far away to count.'

Ryan heaved a mournful sigh. 'It's time to count our losses and hightail it outta here.'

He nodded. 'I'll talk to Dad about getting his patients to safety.'

'Thank you, Warlock Winters, for this and everything else you've been doing to help us.'

'I wish I could do more.'

With heavy hearts, they left the Council Chambers and trudged across the lush garden.

'It will be sad to see such beauty perish,' Ryan mused while waving his hand toward the large sinkhole dominating the garden. 'I assume the Umpherston Cave down the road has collapsed beneath the magma by now.'

'It is likely, Sir. There is only so much we can do and saving lives is our priority.'

Ryan huffed. 'But only certain lives, right? I can't pretend to like High Magus Lane's directive. Not when I have so many human friends in this town.'

He wanted to explain Kieran's reasoning: protecting humans would only anger the dragons more. He bit his lip instead and fell silent for the rest of the walk.

Entering the hall, they found Ross tending to Danny Erling's injuries. The burns were severe but healing fast. He observed the dark circles around his father's eyes. *Dad looks as exhausted as I feel.* 'We need to go.'

Raising his brows, Ross shot him a wide-eyed look. 'We can't. Half these people are out cold, and the others aren't fit to travel by ley line.'

'We'll transport the unconscious in the truck and send each of the others with a pair of warlocks and shamans,' Liam explained. 'Travel along the Coorong[1] and take regular rest stops on your journey.'

Doran rose from his seat beside Erling's stretcher. 'I will help ward the truck.'

'Um….' He hesitated, concerned by Councillor Ryan's caution over the unknown mage.

'It's okay, Liam,' Ross assured him. 'Kieran already vouched for Hugh.'

He exhaled his relief. 'Fine. Mr. Doran—go with your friend and keep the others safe.'

Doran smiled. 'Of course. Oh, and please call me Hugh.'

---

[1] A lagoon along the southern coast of South Australia.

Sensing something was off about Doran, Liam gave him a curt nod. The man was far too friendly, given the circumstances.

A tempest raged within Alannah's mind as she curled up on the sofa with her fluffy white cat. Thoughts and feelings for Brendan whirled about. She wanted to trust him again, but she did not know how. *What the hell did he mean about protecting me? Does he want to shield me from his life of crime? Or is there something else?*

'Hey, are you okay, Alannah?'

She looked up at Amy's gruff voice and forced a smile. In the chaos of her morning spat with Brendan, she had forgotten about the other house guests staying with her at Cailleach Estate. Amy and Jacob had arrived in the middle of the night, just as Liam had left with his parents. She sighed. 'No, not really.'

The butch dwarf sat beside her on the couch. 'Worried about Liam?'

A short, bitter laugh escaped her raspy throat. 'Not as much as I should be. I was thinking about Brendan.'

Amy perked up. 'Oh shit! Really? What happened with Brendo?'

She briefly debated the wisdom of confiding in Amy. They had never been especially close, but that had more to do with circumstance than the woman herself. Yet she did need someone to talk to, and Cara was away helping with the volcano situation. 'Promise to keep a secret?'

'Of course, dude! I'm not a gossip queen, unlike some of your other friends.'

Ignoring the snide remark clearly aimed at Monique Lane and Jessica Ó Máille, she took a deep breath and braced herself. 'I'm still in love with Brendan.'

'Well dah. That much is obvious with the way your eyes glaze over every time his name comes up. I hear he is back in town, though. Has something happened between the two of you?'

Tears trickled down her cheeks as she nodded.

'Oh hell. What did he do?' Amy clenched her fists in her lap. 'Want me to beat the crap out of him?'

She snorted. 'No, but thanks for the offer. I'm upset because of lost opportunities.'

Amy scrunched her brow. 'Whaddaya mean?'

'Brendan left me all those years ago because he thought *I* betrayed *him*.' She explained how Liam had kissed her on the night Brendan announced their soul link, the way Brendan had reacted to the scene, and the Bridey-related aftermath that followed. 'He still wants me, Amy. Brendan never stopped loving me, but I don't know how to trust him anymore—not after the way he jumped to the wrong conclusion so quick, then abandoned me.'

'Fuck, that's heavy stuff,' Amy admitted.

'What should I do?' She sniffled and grabbed a nearby tissue box.

'You should give him a second chance.' The voice to her left startled her. Jacob slouched in the doorway with his arms crossed. Wisps of dark red hair framed the grey skin on his face, although the bangs did little to hide his pointy ears. Only glamour could disguise his unseelie fae origins. 'It's only fair, after the number of times you welcomed Liam back after *he* screwed up.'

'Jacob?' She queried in a mumble. 'I didn't see you there.'

'They don't call me a spymaster for nothing, sweets.' His grin revealed a set of razor-sharp teeth.

Amy scowled at him. 'How long have you been eavesdropping, Bennett?'

'Long enough to know how Alannah truly feels about Brendo.' Jacob drew closer and sat in an armchair facing them. 'That man's heart bleeds for you, Alannah. His soul aches for its other half and I'm sure yours does too. Am I right?'

She sucked in a lungful of air. 'But Bridey—'

'Can suck my cock! Seriously woman, you can't let that bitch keep him from you any longer.'

The doorbell rang, putting an end to their conversation. She sprang to her feet and frowned at Jacob. 'You should hide. I'm expecting Kieran today, so that might be him now. I can't afford to lose his favour. Offering asylum to Unseelie is a sure way of doing so.'

Grinning wide enough to show his razor-sharp teeth, Jacob saluted her. 'Yes, ma'am!' He marched out of the living room and hurried upstairs toward the secret attic hidden by powerful glamour.

High Magus Kieran stood on the doorstep, flanked by two large trunks. His blond hair— usually slicked back—sat a scruffy mess atop his head while days of facial hair covered his upper lip and chin. *The war must be running him ragged.* 'Hi, Alannah. I have more armour for you to imbue.'

'Come in.' She unlocked the screen door and held it open for him as he wheeled the crates inside. 'I finished the last lot.'

'Already? How did you work so quick?'

Leading him through to the family room, she shrugged. 'You said it yourself: I'm a powerful mage.' No way in hell was she going to admit Brendan had helped her.

Kieran chuckled. 'Modesty doesn't suit—' Stopping dead in his tracks, he stared at Amy on the sofa. 'Miss Smith? What are you doing here?'

Leaping to her feet, Amy bowed before him. 'Greetings, Your Honour. Councillor Winters was kind enough to offer sanctuary, Sir.'

'Shouldn't you be helping your parents at the forge. We need all hands on deck right now.'

'Apologies Sir, but my folks and I don't exactly see eye-to-eye.'

Kieran harrumphed. 'With your lifestyle choices, I'm not surprised.' The High Magus was nothing if not ultra conservative. He would never understand the kinkster scene; few pureblood mages did. 'That said, I'd still appreciate your help in the war. The dragons have appeared now, so we need to double down on our preparations.'

'*What?*' Alannah and Amy screeched together.

'Did you just say the dragons are here?' Alannah's voice trembled, revealing the panic thumping in her veins.

'Not in Gaeilge Shores, yet. They are still down in the Southeast, but it's only a matter of time before they descend upon the rest of the state,' he explained.

'I'll go get the first batch of armour and take these to the cellar.' She grabbed a trunk and dragged it toward the stairs.

'I'll give you a hand,' insisted Kieran as he took the other case.

Once they reached the glamoured door hiding the ritual room from the rest of the basement, Kieran seized her wrist. 'Please tell me you aren't sheltering any other lost lambs here?'

Holding his gaze, she schooled her expression. 'No. Amy is the only one staying with me. My other friends are either helping with the war or they have their own safehouses.'

'For your sake, I hope that's true. Spending time with Brendan is dangerous in ways you can't even begin to fathom.'

The hairs on the back of her neck stood on end. Laughing it off nervously, she shook her head. 'I don't know what you're talking about, Your Honour. There's no way I'd let a villain like him back into my bed, let alone my heart.'

He cocked a brow. 'Please be careful, Alannah.'

Gulping, she turned to unlock the cellar.

Wrapping herself in a plush robe, Neve stepped out of the bathroom and crossed Erik and Elna's bedroom to look out the window. The house—a massive log cabin structure—sat nestled in the thick bushland canopy. Letting her mind drift, she spied a koala chomping on the leaves of a neighbouring gum tree. Her own stomach rumbled at the thought of food, but there was something else the koala possessed that she craved even more.

'You're dripping all over the floor, Neve,' Erik grumbled while glaring at her bare feet. Completely starkers, he stood tall, not the least bit self-conscious. Not that anyone would be ashamed of such a finely sculpted body and flawless golden skin.

Lowering her gaze, she glimpsed a few trickles of water trailing down her legs and splattering on the timber floor. She shrugged. 'It'll dry.' Her attention returned to the sleepy marsupial outside. 'Am I a prisoner?'

With a huff, he closed the distance between them and hugged her from behind. 'Is it so terrible here? I thought you enjoyed my company, and Elna's.' He spun her around to face him and smirked. 'You weren't complaining this morning, or this afternoon. I lost track of how many times we made you come.'

Her cheeks flushed as recent memories flicked through like a movie reel in fast forward. 'I... don't get me wrong. The sex is amazing... a great distraction, but I miss my other friends and family. I'm not a fan of being cooped up inside too long, either.'

Erik sighed and released her from his grip. 'You're not my captive, Neve. Feel free to come and go as you please.'

'But your dad—'

'I know what my father said last night, but I won't stop you. I wouldn't advise it, however. The outside world is not safe and every time you step beyond the borders of this property, you risk a toasty fate.'

'What if I hop the ley lines and only go to safehouses?'

Erik laughed drily. 'The only safehouses belong to the Seelie. Your mage friends are fools to think their wards will hold against dragon fire.'

She gasped and dashed to the wardrobe, throwing clothes on the bed in a rush to get dressed. 'Oh Gods! Mum and Caitlin! I can't let them burn—'

13

'Neve, wait! Don't go running off without a care for your own safety.' Erik tugged at the collar of her robe, pulling her back into his arms.

Collapsing under the weight of frustration and worry, she twisted in his embrace and sobbed against his shoulder. 'I need to do something to save them.'

'Don't worry, my love. Dad intends to help your mother if she agrees to the terms of our betrothal.'

She peered up into his impassive green eyes. 'What terms?'

'The legally binding conditions of our betrothal contract. Would you like to read it before or after your mother signs on the dotted line tomorrow?'

Realising she was gaping; she snapped her mouth shut and frowned. 'You make it sound like a financial transaction, as if I'm a piece of property for sale.'

'That's how marriage works in my world. From what I understand, it's not much different for most pureblood mages either. Love and happy endings are luxuries most of us can only dream of, which is why I feel so lucky to have your heart as you have mine.' He stroked the side of her face tenderly and leaned down to kiss her lips.

Erik still hadn't bathed after their day of making love and she tasted her own tang on his lips. It sent tingles through her body and stirred her core.

'And here I thought we were getting ready for dinner,' Elna remarked as she opened the bathroom door. Plumes of steam billowed around her, and a skimpy scrap of terrycloth struggled to conceal her voluptuous curves. 'Looks like the pair of you are ready to go another round.'

Tucking Neve into his side, he grinned at Elna. 'I was just easing our girl's anxieties while you hogged all the hot water.'

'Pfft. Looks like you could use a cold shower anyway, Brother dearest.' Elna glanced at the situation below his waist and smiled smugly.

He pressed his mouth against the shell of Neve's ear. 'Wake me up next time so I can shower with you, sweetheart.' His teeth nipped at her earlobe and she half-squealed, half-giggled as he strode toward the ensuite.

'Hm, I wonder,' Elna mused as the girls watched Erik disappear into the bathroom. 'Are you the reason for the increase in his sex drive?'

'Are you saying he wasn't this…?' She blushed.

'I think the word you are looking for is "horny." And no—before you, he was content with far less.'

'Oh.' She fell silent and shifted her attention to getting dressed.

Once again, dinner was an awkward affair of forced conversation and stiff formality. She wondered if things would remain this way, or if Alvar would eventually warm up to her. After placing her cutlery neatly on her plate, she cleared her throat. 'Excuse me, Your Highness. May I please read the betrothal contract?'

Alvar sipped his red wine and dabbed his mouth with a linen napkin. 'Certainly. It is wise to understand the rules, so you do not break them unknowingly.' He rang the brass bell beside his glass and asked the butler to fetch the document. 'I am confident your mother will agree to my terms. She stands to lose a great deal by refusing, so it is in her best interest.' He handed her the papers.

She felt the blood drain from her face as she read through the extensive list of conditions and her heart skipped a beat when she reached the virginity clauses:

*During the period of betrothal, The Claimed
will submit to a physical examination on an
annual basis to confirm her hymen remains
intact. This procedure will be performed by
an independent party.*

*If The Claimed loses her virginity at any
point prior to matrimony, The Claimant will
lose his claim and the parties responsible will
be charged with treason, punishable by death.*

She didn't need a law degree to understand
the severity of her situation. *If Mum signs that
contract, I'm as good as dead when they check my hymen.
But if she doesn't sign it, her own life and those of
everyone staying at Cailleach Estate will be in danger.*

Alannah awoke with a start beneath the solid mass
of a man's body. She tried to scream, but a hand
clamped her mouth, and she flicked her eyes open.
Within the seconds it took her vision to adjust to the
darkness, his familiar musky scent filtered through
the panic and seeped into her senses. The tension
eased from her muscles, and she stopped
struggling. Another second passed before she
realised Brendan had crept beneath the covers to
straddle her and heat crept across her scantily clad

skin. When she attempted to question him, he tightened his grip against her mouth.

Bringing his chest flush with hers, he whispered in her ear, 'Shoosh, gorgeous. Erect a sound ward first.'

She glared at him but did as he asked. 'Why couldn't you put up your own damn soundproofing?'

'Your wards are much stronger, and they even hold up if someone opens the door.'

'Oh.' The hint of a blush warmed her cheeks. 'So, what do you want to talk about?'

Brendan smirked. 'Why do you assume I want to talk? Maybe I just want to ravish you and spare our guests the embarrassment.'

She arched her brows and gave him a sidelong glance.

'Yeah okay, you got me there. I couldn't care less if they heard your cries of ecstasy, but I do owe you an explanation.'

'And you had to wake me up in the middle of the night? I'm exhausted after a full day of conjuration, and it wasn't easy to get to sleep.'

He gave her a sheepish simper. 'I'm sorry, Lana. I couldn't wait any longer.'

'Okay fine. Let me sit up first because I won't be able to concentrate in this position. I can feel your dick straining against those flimsy trackpants you're wearing.'

He gave her a sly grin. 'At least I'm wearing pants,' Brendan's hand slid up her thigh as he spoke, 'unlike you. I'd forgotten how you tend not to wear panties to bed.' He tugged gently at the hem of her black satin slip before lifting it above her hip.

'Brendan…!' She intended to use a threatening tone, but her warning sounded more like a whimpering plea.

'Hm, maybe the talk can wait a *little* longer.' He brushed his lips across her cheek and thrust his erection against her.

She moaned as her body shuddered and her core flooded. 'Brendan, please.'

'Please what, Lana?' He breathed the words against her lips.

'Please stop.'

'Who are you trying to convince?' His cock pressed hard against her clit.

Closing her eyes, she took a deep breath and blurted out, 'Richard!'

He scrambled away from her and sat on the edge of the bed with wide eyes.

She had never needed to safeword out with him before and it pained her to do so, but they had too many issues to resolve first. Sitting up, she leaned against the headboard. 'I'm sorry, Brendan, but I'm not ready. We really should talk first.'

'Don't ever feel you need to apologise for using your safeword, gorgeous. I'm just surprised is all.' He was panting heavily and took several seconds to compose himself. 'Is it okay if I still hold you while we talk?'

She nodded and moved across to give him space. Sitting beside her, he pulled her into his arms. Slumping down, she placed her head against his chest and listened to the frantic thumping of his heart.

A full minute elapsed before he spoke again. 'The reason I didn't return after gaining my freedom, my excuse for staying away from you all these years, was fear. I'm a coward when it comes to you, Lana—always have been. Yeah, I was scared you'd reject me, but I was even more afraid of losing you to our enemy.'

'Enemy?'

'I still don't know who they are, but I'm pretty sure their identity is part of Tara's big secret.'

'Wouldn't I be safer with you here to protect me?'

He squeezed her tight and pressed a chaste kiss against the crown of her head. 'I wish it were that simple. The enemy doesn't want us to be together. Bridey made that abundantly clear.'

She tensed at the sound of the bitch's name. 'Why? And what does the she-devil have to do with this?'

'I only just learned Bridey is working for the enemy by trying to keep us apart and even spying on me. I don't know the full extent of her involvement, which is why I can't cut ties with her yet. I used to think her dislike for you was personal. When I first gained my freedom, I struck a deal with her. I was still heartbroken over you at the time, so I agreed without question.'

Painful silence followed and she prompted him to continue with a soft voice, 'What did you agree to?'

He sucked in a breath. 'To stay away from you. In exchange for her support in the Syndicate and… continued access to Caleb.'

'Fuck.' The muttered curse slipped out before she could stop it.

'Yeah, I know. I didn't intend to keep my word for long. I dreamed of ways I could sneak away to visit you in secret. But then I started unravelling the doppelganger mystery with Tyler and that threw a massive spanner in the works.'

'I heard about that stuff from Tyler, but what does it have to do with us?'

'Tyler hasn't told you the full truth of the matter because he doesn't even know. I kept my theory to myself.'

'What theory?'

'Then you went and proved it yesterday.'

Goosebumps prickled her exposed arms. 'What theory, Brendan?'

'You're my doppelganger, Lana.'

She sat bolt upright and gaped at him. 'What? How? I'm a woman, I can't be *your* doppelganger.'

He leered at her breasts and licked his lips. 'I'm quite aware of your gender, gorgeous.'

She smacked his arm. 'Quit it.'

Mischief twinkled in his eyes when they returned to hers. 'From what I understand, doppelgangers don't have to be the same sex. We are mystic twins. Your bio dad, whoever he was, must descend from a God of magic—probably The Dagda if he was Irish—but who really knows? That power surge we felt during the ritual yesterday: that was due to our mystical connection. I felt the same with Tyler, but it was much stronger with you, and I think that is why the enemy wants to keep us apart. Because our working together, on top of your Beltane blessing, turns us into a force to be reckoned with. Someone perceives us as a threat, and they'll stop at nothing to keep us apart. We can't fight an unknown enemy, so until we know who they are, we must be extremely careful.'

'If we are such a threat, why not take us out before we become unstoppable?'

'I don't know. I've wondered the same thing. Maybe they have plans for us? Like how the Obsidian Cult used Tyler and me. The value of our mystic connection might outweigh the risks, but this is all conjecture because I have no fucking idea who this dickhead is, let alone how their mind works.'

She inhaled deeply and breathed out through pursed lips. 'Thanks. I understand now. I hate it, but I get it.'

'Yup. It sucks balls alright. Now that I know what really went down with Liam back then, *and* I know how you feel about me, I'm willing to fight for us. I'm sorry it took me this long to grow a pair.'

She sank back into the bed. 'Will you stay with me tonight?'

'Of course.' He held her, stroking her until she fell asleep in his arms.

Chapter Two

Warmth surrounded Alannah as she stirred from her slumber. Her eyes fluttered open, and she rolled over to give Brendan a contented smile. 'You stayed.'

'I said I would, didn't I?' He tucked a stray strand behind her ear and leaned in to kiss her.

Biting her lip, she turned her face, and his mouth met her cheek.

'Lana?'

'Not yet. You want me to give you a chance and that's what I'm doing. But I need to take things slow. Can we keep things platonic while rebuilding the trust?'

Brendan breathed in deeply. 'Yeah, okay.'

The doorbell rang and she cursed under her breath. 'Don't tell me that's Kieran again already. I'm still working through the latest lot of armour.'

'You want my help with those?'

'Yes please. But for now, you should probably hide.'

He rose to his feet, giving her an eyeful of his bare chest. The years had been kind to his figure, although there was a strange scar above his left nipple that she had not noticed before. After pulling on a t-shirt, he gave her a smug grin. 'I'll go hang with Jacob in the glamoured attic.'

'Wait up.' She stood in front of him and lifted his shirt.

Brendan chuckled. 'I'm not sure we have time right now, gorgeous.'

She rolled her eyes and inspected the mark closer. The scar tissue looked like the remnants of a scalding brand and the design resembled an Egyptian cartouche. 'What's the deal with this?'

Brendan sucked in a breath as she ran her fingers over the ridges of flesh. 'Oh that. Set managed to brand me during the ritual where I banished him back to the Underworld.'

'What does it mean?'

The doorbell rang again, and Brendan retreated, yanking his shirt back down. 'It's the Obsidian Cult's sigil. You should probably answer the door.'

She shuddered as he left the room. She did not understand everything that had gone down with the evil Egyptian God, but she knew enough to fear the consequences of such dark magic. Pushing her concerns aside, she promptly dressed and hurried downstairs.

Finding Alvar Elofsson on the doorstep knocked the air from her lungs. 'Fuck! Is Neve okay?'

'Relax, Lady Winters. Your daughter is safe. I have an important matter to discuss with you.'

Letting him inside, she strode into the formal lounge room. 'Is this about Neve or the dragons?'

'Both actually.'

'Can I get you a drink?' Glancing toward the dry bar, she spotted a few bottles of liquor and temptation rattled the chains of her restraint. 'Tea, coffee, or would you like something stronger?' Drawing closer, she surveyed the assortment. 'We have whiskey, gin, vodka, sherry—'

'Tea is fine, thank you. I don't like to drink alcohol before noon.'

Dragging herself away from the hard stuff, she silently thanked Alvar for saving her from a relapse. *I should ask Brendan to hide Uncle Ross' booze while we're staying here.* She made herself a coffee while the teapot brewed.

Alvar sat patiently on a lounge chair and graciously accepted the tea and biscuits.

She took a seat facing him and sipped her drink, letting the caffeine mend the frayed edges of her nerves. 'What do you wish to discuss, Your Highness?'

'My son Erik seeks Neve's hand in marriage.'

'Aren't they a bit young to be thinking seriously about marriage? Neve is only fifteen.'

'She is old enough to fall pregnant. There was a time when girls got married at her age; so no, I don't think she is too young. Obviously, the wedding will need to wait until Neve can legally marry. With your consent, it can happen when she is sixteen. The sooner they marry, the more chance Erik has of claiming the Seelie crown and making Neve his queen.'

She frowned. 'So that's what this is about. Erik is hungry for power.'

'For what it's worth, they are also in love. I don't put much stock in such sentimental notions, but it may comfort you to know my son cares deeply for your daughter.' He reached into the briefcase he had brought with him and produced a manilla folder. 'I have a betrothal contract here for you to sign.'

'Forget it,' she hissed. 'I'm not selling my daughter to the Seelie Court. If those kids truly love each other, they can get married of their own accord when Neve is an adult. I don't agree with your archaic marriage laws.'

Springing to his feet, Alvar crossed the room and dropped the document on the coffee table beside her. It landed with a thud and jiggled the contents of her cup. 'If you sign it, I promise to reinforce the wards protecting this house. They will not withstand dragon fire in their current state.'

'You mean to barter my daughter's life?' she seethed. 'You disgust me.'

'Please be reasonable, Lady Winters. This is an excellent union for Neve and—'

'*Reasonable?*' she screeched, leaping to her feet, standing off against Alvar. 'How is signing my daughter's death warrant *reasonable?*'

He glared at her. 'It is hardly a *death warrant*, Lady Winters. So long as Neve maintains her virginal status, she is perfectly safe.'

Curious. He doesn't know about Jasper. 'What makes you think she hasn't already lost it?'

'She assures me her hymen is very much intact.'

'And you believe her?'

Alvar gave her a haughty grin. 'Yes, I do. Lying to a Seelie noble in his own home is a criminal offence. I will of course arrange for a physical examination upon signing and on an annual basis. This is a standard condition of the contract.'

Oh fuck! 'And if I refuse to sign? What happens to Neve then?'

'I will send her home and the lot of you can deal with the dragon threat on your own.'

'I need time to think about this, and to discuss it with her father.'

'Very well. Call me when you have made your final decision.' He handed her a slip of paper with his phone number.

After showing Alvar out, she raced upstairs to find Brendan.

Shame and sexual frustration churned in Brendan's gut like a toxic cocktail as he left Alannah's room and climbed the stairs in the secret passage to the attic. He knew he would need to explain Set's brand to her eventually, but with everything going on, he did not think it was the right time.

Jacob's snoring greeted him as soon as his feet hit the upper floor.

Good thing this room is soundproofed with one of Lana's wards. His dick stirred at the mere thought of Alannah and before he knew it, he was sporting a full hardon. *Fuck's sake.* He usually had better control of his body's reactions, but the more he tried to will his dick into submission using magic, the more the damned thing resisted. Sleeping with her in his arms after the night they had shared filled him with hope and his sex drive clearly got the memo.

Staring down at Jacob's sleeping form, he considered using the man to alleviate his current urges. He knew Jacob would jump at the opportunity. *What would Lana think though?*

The snoring ceased with a grunt and Jacob flicked his dark grey eyes open. 'Morning, Jet.'

'Ah hell, Red! Your senses are uncanny.'

Jacob gave him a toothy grin. 'That's why I'm your best spymaster, Sir.' His eyes travelled down Brendan's body, bugging out when they reached his cock. 'You want me to take care of that for you, Sir?'

His cheeks puffed out as he exhaled sharply. 'No. I'll deal with it myself. I'd rather hear the latest on the Seelie situation. Shove over.'

'Suit yourself.' Jacob sat up and made room for him on the bed.

Adjusting himself, he got as comfortable as possible, given the circumstances. 'What can you tell me?'

'Not gonna deal with your boner first?'

He groaned. 'Drop it, Red. I'm not fucking you and I'm not about to jack-off in front of you, either.'

'So why are you in my bedroom rather than having a private moment?'

'Lana has an official visitor.'

Jacob nodded. 'Fair enough. Speaking of Alannah, I heard her talking to Amy about you yesterday. She was crying and everything. I haven't seen her that emotional in like… forever.'

'Oh?'

'Yeah man, she was pouring her heart out to Amy like they were best friends.'

'What did Alannah say about me?'

'She mostly talked about the way Liam and Bridey fucked things up for the pair of you, but she also admitted to how much she still loves you.'

His heart swelled with the affirmation. Alannah had told him as much a couple of days ago and Jacob's news was a welcome reminder. 'Best thing I've heard in ages. Thanks, Red.'

'No probs, Sir. Sorry I can't give you better news regarding the Seelie.'

'Hit me with it.'

'I spoke to the dealer who went to that party Neve was drugged at.' He frowned. 'Things don't add up.'

31

'What do you mean?'

'It was Craig Munroe, Locky's little brother. He used his private stash.'

His blood boiled as he clenched his fists. 'That little brat should've known better.'

Jacob winced. 'Yeah well, it's my fault for giving Elna his number. Apparently, she offered to double the money he made on sales at the party on the condition he sold two vials to Jasper Rowan.'

'The fuck? That bitch set them up!'

'Seems that way. I don't get it though. If the Alavarsson twins claimed Neve, why set her up with Jasper knowing she'll fuck him?'

His head throbbed painfully, and he massaged his temples. 'I don't know, Red. Those Seelie shits are an enigma.'

'You look tense, Sir.' Jacob moved behind him and squeezed his shoulders.

'Your powers of observation astound me,' he replied sarcastically.

Jacob chuckled as he started kneading the knots in Brendan's shoulder blades. 'Spymaster, remember?'

A moan slipped out of him as his eyes rolled back. 'Gods that feels good.'

Alannah burst into the room a moment later carrying a stack of papers. Stopping in her tracks when she glimpsed the guys, she let the pages drop and scatter across the floor. 'Am I interrupting something?' she asked in a raspy voice.

'Only the best massage I've ever had. Don't worry gorgeous, I'm not about to jump Jacob's bones, unless you want me to.'

She bit her bottom lip as bright red lust pulsed in her aura.

Hot damn! She's turned on by the thought of me with another guy. He filed that thought under 'future opportunities.'

'Hm, so that's my ticket,' Jacob teased.

He elbowed Jacob in the thigh, toppling him as he cried out, '*Oof!*'

'Um, Jacob, can I please have a private word with Brendan?'

'Sure. I could use a cold shower anyway.' Jacob climbed out of bed, not bothering to hide his own arousal as he strode across the room in nothing but a pair of boyleg shorts.

Shit! No wonder Lana assumed something was going on.

Once the door closed, Alannah smirked at him. 'So, Jacob huh?'

He shook his head. 'Nah. That man's been trying to get in my pants since he discovered I was bi, but it's never gonna happen. Jacob's not really my type. What's with all that?' He gestured toward the mess on the floor.

'Oh right.' Alannah kneeled on the carpet to gather the papers. 'This is a contract I wanted you to look at.'

Dropping to the floor, he helped collect the strays. 'What sort of contract?'

'A betrothal for Neve and Erik.'

He froze. 'Don't bother. You may as well use it as kindling because there is no way our girl is marrying that jerk.'

Tempting as it was to eavesdrop on Brendan and Alannah's conversation, Jacob desperately needed to deal with his own frustrations. He knew lusting after Brendan was a hopeless endeavour, but he couldn't help himself. The man *was* sex on legs, after all.

Lost in his thoughts, he didn't even realise the bathroom was occupied until he opened the door and barged his way inside.

'*Motherfucker!*'

Oops. How'd I forget Amy was staying here too? He stared at the redhead who stood naked in the shower cubicle, all curves and shit. *Ah heck, I'm never gonna get rid of my boner at this rate.* She must've just finished because the water was no longer running.

'Get the fuck out, you perverted arsehole!' She threw a drenched loofah at him.

He caught it and tossed it aside. 'Sorry, shorty. I didn't know you were in here.'

Crossing her arms under her D-cups, she scowled. 'You expect me to believe that? You're innately attuned to senses, dipshit. If you come any closer with that disgusting thing,' she pointed at his dick, 'I'll rip your pissy little balls off.'

'Pfft. Don't flatter yourself, Amy. My state of arousal has nothing to do with you.'

'Maybe not, but I wouldn't put it past you to try something. I know how you fuck everyone who moves.'

Marching up to her, he wrapped a hand around her throat and shoved her back against the cubicle wall. 'Not *everyone*. I'm not a rapist. I suggest you get your facts straight before making outrageous accusations.'

Storm clouds flurried in her wide hazel eyes and for a few glorious seconds the feisty dwarf held her tongue. She gave him just enough time to entertain wild, inappropriate fantasies before pushing him away. 'Fuck off, Bennett. I'm going to need another shower now, to wash your bloody filth away.'

His feet slipped on the tiles, but he reached out and grabbed the soap dish before his arse hit the deck. 'Sounds more like you need to wash your mouth out. I doubt even Alannah swears as much as you.'

'*Out!* Go find another bathroom. It's not like this house is hurting for them.'

'Fine. Whatever.' He sauntered out, slamming the door behind him. Amy had always irritated him, but after the old crew shamed and shunned him for his work with the Syndicate, she infuriated him every chance she got. *It's that goddamned mouth of hers.* Sometimes he wished he could stuff a gag in it. *Or better still, my cock.* He halted in the hallway. *I so didn't just think that. Did I?* He shook away the absurd notion and found one of the many ensuite bathrooms.

Amy collapsed against the wall and slid down the tiles. *What the hell was that?* She shivered as goosebumps danced across her skin, yet she didn't feel cold. *I can't believe that insufferable boggart!* Her pulse was racing as she struggled to suck in enough breath. She stroked her throat, still feeling the pressure of Jacob's fingers where bruises were likely forming. *Why the fuck did that feel so good? I'm not a fucking masochist and I'm definitely not a subby.*

Tilting her head back, she performed some deep breathing exercises to get her heartrate under control. Minutes later, she pushed up from the floor and reached for a towel. She almost slipped on the loofah on her way out of the shower and cursed her own stupidity. *What the hell was I hoping to achieve by hitting him with a wet sponge, for fuck's sake?*

Once she made it back to her temporary bedroom, she found her phone and checked her messages. There were none from Connor, her boyfriend and full-time submissive. Along with every other mage in the state with healing powers, he had gone to the Limestone Coast to help with the disaster relief. Her heart ached for him, for any words he could send to assure her he was okay, so she tapped out a message: HEY BUNNY. EVERYTHING OK? I MISS YOU.

She scrolled through her socials while waiting for his reply. Most of the world was complaining about the volcanoes spoiling all their fun. *Selfish fucktards.* There were some concerns about the devastation and even a few reports of fire raining from the sky. *I guess that's the dragons.*

Connor's message came through several minutes later: HI MISS. THINGS AREN'T GOING WELL.

WE LEFT MT. GAMBIER YESTERDAY, ON OUR WAY HOME WITH A TRUCKLOAD OF INJURED REFUGEES. THE ROADS ARE TOO PERILOUS TO TRAVEL FOR LONG STRETCHES, SO IT'S A SLOW AND ARDUOUS JOURNEY. MISS YOU TOO.

A sliver of hope awakened as she read the words, 'on our way home.' She couldn't wait to see him again. After getting dressed, she headed down to the kitchen for a coffee. Alannah hadn't yet shown her how to use the machine, so she searched for some instant stuff.

'What are you looking for?' Jacob's voice startled her, and she smacked her head on the top rail of the cupboard she was looking inside of.

'*Motherfucker!* Stop sneaking up on me.' Standing upright, she rubbed the bump on her head.

'Sorry. Occupational hazard.' He grinned wide enough to show the tips of his teeth. Although fangs might be a better term for those things.

'I'm looking for coffee.'

'Are you blind as well as daft? It's right there.' He pointed to the coffee supplies on the bench.

'Argh. I'm neither. I just don't know how to use the machine and I didn't want to bug Alannah and Brendan, so I'm looking for instant coffee.'

'Tsk, tsk. They don't stock that crap here. Only the best will do in a bloodline house. You ought to know that, Amy.'

'Fine. I guess I'll have tea for now.' She flicked the kettle on and opened the tea canister. 'Fuck! This is loose leaf. Don't they have teabags?'

Jacob snorted. 'Short term memory loss too, huh? What did I say only seconds ago?'

Ignoring him, she found an infuser and prepared her drink. The moment she sat down at the breakfast bar and started sipping her Irish Breakfast, Jacob started the coffee machine. She glared at him until the grinding noise stopped. 'Fucktard! Why didn't you tell me you knew how to use it?'

'You didn't ask. Besides, it's not all that hard. I would have thought someone attuned to matter like you could have worked it out.'

'Now who's the stupid one? You really have no idea how conjuration magic works, do you?'

'Sure I do. I've seen Alannah at work.' He slumped into the chair beside her.

She sighed. 'We're not all as gifted as Alannah. My talents lie in arcane metalsmithing and imbuing.'

'Don't forget cussing and throwing shit.'

She stifled a laugh. *Wouldn't want him getting the wrong idea, or anything. And why the hell is he sitting so close?*

Chapter Three

Alannah took the last of the pages from Brendan and put the betrothal contract back in the manilla folder. 'With all due respect, this isn't your decision. I came to you for legal advice. I need to speak to Lawyer Brendan, remember him?'

He glared at her. 'My advice is to burn that damn contract.'

With a sigh, she rose to her feet. 'I wish it were that easy. Neve's life is at risk either way.' Leaving the attic that she had turned into Jacob's temporary sleeping quarters; she made her way to Brendan's room.

He followed her and waited while she cast a fresh soundproof ward. 'How is her life at risk if you don't sign it?'

'She lied about her virginity to Alvar, in his own house.'

'Oh hell.'

'*And* if I refuse, Alvar won't protect her from the dragons. He'll send her back to us and apparently the wards on this place won't keep dragon fire out.'

Brendan's eyes bugged out. 'You don't seriously believe him, do you? This place kept Tara out even though she was attuned to nether; why wouldn't the wards hold up against dragons?'

She shrugged. 'I don't know. I'd like to test the truth of Alvar's claims *before* the dragons get here, but I don't know how.'

'I could interrogate him.'

She almost dismissed the idea, then remembered she was not talking to the same Brendan she used to know. 'Do you honestly think it will help? Can you even get to him?'

Closing the distance between them, Brendan clutched her shoulders firmly. 'I can be persuasive when I need to be.'

Shudders transformed into excited tingles as she untangled all the meaning in his words. 'I take it you've mastered all the powers of an enchanter?'

One side of his mouth rose in a lopsided grin. 'And then some. I see your bad-boy fetish hasn't waned over the years.'

'Only when it comes to you,' she confessed.

His grip tightened, sending delicious pleasure-pain signals through her body. 'Gods! You're killing me here, Lana. I'm trying so hard to respect your wishes with this whole platonic thing, so you need to tone down your "fuck me now" signals.'

'Maybe you shouldn't touch me like this then.' Her own resolve was about to give way under the weight of his hands. She was literally five seconds away from dropping to her knees and addressing him as Sir. Four seconds….

'Sure you're not ready?'

Three seconds….

Biting her lip, she nodded.

Two seconds….

Brendan stepped back, plucking the contract from her hands. 'I'll give this a look.'

She released her breath. 'Thank you. You may as well interrogate him. I can't think of any other way to uncover the truth.'

Taking a seat on his bed next to Luna the cat's sleeping form, Brendan sifted through the papers, putting them back in order before he started reading the terms and conditions. Alannah sat beside him and fidgeted with the hem of her short dress.

'Dagnammit!' He handed the contract back to her. 'This thing is airtight. The Seelie Court must have some exceptional lawyers. I stand by my previous advice: please don't sign it, Lana.'

'What if we could somehow rig the medical exams? With your contacts and… powers of persuasion.'

'That would mean infiltrating the Seelie Court,' Brendan explained.

'And?'

'And I've been trying to do that for years to no avail.'

She gaped at him.

'The Syndicate is essentially like the royalty of the Unseelie Court, as you might have guessed. This makes the Seelie our archrivals, so of course I'd look for ways to tear holes in their organisation.'

She huffed. 'No wonder you hate Alvar and his kids so much.'

'Trust me gorgeous, my contempt for them has everything to do with the way they are treating Neve.'

She placed her hand on his knee and looked deep into his eyes. 'You really care for her, don't you?'

His own large hand engulfed hers. 'Yeah, I do. I really want to step up and be a proper father for Neve, regardless of what happens between us.'

Tears welled in her eyes. 'You have no idea how much that means to me.'

Shuffling around to face her, he moved his hand up to cup her cheek. 'Yeah, I kinda do. Enchanter, remember?' His thumb brushed away her rogue tear before it travelled far.

A smile blossomed on her face. 'You make it hard to forget. For the record, I was talking figuratively.' They remained locked in a heated stare for several seconds until the gravity of Neve's situation returned to the forefront of her mind. 'I'm really fucking scared, Brendan.'

His hand slid around the back of her head, fingers lacing between strands of her long, black hair as he dropped his forehead against hers. 'So am I.' He inhaled a deep breath. 'I don't know exactly what Erik and Elna are playing at, but I'm pretty sure they want to hurt Neve.'

'I don't trust them either,' she admitted.

Brendan sat upright and shook his head. 'There's more to it, Lana. They set Jasper up at that party. According to the dealer who worked there, Elna wanted Jasper to get his grubby hands on two Rhapsody vials. I also saw the twins talking about it on the video footage from Neve's hidden camera. Elna said "It'll be a pity to destroy them." Also… I think they were the ones who posted Neve's sex tape online.'

'What?' Her brows rose sky high.

'I'm not certain yet, but I know Jasper didn't do it. I paid the little shit a visit the other day and got the truth out of him. He only broke up with Neve because Erik threatened both their lives.'

She sprung to her feet, her heart beating frantically and her sudden movement startling Luna, who dove under the bed. 'Holy fuckin' fuck! We need to get her out of there, Brendan.'

'I'm glad we're on the same page at last.' Standing before her, Brendan pulled her into his arms. 'Why don't you let me deal with Neve while you work on that armour? Maybe get Amy to help you while I'm busy.'

'Crap! I'd almost forgotten about my conjuration work.'

The hint of a smile touched his lips. 'There are much better ways to forget our troubles.'

With a snort, she backed out of his arms. 'I'll be sure to find you when I need a distraction.'

His eyes darkened with lust.

Turning on her heel, she strode toward the door. 'Keep me updated on your progress.'

Nothing killed the mood quite like facing certain death. After reading the betrothal contract the previous night, Neve had retreated into herself, refusing to sleep with the twins. Her sour mood had continued the next day despite Erik's numerous attempts to cheer her up. Normally, when she felt depressed, Neve preferred to eat ice cream from the tub while watching stupid movies. But the closest thing she had found to ice cream was some weird blossom sorbet and the Alvarssons didn't even own a TV.

She had managed to find a large library full of antique shelves. They were the sort she'd only seen in fairytale movies. There was even a reading corner with some comfortable armchairs beside a large, rustic window. To her surprise, there was a decent assortment of fantasy fiction, so she curled up with a book and escaped reality for the better part of the day.

'There you are. I've been looking all over for you.' Erik's deep voice startled her, and she dropped her novel on the floor.

'Fuck! Now I've lost my place.' She stooped to pick it up, but he beat her to it.

Kneeling before her, he read the cover: '*City of Bones* by Cassandra Clare. I didn't even know we had this in our collection. Elna must have bought it.' He handed the book to her and sighed. 'Talk to me, Neve.'

She turned away from his stupidly beautiful face and glanced out the window. The sun had already dipped beneath the horizon and fairy lights were twinkling in the trees, casting eerie shadows on the ground.

'What's wrong, sweetheart?'

Neve scoffed and glared at him. 'Stop playing dumb, Erik! You've seen that contract and I know you can read my mind. Why didn't you warn me about the chastity exam? You know I can't—'

He clapped a hand over her mouth. 'Hush! Keep it down.' He lowered his own voice to a whisper. 'I didn't warn you because I honestly didn't know my father was going to insist on it. Such archaic practices haven't been performed in my family for decades. I guess he is serious about ensuring the legitimacy of my bid for the crown. The Seelie Court have other... tests.'

When she tried to peel his hand away from her mouth, he caged her between his arms and leaned in closer.

'I doubt my mum will sign it,' Neve explained quietly.

'Good. That buys us some time.'

'What are you talking about?'

'I'm looking into hymen restoration.'

Neve gasped. 'Is that even possible?'

'Technically, yes. I know human plastic surgeons can do it, but I'm not sure there are any close by and well… the human world is under attack at the moment. I'm hoping to find a magic practitioner who can help. I won't let anything happen to you, Neve. I promise.' His lips brushed across her cheek as he brought them to her mouth, and he kissed her sweetly. 'You should eat something. I saved you some dinner.'

After a moment of hope, her heart sank again. 'I'm not hungry.'

'Will you at least come to bed with me and Elna?'

'Maybe later. I'm not in the mood for anything sexual.'

He nodded. 'Of course. It's the furthest thing from my mind too right now. I just want to hold you, my love.' Erik's new soppy side unnerved her.

'We'll see.'

Rising to his feet, he growled slightly and stormed out of the room.

She sighed and resumed reading, letting the *Shadowhunters'* troubles distract from her own until her phone buzzed on the table beside her. The screen displayed an unknown number. Curious to know who would ring her at such a late hour, she accepted the call. 'Hello?'

'Evening, princess,' replied Brendan.

'Um, hi. What's up?'

'Is now an okay time to talk, and are you alone?' The urgency in his voice bristled the hairs on the back of her neck.

'Yeah, I am. What's wrong?'

'You need to get out of there, Neve. I think those twins are planning something nasty.' He told her about all the dirt he had uncovered on the Rhapsody plot. 'To make matters worse, I suspect they posted the video of you, but I can't dig up any proof. I forced the truth out of Jasper, so I know he didn't do it.'

Pain stabbed at her chest like thousands of sharp needles. 'But how? Erik showed me his aura when I asked him about it. He wasn't lying.'

'The Seelie are skilled manipulators and deceivers, princess. He could've been portraying a false aura. It's a trick I use all the time in my line of work.'

'I'm really starting to hate boys,' she grumbled. 'Maybe I should've hooked up with Caitlin.'

Brendan snorted. 'We're not all bad, just most of us.'

'Is it safe to travel by ley line?'

'Yes, for now. The dragons have risen, but they haven't reached the Peninsula yet. I'm staying with your mum at Cailleach Estate and we both agree that you should come back here.'

'Will we be safe there? Alvar said—'

'I know what that tosser told your mum, but I'm confident he was lying. The wards over this place were built by generations of kick-arse mages. They are stronger than most. Not even spell-breaking magic can take them down.'

Neve breathed a sigh of relief. 'Okay, I'll try to leave this place. Erik told me I'm free to come and go as I please, but now I'm questioning everything he's ever said.'

'Good. Best of luck.'

'Thanks... Dad.' After hanging up, she debated the wisdom of retrieving her school bag from Erik and Elna's room. The only thing of value she recalled leaving in it was her laptop and she didn't think it was worth risking her life over. All she really needed to take with her was her phone.

Now to find a way to sneak out. The library window was big enough to fit through, so she slipped outside and climbed down the large tree

51

supporting that side of the house—an easy feat for an expert gymnast like Neve. Sticking to the shadows, she crept along the driveway, breathing easier when she spotted the road ahead. After another two steps, she hit an invisible barrier that zapped her, knocking her back on her arse. *What the hell?* She crossed to the other side of the path and inched forward. Another electric shock forced her back. *Dammit! This must be a ward, but why can't I pass it? So much for not being a prisoner.*

After several more failed attempts at different points around the perimeter, she gave up and headed back inside. Every muscle in her body ached from so many jolts and she was exhausted, so she found the nearest guest room and collapsed on the bed. The last thing she managed to do was send Brendan a text message: I CAN'T GET PAST THE WARDS. I'M TRAPPED. PLEASE HELP.

Then sleep overwhelmed her.

Liam followed the trail of death and destruction from Mount Gambier to Murray Bridge, passing lots of human military trucks on the way. The dragons had not lingered long in the small towns, focussing instead on the more populated areas. He headed straight for the mage garrison, a large red brick building on the southern outskirts of town. It was one of several mage forts at strategic locations in South Australia, each disguised as country estates. When he arrived, a warlock guard ushered him to the war room.

High Magus Kieran rose from his seat at the table, along with several other high-ranking mages. 'Please join us, Warlock Winters.'

'Thank you, Your Honour.' After shaking hands with all the other men as they introduced themselves, he sat beside Kieran. 'I see the human Defence Force has responded.'

'Yes. The 9th Brigade has deployed a task group to assist emergency services and the human communities,' Kieran explained.

'Will they interfere with our efforts?' Liam asked.

'No. I have been in regular communication with their commander to coordinate matters. They have evacuated this town for us so we can fight without fear of detection. I also have the State's best illusionists working on a cloaking ward to keep the humans out. We need to hit the dragons hard and fast before they move closer to the city. I hate to imagine the bushfires that will result if they attack the Hills.' Kieran pressed a button on the control panel in front of him, displaying a three-dimensional holographic map of the region, which covered the whole table. It showed fires burning and brown spots circling the town. 'The data on this Holo-Map comes from several mystic cameras in key locations and it updates every five minutes, so it is the closest thing we have to a live feed.'

Liam touched one of the brown dots and the map homed in on a large red dragon. 'I assume each of these represents a dragon?'

'Yes,' Kieran replied. 'And the smaller coloured dots are our guys. Gold for warlocks, silver for conjurers, green for shamans, blue for abjurers, black for alchemists, and…,' he zoomed out and gestured to a red clump within the garrison, 'these are the illusionists working on the cloaking ward.'

'Do the dragons know we are here, in this fort?'

Kieran sighed. 'I'm not sure. They haven't shown any interest in the place yet, so that's a promising sign. We might have the element of surprise on our side. I want you to stage an assault from here.' He pointed to a large, open field east of the town. 'Gear up and head out as soon as you are ready.'

'Yes, Your Honour.' Liam bid the councillors farewell and strode into the armoury to meet the troops. 'Alright men—'

One of the female conjurers cleared her throat.

'And ladies,' he added quickly. 'It's our time to shine. Warlocks—pair up with a conjurer. I want archers up front. Shamans and abjurers in the rear guard need to focus on fire control while the alchemists transmute the campsite. Is that clear?'

They all saluted him. 'Yes, sir!'

As he stepped up to a bench covered in weapons, a conjurer approached him. She wore a helmet with a full-face shield and the only way he recognised her gender was by the shape of her breastplate. She was also the woman who had corrected him earlier, and the silver insignia on her arm suggested she was a council member.

'What can I do for you, Councillor?'

'With your wife stuck at home in reserves, I assume you'll need someone else to stand by your side.'

He gaped at her. 'What the hell, Monique? Does your dad know you're here?'

She huffed. 'Of course not. Your uncle James[2] snuck me in.'

'Go home,' he ordered through gritted teeth.

---

[2] James Maher is Steve Maher's father, Monique's father-in-law, and Liam's uncle on Nora's side.

'No!' She crossed her arms in a defiant stance.

He growled at her. 'Kieran will kill me if anything happens to you.'

'No, he won't. Dad loves you too much. Besides, you don't have to tell him you know I'm here. Come on Liam, you need the support of a powerful conjurer and with Alannah on the bench, I'm the best alternative.'

'Fine. Don't make me regret this.' He slung a quiver and bow on his back and affixed a sword to his weapons belt.

Monique did the same and followed him outside.

Crossing the courtyard, he studied his battalion with a heavy heart. Some of them were just kids, most of them were unlikely to come out of this unscathed, and all of them looked to him for guidance. *I suppose I should give them a motivational speech before sending them to their doom.* 'As mages, we have spent our lives training for battle, to guard the world from the forces of darkness. The monsters we face today claim to have the same motives, but they are nothing more than a bunch of zealots who would rather burn the world than help us save it. We will not let the dragons destroy everyone and everything we have worked hard to protect. Today we fight for order. *What do we fight for?'*

'Order!' the crowd hollered.

'Today we fight for justice. *What do we fight for?'*

'Justice!'

'Today we fight for our very fucking lives. *So let's fight!'*

They all roared and cheered, thrusting fists and swords into the air.

Taking point, he led them along the ley lines to the designated battleground. He stood amidst blades of yellow, overgrown grass with a large open field between them and a scene out of some doomsday movie. Beyond the haze of sweltering heat, shops and houses burned in a furnace that coloured the sky like an eerie sunset. Once his ranks re-formed, the thunder of twenty dragons shifted their attention from the town centre and flew toward the mage army. He gulped as he watched them approach like a thick blanket of smog blocking out the sun. Not wanting them to gain too much ground, he nocked an arrow. *'Archers, ready!'*

As the frontline of beasts entered his range, he drew his bow. *'Archers, aim!'*

'Archers, fire!' Loosing his arrow, he let it fly at the closest dragon. He was already preparing the

next one when the flurry of projectiles hit an invisible barrier inches from their targets and fell to the ground. 'Shit! The bastards have warded themselves.' Before he had time to prepare a new strategy, the dragons returned fire.

Brendan sat up in bed with his laptop, clicking between windows as he researched everything from bypassing magical barriers to reinforcing them. Finding reliable information online was difficult at the best of times, but it was harder still when delving into the mystical dark web. Neve's message had distressed him and while his newly acquired paternal instincts screamed at him to rush to her aid, he knew better than to blunder blindly into a Seelie death-trap. He needed to arm himself with knowledge and devise a solid plan.

Several hours into the search, the screen turned blurry, and his eyes drooped. Letting out a frustrated groan, he shut down the computer and stripped out of his clothes. He slipped under the top sheet and turned out the bed lamp. It was a hot summer night, so he did not bother with the quilt. Despite his physical exhaustion, sleep evaded him. His overactive mind ran through its monologue of bullshit while he tossed and turned. Eventually, he resorted to mindfulness just to shut the damn thing up.

He got halfway through his breathing exercises when the door creaked open, and a familiar musky scent wafted across the room. Keeping his eyes closed, he remained perfectly still and pretended to be asleep. His heart thumped a manic beat in response to her presence and he knew there was no chance of fooling her if she was channelling senses mana. Still, he needed to try because if she so much as touched him, his willpower would likely crumble.

'Brendan?' she whispered.

Biting his lip, he kept up the charade. The silence did not deter her, however, as she slid under the sheet and nestled into his side. *Fuck!* His nerves sparked and sizzled like live wires, and he leaped into action, pinning her to the mattress. 'Does this mean you're ready, Lana?'

She shook her head despite the lust pulsing in her aura like a neon sign.

'Then why the hell are you climbing into bed with me?' He pressed his hard cock against her for effect, eliciting one of her delightful whimpers.

'I couldn't sleep,' she rasped. 'I need you to hold me.'

He felt like a royal douchebag for pushing her when she just needed to feel loved. Brendan collapsed beside her and let her snuggle against him. 'I'm sorry, gorgeous. I haven't had sex in days and your body is like an open flame in a tinderbox.'

'Pfft. Only days? Try going for months, then I might pity you.'

'I'd rather not, but I will if that's what it takes to win back your trust.'

'I don't mind if you fuck men in the meantime,' she admitted in a gravelly voice.

Brendan chuckled. 'I bet you'd prefer to watch though, right?'

'Hm.' Her hand skirted across the ridges of his abs as she contemplated the idea. 'Yes. Definitely.'

'Ah hell, Lana. Unless you intend to use your hand to ease the ache in my balls, could you *please* stop touching me like that?'

She jerked her hand away. 'Sorry. I... I won't stop you if you want to take care of it yourself.'

Rolling onto his side, he stared at her with wide eyes. 'For real?'

'Yeah,' she replied breathlessly. 'I'll even give you some visual stimuli if you like.'

'Hot Damn! I'd fucking love that, but... you don't have to.'

'I know, but I want to. You're not the only one here with an itch to scratch.'

An almost orgasmic moan escaped Brendan's diaphragm. 'Christ, Lana! You've just made my day. No, scrap that. You've made my year!'

Throwing the sheet aside, she kneeled back on her haunches and flicked on the lamp. 'I hope you're exaggerating because I'd like to think the real deal will be better than your own hand.' She gradually lifted her black slip in a deliberate, teasing manner.

As soon as her breasts filled his vision, Brendan's dick twitched, and he groaned. 'Believe me, gorgeous—nothing compares to sex with you.'

Her hungry eyes devoured the sight of his naked body, and she licked her lips. 'Gods, I've missed your cock, Brendan.'

Keeping his eyes glued to the goddess before him, he gripped his erection firmly. 'Fuck! I've missed every part of your delicious body, Lana.'

Still kneeling, and with one hand fondling her left nipple, she slipped a finger between her legs and toyed with her clit.

The sight heated his already hard flesh, bringing him close to boiling point as his extremities tingled. 'That's it, gorgeous. Make yourself come for me.' Even though his own climax was fast approaching, he wanted to wait for her, so he slowed his own strokes.

Plunging two fingers into her core, she threw her head back and let out an inarticulate cry of pleasure.

'Fuck, I love that sound!' Intense heat radiated through his body as the tension built.

She dripped and squelched; the heady scent of her arousal flooding his senses. The orgasm took hold, possessing her body like a demon of pleasure as she shuddered and screamed. Brendan cut the tethers of his own restraint and toppled over the edge.

Alannah crumpled onto his chest in a hot, panting mess, and they both fell into oblivion together.

Chapter Four

Oh Shit! So much for taking things slowly. Alannah chided herself as she woke up in Brendan's bed. In a moment of weakness, her plan to keep things platonic had fallen in a heap. She looked at the man sleeping peacefully beside her and briefly considered taking advantage of his obvious morning wood. Then the doubts crept in. Giving her body to Brendan also meant giving him her heart again. Rather than risk it, she eased herself out of bed and glanced around for her nightdress. When she could not find it, she stole one of the t-shirts Brendan had discarded on the floor instead.

Tiptoeing across the room, she got as far as the door when his gravelly morning voice stopped her: 'Leaving so soon, gorgeous?'

Dammit! Wearing a sheepish grin, she peeked over her shoulder.

Having tossed the sheet aside, Brendan sprawled out across the mattress, lacing his fingers behind his head, showing off an eight pack and a ten-inch cock, all as hard as granite. 'I didn't take you for the sexit[3] type.'

Sighing, she turned to face him properly, leaning against the door. 'I wanted to avoid temptation.'

'If you're so tempted, why fight it?'

She closed her eyes to stop herself gawking at him. 'Because my libido is at odds with my heart and I'm still not ready to trust you completely.'

'Hm.' A painful silence filled the room, so she opened her eyes to see what he was doing and jumped when she found him standing directly in front of her. Brendan pulled her into a comforting embrace. 'Let's make a deal. When you're ready to take the next step, you can give me a codeword, like a safeword in reverse. Until then, I promise not to let things go too far, no matter how much they heat up between us. Sound fair?'

She basked in his musky scent and the warmth of his arms. 'That will definitely help. Did you have a codeword in mind?'

'How about a phrase like… "fuck me to the moon and back." Not brilliant, but it's the best I

---

[3] Sexit is the morning-after-sex exit that someone makes before the other person wakes up.

could think of at short notice. If you think of something better—'

'It's fine. Thank you, Brendan.' She glimpsed the digital clock on the bedside table. 'Fuck! It's nearly noon. I can't believe how late I slept. I should get to work.' They shared a heated stare for several seconds. Reluctantly, she stepped out of Brendan's arms.

'Me too,' he agreed. 'I'm getting Neve back from Alvar's today.'

A spark of hope hummed in her chest. 'Good luck. You'll want to take a pair of my glamour-piercing glasses with you, otherwise you probably won't find the place.'

'Glamour piercing glasses?' he asked with a sidelong glance.

'Yeah. A conjuration invention of mine. There's a bunch of them in the cellar. They look like sunglasses.'

'Okay, thanks.'

They gazed into each other's eyes a moment longer before she turned and left his room. After a quick shower, she entered the kitchen and switched on the television to watch the midday news while she drank her coffee.

Jacob joined her a moment later. His feet were still bare, and he wore ripped, dark denim jeans and a faded band shirt. 'Sounds like you and Brendo worked things out last night.'

Oops! I must have forgotten to put up a sound ward. She smirked at him. 'What makes you think Brendan had anything to do with that?'

'You were in his room, right? So—'

Brendan's laugh drifted across the room from the doorway where he leaned against the frame in a sexy arse pose. 'Give me some credit, Red, if I had been fucking Lana, there's no way I would've stopped at one orgasm.'

She felt her cheeks flush, and Brendan rewarded her with a wink before heading out.

Jacob's brow furrowed. 'Then how—'

'Shoosh!' Something on the news caught her attention. Grabbing the remote she turned up the volume. A female reporter stood in front of a burning Sydney skyline:

> *This scene of devastation you see behind me is just one of many from across the globe, thanks to a new weather phenomenon many have dubbed 'Doomsday Rain.' Literal showers of fire have caused widespread panic and uncalculated damage to towns and cities across the world.*

The camera panned to a cluster of people holding propaganda placards with messages such as JUDGEMENT DAY IS HERE! and ATONE FOR YOUR SINS BEFORE IT'S TOO LATE!

> *It's no wonder so many religious groups are banding together during what they claim to be the apocalypse. We are advising all civilians to stay indoors as we enter a nationwide lockdown....*

She turned off the television. 'Crap! The dragons have already reached Sydney. I hope Tyler and Sam are okay.'

'Tyler's a warlock, right?' Jacob asked and she nodded. 'I'm guessing he's probably fighting the dragons, just like Liam is.'

'Yeah, probably. Speaking of which, I ought to finish that armour.' She swallowed the last of her coffee, wincing as it burned her gullet, and slid off the breakfast bar stool. When she reached the basement stairs, the doorbell rang. She waited for the sound of Jacob scurrying up to the attic to finish before answering.

High Magus Kieran greeted her with a weathered frown and another two trunks. 'I have bad news, Councillor.'

Her heart skipped a beat as she let him in. 'Is Liam okay?'

'Yes, thanks to you. Unfortunately, not everyone was wearing your armour. We lost a lot of mages out there. The rear guard were lucky enough to escape back to camp and the frontline bore the brunt of the onslaught.'

'Oh gosh! Is that more armour for me to work on?' She pointed to the trunks beside him. 'I still haven't finished the last lot.'

'Actually, no. These are arrows. I need you to imbue them with spell breaking. The dragons are able to ward themselves mid-flight.'

She gaped at him. Immense mystic power was needed to shield a moving sentient being against any form of magic and she knew other conjurers had instilled those arrows with various spells. 'I hate to suggest this, but it sounds like you could use some dark mages on the battlefield.'

Kieran scowled. 'Over my dead body!'

'Let's hope it doesn't come to that then.'

He sighed. 'Please just get these and the rest of the armour done ASAP, then coordinate delivery with Liam. After that, I want you to work with the dwarves to ensure a regular supply of imbued weapons and armour reaches the mage army. Focus on the nether based spells. Our frontline conjurers will handle the rest.'

'Yes, Your Honour.'

Ironic, Brendan thought as he approached the Seelie property wearing a pair of magical sunglasses. Learning about Alannah's conjuration invention had stirred a memory. After giving it more thought, he realised they were probably the glasses Tyler's crew had worn when catching him at the museum heist a bit over fifteen years ago. He never thought he would be thankful for the existence of such an item, yet there was no way he could have seen Alvar's house for the trees without them. It had not taken much for him to bypass the wards—nothing a little spell breaking could not fix. The real challenge presented itself as he studied the enormous wood cabin and wondered how to break in undetected.

'Let me save you the trouble,' commanded a tall blond man in a menacing tone, who stepped out from behind a large gum tree.

Fuck! Is the man an illusionist or something?
'You must be Alvar Elofsson,' he sneered.

'And you must be trespassing on private property, mage scum. I suggest leaving before I show you how the Seelie handle criminals.'

He huffed. 'I'm perfectly aware of the underhanded methods you lot employ and I'm not the least bit scared of you, *Your Highness*.'

'Is that so? I guess you leave me no choice.' Alvar snapped his fingers and tendrils of bark shot out from the tree behind him, trapping him in their writhing mass.

'So you're an alchemist then,' he mused.

'What are you doing here, mage? I'll happily feed you to the dragons if you even think about lying.'

'I have come to take my daughter home. Her mother and I refuse to sell her to a bunch of arseholes who think they can use her to advance their position in the Seelie Court.'

'So, you're the great Liam Winters,' Alvar remarked drily. 'I honestly thought you'd be taller.'

'Please don't insult me.' He spat at the ground before Alvar's feet. 'No, I'm Neve's *real* father.'

'If that's the case, you are nothing more than a Beltane sperm donor. You have no legal claim over the girl, and I will not release her into your custody. If Lady Winters is not intending to sign the contract, she can come see me herself.' Alvar turned to leave.

Drawing on his open connection to the stygian element, he broke free of the magically animated vines and charged Alvar. Catching the man in a chokehold, he ignited crimson flames of hellfire on his fingers and let them dance in Alvar's peripheral vision. 'You have no fucking idea who you're dealing with, *princeling*.'

'So, you've gone a little dark.' Alvar's shoulders rose in a partial shrug, the best he could manage with Brendan's arm restricting his movement.

He chuckled at Alvar's observation.

'I'm still not handing her over. If you kill me, the wards will expel you from this property and you'll have no hope of seeing your precious girl ever again.'

'Who said anything about letting you die?' He brought the flames closer to Alvar's cheek. 'I will, however, enjoy hearing you scream in agony as I singe your soul.'

'I'm not so easily swayed,' Alvar croaked. 'Besides, it's not up to me. You cannot interfere with the sacred laws of the Seelie. I did not create the barrier holding her here, nor can I control it. And before you ask, not even your dark magic can break it.'

'Fine then. Let's play a little game of Truth or Burn instead.' He tightened his grip around Alvar's throat. 'I should warn you, I'm a powerful enchanter, so I'll know if you're lying. Do you understand?'

'Yes.' Alvar's voice betrayed no emotion, but grey blobs of fear oozed like mud dripping from his aura.

'Is it true that the wards over Cailleach Estate won't withstand dragon fire?'

'It's true,' Alvar admitted. 'None of the current wards over the mage estates will protect you.'

'Even though not even nether can break through the Cailleach wards?'

'Dragon fire is pure primordial,' Alvar scoffed. 'It is far more powerful than all other mana.'

'So how do we beat it?'

Alvar sniggered. 'I'm not revealing Seelie secrets without a signed betrothal contract.'

He attempted to manipulate Alvar's thoughts to force it out of him, but he came up against a mammoth-sized mind shield—and not the temporary sort produced by pathetic little pendants. Not even his attunement to nether helped him penetrate the powerful defence.

Again, the man just laughed. 'Nice try, enchanter. We guard our secrets well. Do what you like to me, I'm not betraying my people.'

Hot hatred boiled his blood. '*Mages* were your people and you willingly betrayed them. Why did you do it? Why turn your back on the people who gave you life?' His hands trembled with rage and a flicker of hellfire seared Alvar's cheek.

A blood-curdling cry slipped from his throat, and it took him a moment to settle his breathing. 'B-because I discovered the covenant. A friend of mine warned me the dragons were coming, so I chose the winning team.'

He hovered close to Alvar's ear. 'You know what that makes you?' He paused, not caring if the bastard answered. 'It makes you a disgusting coward. Take me to see my daughter. I refuse to leave this place before knowing she is okay.' He burned a strand of Alvar's hair, reminding the man what failing to cooperate would cost him.

'Fine!' Alvar spat. 'Follow me.'

Not even the wondrous world of fiction could hold Neve's attention as she slipped further into depression, so she tossed her book aside and let the misery take her.

'*Hi princess, I'm coming. Whatever you do, don't mention my name to these jerks,*' said Brendan within her head.

The magic communication startled her out of her funk, and she sat bolt upright. '*Are you taking me home?*' She hadn't yet mastered telepathy, so she hoped he could read her thoughts from wherever he was.

'*I'm sorry. I can't free you from the magic binding you to this place, but I can help you get the truth out of the Alvarssons while I'm here. Then you can decide if you want your mum to sign the contract or collect you herself. Get the twins and bring them to the front sitting room.*'

'*Okay.*' She dashed from the library and up some spiral stairs to Erik and Elna's room. There was no guarantee she would find them there, but it was where they spent most of their time when at home. *Doing Gods knew what as they concoct their vile schemes.*

Erik sat alone on the suede couch, reading a novel. He looked up from his book and smiled. 'Have you decided to make the most of your situation, sweetheart?'

'No. We have a visitor. Where's Elna?'

'Out.' He rose and crossed the room, wrapping her in his arms. 'Who's our guest?'

Squirming out of the embrace, she turned away from him. 'You'll see.' As they walked alongside one another, she asked, 'Why did you lie about my freedom to leave?'

Erik sighed. 'I didn't know the Seelie Court would use magic to keep you here.'

'Likely story,' she hissed.

'I'm telling the truth. The Seelie Court of Australia is a large, powerful organisation with lots of archaic laws and practices. I hope to change them one day by becoming the king, but until then, I'm stuck under their thumb.'

'How do you become king?'

'By creating a marital bond stronger than any of my rivals. For that, I need a powerful wife. I need you, Neve.'

'Seelie politics sounds complicated,' she mused.

Erik snorted a cynical laugh. 'To put it mildly.'

When they reached the sitting room, she ran toward Brendan and threw her arms around him. 'Thank you for coming.'

'Anytime, princess.' He hugged her tight. 'Where's Elna?'

'Visiting family,' Erik explained. 'Who the hell are you?'

'Family,' Brendan replied in an equally aloof tone as he released her. 'I have a few questions about your recent… activities, Erik.'

Erik glanced at Alvar. 'May I have some privacy, please Sir?'

Alvar gave Brendan a wary look.

'It's okay, Father,' Erik assured him.

When the door shut behind Alvar, Brendan closed his eyes and began concentrating.

'What—' she began.

'He's casting a soundproofing ward over the room,' Erik explained.

'Stay out of my head, kid,' Brendan warned. 'Or I'll tell your old man about all the inappropriate things you've been doing to Neve.'

Erik scowled. 'You're bluffing.'

Brendan's eyes shot open, and he glared at Erik. 'You really wanna try me? How about we start with why you and your sister bribed an Unseelie dealer to sell Rhapsody to Jasper? What did you stand to gain by setting them up to fail your fucked up loyalty test?'

Turning a deathly shade of pale, Erik gaped at him. 'How—'

'Answer the fucking question, Erik. And don't even think about twisting the truth, because I'll know.'

The way Brendan put Erik in his place made her grin proudly.

'I wanted blackmail material on Jasper, to keep him away from Neve.'

She gasped. 'You *did* break us up?'

He nodded stiffly, as if it physically hurt him to admit the truth.

'And when the prospect of losing his own life wasn't enough to incentivise Jasper, you threatened to harm Neve, didn't you?'

'Wait, what?' Brendan hadn't told her that huge detail.

'I didn't intend to follow through with my threat, I swear. I just needed Jasper to believe me, so he'd stay away.' Erik's voice was trembling. He gazed into Neve's eyes. 'I mean it, sweetheart. I love you and I would never harm you.'

Brendan shook his head. 'You sure have a perverse way of expressing your love, kid. What about the sex tape? I know for a fact Jasper didn't post it online. Do you know who's responsible?'

'No,' Erik replied through gritted teeth. 'I definitely had nothing to do with that.'

Stomping up to Erik, she seethed in his face. *'If you didn't do it, then who did?'*

His eyes mirrored the rage fuming in her own. 'I don't know, but I intend to find out.' He reached out to grip her shoulders, but she jerked away, and his hands fell short.

'Don't touch me, *sicko!*' A few tears dripped down her cheeks.

His jaw locked and his fists clenched. 'Neve, please. I'm sorry, okay?'

'Sorry? You're not sorry. You had no right. Go find some other virgin bride to help you take your stupid crown. I'm done being your plaything.' She stormed out of the room and slammed every door she walked past. When she reached the guest room she had claimed, she collapsed on the bed and bawled her eyes out.

Playing it safe for once, Alannah retired to her own room with a conviction to stay there. Her day had been long and draining, and while she craved the comfort of Brendan's bed and the familiarity of his scent, the temptation was too strong. The fact that he had not yet returned also worried her. *What's taking him so long, dammit?* He had left to help Neve twelve hours prior without sending her so much as a text update since. *Don't tell me he skipped town again!*

After tossing and turning another hour, she let her thoughts drift to the bottles of liquid solace in her uncle's sitting room. *What harm could one nightcap do?* Sliding out of bed, she donned her silk dressing gown and plush slippers before sneaking downstairs. It was absurd really; like who was going to tell her off for drinking? The only other people in the house were unlikely to care. Still, she did not want to disturb them, so she left the lights off and crept on tiptoes. Grabbing a whiskey tumbler, she poured a double shot and curled up on the sofa in the family room. The first sip tasted like the loving arms of an old friend welcoming her home. The second warmed her insides and soothed her aching muscles. Before she knew it, she had finished and poured herself another.

'Lana?' Brendan asked softly as he flicked on the light.

Blinking several times, she adjusted to the brightness before taking in his bruised face and dishevelled attire. 'Hmph. You came back,' she slurred.

'Oh fuck! You've been drinking.' He rushed forward and snatched the glass from her hand.

'Hey! No fair! Get your own damn drink.' Flailing her arms about, she tried to grab it back.

'I know your history with alcohol, Lana. I don't think you should be having this.' He knocked back the shot himself and sat beside her.

'Yeah, well it was your fucking fault! Yours and Liam's.'

Brendan embraced her firmly. 'I told you: I'm not going anywhere. I'm sorry I got back so late. Something… detained me.'

Spotting a tear in his sleeve, she sighed. 'Looks like you got in a fight.'

'I did.'

'What happened?'

'It's a long story. Maybe we should get comfortable, in my room.'

Biting her lip, she nodded and let him lead her by the hand. Once the door closed, she cast a sound ward and shrugged out of her dressing gown, letting it pool on the floor.

After stripping down to his boxer shorts, he stared lasciviously at her in nothing but a black chiffon babydoll. 'You're really testing my limits in that thing, gorgeous.' Pulling her flush against him, he traced the spaghetti straps of her nightie with his fingertips while holding her heated gaze. 'I'm dying to kiss you right now, but I won't push my luck. I want you to make the first move when you're ready.' Stepping back, he dropped onto the bed, bringing her down onto his lap.

As soon as she felt his hardness nudging against her, she clambered out of his grip and climbed under the quilt. 'Tell me what happened first.'

Exhaling sharply, he snuggled in beside her. 'Well to start with, I wasn't able to bring Neve home, but you should have no problem retrieving her yourself. Alvar wants you to reject his contract in person.' His brow furrowed. 'I'm sorry, Lana, but the wards over this place won't stop dragon fire. Apparently, they breathe pure primordial. That said, Neve doesn't want to stay there any longer. After getting the truth out of Erik, she despises the arsehole.'

'It's okay. I think I know a way to reinforce the wards. Turns out the armour I imbued for the mage army can stand up to dragon fire. I just need to use the same approach on the wards.'

'Good, that's a huge relief. Anyway, I helped Neve shake the intel we needed from Erik.' He related their conversation wherein the only crime Erik denied committing was uploading the sex tape. 'After Neve stormed out the room, I squeezed another truth from the Seelie fucker. He confessed to pushing the Rhapsody knock off. When I asked for his source, he told me it came down the chain of command from the king himself.'

'Oh crap!'

'My thoughts exactly. Anyway, I punched the kid's nose before taking my leave. I was in the middle of texting you as I left Alvar's house when someone appeared out of nowhere and knocked me out cold. When I came to, I was sitting in an interrogation room with a couple of enlightened guys. They wanted to know who I was and how I knew about the fake Rhapsody. When I refused to talk, they used my own fucking mind tricks to force it out of me. So now the Seelie Court knows I'm the Syndicate Boss and that I'm Neve's bio dad. I think they even have my business phone.'

Her heart hammered as she listened. 'How did you escape?'

'The guards made one huge mistake when transporting me to their dungeon: they didn't use cold iron cuffs, so I blasted the bastards with hellfire and hightailed it outta there. When I got outside, I found myself in a rainforest I didn't recognise. It took a bit of trial and error along the ley lines to get back to civilisation. Turns out I was in the Daintree, home of the Seelie throne.'

She gaped at him. 'You hopped the ley lines all the way from Queensland? In the middle of a war with the dragons. *Are you insane?*'

He smirked. 'Yeah, probably a little.'

'Thank fuck you made it home in one piece.' She flung her arms around him and sobbed. The thought of losing Brendan again after she had just got him back was more than she could bear. That was when it hit her. Despite the shadow of doubt lurking in the back of her mind, her heart needed him as much as her body wanted his. She was sick of holding out on him.

'I'm sorry for making you worry, gorgeous,' he whispered against her ear.

Her cheek brushed against his rigid jawline as she brought her mouth a hair's breadth from his lips. Their eyes locked together for a second and the air between them sparked with electricity. Then she kissed him, breathing him in like he was her oxygen. The hint of whiskey on his lips tasted delicious, urging her to straddle him and deepen the passion. He echoed her desperate moans with fervent groans and by the time she came up for air, they were both panting frantically.

'Brendan I—'

'Shoosh.' He placed a finger over her lips. 'As keen as I am to bend you over and make you scream my name fifty million times, I think you should wait until you're completely sober before taking things any further. Last thing I want is you waking up with regrets.'

A fresh wave of tears brimmed in her eyes. 'Fuck I love you, Brendan.'

He chuckled softly. 'I love you too, Lana.'

Chapter Five

With her face to the porcelain throne, Alannah rid herself of the toxins she had imbibed the night before. She had barely made it to the ensuite bathroom in time.

Brendan kneeled beside her and gathered her hair in his hands. 'Hey Lana. Jacob is getting the green goop for you.'

'Thanks,' she rasped before giving another offering to the God of hangovers. *Is that even a thing? Fuck I don't miss this aspect of drinking.*

'Ah shit!' Jacob appeared a minute later, handing her a shot glass of Uncle Ross' elixir. 'Don't tell me you had a relapse, sweets?'

Grabbing the potion, she knocked back the bitter medicine and gave Jacob a sheepish grin. 'Okay, I won't.'

He shook his head. 'What tipped you off the wagon?'

Lowering her gaze, she muttered, 'I thought Brendan had skipped town again.'

'Why—'

Brendan cut him off: 'I had a run-in with the Seelie Court yesterday. The bastards seized me when I wasn't paying attention and took me to Queensland. I'll fill you in later, Red. Right now, Lana and I need to reinforce the wards on this place so she can pick up Neve.'

'No worries, Sir. I'll leave you to it.'

'It's so weird hearing him call you Sir,' she mused as she lurched to her feet, bracing herself against Brendan when she staggered. 'Ick! I desperately need a shower before we get to work.'

'Want some help? You still seem a little unsteady on your legs.' His eyes skimmed across her body, and he gave her a sly grin. 'Or some company?'

She snorted. 'And how is that going to help me regain stable footing?'

'Fair point. You'll be walking funny for days the next time I have my way with you, gorgeous.' Holding her firmly, he helped her toward the shower cubicle and turned on the water. 'I'll stay out here and... keep an eye on you.'

'I don't have any of my hair or body products in your shower,' she protested.

'Just use mine for now. As a bonus, you'll get to smell like me all day.'

Well damn! He had her there. 'Fine. But if I'm going to make a habit of staying in your room, I should move my toiletries in here.'

'Agreed. Now get to it, gorgeous. Water's a-wasting.'

Rolling her eyes, she removed her nightie. 'You're just overly eager for the show.'

He laughed as she stepped under the water. 'I can't deny how much I enjoy the sight of your naked body, Lana.'

Their banter continued through her shower, then through his, easing her into a sense of serenity. For several precious minutes she forgot about the world crumbling around them.

After breakfast, they entered the ritual cellar together. Their ancestors had built the room over a ley line nexus, making it a power hub for the protections surrounding Cailleach Estate.

'I'm going to start by tapping into the wards,' she explained. 'Once I access them, we should open a mutual nether connection. That's when I'll need your help, like we discussed over breakfast.'

Brendan nodded as he shamelessly stripped out of his clothes.

When she did the same, the heat of his gaze tingled her skin. They usually wore robes for rituals, but she wanted to use the tension mounting between them to enhance the magic. Sexual energy was a powerful medium for the stygian element. Moving around the room, she cast the circle, calling upon the guardians of the watch towers and invoking their names.

When they sat upon the cushions, she closed her eyes and cleared her mind as best she could. Awareness of Brendan's naked body did not help matters. She eventually connected with the primordial, using it to reach out and detect each of the magical shields surrounding the property. Opening her third eye, she studied the threads of multi-coloured light, weaving and flowing together in intricate patterns. 'Fuck! There's so many.'

'I'm not surprised. Every generation of the Winters clan has added to them,' he reminded her.

'Okay, let's do this.' She drew on the power of her nether connection and opened her mind to Brendan as she crossed into his. The surge still winded her despite anticipating it this time, but she recovered sooner, letting the ecstasy quiver through her.

'Are you ready?' he asked in a husky voice.

'Yes,' she replied breathlessly as she reclined back onto her elbows and opened her legs. In the past, she had taken care of herself during stygian rituals, but the immense power they were drawing on called for more intensity.

His warm breath tickled her sensitive flesh seconds before his velvety tongue traced a trail of goosebumps between her folds. She bucked against his mouth as a guttural noise escaped her. As the pressure increased, she directed the sizzling heat in her blood through her magical conduits which created a feedback loop with the intoxicating sensations rippling through her. The air sparked and crackled around her, lifting the tiny hairs all over her skin. Concentrating as best she could, she pushed her desire to protect her home into the tightly woven mesh of mystical energies, spinning her own crimson tessellation. Each time she teetered on the edge of her climax, Brendan drew back, prolonging her sublime torture until she was ready. As the final filaments tangled together, she trembled with wanton need. 'At last,' she mewled. 'Fucking finish me, dear Gods!'

He growled into her core, not hesitating in the slightest as he sent tidal waves of pleasure rippling through her with his deft fingers and slick tongue. Quaking from the explosion in her nerves, she locked the stygian strands into place before her limbs collapsed and euphoria blinded her.

As her senses returned, Brendan hovered above her, concern drawing lines on his brow. 'Are you okay, gorgeous?'

'Yeah, I'm great. That was extraordinary.' She spoke gruffly with her parched throat.

'Did it work?'

'I think so.'

Brendan seized her lips in a fervent kiss, giving her a luscious taste of herself. As their bodies entwined in passion, temptation tapped her on the shoulder.

'Gods! I'm so close to asking you to desecrate this sacred space with me,' she admitted. Sexual acts in the name of magic were one thing, but rutting like animals inside the ritual circle would likely anger the Gods.

He smirked. 'Wouldn't be my first time.' As her eyes widened, he laughed. 'Please don't ask. You really don't want to know.'

Biting her lip, she nodded, wondering if it had anything to do with Bridey.

'Much as I'd love to fuck you senseless here and now, you still need to save Neve.' He sat back on his heels and drew his athame across the painted perimeter.

'I know. That's why I'm not begging for it yet.' Rolling onto her side, she broke the circle with her own blade.

When she rose to her feet, Brendan embraced her, whispering in her ear, 'Come to my bed tonight and I promise to make up for lost time.'

Delightful shivers danced across her neck and shoulders to the tune of anticipation. 'Okay.'

Brendan's nerves hummed with excitement like high-tension wires. After hopping the ley lines to his car on the esplanade, his thoughts returned to Alannah as he drove to his property. *In several hours, she will be mine again. Is it too soon to suggest repairing our broken link*? He had felt the tug of her soul during the ritual that morning and he knew she did too, although neither of them had brought it up after.

Before parting ways, he had explained his plan to return home briefly. He needed more clean clothes and wanted to check on the Hawthorns. A flicker of doubt had clouded her countenance when he told her, so he assured her Bridey no longer had a place in his heart or bed. Caleb was a different matter, however, and while Alannah had given him her blessing as far as men were concerned, she did not understand the complicated dynamics of his menage with the Hawthorn siblings. He just hoped he could fool Bridey long enough to steal Caleb from under her nose.

Bridey greeted him in the kitchen with her arms crossed. She looked the part of a stern housewife, although she had never lifted a finger for anything as menial as chores. 'Where have you been these last few nights?' she accused.

'Working,' he snapped. 'Some of us still have empires to run.'

'Puh-lease, Jet, I can see the glimmer of sex in your aura, so I know you've been getting some on the side. I warned you not to mess—'

'Enough!' he roared as he crowded her personal space. 'I haven't been messing around with Lana. Stop acting like an insecure brat.'

Narrowing her eyes, she ground her teeth before replying, 'If not her, then who's responsible for that satisfied afterglow in your aura?'

He huffed. 'Red. I've been working closely with him on the Seelie potion issue.' It was not a complete lie.

Her eyes widened. 'Seriously? I didn't think you felt so inclined.'

Shrugging, he wandered into the bedroom to start packing his suitcase. 'When needs must… and all that jazz.'

Bridey followed him, getting comfortable on the bed as she watched him. 'What's with the luggage?'

'I'm taking a trip interstate. I've tracked the source of the Rhapsody fake to the Seelie king himself. I need to destroy their supplies and hopefully find enough evidence to discredit them.'

'Can't you get one of your spymasters to do that?' she asked, raising the pitch of her voice enough to betray her fear.

'No. The wards around the Seelie Court are impenetrable to Unseelie. I can only pass them because of my bloodline. A large portion of their nobility are pureblood mages, after all.'

'What about the taint on your soul?'

He smirked. 'Turns out they aren't so innocent themselves. I won't even have the blackest soul there.'

Gasping, she shuffled to the edge of the bed. 'Wait! You've been there already?'

'Yu*p*,' he replied, popping the p. 'Where's Caleb?'

'Hanging out the washing,' she replied with an exasperated tone. 'We could really use some servants around here. A housemaid and cook in the very least.'

He sighed. 'I'll look into it after the dragon war. No point hiring anyone to look after an empty house. That's if this place is even standing by then.'

Bridey gaped at him. 'You want us to come with you?'

'No. It's far too dangerous. I want you and Caleb to hide until this all blows over. Use your underground connections to find a safehouse.'

The rear sliding door swished across its tracks and Caleb appeared a moment later. Dropping the washing basket with a thud, he rushed into Brendan's open arms. 'Gods I've missed you!'

He kissed Caleb deeply, drawing back only when the heat growing between them suggested they were both at risk of fucking each other senseless for the rest of the day. 'I need you to go with Bridey.'

Caleb sucked in a sharp breath. 'What do you mean? A… are you leaving us?'

'No,' he replied while shaking his head. 'This is just temporary, while I sort out a few things. I'll join you as soon as I can, but this place won't protect you from the dragons. Find a safehouse and make sure the wards include spell breaking.'

Bridey gave him a sidelong glance. 'How would you know what sort of mystic shields are needed?'

Fuck! Schooling his expression, he hid his panic. 'Call it a hunch.'

Still eyeing him warily, she rose from the bed. 'I guess I'll message you once we've sorted our accommodation.'

'Oh shoot! I almost forgot: the Seelie took my phone, so we need to change our numbers.' He marched across the house to the study, where he withdrew a fresh set of burner phones for the three of them. Leaning against the edge of the solid desk, he set up the three devices. 'Send me all our Syndicate contacts once you've added them to your phones.' After handing them over, he drew Bridey into his arms. 'I'm sorry to be running out like this Bry, but the situation is urgent.'

'So, this is goodbye for now?' she asked, adopting a neutral expression, and locking herself up tight.

It frustrated him to no end when she did that because he knew she was hiding something, but it was not like he had room to complain anymore. 'For now, yes.' He leaned in to kiss her, but she turned away. 'Bry?'

'Save it for Caleb.' She stormed off toward the back of the house. The sliding door whizzed open and closed with a *bang!*

'What the fuck's her problem?'

Caleb slid his hands over Brendan's shoulders and down his chest. 'She's scared of losing you, as am I. We just deal with our fear differently.'

He spun around in Caleb's arms, holding him tight against his own chest. 'I swear to the Gods I'll return to you, Thornsy.' Their lips collided in another passionate kiss, and he prayed it would not be their last.

After taking his leave, he hopped the ley lines back to Cailleach Estate. There was no point driving since the car would draw unwanted attention to his whereabouts and he found it easy enough to traverse the short journey, even with luggage in tow. Alannah was still out when he got there, so he searched the house for Jacob, finding him sprawled out on the bed in the attic.

The boggart was reading a novel when he looked up. 'Hey Boss. How did things go back home?'

He shrugged. 'Bridey cracked the shits with me, and Thornsy clung to me like a needy child.'

'Sounds like a normal day in that household.'

'You're not wrong,' he huffed. 'We need to talk about the fake Rhapsody situation. I found the source and we need to act fast if we're going to shut down their operation.'

The library window had beckoned to Neve. While she no longer cared to read, she still found solitude in the vista. A pair of small birds with long beaks flitted about on the branches of the tree, displaying flashes of bright yellow plumage. A quick internet search told her they were probably honeyeaters. *Oh, to be as free as a bird.*

After a brief knock, Alvar entered the room, scowling more than usual. 'There's someone here to see you.'

Another figure stepped out from his shadow and her spirits lifted. 'Mum!' Springing to her feet, she dashed across the intervening space and barrelled into her mother.

'Hi hun. I've missed you too.' Alannah pecked her cheek with a dainty kiss. 'Can we talk in here?' she asked Alvar.

'May as well. Should I summon my children?'

'No, that won't be necessary,' her mum insisted, taking her hand, and leading her to the chairs by the window.

Alvar sat with them. 'Have you made a decision concerning the betrothal contract?'

'Yes. But first I would like to ask my daughter to confirm her own wishes. When we last spoke, she sounded head-over-heels in love with Erik, but I understand things have changed?'

She nodded frantically. 'I don't want to marry Erik. He is a horrible person.'

'Then it's settled.' Alannah shoved a folder at Alvar's chest, barely giving him time to grip the pages. 'You can shove this fucking betrothal where the sun don't shine. I refuse to sign it. Come on hun, let's go.' She rose abruptly and waited for Neve to follow before leaving.

Beaming with pride after her mother's assertive display, she welcomed the drops of sun on her face as they stepped outside. But then she remembered their predicament. 'What happens when the dragons get here? Alvar said the wards—'

'Don't worry about that,' Her mum assured her as they climbed into the car. Their seatbelts both clicked in unison. 'I've reinforced the estate with a spell breaking ward that ought to hold up against dragon fire.'

The tension fled her body with each breath she exhaled. 'I'm so glad. Thank you, Mum.'

After offering a slight smile, Alannah started the engine and drove in silence for a few minutes. 'I should warn you: we have some guests staying with us. You remember Amy and Jacob?'

'The dwarf chick and boggart bloke?'

'Yeah, them. Unfortunately, they don't get along very well, so there may be some tense moments.' Alannah sighed. 'Brendan's there too.'

She gasped. 'Are you two... back together?'

'Sort of. I don't know; it's complicated.'

'Gawd, please promise to soundproof the bedroom if the pair of you go at it!'

Alannah snorted, her mouth twitching. 'We'll try. Apologies in advance if the heat of the moment makes us forget.'

Good Gods. She prayed it never came to that. 'Um... Mum?'

'Just spit it out. What do you want?'

She bit her lip. 'I'd like to invite a couple of my own friends to stay with us.'

'Who?'

'Cat, for one. I can't bear to think of the dragons getting her.'

'Yeah fine,' her mum agreed. 'I should probably reinforce the Maher wards anyway. It's the least I can do for Nora and Monique. I assume the other friend is Fiona?'

'Um no. I'd like to mend things with Jasper.'

'*No fucking way!*' she screeched. 'That little shit—'

'He's not all bad, Mum! Erik set him up and Jas had nothing to do with that sex tape.'

'Fine. But I want you both in separate rooms and no funny business under my roof, you hear? I still don't trust any boys from the Rowan clan.'

Crossing her arms with a huff, she slumped back into her seat. 'Whatever.' *It's not like Mum will pay attention to us anyway if she has Dad to distract her.*

Rather than heading straight home, Alannah detoured via the Maher family estate. Most of the adults had gone to war, but Neve's great-grandparents—Nora's parents—had stayed home to look after the kids. The girls greeted each other with excited squeals, bouncing on their toes as they hugged each other until Great Grams ushered them all inside for a cuppa. With hot chocolates in hand, the girls went to Caitlin's room.

'What's going on?' Caitlin asked, perching on her bed.

She sat beside Caitlin. 'I was hoping you could come stay with me during the war.'

Caitlin's eyes lit up. 'Really?' The excitement fled from her expression. 'Wait, what about the Alvarssons? I thought you were staying with them.'

'Not anymore. Things went pear-shaped.'
She explained the nasty things Erik had done.

'Yikes! I always knew there was something
dodgy about those twins. I'm glad you got out
when you could.'

She nodded her agreement. 'I'd like to patch
things up with Jasper, too. I convinced Mum to let
him stay at our estate, although she insisted on
separate bedrooms.' She rolled her eyes at the
absurdity and hypocrisy of the request, very much
doubting her mother was staying out of Brendan's
bed.

A frown creased Caitlin's brow.

'Come on, don't tell me you still have a
problem with Jasper?'

'It's not that,' Caitlin sighed. 'The Rowans
left the state. They went to stay with family in
Queensland.'

Something heavy constricted her chest and
she wheezed. Grabbing her phone from her bag, she
dialled Jasper's number. It rang once before going
to voicemail. Hanging up, she tried again. One dial
tone then the prompt to leave a message. 'Dammit!'
She dropped her phone back in her bag.

'He probably blocked your number,' Caitlin
suggested.

A glimmer of hope sparked in her heart. 'What if you ring him?'

'I doubt I'll get anywhere, but I can try.' Caitlin's attempt yielded the same result. 'He would've known you'd resort to other people's phones. You should get a burner or find someone he won't connect to you.'

Her shoulders slumped. 'If he really doesn't want to hear from me, he'll screen his calls. I've lost him, Cat.' A few tears trickled down her cheeks. Thinking about the insufferable faerie responsible for her predicament, her mood turned as salty as the grief on her lips. 'Fucking Erik! It's all his fault! I could've been happy with Jasper. Those twins must pay.' She sprang to her feet.

Caitlin jumped in front of her, blocking her path to the door. 'Woah! Hold up. I get it, I do… but don't run into battle unprepared. Take some time to devise a strategy.'

The dam broke and she collapsed into Caitlin's arms, heaving and sobbing.

After knocking briefly, Alannah entered the room and gasped. 'Oh hun, what's wrong?' Flanking Neve, she embraced her from behind.

'Jasper left town,' Caitlin explained, 'and she can't get hold of him. I think he blocked our numbers.'

'I'm sorry, sweet pea.' Her mum stroked her hair soothingly and kissed the crown of her head. 'Caitlin, honey, your Grams said it's okay for you to stay with us. Can you pack a bag, please?'

'Okay. Thanks Aunty Alannah.' Caitlin turned Neve to face her mother before releasing her.

Immersing herself in the warmth of her mum's arms, she cried her heart out.

After setting Neve and Caitlin up with a metric shit-tonne of junk food and a pile of B-grade movies, Alannah excused herself for the night. Grabbing a few toiletries from her bathroom, she halted on her way out to look at the bed she had once shared with Liam. A sharp pain cinched her chest as she thought about him.

'You're not having second thoughts, are you?' Brendan slouched against the doorway, wearing nothing but a pair of black satin boxer shorts.

She sucked in a breath at the sight of him, feeling warmth spread through her body. 'No. But I do feel a little guilty.'

Closing the distance between them, he placed one hand on her hip and cradled her cheek with the other. A fire blazed in his bright green eyes. 'Liam's the only guilty party here. He never should have touched you. Ever. You've always belonged to me, Lana, and the sooner you both come to terms with this, the better.'

Her heart leapt into her throat, and she swallowed against the throbbing lump. 'Okay,' she rasped.

'Good. Let's go.' Stepping back, Brendan spun on his heels and sauntered down the hall to his own room.

She took a deep breath and followed him, regaining her confidence with each stride. Closing the door behind her, she dropped her toiletries bag in his ensuite and cast a soundproofing ward. Glancing at the bed, she spotted the leather straps Brendan had tied to each of the four posts, then she shifted her gaze to the man himself. He sat up against the headboard with his hand resting casually on his knees while watching her intently. Desire pooled in her core as she drew closer.

A lopsided grin tugged at one side of his wicked mouth. 'Lose the clothes, gorgeous. All of them.'

Her heart slammed into her ribs as it took off at full speed. 'Yes, Sir.'

A groan slipped from his throat and his eyes darkened.

She loved the beautiful irony of feeling empowered through her submission. Removing her knee-high boots and thigh-length dress, she paused to give Brendan the opportunity to appreciate her lingerie: a crotchless body harness with strappy pentagrams on her thighs and belly, and another plunging into her cleavage. She had bought it on a whim a year ago, intending to surprise Brendan's doppelganger—Tyler—with it, but this was the first time she had used it.

'Holy fuck!' Brendan's eyes bugged out as he sprang to his feet. He tugged on the black bands crossing her midriff. 'I love this. It can stay.'

She smirked. 'Thought you might say that.'

Mesmerised by the harness, he traced the design with his fingers and her skin hummed. He let out a guttural noise when he reached her breasts. 'I especially love how it exposes these.' He flicked her nipples before dipping his hand between her legs. 'And this. Gods, Lana, I hope you use your codeword tonight because I need to fuck you in this thing.'

'Do you honestly think I'd be so cruel as to put this on if I didn't intend to let you have your way with me?'

Pulling her tight against him, his lips claimed hers. He walked her backwards as she returned the kiss with equal fervour. Cold glass touched her bare flesh seconds later, startling her. He had pinned her up against the window. 'I think you missed the bed,' she teased.

Mischief twinkled in his eyes. 'What makes you think I was aiming for the bed?' He spun her around to face her reflection in the full-length casement. 'Do you see how incredibly hot you look right now?'

Taking in the sight of her body pressed against Brendan's, she had to agree. 'Yes, Sir.'

'I'm going to make you feel good tonight, gorgeous, but I promise I won't fuck you until you say the codeword. Understood?'

'Yes, Sir,' she replied huskily.

'Good girl.' He rammed her front up against the window.

She inhaled sharply when her nipples pebbled against the icy surface and chills tingled across her simmering skin. 'I-is it a good idea to play here? In full view of the world?'

'Who the hell's gonna be looking right now? Besides, this place has the best wards in town,' he assured her while trailing kisses down her neck. 'We'd know if any uninvited guests crossed the perimeter.'

Conceding his point, she relaxed into the moment, mewling when he reached around and stroked her clit. Her eyes began to droop until she spied the tell-tale glimmer of glamour directly outside and stiffened.

'Is something wrong?' Brendan asked softly in her ear.

'*I don't know,*' she replied telepathically. '*I think someone is watching us. Don't make any sudden moves. Continue what you're doing.*' She felt him tense slightly, but he otherwise complied. She moaned loudly when his fingers slipped between her slick folds and invaded her sanity. Inhaling deeply, she concentrated on piercing the glamour. She thanked years of experience and powerful magic for making the task simple, despite the erotic distraction. As the veil lifted, she gasped.

He stood flush against the window, balancing on the outer ledge with only a few millimetres of glass separating them. His black eyes dilated such that no white shone through as his attention flitted across her naked body.

'*What is it? What do you see?*' Brendan asked within her mind.

She took a moment to study their prowler who remained oblivious to her discovery, too entranced and aroused by the live show. She had not seen him in years and even then, she was not used to seeing his true form. In her youth, she had been too shallow to accept other magicals for what they really looked like, making a habit of looking at their glamoured forms instead. But she had since adjusted and accepted everyone—warts, horns, claws, and all. Looking at the man before her, she admired the beauty of his silver skin, shimmering in the moonlight. Even his black claws and sinister eyes, while spooky to some, only sparked desire in her nerves. Hooking an arm around the back of Brendan's neck, she bucked against his thrusting fingers.

'Oh hell, Lana. Tell me what you see.'

'Make me come first,' she pleaded.

'No! Not until you tell me.' He withdrew his fingers and rubbed her backside.

Dammit! She figured Brendan would stop touching her as soon as he knew who stood on the other side of the glass, but she did not want the fun to end.

'Christ! Are you suggesting a peeping Tom is just outside this window, perving on you right now?'

'Oops, I guess you read my mind. I doubt he intended to perve, but he's clearly enjoying what he's seeing.'

'Who is he?' Brendan demanded.

'Caleb,' she whispered, locking eyes with the Unseelie man himself.

Chapter Six

Caleb had always fancied Alannah. Most guys with eyes did. Yet in that moment—with her bare tits squashed against the glass as she writhed thanks to Brendan's fingers—his beloved sister paled in comparison. Add the fact that Brendan wore next to nothing as he pleasured her and *bam!* Caleb's dick throbbed in his trackpants, pressing up against the cold glass. *What I'd give to be in the room, sinking inside either of them.* But he couldn't let Bridey down, so he kept quiet and maintained his cover.

Lifting his gaze, albeit hesitantly, he met Alannah's gorgeous green eyes—the same shade as Brendan's—and realised a moment too late.

Brendan spun her out of the way before yanking the window open. He hoisted Caleb inside, throwing him on the floor before slamming the window shut. The glass rattled in the pane. 'What the fuck are you doing here? You were meant to be finding safety with Bridey. And how the hell did you get past the wards without alarming us?'

'His open invitation still stands,' Alannah reminded him. 'From when your dad thanked our friends for their help fighting Tara back when we were still in high school.'

Scrambling back along the floorboards, he tried to rise to his feet, but Brendan straddled him, effectively pinning him to the polished timber. He caught a glimpse of Alannah perching on the end of the bed before Brendan forcibly shifted his attention front and centre with a firm grip of his chin.

'Answers. Now!' Brendan demanded in a stern, no-nonsense voice.

He scowled. 'Bridey was right! You *are* betraying her with Alannah. Does this mean you intend to leave us? How long were you planning to string us along? Or are you only toying with Alannah?'

Brendan growled as Alannah let out a tiny gasp. 'I'm the one asking questions here, Thornsy. Did Bridey send you to spy on me? *Again*?'

He responded with a defiant smirk. 'Does Alannah know about *us*?'

Grinding his teeth, Brendan pressed his weight into Caleb and clamped a hand around his throat. 'Leave Lana out of this.'

Alannah snorted as she drew closer. 'It's a bit late for that, babe.' She knelt beside them. 'To answer your question Caleb, yeah, I know all about your menage. I can't say I approve of Brendan's choice where your sister is concerned, but....' Leaning closer, she brushed his arm with her massive breasts as she hovered above him. 'I'm absolutely fine with the thought of him fucking *you*.' She laughed when he gulped. 'You should let me handle this interrogation, Brendan. I seem to be unnerving him more.'

'Turning him on, more like,' Brendan pointed out. He wasn't wrong, and his prime position told him just how much the situation aroused Caleb.

'It's not like you can talk, Winters. You might come across more intimidating if it didn't feel like you're about to shove that boner deep into my arse.'

Fury blazed in Brendan's eyes. 'I won't be putting my dick anywhere near you if you don't fess up. Why were you spying on me?'

He sighed. 'Bridey thought you were betraying us. I guess her fears were justified.'

'Don't play dumb, Thornsy. It doesn't suit you,' hissed Brendan. 'I know Bridey has been feeding intel to my enemy. What's her interest in Lana? Why is she hellbent on keeping us apart?'

Pursing his lips, he remained silent, holding Brendan's lethal stare.

'Let me try,' suggested Alannah.

Brendan gaped at her. 'No!'

'Don't make me pull rank on you, Brendan.'

Caleb sniggered, earning daggers from them both. Shoulders sagging with resignation, Brendan rose to his feet. Before Caleb could follow, Alannah took Brendan's place, only instead of a menacing glower, she adopted a lascivious expression. His heart hammered in his chest when her tongue traced a seductive line along her lips. She was still wearing the sexy-as-fuck harness and *nothing else.*

'Caleb, sweety,' she began with a saccharine voice, 'let's make a deal. You tell me and Brendan everything you know about Bridey keeping us apart, and I'll reward you.'

He huffed. 'You think I care for your money?'

'I wasn't talking about money.'

'What could you possibly offer me then?'

Grinning, she slid her hands across her tits and tweaked her nipples. 'Me.'

His eyes widened. *Is she messing with me?*

'Tell us what we want to know, and I'll fuck you every which way, right here, right now.'

'No way!' Brendan roared, pulling Alannah off him and sitting her on the bed. 'I'm not letting you jump Caleb's bones when I still haven't had the pleasure in like sixteen years.'

'You are not the boss of me, Brendan!' she snapped. 'You don't get to decide who I invite into my bed!'

Brendan towered over her. 'Maybe not, but I am Caleb's boss and his Dom, so I do get a say in who *he* sleeps with.'

Caleb took the opportunity to stand up. He considered making a break for it, but curiosity and desire got the better of him, so he leaned against the bathroom door and watched them bicker.

'I was just trying to help. I figured the three of us could've had some fun. Why do you have to be such a grumpy jerk about it?'

'You were encouraging his bad behaviour,' seethed Brendan.

'I wasn't! Rewarding good behaviour beats punishing the bad any day.' She crossed her arms beneath her breasts, lifting them further and diverting Brendan's attention.

'You guys make the best parenting team,' Caleb added with a snicker. 'You gonna smack me before or after sending me to my room?'

'Don't fucking tempt me!' Brendan spat.

'Actually, that's not a bad idea,' mused Alannah. Her hands flew up in supplication when they both stared at her. 'Not the spanking, 'cause I know he'd enjoy that too much. We can't let Caleb leave here and run back to Bridey with evidence.'

Brendan nodded. 'Have you got any cold iron cuffs?'

'I think Liam keeps a spare pair in his room.' She covered herself in a robe before disappearing from the room.

Caleb dashed toward the window, but Brendan grabbed him, wrestling him to the ground. 'Stop pushing me, Thornsy. For the record, I'm still madly in love with you and that's the only reason I'm not pushing the truth out of you with magic right now. Using mental manipulation will shatter the frayed bonds of trust between us and I pray to the Gods it doesn't come to that. I hope you will find it in your heart to open up to me because if you don't, our relationship is over.'

Tears welled in his eyes. 'W-what about Bridey?'

'She's dead to me. The traitorous bitch never should've come between me and my soulmate.'

Alannah gasped from the doorway.

'I fucking mean it, Lana. I'm not letting anybody ruin things for us again.' Brendan flipped Caleb over and cuffed his wrists.

He staggered as Brendan pulled him to his feet.

Turning Caleb to face him, Brendan spoke in a deadly tone, 'It's time to make a choice, Thornsy. Us.' He gestured to Alannah and himself. 'Or your deceitful whore of a sister.' He shoved him out the door and led him up a flight of stairs.

When they entered the attic, the sight of Jacob and Amy playing videogames together surprised him. The pair looked up from their gritty shooter with wide eyes.

'I have a job for you, Red. I caught Stirling spying on me and Lana. He is withholding important intel, so don't let him leave this house.' Brendan meant business if he was using both their Syndicate names. 'Chain him up if you have to.' He pointed to the shackles in the corner of the room before returning his attention to Caleb and whispering, 'Let Red know when you're ready to talk. Until then, our relationship is on ice.'

Erik stirred restlessly, feeling the void Neve had left, not only in the middle of the bed, but at the centre of his life. He glanced across at Elna, who sat up, reading a smutty romance novel by faerie light. 'You don't seem too upset by her absence,' he observed.

Looking up from her book, she frowned. 'Maybe I'm just better at masking my emotions than you give me credit for?'

Narrowing his eyes, he studied her aura more closely. Not only was it missing the dark clouds of grief, but she also glowed with positivity and success. He glared at her. 'What did you do, Elna?'

'Excuse me?' Her voice rose in pitch ever so slightly.

Sitting upright, he shuffled closer to her. 'Your aura is practically gloating, so don't play dumb, Sister dearest. Tell me what you did.'

She grinned. 'I found us another prospect.'

'Are you kidding me? I'm not done fighting for Neve.'

'Give it up,' she scoffed. 'The girl's not even a virgin. There's no way they'll accept your claim.'

'*Our* claim,' he reminded her.

She shrugged. 'Same difference.'

'No, it's not. We agreed to work together on this.'

Snapping her book shut, she flung it at the nightstand, where it slid to the floor. 'Really? If that's the case, why didn't you ever ask me if I liked Neve? Hmm?'

'Oh crud!' Grabbing Elna, he wrestled her into a submissive position and pinned her to the mattress. 'You released that sex tape of Neve, didn't you? It makes sense now I think about it. You had access to it, and you have the hacking skills to infiltrate Jasper's email.'

She pursed her lips.

'Did you do it?' he demanded.

Her eyes brimmed with tears as she nodded.

'You stupid little bitch!' He slapped her hard across the cheek. 'Why did you sabotage this for us? Come to think of it, involving Neve in the Rhapsody plot was your idea in the first place, wasn't it? I only intended to set Jasper up that night.'

She squirmed helplessly beneath his firm grip. 'Because you never once considered what or who *I* want!'

He gaped at her.

'You were so obsessed with Neve Winters; you didn't even notice the moment I fell in love with *someone else*.'

'Who?' he asked coldly.

'Finn Doyle.'

'As in Rónán's older brother?' When she nodded, he brought the guy to mind. 'Isn't he a senior? What are the chances *he* is still a virgin?'

'I've already tested him, so I know he is. He told me he is saving himself for the right girl.'

Jealousy wrapped its claws around his heart as he slumped beside Elna. 'Pfft! The boy sounds like a pussy.'

'Get over yourself, Erik! He's a decent guy.'

He huffed. 'Does he know you and I are a package deal?'

'Yes, of course. He assures me he is bi. Gosh I can't wait for you both to hook up, he is so sexy. He does this thing with his tongue....'

Sighing, he rolled onto his side and studied her features closely. Strands of green and platinum hair framed her delicate face, her vibrant eyes sparkled as she talked about him. 'Top or bottom?'

She blinked. 'Sorry, what?'

'I asked if he is a top or bottom with guys.'

'Oh.' She laughed nervously. 'He doesn't know yet, being a virgin and all, but figures he's probably a top.'

He groaned. 'That's hardly going to work for *us* now, is it?'

'Would it hurt you to try something different for once?'

He snorted. 'Bad choice of words, Sis. *That* probably would hurt.'

'Argh! Only because you're always so uptight. It's actually quite enjoyable when you relax.'

Gaping, he stared at her with wide eyes. 'How would you know?'

'Finn and I play with toys,' she replied nonchalantly.

Closing his eyes, he took a deep breath. 'Fine. If it makes you happy, I'll give *it*, and Finn, a go.' He already knew he was going to hate the guy, but she did not need to know that yet. Elna had failed to realise he viewed *all* other men as a threat to his plans and… competition for his place in her heart.

Alannah's foul mood followed her into the next morning. After locking Caleb away in the attic the night before, Brendan had done a full perimeter sweep before collapsing in bed beside her. Neither of them had spoken for a while and she had wondered if he'd fallen asleep. Then he had turned to face her, and she saw the sorrow in his glistening eyes.

'I'm sorry, Lana,' he had said. 'After everything that just happened, I don't think I can give you the good time you deserve tonight. Raincheck?'

After wiping away a stray tear from his stubbly cheek, she had agreed to wait. She knew what had upset him without him saying as much: the thought of losing Caleb was breaking his heart. She had changed out of the harness and slipped into a silk nightgown before curling up in his arms. Sleep had evaded her for the better part of the night, however. Even without their soul link, she could feel Brendan's dark emotions, sending her into her own spiralling funk.

Groaning when her phone alarm sounded, she rose and stumbled into the bathroom. At least she had her own shower gel and hair products. She needed to meet Liam that day and smelling like another man would not go down well, even though they had agreed to take a break. She used the flow of hot water over her skin to ground herself, letting it wash the negativity away as she practised her mindfulness breathing. By the time she stepped out of the ensuite, her misery had drifted away with the plumes of steam.

'How are you already up and about?' whinged Brendan from beneath the quilt as she towelled herself at the foot of the bed.

'I can't afford to sleep in,' she replied. 'There's conjuration work to get on with, then I need to deliver some weapons to the frontline.'

'Oh shit!' He sat bolt upright. 'I thought Kieran wanted to keep you out of harm's way?'

'Don't worry—I'll wear armour and coordinate the drop off with Liam so I'm not in direct contact with any dragons.'

Leaping out of bed, he stalked toward her. 'If there's nothing to worry about, why are you leaking fear like it's oil oozing from a poorly tuned car?'

'I guess there are still risks,' she admitted. 'I'll be going out into the middle of a warzone. I don't exactly know what to expect. This won't be like our skirmish with Tara, or the time I took on Richard.'

He slipped his arms around her waist, dislodging the towel from her breasts without his attention straying from her face.

How very un-Brendan.

Gripping her hips firmly, he stared intently into her eyes. 'Promise me you'll be careful.'

'Promise,' she whispered.

His lips crashed into hers, consuming her in a whirlwind of emotions that barrelled through her chest, cramped in her stomach, and tingled in her toes.

'Come back to me in one piece, Lana.' He disappeared into the bathroom before she could reply.

Before she could tell him—

The door swung open, and he rushed forward, sweeping her up into another dizzying kiss. 'I love you too, gorgeous,' he rasped as they pulled apart. 'Give me ten minutes and I'll help you with the rest of that work, okay?'

Speechless, she nodded and watched him return to the ensuite. *I think I really am ready to trust him again.*

A black haze of smoke clouded Alannah's vision and stung her eyes as she reached the Murray Bridge frontline, impairing visibility beyond six meters.[4] Dark shadowy figures were rushing around in the distance, and it was impossible to make out Liam from the other tall, muscular forms. Sighing, she moved closer. *At least they are not in the middle of battle.*

The stench of blood and decay assaulted her masked nose as she neared a series of portable cabins, and she fought the urge to empty her stomach. Whimpering voices mumbled a dismal

---

[4] 6m = 40 feet

chorus of pain, and a shrill scream rang out through the muted cacophony. Her pulse quickened as she pictured Liam lying dead or injured on this field of ruin. *Fuck! I hope I'm not too late.* With trembling hands and weeping eyes, she retrieved her phone from her belt pocket and tried to type a quick message.

'Lana?' Liam's voice startled her, and she juggled her phone, almost dropping it. 'I thought we agreed to meet at the ley line nexus near the garrison. It's not safe here.'

Her hood fell back as her head jerked up to meet his piercing gaze. 'Liam? Thank the Gods you're okay!' She barrelled into him, throwing her arms around his solid chest.

Returning the embrace, he remained silent a moment.

'You missed the meeting time, then when I saw the smoke over here, I panicked.'

He sighed. 'I'm sorry, babe. A dragon swooped over and ambushed us about an hour ago. I've been dealing with the aftermath.' He waved his hand toward the bodies lining the scorched ground.

'Oh hell!' She had not noticed them before. 'Are they…' She gulped, supressing a wave of nausea. While death was not new to her, she had never seen so much at once and the acrid smell of burning flesh turned her stomach.

'Dead? Afraid so. The injured are back at camp and we are doing the best we can to ease their suffering. I regret sending our best abjurers home now.'

'What?'

'Someone needed to care for the injured folk we evacuated from Mount Gambier. How is Dad doing with our refugees?'

She gaped at him, although her mask covered her open mouth. 'I wouldn't know. I haven't seen him.'

'Shit! Something must have held them up. I hope they're okay.' He combed his fingers through his hair, the dishevelled mess showing signs of frequent abuse. 'They took a truck back to Gaeilge Shores.'

'They?'

'Mum, Dad, and Connor, plus a dude by the name of Hugh Doran, are transporting several unconscious mages from the Southeast. One of them…' Liam paused. 'One of them looks like Tyler, but his name is Danny.'

She gasped and lowered her voice. 'Another doppelganger?'

Liam nodded.

'Fuck! Does anyone else know about him and where he's headed?'

His brow furrowed. 'No. Why?'

'I can't say. Not here. Just that, if a certain party knew who was in that truck… dragons would be the least of their concerns.'

He nodded. 'I'll keep it under wraps. What have you got for me?'

'Four trunks in total. Two of them full of spell-breaking arrows. They are all back at the garrison. It took me a couple of trips to get them there, so I wouldn't mind a hand to bring them across.'

'Of course. I'll send Cara with you. Once you're done with the delivery, you should head straight home.'

'I wish I could stay and fight.' Seeing so much pain and devastation riled her inner warrior. 'I'll speak to Kieran about deploying me as soon as possible.'

Nodding, Liam pulled out his radio. 'Shaman Hughes, this is Warlock Winters. Do you read me? Over.'

'I read you Warlock Winters. Over.' A glimmer of hope shone through the darkness when her best friend's voice travelled across the airwaves.

'Meet me at the Southern camp. Over and out.'

'Copy that. Over and out.'

He looked into her eyes. 'I wish *I* could go with you, but….'

'I know,' she murmured. She understood he did not just mean back to the garrison. Seeing the yearning in his eyes tightened the muscles in her chest. Unspoken words passed between them, yet she did not have the heart to deliver her final blow, not while he stood on a battlefield surrounded by his dead and dying comrades.

'Alannah?' Cara screeched as she removed her helmet. '*Oh my Gods!*' Charging forward, Cara seized her in a bear hug.

'Hey, Cars.' Stepping back to look at her bestie, she noticed a large burn scarring the left side of her face. 'Oh hell! That looks painful. Are you okay?'

Cara shrugged. 'I'm one of the lucky bastards.' She turned to Liam. 'What's with the reunion?'

'I need you to help Lana move the latest shipment of arms from the garrison,' he explained.

Cara's eyes scanned the armour she wore. 'Are you here to fight with us? We could definitely use some of your kickass power.'

Feeling another pang of guilt clamp around her ribs, she exchanged a glance with Liam, who shook his head. 'Sorry, hun. Kieran has me on the bench still.'

Her shoulders slumped. 'I don't get it. You're the most powerful mage we have. Why do you care what the High Magus says? His own fucking daughter is out there fighting with us, despite his orders.'

Bailey hobbled up to them, using a walking stick for support. 'Hey Cars, what did—' He stopped the moment his eyes met Alannah's. 'Oh, it's you. Finally here to help, huh?'

'Not bloody likely,' spat Cara. 'This is just a passing visit before she returns to her cosy nest.'

She gasped. 'Cara, you know it's not like that!'

'Whatever. Let's go get this stuff before the next assault. Then you can go back to warming dickhead's bed.' She stormed off toward the ley line nexus.

Her jaw dropped as she watched Cara walk away. She glanced at Bailey's bandaged foot. 'What happened?'

'What the fuck do you think? My boots weren't spell-resistant.' He limped back toward the cabins.

Tears brimmed her eyes when she looked at Liam. 'Do they all think I'm a deserter? Why haven't you explained the situation to them?'

He clenched his fists. 'Cara has a point, and I can't really blame her or Bailey for feeling how they do. You don't know what it's like out here for them. They're constantly putting their lives on the line, seeing others perish, all while our best hope, their *friend*, sits at home.'

'It's not like I'm idly twiddling my thumbs! I've been wearing myself thin imbuing weapons and armour. Not to mention saving Neve from certain death at the hands of the fucking Seelie Court.'

Liam sighed. 'Sorry Lana, but I do think you would be able to help us more out here, despite what Kieran says. Unfortunately, pulling rank and demanding you join us would directly contravene his orders, which I'm not at liberty to do.'

Tears began to trickle down her face. *They all think I'm a compliant coward.* 'Why did Cara infer I'm…'

'Sleeping with Brendan? I told her we're taking a break… as well as the other stuff that's been going on with you and him. Is she wrong?'

When she hung her head, she heard him suck in a sharp breath. 'We haven't... not yet. But....'

'I don't want to hear it. I've got more important shit to do. Go help Cara move the gear. We'll talk when this is all over.' He strode away without so much as a goodbye.

Chapter Seven

The moment Alannah entered the dining room, Brendan sprang to his feet to wrap her in his arms and breathe her in. 'Hey you,' she mumbled against his neck. His warmth soaked into her tense muscles and aching bones, although she was still some way off relaxing.

'Thank fuck you're okay.' He kissed her passionately until a chorus of throat clearing, dry retching, and 'get a room' heckles broke them apart. 'Shall we then? Get a room, that is?'

She sighed, removing her hooded cowl and tossing it on the sideboard. 'I'm too wired after everything I saw out there. It was horrendous nightmare fuel. I need some time to unwind before retiring tonight.' Glancing at the table, she noticed everyone had been sharing a meal. Even Caleb sat with them, although someone had chained him to his seat. 'Dinner smells nice. Who cooked?'

'I did,' Neve piped up. 'With Caitlin's help.'

'Thanks girls.' She ambled into the kitchen to serve herself a plate.

Brendan trailed closely behind. 'Why don't you sit down, and I'll get you something to eat?'

She gave him a sidelong glance. 'Brendan Winters! Are you trying to butter me up for later?'

'You know me: any excuse to get you off your feet.' Grinning, he walked her back to the dining table and pulled a chair out for her, returning a minute later with a large bowl of spaghetti bolognaise and slice of garlic bread.

'What was it like out there?' asked Amy.

'I'd rather not talk about it tonight.' The stench of residual smoke still clung to her, and she considered ducking upstairs to shower and change. But her stomach grumbled as the delicious scent of garlic and Italian herbs wafted up to her from the steaming bowl of pasta, so she dug into her meal instead.

'That bad huh?' Amy gave her a sympathetic simper. 'It's okay. We've all been on edge tonight, worrying about you and the fate of the world in general.'

'I have an idea!' Jacob dashed out of the room.

'Uh-oh,' replied Amy, rolling her eyes. 'This can't be good.'

When he reappeared, Jacob placed a black briefcase on the table. 'We could all use a break tonight, yeah? Something to take our minds off our own personal dramas, as well as the approaching apocalypse. How about a game of Texas hold'em?'

'I dunno, Red. There are minors present. I'm not sure we should be teaching the girls how to gamble.' Brendan was really taking his parenting responsibilities seriously and it warmed her heart. 'How about a family-friendly game, like Monopoly?' he suggested.

Neve snorted. 'Are you for real, Dad? Have you seen Mum and Liam playing that game? It's anything but friendly.'

Caitlin giggled. 'Didn't Liam burn all the Community Chest cards?'

'No, only the ones that annoyed *him*,' Alannah explained.

'And that's why we don't allow magic at the gaming table.' Jacob produced a set of collars. 'I don't know what magic tricks y'all use, but I'm confident we have *at least* one mind reader at the table. These ought to level the playing field.'

She studied the collars. Unlike the leather ones adopted by kinksters, these were pure cold iron, but they still reminded her of the time she had submitted to Brendan. Glancing at him, she met his dark gaze and knew he had been thinking the same thing. *Either that, or he read my mind.* The ache between her legs grew and she clenched her leather-clad thighs together.

Brendan cleared his throat. 'How do you feel about the girls joining the game, Lana?'

'I appreciate the fatherly concern, Brendan, but I actually think there are some valuable life skills to learn in a game of poker and this is the best environment to expose Neve to such games. We can bankroll the girls and they can pocket their own winnings.' It had been years since she had played a decent game of poker and the opportunity excited her more than she cared to admit.

'Yesss!' Neve pumped her fist.

'Coolest Mum ever!' chimed Caitlin.

'Wait! What am I missing here?' asked Amy. 'Why are you all referring to Brendan as Neve's father?'

'Man, you are so out of the loop, shorty!' Jacob scoffed. 'Must be hard to hear the latest news all the way down there.'

She scowled at him. 'I'm surprised you can hear anything at all with your bloated ego ballooning past your ears.'

'Why don't we make this game even more interesting,' suggested Brendan. 'For each hand a player loses, they must reveal a secret concerning themselves that at least one person at the table doesn't know.'

'So long as one of you tells me about Neve's baby daddy, you're on!' Amy grinned, smacking the table.

After everyone had cleared their dishes, they put their collars on and dropped their money in the lock box. Still chained to his chair, Caleb needed help from Brendan.

Jacob began setting up. 'Alright, the rules are no-limit, Texas hold'em poker, buy-in is two hundred bucks, tournament style, no cash,' explained Jacob as he glanced at Neve, 'to make this fair for the kiddies.'

Neve rolled her eyes. 'Seriously dude. I'm not a kid anymore.'

'True that,' Jacob agreed, snorting. 'I heard about what you got up to with Jasper Rowan.'

'Zip it, Red!' Brendan boomed as Neve's cheeks blazed ruby red. Pulling a switchblade from his pocket, he pointed it at Jacob. 'If you watched *any* of that footage—'

The mere thought sent a red haze across Alannah's vision, and she glared at Jacob.

'Woah! Chill, Boss! Quite besides the fact I ain't into kiddy porn, I promised you I wouldn't look at anything featuring Neve, and I kept my word. Can we get on with the game now, please?' Brendan relaxed into his seat as Jacob distributed the chips. 'Minimum bets are $1 small blind, $2 big blind.'

'Excuse me Jacob,' Neve squeaked. 'What's the no-limit bit mean?'

Emptying the dregs of a bottle into her glass, Amy growled. 'It better mean unlimited whiskey if I'm to survive a games night with Jacob, Brendan, *and* Caleb.'

'I'm pretty sure it means there's no limit to the stupid shit Amy says,' deadpanned Caleb.

Jacob sighed. 'It just means there's no limit to how much you can bet each round, other than what you have left, of course.' Claiming the dealer button, he dealt the first hand, explaining the rules in more detail to the girls.

Alannah had a K♣ and 4♣. It was not much to work with unless more clubs showed up, so she decided to play it safe for the time being. After Caleb and Brendan placed their blind bets, she called and tossed in a $2 chip. When Neve raised to $4, Alannah cast her daughter a sidelong glance, but she maintained the perfect poker face. *Damn! This kid's a quick learner!*

Looking up from her hand of cards, Caitlin shrugged. 'Go fish?'

Jacob chuckled. 'Does that mean you fold?'

'I guess?' She discarded her cards.

The betting continued with Amy and Jacob both calling, then Jacob revealed the flop: 10♦ A♥ J♦.

Not a great start considering Alannah's cards, and when Brendan raised the bet to $10, she folded. Sitting back, she watched the rest of the hand playout. Brendan won with two pairs.

'Now for the secrets.' Brendan stared intently at Caleb, who in turn smirked.

'I love takin' it up the arse,' admitted Caleb.

Caitlin started coughing while Neve turned a brilliant shade of red.

'Oh hell, Thornsy!' Brendan chided. 'Do you have to be so crass in front of the girls?'

'You're the one who added the secrets rule, *my love*.' Caleb sat back and folded his arms.

Amy smacked her hands on the table. 'Oh my Gods, Brendo! When did you go bi?'

'About sixteen years ago,' explained Caleb. 'When I first fucked him.'

Picturing the guys naked together, their firm bodies writhing in bed, she felt liquid lust pooling in her core.

Brendan sighed. 'Your turn, Lana.'

'This is for Amy's benefit, since most of you know. The year I conceived Neve, Brendan was my only partner at Beltane.'

Lowering her head in shame, Neve confessed to sneaking out of her window at times when she wanted to see Jasper.

Caitlin dropped quite the bombshell: 'I'm a lesbian.' When everyone except Neve gaped at her, she scoffed. 'Seriously guys, considering your own sexual preferences, how is this a big deal?'

'It's not that,' Alannah assured her. 'We're not used to hearing young teenagers making such bold proclamations. I'm proud of you, hun.'

'Since we're on the topic,' Jacob added, 'I'm pansexual.'

'W-what's that mean?' Neve asked. The poor girl looked like she was on the verge of a stroke.

'He fucks anything that moves,' Caleb explained.

Alannah rolled her eyes. 'Only if they're willing, right?'

Jacob nodded. 'And legal. I'm not fussed about gender identity.'

While Caleb shuffled the deck, Amy rose, holding the empty whiskey bottle. 'Yo, Brendo! Mind if I raid your parents' stash?'

'Go for it. Just keep it away from Lana.' His eyes met her arched brows, and he smiled. 'What? I'm looking after you, gorgeous. *Get me a glass too!*' he called after Amy.

The next hand was a bit of a dud. Everyone except Amy and Caitlin folded, the latter taking the win because her full house ranked higher than Amy's. Most of the secrets were rather pedestrian too, although Caleb, true to form, shocked the girls by admitting to his incestuous relationship with his sister. Alannah could see the irritation rise in Brendan's demeanour; his plan to get Caleb spilling the beans clearly backfiring.

Much the same happened during the third hand. When Amy claimed her winnings, thanks to a pair of nines, Neve exchanged a look with her best friend before asking the table at large, 'Is it okay if Caitlin and I bail?'

'That's fine.' Jacob counted their chips and gave them their winnings in cash.

Once they had pocketed the money, the girls politely excused themselves. When Neve gave Brendan a goodnight hug, he grinned. 'Make sure you soundproof your room, princess. We don't need to hear you both screaming.'

'*Dad!*' Neve practically collapsed as the heat rose in her cheeks.

Caitlin huffed. 'Speak for yourself.' Spinning on her heels, she grabbed Neve's hand and led her away.

'What was that about?' Alannah inquired.

Caleb snorted. 'Come on, as if you didn't see the way they were eye-fucking each other.'

She gaped. 'I had no idea Neve was so inclined. Last I heard, she was still lusting after Jasper *Rowan*.' Alannah spat the name she detested so much.

As soon as her feet hit the stairs, Caitlin sprinted to Neve's room. They both collapsed on the floor in a fit of breathless giggles. 'OMG, your mum's friends are so crazy!'

'I know, right!' Neve leaned back against her door. Once she had composed herself, she reached up and flicked the lock, biting into her lower lip as she looked at her. The air crackled between them.

'What?' she asked, feeling her cheeks flush. There was something unfamiliar in the way Neve looked at her.

'I'm totes horny right now.' Neve crawled across the carpet to her, stopping less than an inch away.

Tucking her legs to the side, she gulped. 'You don't mean to....'

Neve grinned. 'Uh huh. Quite beside the fact Elna is a horrible person, I did enjoy the sex with her. She opened my eyes and now when I look at you, knowing how you feel about me....' She trailed her fingers along Caitlin's cheek, down her neck, and dipped them into her cleavage.

Breath hitching, she stared at Neve's lips: they looked so ripe and succulent. Yet nothing scared her more than the possibility of getting exactly who she wanted. 'You know I've never....'

'I know,' Neve whispered. 'You tell me *all* your secrets, remember? I'd know if you ever... went that far with anyone. I can guide you through it.'

Her chest rose and fell with shallow breaths. 'I don't know. What if this ruins everything? I can't lose you, Neve.'

As Neve's finger flicked her nipple, their moans echoed in a chorus. 'I don't think it will. If anything, this will strengthen our bond. I love you, Cat, so what's wrong with expressing our feelings in the best way possible?'

A nervous laugh slipped out. 'Well, when you put it that way.'

Neve helped her to her feet, wrapping her in a firm embrace the moment they both stood upright.

Trembling, she inhaled Neve's sweet vanilla scent. 'What if I'm not enough for you?' she asked in a quavering voice. 'I know how much you still want Jasper—'

Neve silenced her with a kiss. Not a chaste peck on the lips, but a deep, probing kiss that stole her wits. Cool mint contrasted with hot passion as their tongues danced and sparks shot through her nerves. When they came up for air, Neve smiled. 'That was incredible. Please tell me you want more because—'

This time, she cut the conversation short as she claimed Neve's lips and pushed her back toward the bed. With the first kiss out the way, her jitters subsided, and a new wave of confidence spurred her on. Forget Jasper—she was determined to prove Neve did not need a man in her life.

Alannah's ears twitched as she heard the girls running up the stairs and slamming the bedroom door. *Are they really about to have sex?*

Handing her the deck of cards, Brendan rubbed the back of her hand to get her attention. 'It's your turn to deal, gorgeous.'

Simpering, she took the cards and continued playing. As soon as she revealed the 10♥, 10♣, and 3♦ in the flop, she knew her K♣ and 7♥ were not going to cut it, so she folded. She gave some thought to the secret she would disclose. During the fourth round of betting, Caleb went all-in with $153, and she sat forward in the edge of her seat, eager to see how Brendan would respond.

He scrutinised Caleb's expression for a few tense seconds before smirking. 'I'm totally calling your bluff, Thornsy.' He pushed an equal number of chips into the centre of the table.

Caleb dropped his hand of cards face up, showing the best he had was a single Queen. 'Screw you, arsehole.'

Brendan smirked. 'Not until you tell me what I want to know.' He glanced at Caleb's cards and let out a short laugh. 'Holy shit that was close! King beats Queen. Please tell me you have no higher than a Jack, Jacob.'

'Lucky for you, my highest is a seven.' Jacob threw his cards in the muck.

'Fess up now, Thornsy.' Brendan ran his hand along Caleb's thigh as he stared into the man's eyes.

'Bite my arse, Winters. I'm not betraying Bry.'

'But you'll happily betray me?' Brendan grit out between clenched teeth.

Caleb scowled. 'I'm not exactly happy about it. You know how much I love you.'

'Fuck's sake guys! I don't need to see your damn foreplay. You're making me nauseous here,' Amy complained.

'Nah, pipsqueak, that's just the alcohol,' teased Jacob. 'You have a lousy constitution for a dwarf.'

Alannah observed the heated daggers they exchanged.

'Maybe it's jealousy,' suggested Caleb. 'Amy used to crush on Brendo just as much as I did back in the day. She's probably sour that she's the only person at this table he hasn't fucked.'

Jacob sprayed his mouthful of cola across the table. 'She ain't the only one, dude. As much as I'd love a piece of Brendan, he's never done me the honours. That's totally my secret this round, by the way.'

Caleb furrowed his brow at Brendan. 'But you told Bry….'

Brendan shrugged. 'So I lied. Sue me. It's still nothing on her deceit.'

'Wow. Who needs daytime soap operas with real-life drama this good?' scoffed Amy.

'So, what's your secret, Amy?' Brendan asked.

'Caleb already told you.' Throwing back another shot of whiskey, she avoided Brendan's gaze. 'Doesn't mean I want you now though,' she added hastily.

Nonplussed, Brendan turned to Alannah. 'Your turn.'

She bit her lip and glanced at Jacob, seeking his permission.

Jacob gulped. 'Yeah fine, may as well get it out in the open.'

Brendan tensed. 'Don't tell me you've been keeping more shit from me, Red!'

Jacob put his hands up in surrender. 'She swore me to secrecy, and it wasn't really your business at the time.'

'It's true,' Alannah explained. 'Until recently, who I slept with was none of your business, Brendan.'

His wide eyes darted back and forth between them. 'When? How often?'

'Just once, almost a year ago when Tyler was overseas. I almost fell off the wagon, but Jacob talked me down. Then one thing led to another.'

'Fuck,' Brendan cursed under his breath. The table went deathly silent while Amy shuffled and dealt the next hand. When Jacob won with two pairs, Brendan asked Alannah, 'Why only once?'

She sighed. 'Things felt awkward after and we both agreed it was better to keep the friendship platonic. Besides, Jacob may be a switch, but he couldn't dish out nearly enough pain.'

Brendan sucked in a sharp breath and his eyes darkened with lust.

'Hear that, Jacob,' Amy jibed. 'Sounds like you should leave the sadism to us Doms.'

Jacob snorted. 'Be my guest, *darling*.'

Clamping her mouth shut, Amy stared at him, her eyes popping from their sockets.

The poker game continued, and Alannah even managed to win a hand, although the pot was not worth much at the time. Flipping the turn on the eighth hand, she revealed a K♦. 'Gods fucking damn it!' She had been hoping for a fourth spade to show up.

Jacob laughed. 'Nice poker face, sweets.' He raised the bet Amy had just placed.

Amy slammed her glass on the table, a few drops of her drink sloshing out. 'Shut up, Jacob. I don't see you doing any better.' Her speech slurred a little as she spoke.

'And how many hands have you won so far, *Miss Smith*?' Jacob laced his tone with ridicule.

After Brendan called, Alannah folded. She flipped the final card, completing the river and watched with amusement as Amy tried hard to hide the dismay on her face.

'*Naw, what's up Amy poos*? You losing again?' Jacob taunted.

'You're such a dick, Jacob!' Springing to her feet, Amy threw her cards down and stormed off, Jacob and Caleb both chortling in her wake.

When Brendan won the hand, Jacob cashed out. 'Well that was fun.' He untied the shackles from Caleb's chair. 'Come on, Thornsy, it's your lucky night 'cause I'm desperate for release.'

Frowning, Brendan watched as Jacob dragged Caleb up to the attic to do Gods knew what.

Alannah cleared her throat, bringing his attention back to her. 'I guess it's just you and me now, huh?' she rasped.

His countenance transformed as he adopted his best bedroom eyes. 'Indeed.'

'Why don't we change things up a bit?' Brendan suggested.

Propping her elbow on the table, she rested her head against her hand and faced him with hooded eyes. 'What did you have in mind?'

'Instead of revealing secrets, we shed layers of clothing.'

She cocked her brow. 'You intend to continue the poker game?'

'Why not? It'll be great for building tension.' While keen to ravish Alannah, he needed a breather after watching another man take *his* boyfriend upstairs for a night of untold passion. He could have insisted Jacob take care of himself to further deprive Caleb, but he was not feeling *that* cruel. Not yet.

'Okay fine. Deal 'em out, baby.' Shifting her gaze to the doorway while he shuffled, she lost herself in thought a moment and he cursed the collar around his neck for keeping her thoughts private. 'Those two totally want to fuck each other,' she mused.

He sighed as he handed her two cards. 'Can we *please* not talk about Caleb for the rest of the night?'

'I'm not referring to Caleb. I meant Jacob and Amy.'

His brows rose sky high. 'No way! Those two would sooner kill each other.'

She glanced at her cards. 'There's a fine line between love and hate, and lust often straddles it. I'm surprised you of all people didn't notice the sexual tension between them.'

He tugged at the collar. 'Being cut off from my magic is like losing a limb. I rely heavily on it when it comes to reading people. Besides, I was paying more attention to our daughter's… interests.'

'Hm, I guess getting initiated late has some advantages. Makes me better at reading nuance in body language and tone.' When he revealed the first three cards on the board, Alannah bit her lip. 'I'm throwing in $10 this round.'

'Fine, I'll call it. I've gotta say, you've been off your game tonight. I wonder if that skin-tight armour you're still wearing has anything to do with it.' His fingers traced the seam of her leather jacket, stopping shy of her right breast. 'The sooner this goes, the better.' He flipped the fourth card.

'Why? Don't you like this look on me? It's surprisingly comfortable, made for manoeuvrability and all.' She pushed another $10 into the pot.

He snorted. 'Are you kidding me? I love it. Not as much as that harness you wore last night, but you look hot as hellfire in it. Still, if I'm going to fuck you tonight, it needs to go.' Matching her bet as she sucked in a breath, he drew the final card.

'$20.' She slid her chips forward. 'I had planned to change after dinner but forgot all about it as soon as Jacob suggested poker.'

'Calling it.' After placing his bet, he tilted his head to study her. 'You're not addicted to gambling too, are you?'

'Nah. I've just got a hard-on for Texas hold'em.' When they reached the showdown, Alannah revealed a straight, knocking his two pairs right out the water. She scanned his attire. 'I suppose you'll be losing the shoes first?'

He gave her a sly grin. 'To hell with that. I'm going for maximum distraction.' He tugged his t-shirt over his head and tossed it aside.

A mewling whimper slipped from her salivating mouth. 'You play dirty.'

He laughed. 'Is there any other way?' It did not help him much though, as he lost the next two hands, along with his boots and jeans.

'And here I thought you wanted to get *me* naked,' she scoffed playfully.

'Oh, I will. Your streak can't possibly last. Seriously, what are the odds of getting two straights in a row followed by a flush?'

She shrugged. 'Beats me. Maths was never my strong suit.'

As luck would have it, he won the next two hands.

'I'll need help getting out of this thing.' Sliding into his lap, she gave him access to the front of her jacket.

Groaning as his dick sprang to life beneath the weight of her, he unzipped the jacket and slid the sleeves down her arms. Staring at her chest, he watched her braless breasts spring free. He licked his lips and cupped them in his hands. Jolting from the contact, she ground against his erection, so he bit into the crook of her neck.

'Oh Gods!' she cried out. 'Forget the game. I desperately need you to fuck me to the moon and back. Right now!'

He kissed her passionately before rising to his feet, lifting her in the process. Her thighs clamped around him, reminding him of the first time they made love at Beltane. They continued to kiss as he stumbled into walls and furniture on his way upstairs and down the hall to his bedroom. Sure, it would have been easier to let her walk, but there was no way he was letting her go any time soon. Gently dropping her onto the bed, he removed their collars and the last of her clothes, struggling a little with the pants. 'Fuck! Who makes these things? I need to have a word with them about ease of access.'

Alannah laughed. 'That'd be me. I'll take your feedback on board.' She cast a soundproofing ward in the time it took him to wrench the pants off her legs.

He stood back to admire the glorious curves of her body as she sprawled out before him. 'Birth control?'

'On it,' she assured him.

He could not decide which way he wanted to take her first. Years of hoping for this moment, of imagining how it would play out had filled his mind with too many options.

'What are you waiting for Brendan?' she asked with a husky voice.

Blinking, he stopped overthinking it and straddled her legs. 'Nothing. I'm done waiting.' He plunged two fingers between her slick folds, and she bucked against his hand. 'Already so wet and ready for me.' Pumping his hand a few times tipped her over the edge.

She arched her back as she clenched tightly around him and cried out, 'Fuck yes!'

Lining himself up at her entrance, he stared into her hooded eyes and smiled. 'I love you, Lana.' Plummeting into her depths, he added, 'So madly in love with you.' As their bodies merged, the core of his being rattled and reverberated, reaching out for its other half.

Gasping, Alannah stared into his eyes. 'Do you feel that?'

He nodded. 'Our souls are trying to reconnect.'

She frowned. 'Brendan I'm not—'

'Shoosh.' He pressed a finger to her lips. 'Don't worry. I'm not ready for that either. Small steps, gorgeous. Let's focus on the here and now.'

'Okay,' she rasped. 'You better fuck me hard then.'

The left side of his mouth quirked up. 'As you wish.' After pulling out to the tip, he drove himself back inside her with his full force.

Arching her back, she closed her eyes and welcomed him home with a moan of approval.

Yes, I'm home. After savouring the moment, he picked up the pace and sent them both into a grunting, screaming frenzy that lasted for hours.

Chapter Eight

Utterly spent, Neve snuggled into the crook of Caitlin's arm. Her eyes fluttered closed and when they opened again, the room was dark, yet she could see the shadow of a man standing beside her bed. Her breath hitched and she froze, watching him sit on the mattress. A familiar earthy scent greeted her as Erik's grinning face came into view. 'What are you doing here?' she hissed.

'I'm here to pleasure you, sweetheart.' Gruffness replaced the usual singsong cadence of his voice.

She huffed. 'Won't be necessary.' She pointed to the girl sleeping beside her. 'As you can see, Caitlin already took care of me. I don't need you, Erik. How did you even get in my room? This house is warded.'

'Don't be silly, my love. I can see the hunger in your aura. If anything, your friend here was merely an appetiser, making you crave what only *I* can offer.' Dropping his open shirt behind him, Erik revealed the bulging muscles of his chest and arms. He stood to unfasten his pants, letting his erection spring free. 'I know you miss me, baby. There's no point denying it.'

She gulped as she admired the perfect specimen of a man before her, heat spreading through her body, recent memory fuelling the fire. *No not perfect! He's an arse—*

Erik chuckled. 'What's that about my arse?' Turning, he bent over to give her a view of his finely sculpted backside as he removed his pants entirely. 'I can hear your thoughts, sweetheart.' Sitting down again, he slipped under the covers and straddled her. He pressed his mouth to the shell of her ear and whispered, 'And I can smell your arousal.'

A whimper escaped her lips. Still naked from her night with Caitlin, she was defenceless against Erik and her willpower was rapidly depleting.

His fingers found her slick centre and he tickled her bundle of nerves, giving her a glimpse of the stars that she couldn't reach. 'If you don't want me to fuck you here and now, you better hurry up and tell me to leave.'

'I-I can't,' she squeaked as her body shivered and shuddered.

'What's that my love? I didn't quite hear you.'

Arching her back, she pushed against his hand, hoping to increase the pressure where she most wanted it. 'I need more.'

He smirked. 'You *do* need me after all, hm?'

As soon as she whispered 'yes,' he thrust himself deep inside her and their bodies climbed peaks that rose into the heavens. A particularly powerful orgasm took hold, elevating her enough to dance among the brilliant orbs of white-hot flame. She screamed his name before blacking out. When consciousness returned a few seconds later, he was shaking her. No, not him; *her*.

Caitlin hovered above, frowning. 'What the hell, Neve? Why are you having wet dreams about that vile man right after the amazing night we shared?'

'Wha—?' She looked about, confused and disoriented. *Where is Erik?* 'Th-that was a dream? It felt so real.'

'I'm not surprised,' scoffed Caitlin as she sat back against the headboard on her side. 'You were writhing about and crying out his name. I'm pretty sure you climaxed too.'

It was true, if the damp mattress was any indicator. She turned to face Caitlin. 'Are you seriously mad at me for dreaming about someone else? It was *just* a dream.'

'Can you honestly tell me you didn't *want* it to be real?' Caitlin's eyes glistened with unshed tears.

Averting her gaze, she recalled the vivid vision that had plagued her sleep. She knew dreams shouldn't be interpreted literally, but Erik's presence had been so potent. And the sex… 'I… I don't know.'

The waterworks gushed from Caitlin's eyes. 'See, I knew it! I'll never be enough for you!' She jumped out of bed and found her clothes.

'No, Cat! It's not like that. Please—'

'*Stopit!*' she screeched. 'I don't need your excuses or your pity. I'm taking one of the guest rooms, then I'll go home tomorrow.' Grabbing her backpack, she strode into the hall and slammed the door behind her.

Curling up in a ball, she sobbed her shattered heart into dust.

Hours later, when the tears dried, she thought about the dream and what it meant to her. She had heard something about the subjects of sex dreams reflecting your own hidden qualities. *What's so good about Erik though? I mean, aside from his insanely hot body. And the way he touches me.* She sighed. The man was arrogant, cold, and ruthless, but his confidence and charisma were admirable. *Could that be it? Or do I really miss him?*

Eerie silence surrounded Liam as he waited with bated breath. The day had been a summer scorcher, yet the night air sent a chill shivering through his bones. Temperature extremes wreaked havoc with his nerves, and he missed the moderate climate of his coastal home. The frontline had moved further into the Hills, advancing via a series of underground tunnels the alchemists had dug for them, and they hid among the trees, waiting to ambush the dragons. Their scout warbled a shrill birdcall, signalling dragons were approaching. Liam readied his bow along with the other archers, loosing his arrow as soon as the gargantuan shadow flew overhead and blocked the moon.

Quivers of arrows whistled through the air, punching through an invisible barrier with an almighty whoosh before striking the belly of the beast. It crashed to the ground with a crunch, felling a copse of trees.

He charged forward, drawing his sword, although when he reached the dragon, he had no need for his blade. The monster had already died. Cheers erupted throughout the woodland as he stood in awe, studying the corpse. *Our first windfall.* Massive shimmering scales of red and black coated the beast's limbs, tail, and torso, while the wings resembled the membranous leather of bats, articulated by a series of bones.

Monique flung herself at him, hugging him tight. 'We did it! We took the bastard down!'

He chuckled softly in her arms. 'Yeah, we did. Go team!' As soon as they got back to camp, he rang Kieran to share the good news.

'Excellent work, Warlock Winters. It's a huge relief to know Alannah's conjuration efforts paid off, too.'

'Thank you, Your Honour. That's most of our spell-breaking arrows gone though, so we'll need to restock before staging our next assault.'

'Good point. You may as well head home and rest up while we wait for her to finish imbuing more arrows.'

Dread curled his stomach when he thought about the conversation waiting for him at home. 'That won't be necessary, Your Honour.'

'Nonsense. You've been working around the clock. I need you well rested for the next blitz. Go home, Liam. I insist. Spend some quality time with the missus.'

He sighed. 'Very well. I may as well take another two cases of arrows with me to make my trip worthwhile.'

'I've never heard a man so reluctant to leave a warzone,' Kieran remarked. 'Trouble in paradise?'

'Yes, Your Honour. To put it mildly.' *More like banished from paradise.*

'I'm sorry to hear it, son.' The familiarity in Kieran's tone made him smile. 'Best go patch things up with her. Happy wife, happy life, and all that.'

He snorted at the irony. Kieran had no idea what it would take to make Alannah truly happy. *It certainly won't make me happy.*

Tiptoeing through the slumbering house with bare feet, Jacob made his way to the kitchen. He found Amy slumped over the table, nursing her head, and rubbing her temples. Rather than alert her to his presence, he crept across the room to the coffee machine. As soon as he turned on the grinder, her head jerked up.

'What the fuck, dude! You scared the crap outta me.'

He smirked. 'Kinda the point, shorty. What are you doin' up so early? After all the booze you inhaled last night, I figured you'd be snoring away for another few hours.'

'Head hurts too much to sleep,' she whined.

Opening the fridge, he searched the potion shelf for Ross' hangover cure. He poured a shot of the green goop and placed on the table beside her. 'Drink up.'

She glared at him. 'Isn't it rude to raid their potion stash?'

He shrugged, wondering when the concept of propriety had bitten her in that cute little tush. 'No worse than stealing their top shelf whiskey.' He finished making his coffee before sitting across from her.

Groaning, she downed the bitter medicine. 'Where's your prisoner?'

'Sleeping. Don't worry, I've chained him to my bed. He ain't goin' anywhere.' Memories of their nocturnal activities filled his mind and one side of his mouth quirked up. 'Not that he'd want to after last night.'

Her brows shot up. 'Are you fucking him?'

Propping his elbows on the table, he leaned forward with his chin in his hands. 'What if I am? Would that make you jealous?'

'Not on your life! You both disgust me.' Her cheeks resembled beautiful peaches.

Reclining in his chair, he crossed his arms over his bare chest and stared at her. 'I'm not so sure. Why else would you be interested in *my* sex life?'

Her gaze shifted away from him as she replied, 'How does Brendan feel about it? He seemed pretty upset with Caleb last night.'

A sliver of disappointment soured his mood. 'So, this is about Brendo? Thought you said you were over that crush.'

Her chest heaved, briefly drawing his attention to her full breasts. 'Why do you assume this has anything to do with how I feel about any of you?' She spoke with an exasperated tone. 'You're so infuriating, Bennett. I'm content with Connor and have no desire to fuck any other guy in this town.'

He sipped his steaming coffee, although it had nothing on the fury burning in Amy's eyes. 'Fine. You wanna know how Brendan feels? He's heartbroken over Caleb's betrayal because he's in love with the guy, but that's nothing compared to the depth of his feelings for Alannah. He'd do anything to protect his soulmate, even while their link remains severed. My primary job as his spymaster has been looking out for her these past fifteen years. Yeah, I've shacked up with Thornsy whenever I could, but it was only ever empty sex, and Brendan knows that. I haven't had a meaningful relationship since….' His voice trailed off as he realised why Amy had suddenly sparked his interest. Aside from the physical resemblance, she also possessed the same fierce temper and passion as Cara.

A tense silence hovered in the air between them, the seconds ticking by on the deafening kitchen clock.

'Do you still love her?' Amy whispered.

He nodded.

She sighed. 'You have to move on, dude. I know it's hard, but you won't find peace and happiness while clinging to the past.'

Scowling, he sprang to his feet, clutching his mug of coffee to his chest like it was his Linus blanket. 'Unless you're planning to fill the void, I suggest keeping your nose out of my fucked-up love life.' He spun on his heels as her jaw dropped and stomped toward the stairs.

'Jacob, wait!' A chair scraped against the floorboards as she rose and charged after him. 'What the hell was that supposed to mean?'

They reached the hall by the time she caught up to him. Turning to face her, he set his coffee down on a nearby cupboard and marched up to her, inhaling the sensual scent of leather that always surrounded her, even when she wasn't dressed like a dominatrix. He grasped her throat, retracting his claws and taking care to avoid crushing her windpipe. 'Are you daft, woman? I've had a raging hardon for you since stumbling upon you in the shower, so fuck me, or fuck off.'

Her eyes widened with each syllable of his confession to the point of bugging out. 'I—' Breaking free of his grip, she fled, sprinting out the front door as fast as her little feet could carry her.

'What the hell was that about?' Brendan asked as he sauntered down the stairs, his feline friend trailing behind him. He looked every part the sex God he was, with ruffled hair and trackpants clinging to *all* the bulges. You could've lit up a concert hall with the radiant glow of his skin.

'Mornin' Boss. You look awfully pleased with yourself. I take it things went well with Alannah last night?'

A massive grin took over Brendan's face. 'You might say that. Now tell me what's going on with Amy.'

'I dunno, man. She's a tough nut to crack.' Jacob picked up his coffee and gulped a mouthful of the tasty drink. He followed Brendan into the kitchen.

'So, you do want her then?'

He cocked his brow at Brendan. 'Do *you* really need to ask?'

'Contrary to popular belief, I don't always pry into people's thoughts and emotions.' Brendan flicked on the coffee machine. Once the noise had subsided, he added, 'Besides, I've been distracted lately.'

'Fair point.' Hoisting himself up, he perched on the breakfast bar and watched Mr. Sex-on-Legs strut around the room in nothing but meat vision pants.

'What's your interest in Amy?' Brendan asked, ignoring his less than subtle ogling. 'You looking for a casual hook-up, or have you caught genuine feelings for her?'

He contemplated his body's response to Amy. The dwarf girl's inner flame could have heated her parents' forge alone, not to mention her smokin' curves. It was more than a physical attraction, he was certain. 'I'm not about to write sonnets and sing ballads, but I definitely feel something other than pure lust for her. Problem is, I don't know if it's 'cause she reminds me of Cara, or if I genuinely like *her*.'

'Hm, 'fraid I can't help you much there. For what it's worth, I do know she wants to jump your bones.'

He gasped dramatically. 'You *were* paying attention! What ever happened to your staying quiet policy?'

Brendan snorted. 'You know I tossed that stupid fucking rule out the window years ago. Anyways, Lana was the one who noticed the chemistry between you two. As for myself, I thought you hated each other until I witnessed your confrontation this morning.'

'Oh, we do. At least we love to hate each other, but Alannah's right about the sexual tension.' His eyes glazed over as he imagined what it'd be like to battle for supremacy in bed with Amy.

A strong hand clamped over his shoulder. 'Good luck then, yeah? Just don't let her distract you from your prison guard duties.'

He sported a big-arse grin as his thoughts turned to taking Amy in front of Caleb. 'Don't worry Boss. If things go my way, they could work in your favour too. A bit more incentive for Thornsy, ya know?'

Brendan's expression darkened as he nodded. 'Anything to report on that front?'

'Zilch. Sorry, man. The only words I could get outta Caleb last night were cries of "fuck me harder."'

Wincing, Brendan shifted his attention to the fridge as he started preparing some food. He did *not* want to think about Caleb with Jacob. A full night of debauchery with Alannah had left them both famished, so he had offered to cook a protein and carbs-loaded breakfast.

'Ah shit! I'm sorry man. That was super insensitive of me.'

'Drop it, Red,' he growled. When Luna circled around his legs and mewled into the open fridge, he retrieved a tin of cat food and spooned a portion of it into her bowl, gagging over the fishy stench. He glanced at her, bowl still in hand. 'How the hell do you eat this stuff, girl?'

'Meow.' Luna reared up on her hind legs and batted the air.

He smiled at her cute gesture and placed the stinky stuff in front of her before getting to work on everyone else's meal. Slicing a cluster of mushrooms, he glanced up to see Alannah amble into the kitchen. His hand on the knife paused as he admired her dishevelled state, complete with smudged eye makeup and frizzy bed hair. There was a definite stagger in her gait, too.

Her eyes met his straight away and she beamed. 'Where's that coffee you promised me?'

'Kiss first.' He tugged at her old whiskey t-shirt, pulling her flush against him to feast on her lips.

'Naw, you guys are adorable,' teased Jacob.

Refusing to end the kiss prematurely, he showed Jacob the middle finger behind Alannah's back. Breathless and hungry for something other than food, he came up for air and handed Alannah her coffee.

Studying the unicorn mug, she smiled and whispered, 'You remembered my favourite cup.' Not waiting for his response, she turned and cast her eyes in Jacob's direction. 'Christ, Bennett! Get your filthy arse off the breakfast bar. People eat food off that.'

Simpering, he slid off the bench. 'I'll go get Caleb.' Jacob disappeared, leaving them to their domestic bliss.

The smell of fried food drifted through the house and summoned the girls, although their separate arrival surprised Brendan—Caitlin appeared first, followed by Neve. They sat at opposite ends of the table and glared at each other. Seeing the obvious conflict between them, he shot Neve a questioning look, but she shook her head. Jacob returned a moment later and chained Caleb to a chair. It was Brendan's turn to share a tense gaze as he placed the butter on the kitchen table. 'Are your lips feeling any looser this morning, Thornsy?'

'Not especially,' he replied with a smirk. 'A bit swollen though.'

They all ate breakfast in silence until the hairs rose on the back of his neck and the *aroogah* of a klaxon tolled inside his head. *The wards.*

Alannah's eyes widened. 'We have an uninvited guest, Unseelie by the sounds of it.'

'Shit! Amy's outside,' Jacob announced in a panicked voice.

Brendan grabbed Alannah's arm when she began heading for the door. 'Wait! They might be Syndicate. Let me deal with them. Probably best if they don't see us together either. Take Caleb and the girls to the cellar and keep them safe. Come on Red, I might need backup.'

'Yes, Sir.' Jacob trailed after him, the ancient floorboards creaking under his bare feet.

The front yard was clear at first glance, so he donned the glamour piercing glasses he had taken from the hallway and gave a pair to Jacob.

Jacob stopped behind him and whispered. 'I can't see anything. You want me to check out back?'

He began to nod when something caught his attention. Shimmering light refracted around a hulking gum along the fence line. Clutching Jacob's arm tight, he halted the man's retreat. 'Three o'clock.' They both turned to face the tree slowly. Whoever concealed themselves was hiding behind the thick trunk. Instinctively, he summoned flickering flames of hellfire in his hands. 'You're trespassing on Syndicate territory! Show yourself now before you make some powerful enemies.'

A melodic laugh rang out as she stepped out from her hiding place. 'A bit late for that, handsome.'

He sucked in a breath. 'What are you doing here, Bridey?'

'Caleb didn't come home last night.'

He maintained a passive expression, refusing to give away the game. 'Get to the point, woman.'

She closed the distance between them. 'I tracked his phone here, so I know he's inside, along with that bitch who broke your heart.'

'The only bitch around here is you, Bry. Caleb told me *everything*,' he bluffed. The way she paled told him Caleb had indeed withheld valuable intel.

'There's no way he would have betrayed me like that,' she insisted, despite the doubt wavering in her voice.

'No? Why not? Do you honestly think he loves you more than me?'

She shook her head violently as tears pooled in her eyes. 'You don't understand. It's *because* he loves you. We're both trying to protect you.'

He clenched his jaw. 'Consorting with my enemy is a real nice way of showing your love.'

'I didn't have a choice,' she screeched. 'Please don't do this. You don't understand the danger you're in.'

'Oh, I'm fully aware of the risks and I'm done depriving my heart and soul of the person they need. Either get on board with my decision or get the hell out of my life.'

Bridey gasped. 'So that's it then? You're throwing away our years of happiness together for what's under Alannah's skirts?'

'You know she means more to me than that. Lana's my soulmate.' Given the connection they had felt the night before, it was only a matter of time before he would repair their broken link.

Bridey glanced at Jacob, who stood silently beside him. 'Red—go fetch Stirling for me, would you?'

Jacob did not budge.

Folding his arms across his chest, Brendan gave her a smug grin. 'Caleb stays with me. And you can kiss your Syndicate job goodbye.'

'*Fine!*' she huffed. 'Don't say I didn't warn you!' Bridey strode away, tearing up the turf with her spikey heels.

'Follow her, Red,' he ordered. 'I want to know where she goes and who she talks to.'

'Yes, Sir.'

He watched Jacob slink away before heading back inside.

Chapter Nine

'Were you expecting company, Caleb?' Alannah glared at him as they sat on opposite sides of the stone-cold floor amidst racks of quality red, awaiting the all-clear. She was not much of a wine drinker, but she still heard the alcohol within those bottles whispering words of temptation. Ignoring her craving, she focussed her animosity on the traitorous endarkened man.

He slapped his head dramatically, rattling the chains shackling him to the bolt on the wall. 'Oh shit! I forgot I'd invited the Seelie Queen for tea and scones! My bad.'

She sighed. 'Why are you doing this to Brendan? Don't you see how much he loves you? You're breaking his heart.'

'Hardly,' he scoffed. 'He doesn't need me now he's got you back.'

'His love for me doesn't diminish his feelings for you and I won't stand in the way of your relationship with him. Stop acting like an insolent child and be a man about this, Caleb.'

The door swung open, and Brendan appeared. 'Coast is clear. That was just Bridey, and she's gone now. Things are officially over with her and me. If she interferes with my life again, I'll kill the whore.'

Gobsmacked, she clasped her hands over her mouth. She studied him, wondering if he was exaggerating. The red hue of his face, taut muscles in his shoulders, and throbbing vein in his neck all implied a real threat.

He looked at Neve and Caitlin huddled together in the corner, their prior grievances apparently forgotten. 'You girls are safe to head upstairs. I need a private word with Lana and Caleb.' As soon as they left, he locked the door and stalked across the room to Caleb. 'Get up!' When Caleb refused to obey, Brendan grabbed his cold iron collar, lifting him and pinning him against the wall. 'This is your last chance, Thornsy. Red's following Bridey as we speak, so he'll soon uncover the identity of this mysterious enemy she's cosied up to.'

Caleb snorted. 'Red's wasting his time. Bridey doesn't even know who they are.'

'They?' she asked, drawing closer.

He snapped his mouth shut.

Brendan growled. 'Spit it out, man, before I force it out of you.'

'Kiss me first,' demanded Caleb. 'Show me how much you love me, that betraying Bridey will be worth it.'

'If you insist.' Brendan pressed his body against Caleb's as their lips locked together.

Heat scorched her blood and pooled in her core as she watched them. Seeing the way Brendan devoured Caleb's mouth with a savage hunger, possessively claiming the man, reminded her of what it felt like to surrender herself to his touch. *If this is what it's like watching them kiss, I can't wait to see them fuck.*

'Convincing enough?' Brendan asked Caleb, whose eyes glazed over.

Caleb nodded. 'What do you want to know?' he asked in a gruff voice.

'Everything about Bridey's scheme of keeping me and Lana apart.'

'Levi first approached Bridey with the job when you were making Rhapsody for the Syndicate, but before you signed the contract. He represented an interested party who wanted to remain anonymous, and she didn't question this at the time. Her initial role was to get close and appeal to your baser instincts. Naturally, she figured it would be easy enough. Besides the fact she's an expert in the art of seduction, she'd already shared a night of passion with you.'

Alannah winced as she recalled how easily Brendan had fallen for Bridey's tricks.

'Wait, I thought Levi was one of her seven?' Brendan asked. 'One of her slaves,' he explained to Alannah.

'I thought so too,' replied Caleb. 'I later learned he'd planted himself in her household to keep an eye on you both.'

'Fuck!' Brendan paced the room. 'Go on.'

'With her footing established in your life, her job evolved into spying on you and Alannah. He wanted to know how close you were. When you both hooked up after Alannah's trial, he sent Bridey to break the pair of you apart, insisting you must not form a soul link. I was frequenting her bed at the time and Levi knew how much I meant to her, so he threatened to hurt me as well as Bry should she fail to keep you both apart.'

'*What the hell?*' Brendan's voice boomed in the cramped wine cellar. 'She never told me your lives were at risk because of this.'

Caleb shrugged. 'I didn't find out for myself until the night you both showed up at her parlour looking for Red. Observing your soul link, she panicked and broke down in my arms. She told me everything about the threats to our lives and asked me to help end your relationship.' He hung his head. 'I'm really fucking sorry.'

An icy shiver prickled her skin.

'What did you do?' Brendan asked.

'The night you shared a meal with your family, to formally break the news to them, I snuck into the house and drugged your meals with Bridey's potion.' Each syllable of Caleb's confession lowered her opinion of him, sinking it well below sea level as he drowned in his own duplicity.

'What potion?' Brendan ground out through gritted teeth.

'Something to do with heightening everyone's emotions, to make you all overreact. Bridey had already planted the seeds of doubt in your mind, and she'd also whispered in Liam's ear about fighting to win Alannah back.'

She gaped at Caleb, struggling to believe the lengths he and his sister had gone to. Where her own visage turned as white as a sheet, Brendan's flushed a vibrant red as he clenched his fists, ready to punch something or someone.

'*Un-fucking-believable!*' Brendan roared. 'And here I thought you both genuinely cared about me.'

'We do!' Caleb protested, his eyes brimming with tears. 'My love for you is real, Sir. Once you had fallen for me and Bry, Levi changed the rules. Not only were our own lives at risk, but yours and Alannah's were on the line.'

Brendan sniggered drily. 'You can be so dense sometimes, Thornsy. Lana and I were always at risk, Levi just kept that detail from you until he could manipulate you with it.' He combed his fingers through his hair and exchanged a sorrowful look with her.

She returned her attention to Caleb. 'Do you know why Levi wanted to drive us apart?'

Caleb shook his head, tears streaming down his face. 'Levi doesn't even know. He was just following orders.'

'Hm. Explains why he didn't try to stop me meeting Tyler,' mused Brendan.

Caleb's brow furrowed. 'What's Tyler got to do with any of this?'

'That's none of your damn business,' snapped Brendan. 'Are you done, or do you have more nails to hammer in?'

'That's all I know,' Caleb replied with downcast eyes. 'I'm really fucking sorry for my part in all this. I only ever did it to protect you and Bry. I love you, Sir.'

'Are you kidding me? You know *shit* about real love, Thornsy,' Brendan spat as he stormed out the cellar.

'Alannah? Please.' Caleb choked on a sob as he gave her a pleading look.

Her heart ached for Brendan, and she fought hard to supress her protective instincts. *I don't need a fucking murder case on my hands, and I doubt Brendan will appreciate me killing Caleb.* 'Bridey may have steered you down this path, but you chose to follow her and it's time to reap the devastation you sowed. Your actions did a lot of damage to my life as well as his, but I'm not the one you claim to love. I can only begin to fathom how he must feel about your betrayal.' She left him sulking in the cellar and went in search of Brendan.

Amy rose from the couch in the family room as Alannah emerged from the cellar. 'What's going on? I just saw Brendo fly outta there like his arse was on fire.'

'Caleb spilled the beans, and they were darker than my coffee roast. Suffice to say, Brendan's royally pissed at Caleb right now. I'd love to stay and chat, but I really need to comfort Brendan. Did you see what direction he went?'

Amy nodded. 'Upstairs. Where's Jacob?'

A slight smile tugged at her lips. 'He's out tracking someone for Brendan. Why do you ask?'

Her cheeks flushed. 'Oh, no reason.'

She cocked a brow at Amy. 'Uh huh.' On any other occasion she would have stayed to wheedle the truth out of Amy, but she left her alone and sprinted up the stairs, taking the steps two at a time. She found him wearing a hole in the rug lining his bedroom floor.

He looked up as she closed the door. 'I'm not great company right now, Lana.'

'No shit, Sherblock[5],' she huffed. 'But I'm not leaving you to deal with this alone. Being together means supporting each other through the lows as well as enjoying the highs. What do you need?'

'I probably need a punching bag. I'm so fucking angry.'

Halting his path across the floor, she wrapped her arms around him. 'I'm right here, babe. Take your rage and frustration out on me.'

His eyes bugged out. 'That's not a good idea. I won't be able to hold back, and I might go beyond your threshold.'

---

[5] This is not a typo, but a personal joke between Brendan and Alannah from one of their drinking sessions in *Winter's Maiden 2*.

'It's okay,' she assured him. 'I can take a lot more pain these days and I've been craving a good caning like you wouldn't believe. I can always use my safeword if it comes to it.'

He took two deep breaths. 'Do you have our box of gear?'

'Yeah, it's in my room. I brought it just in case.' She tugged on his hand, leading him down the hall. Retrieving the black plastic tub from beneath the bed, her insides tingled with anticipation. Setting it aside on the dressing table, she opened the lid and cast her eyes upon the bondage equipment and impact play toys. Her nerves hummed like high tension wires at the sight.

Brendan drew close behind her, caging her in his arms as his breath tickled her ear. 'Are you sure about this, Lana? I'm not in my right mind now. What if I don't hear you using your safeword?'

Twisting in his arms, she looked into his dark gaze, recognising the sparks of desire. 'I'm certain. Trust me, I can take it. I want to do this for you, for us. I doubt I'll even need my safeword, but if I do, I promise to scream it loud enough for you to hear me.'

A deep guttural groan slipped from his throat, and he kissed her deeply. 'Lose all the clothes, then kneel on the bed for me, gorgeous. On all fours.'

'Yes, Sir.'

Amy perked up from her couch potato boredom when she heard the front door. Springing to her feet, she strode through the house to meet the new arrival. *Shit! If it really is Jacob, I don't want to appear desperate.* She slowed her steps as she entered the kitchen, stopping altogether when she realised the cacophony was due to several people. Recognising a couple of voices as Brendan's parents, her heart began to hammer against her ribs. *Does that mean?*

She entered the front hall, spotting Ross and Nora first. 'Oh, hey Lord and Lady Winters.' Then Liam, to whom she gave a curt nod. When her eyes landed on Connor, she grinned widely, admiring his tall, muscular form. Her man looked even scruffier than usual, sporting at least a couple weeks of facial fluff, but she didn't care. He was home. She closed the distance in a few quick steps and embraced him. 'Oh Bunny! Thank the Gods you're okay!'

Liam snorted. 'Dude, she calls you Bunny?'

'Shut the fuck up Winters,' Connor grumbled, his arms still wrapped firmly around her.

Seeing a warlock home from war so soon surprised her. 'Don't you have dragons to kill, Winters?'

Liam shrugged. 'Kieran sent me home. Compulsory leave while we wait for more arrows. I need to speak to Lana straight away unless she's busy in the ritual room?' When Amy shook her head, he dashed upstairs before she could warn him.

'Oh shit! That's not gonna go well,' she whispered under her breath.

'What do you mean, Miss?' Connor asked her.

An extremely tall man marched in through the front door, carrying another guy in his bulging arms. 'Where should I put our patient?' he asked in a deep, commanding voice with an accent more like King's English than any other South Australian she'd ever heard. Aside from the charm of his British accent, he towered over them at a good six foot six and glowed with golden beauty.

'Holy fuck,' she muttered.

Connor's chest rumbled against her. 'Amy, this sexy giant is Hugh Doran.'

Hugh smiled warmly. 'It is a pleasure to meet you, Miss Amy. I would shake your hand, but as you can see mine are quite full.'

'Take him into the family room for now,' instructed Nora, leading the way. 'Lay him down on the couch. Where's Brendan? I think he'd like to meet Hugh and our patient here.'

As Amy drew closer to the unconscious figure on the couch, she sucked in a breath. Hairstyle and absent eyebrow piercing aside, he was a dead ringer for Brendan. She looked up into Nora's eyes. 'Brendo's… um… busy.'

'And Alannah?' Ross asked.

She gulped. 'With Brendo.'

A second ticked by until realisation dawned on Ross and Nora's faces.

'Oh,' they replied in unison.

'What am I missing here, Miss?' Connor asked.

Pressing her lips to the shell of his ear, she whispered, 'Brendo is *busy* with Alannah.'

Connor gaped at her, understanding lighting his eyes.

Ross heaved a sigh. 'I need a bottle of wine.' He took off for the cellar before she could warn him. When he returned minutes later, his eyes narrowed on her. 'Mind telling me why Caleb Hawthorn is chained up in my wine cellar?'

'What the blazes?' Nora squeaked.

She sighed. 'Brendan caught Caleb spying on him and Alannah, so he locked him up for interrogation purposes.'

Ross shook his head in disgust. 'Next time I see that boy....'

'Oh, leave it be, sweetheart,' insisted Nora. 'He's been through enough over the years. I do hope he has patched things up with Alannah. They deserve to be happy together.'

'And what of *our* son, Liam?' Ross demanded.

Amy thought the inflection in his voice was curious but didn't dare question it.

'Liam and Alannah were never suited for each other,' argued Nora. 'Liam would be much happier with a compatible partner.'

Connor's proximity was driving Amy to distraction, and she didn't care much for the Winters' family feuding, so she excused herself and dragged her boyfriend out into the back garden. 'I've missed you so much.'

'Likewise,' he agreed.

She climbed his body like a monkey, wrapping her thighs around his waist so she could claim his succulent lips in an ardent kiss.

'Mm, this is a much better welcome home,' he mumbled into her mouth. 'Don't you think we should take this somewhere private before things heat up much more?'

'Probably.' She kissed him again before dropping her feet to the ground. A flash of movement caught her attention, so she glanced toward the rear of the yard, spotting Jacob reclining against a tree. *How long has he been there? Was he watching me with Connor?* Scowling at him, she turned on her heels and led her man toward the guesthouse.

There was no point delaying the inevitable any longer. Liam sprinted up the stairs and paused outside the room he had shared with Alannah. It was as good a spot as any to start his search. *If she isn't working, she might be resting.* Taking a couple of deep breaths, he opened the door a crack and froze.

It was not the sight of Alannah's wrists and ankles tied to the bedposts with rope, although seeing her bound and helpless did not help. Nor was it the sight of Brendan thwacking her backside with a cane that left bright red welts across her skin that angered him the most. Hearing Alannah's bloodcurdling scream was what did it, filling his vision with a red haze that seeped into his mind and took control of his limbs.

Electricity arced between his fingertips as he stalked silently forward. Once he had a clear shot that would not put Alannah at risk, he zapped Brendan with the full force of his fury, knocking the sadistic freak unconscious.

Jerking her head to the side, Alannah glanced at Brendan's body slumped on the ground and she screamed louder with tears streaming down her face. '*Oh Gods! Brendan!*'

Liam rushed to her aid, freeing her from her tethers. 'Hey, Lana, it's okay. I'm here. He won't hurt you like that again; I promise.'

The moment her hand slipped free; she shoved him away. 'Hurting me was the whole point, you moron! How many times do I have to explain my love of pain?' She untied her other hand, then her ankles, and slid to the floor beside Brendan.

'It didn't look like you were enjoying *that*,' he spat.

'Please just stop!' Glaring at him, she shot daggers at his heart. 'Would you quit messing things up for me and Brendan?' She pressed her fingers to his neck. 'Fuck! What've you done?' she croaked out. 'I c-can't f-feel h-his p-pulse.'

His jaw dropped. *No way! He can't be…* 'I-I.' Snapping his speechless mouth shut, he stumbled forward, hoping he could revive Brendan before it was too late.

'Don't touch him!' she shrieked. '*Get out, get out, get out!* I never want to see you again!'

Clutching the wall for support, he staggered out of the room and down the hall to a guest bathroom. He emptied the contents of his stomach into the toilet and prayed silently: *Please don't let him be dead. I can't be a murderer. Please Gods.* Footsteps pounded through the house as Alannah cried out to the world for help. After rinsing his mouth and washing his hands, he crept out of the house and hopped the ley lines to his sanctuary. Even without his surfboard, the ocean called to him, so he stripped down to his underpants and waded through the shallows. With long, powerful strokes, he swam out to his usual surfing spot. Splaying his limbs out, he floated on the current, letting the slight swell ebb and flow naturally beneath him.

Several minutes later, the surface rippled, and a smiling face broke through to greet him. 'You don't have your board or boat,' Saoirse observed.

'No.' Dropping his legs beneath the surface, he began to tread water so he could face her.

Saoirse's brow furrowed. 'What's wrong, Liam?'

Throwing his arms around her, he let the deluge flow from his eyes into the crook of her neck. 'I think I murdered my brother.'

She tensed in his arms. 'What? Why? How?'

He explained the scene he had walked in on, how he had grossly misjudged things and lost control of his temper. 'Shit! If he is dead, I'll need a safe place to hide. I don't want to go to prison, Saoirse. This will ruin me!'

Hugging him tighter, she attempted to soothe him with cooing noises. 'It'll be okay, Liam. You can stay with me, like I promised. My home is always open to you.'

'Really? Like now?'

She nodded. 'Wait here a moment, I'll fetch my aunt. She can perform the ritual.' Saoirse dove into the depths.

A tempest bubbled through his blood as images of Brendan's lifeless body plagued his mind.

Saoirse returned several minutes later, introducing her aunt Sionainn. The older woman remained aloof, silently scrutinising him. Luckily, her long, dark grey curls covered her otherwise bare chest because staring at her breasts would not have done him any favours. It would take some adjusting to a world where nudity was the norm.

Power emanated from Sionainn's aura. 'What are your reasons for seeking the transformation?'

Exchanging a glance with Saoirse, he saw the unspoken warning, reminding him that merfolk warriors were not meant to be lovers. 'I need refuge from the perils of my own world.'

Sionainn cocked a brow. 'You are a warrior, no? Why desert your people in their hour of need?'

Fuck! He had not been excepting the Spanish Inquisition. 'I grow tired of my own people, as they do of me. I feel I can better protect your realm, My Lady.'

'Are you certain you want to do this? While the change is reversible, it still takes its toll on your body. Even the strongest of men have perished in the process, for it takes not only physical endurance, but mental fortitude as well.'

'I-I'm sure. I do not fear death, My Lady.' *There are worse fates.*

Sionainn smiled. 'Good. For this ritual, you must shed your land-dweller clothing. All of it.'

Gulping, he tugged at his underpants, removing them entirely and letting them float away. 'Done.'

Both women blatantly gawked at his lower body and heat rose in his cheeks. Saoirse checking him out was one thing. *But her aunt?*

'Pity you're a warrior, young man,' remarked Sionainn. 'You'd make fine breeding stock.'

Saoirse gasped. 'Aunty! You're embarrassing him.'

Sionainn snorted. 'He had better shed his shame, too. No place for that where we're going.' She drew close to him, clutching both of his arms in her webbed hands. 'Take a deep breath.' As soon as he had sucked in a lungful of air, she dunked his head beneath the surface and began chanting in Gaelic.

Clamping his eyes shut eased the salty sting but it did not stop the images flashing before him: a field of scorched corpses, Alannah's look of bitter contempt, Brendan's body lying lifeless on the floor. His head turned fuzzy, and he flailed about, struggling against the immense weight dragging him down.

A sweet voice whispered in his mind, '*Let go, Liam. Everything will be okay.*'

Giving in, he dropped his arms to his side and let the darkness take him.

191

Chapter Ten

'Oh Gods! *Somebody, please help!*' Alannah screamed at the top of her lungs as she frantically searched Brendan's body for signs of life. Not yet adept at the level of magical healing necessary, she tried to recall her first aid lessons. The source of electricity had stumbled out the door, so it was safe to touch him. *Shit! I probably should've thought of that before.*

Straddling him as she prepared to start the chest compressions triggered memories of CPR disco music. For the first time in her life, she voluntarily let the Bee Gees play their music in her head and she sang gruffly to keep herself in time:

> *Whether you're a brother, goddam your fuckin' brother*
> *You're stayin' alive, stayin' alive*
> *Feel how I'm breakin' and I'm totally shakin'*
> *You'd better be stayin' alive, stayin' alive*

*Come on now, Brendan, you're, stayin'
alive*
Ah, ha, ha, ha, stayin' alive...

Glancing up, she met Neve's wide eyes as she halted in the doorway. 'What happened?'

'Liam,' she choked out.

Ross and Nora hurried in a second later. Her uncle frowned as he knelt by Brendan's left side, while Nora collapsed to the floor on his right, tears gushing from her eyes, muttering incoherently about her baby.

'Liam shot him?' Neve asked in a tiny, wavering voice.

She nodded before giving Brendan two resuscitation breaths. His lungs still refused to breathe, and another part of her heart crumbled away. *Come on babe, please wake up for me.*

Ross gently picked up Brendan's hand. 'Continue the CPR while I use my magic to revive him. Neve, why don't you find your mother a dressing gown?'

She had not given a thought to her state of undress, let alone Brendan's. She had more important things to worry about. *Like saving my soulmate's life.* Yet, she did not refuse the robe Neve slid over her shoulders, slipping her arms into the sleeves once she had finished her fifth cycle of compressions. Another two breaths. 'He's not….' Tears blurred her vision as she stared at Ross who continued meditating, intense concentration creasing his forehead.

Brendan's chest rose and fell beneath her hands.

'Oh, thank fuck!' She peppered his face with kisses.

'He's not out of the woods yet,' advised Ross with a weary voice. 'His heartrate remains weak, and I detect extensive cerebral damage. This is already pushing the limits of my abilities. Do we have any healing potions in the fridge?' He directed the question at Nora.

'I'll go check,' Nora rasped before dashing from the room.

'Let's move him to the bed,' Ross suggested.

Alannah took Brendan's legs while Ross hugged his upper body, hoisting him up and bearing the brunt of Brendan's considerable weight. They passed a trembling Neve, who backed up against the dressing table to grant them access to the bed. With a gasp, she leaped away on spring loaded feet, squeaking, 'What the hell?'

After tucking Brendan beneath the covers, Alannah looked at the mess on the floor and blushed. Neve must have knocked the tub from its place on the dressing table, scattering the contents which she had stooped to gather up. 'Christ! Don't touch those, hun. Sit with Brendan while I clean them up.'

Ross snarled in disgust as he watched her return the sex toys to the plastic crate. 'Such unsavoury behaviour. I'm not surprised Liam reacted the way he did.'

Placing the lid on the box, she gaped at him. 'How can you say that? About your own son, no less? I know Liam was always your favourite, but he almost killed Brendan and there is still a chance he could die from his injuries.' She slid the tub back under the bed and perched on the mattress, embracing Neve as much for her own comfort as she did to support her trembling daughter.

'What of your marriage vows?' asked Ross.

She huffed as her blood boiled. 'I should have made them with Brendan, and I would have if other parties hadn't interfered. Liam had no right to come between us then or now. You have no idea what Brendan's been through these last sixteen years, so get off your fucking high horse.'

Nora broke the mounting tension when she approached Ross with a clear glass vial in hand. 'Here.'

Using the pipette inside the lid, he dripped the magical medicine beneath Brendan's tongue. Rising to his feet, he handed her the vial. 'That's all I can do for now. Give him six drops of this every four hours. Neve knows how to make it if you need more.'

'Wait, you're leaving?' she asked incredulously.

Ross sighed. 'I have other patients to treat, and I need to rest my conduits before attempting more magic.' He turned from her and strode out the room.

Day turned to night as she maintained her bedside vigil, refusing to budge even when Nora tried to coax her away for dinner. Her appetite had ceased to exist anyway. Even Luna had curled up in Brendan's armpit, choosing his company over food. As the shadows lengthened, a sense of déjà vu washed over her, and she tried to place the familiarity. *Is it due to the time Brendan overextended himself with his magic in high school? No that can't be it. Liam sat with us then.* Then it struck her. She had seen Liam strike Brendan with a lightning bolt before. Not in reality, but in a clairvoyant vision. Everything had played out exactly as she had predicted, from the intense BDSM scene to the way Liam reacted when he walked in on them. *Fuck!* She assumed her vision had warned her to make a clean break from Liam before starting things with Brendan, and she did exactly that. The first time anyway. *Maybe it's time to start paying more attention to my cosmic mana connection.*

Amy tried to conjure up a stronger word than 'awkward' to describe the dinner table that night. *'Strained'? 'Edgy,' maybe?* Brendan's parents sat at opposite ends of the long table, glaring at each other when Ross wasn't sending Jacob filthy looks. Just as well Caleb had declined to come up from his prison in the cellar after hearing the news of Brendan, and Hugh was too busy looking after Danny.

Ross even mumbled, 'Unseelie scum' under his breath before addressing Jacob directly, 'What are you doing here, boggart?'

Shoving a chunk of steak into his mouth, Jacob gave Ross a toothy grin as he spoke with a mouthful of food. 'You invited me, remember?'

'That was years ago. Times have changed.'

'Too bad you ain't the head of the family anymore, huh?' He washed his meat down with a swig of beer and shot Amy a hungry look before chomping on some carrots. This was the other source of unease. Jacob sat directly across from her, frequently nudging her toes under the table while undressing her with his eyes.

Easy enough when he knows exactly what I look like naked. Squirming under his scrutiny, she averted her gaze, hoping like hell Connor didn't pick up on the palpable sexual tension.

Ross sipped his wine and blotted his lips with a napkin like a toff tosser before responding. 'Alannah's judgement is severely lacking these days. I pray to the Gods she does not become the next High Magus.'

Nora gasped but held her tongue, and Amy glimpsed the tears brimming in her eyes.

Curious. Is this a new development, or did I just fail to notice the rift between Brendan's parents before?

A bare foot inched up her shin, the contact startling her, and she jerked back. When she shot daggers at Jacob, he responded with a smug grin.

Cutlery clattered on Nora's plate. 'Please excuse me, everyone. I seem to have lost my appetite.' She rose abruptly.

'I'm sorry.' Jacob stood to face her.

Nora forced a slight smile. 'It's okay, Jacob dear. It's not your fault.' She glanced at Ross before leaving the dining room.

Heaving a sigh, Ross abandoned his own meal and followed his wife.

'What do you suppose that was about?' asked Connor.

Amy stared at Nora's half-eaten meal. 'I have a few theories, but they're all conjecture.'

'Ooh, that's a big word for a little person,' taunted Jacob.

She glared at him. 'Yet I'm not at all surprised an imbecile like you would say something so childish.'

Jacob snickered. 'Such a smart mouth. I wonder what else it's good at.'

Amy's cheeks burned. 'Keep dreaming Bennett, 'cause you'll never know.'

Pushing his empty plate aside, he licked his lips and leaned on the table. 'Thanks, Shorty. I'm always looking for new material to go in the spank bank.' The chair scraped against the floor as Jacob rose. ''Scuse us, I'm gonna take some food to Thornsy and check on Brendo.'

She shovelled the last of her peas 'n' mash into her mouth.

Connor squeezed her thigh, his spicy scent bombarding her senses as his breath tickled her ear. 'You like him, don't you?'

Coughing and spluttering, she sprayed a mushy mess across her plate. 'Fuck no!'

'It's okay, Miss. I'm totally fine with you fucking him, or anyone else for that matter. Just because I choose to remain monogamous, doesn't mean you have to,' he reminded her.

'Yeah, but Bennett?' she scoffed.

'I know we've had our differences over the years, but Jacob can't be all bad if Alannah's still friends with him.' He tentatively traced circles on her inner thigh, heating her to the core. 'I know you intimately, Miss, so, I can tell when something, or *someone*, turns you on. Don't let me stop you taking what you want.'

She grinned at him. 'You got a cuckolding fetish you haven't told me about, Bunny?'

His cheeks flushed as he lowered his gaze submissively. 'Yes, Miss.'

Hot fucking damn. 'I'll keep that in mind if I ever do hook up with someone else. Would you want to watch me fuck Bennett?'

'Yes, if it pleases you Miss.'

The air whooshed out of her lungs. *Connor wants me to pursue Jacob, which begs the question: how do I really feel about that impish boggart?*

Pressing his thumb against the beautiful bud flowering between her legs, Erik grinned with satisfaction as Neve writhed beneath him.

'Not now,' she pleaded.

He applied more pressure. 'Stop denying yourself the pleasure I can bring you. Come for me sweetheart.'

'I can't. Not here.'

'Why not?'

Her head lolled to the side, and he followed the direction of her hooded gaze. The shadows of her surrounds slowly took shape, revealing the figure of another man in her bed.

Snatching his hand back, he clenched his fists and began to scowl, but then the man's features became apparent. Recognising Neve's father, he paled. 'What the fuck? Why are you....' He gulped, unable to put his disgust and horror into words. *It's one thing to share a bed and fool around with a twin sibling, but parents?* Deep seeded hate for the dark mage arsehole took root in his gut. As tears trickled down her delicate face, he teetered between murderous intent and comforting Neve. 'It's okay, sweetheart, I'll save you from him.'

'What?' Her brow furrowed, then leaped off her face as realisation dawned. 'No, you idiot! Dad is injured, possibly dying. I refuse to leave his side until he wakes up, or....'

'Fuck! I'm sorry. Can I hold you?'

Sniffling, she nodded. 'Please do.'

Covering her body in head-to-toe silk pyjamas, he resituated himself at the head of the bed and drew her into his arms. Recalling a tune his mother had often soothed him with, he sang to his sweet girl:

Tha Mi Sgith: Faery Love Song
Traditional Celtic (Scottish) Folksong by Anonymous

Tha mi sgìth 's mi leam fhìn,
Buain na rainich, buain na rainich
Tha mi sgìth 's mi leam fhìn,
Buain na rainich daonnan

'S tric a bha mi fhìn 's mo leannan
Anns a' ghleannan cheothar
'G èisteachd còisir bhinn an doire
Seinn sa choille chòmhail;

Tha mi sgìth 's mi leam fhìn,
Buain na rainich, buain na rainich
Tha mi sgìth 's mi leam fhìn,
Buain na rainich daonnan…

Ciod am feum dhomh bhi ri tuireadh?
Dè ni tuireadh dhomhsa
'S mi cho fada o gach duine
B' urrainn tighinn gam chòmhnadh?

She sighed when he finished. 'Thank you, Erik. Your voice is beautiful.' Turning to mist, she whispered, 'Sing to me again next time.'

Reaching out, he tried to catch the coils of her fading dream, calling out, 'I love you, Neve.' His eyes fluttered open, and he smiled at the ceiling of his bedroom. *She wants me back.* Music had been the key to her heart, and he would make a point of wooing her with his lilting voice every chance he got.

A soft moan traversed the bed, drawing his attention to Elna as she stirred from her slumber. Green flecks of light shimmered in platinum locks as they cascaded around her voluptuous curves. 'You're awake?'

As much as he hated the distance between them, he appreciated the need for a buffer in the form of the young man who slept soundly beside him. She was far too tempting otherwise, and he feared walking that treacherous path of sin before his plans came to fruition. 'I woke from a rather vivid dream,' he lied. The only one who had been dreaming through that encounter had been Neve, but he was not about to let Elna in on his plans to win Neve back through oneironautics.

Her gaze scanned his naked flesh and she grinned. 'A hot dream, I take it. Would you like Finn to take care of that for you?'

Erik sighed. 'I suppose it's preferable to my own hand.'

Nudging his arm, she warbled in the sleeping man's ear, 'Finn, honey? Your *services* are needed.'

Wiping his eyes, Finn grumbled something about insatiable appetites. His lids remained closed as he spoke gruffly, 'Just sit on my face, sweet pea.'

Erik's hard dick twitched at the thought.

Elna giggled. 'As much as I'd love to, Erik is the one who needs… attention.'

'Then *he* can sit on my face,' Finn rasped.

Fuck! At this rate he would not need much… attention. 'You sure about that?' he asked. 'You're still half asleep. I wouldn't want to choke you.'

Sliding down the mattress slightly, Finn snorted. 'Dude, it's fine. Get over here.'

Gripping the headboard firmly, he hovered above Finn's stubbly face. Two large, muscular hands grabbed his bare arse cheeks, guiding him down into Finn's gaping mouth. As soon as those full lips clamped around Erik's cock, a bristled chin brushed against his balls, and he bucked wildly. 'Holy Goddess!' Being fae, he would never grow facial hair, but he was beginning to understand the appeal. Finn moved one of his hands, squeezing the base and humming while his tongue massaged Erik's shaft. Together, they found a synchronised rhythm as he threw his head back and closed his eyes while undulating his hips.

He normally preferred a woman to provide visual stimulus when he hooked up with guys, and lately he had resorted to imagining Neve, but neither were necessary as he lost himself in the intensity he shared with Finn. Pure pleasure coursed through his veins like a potent drug, surging up from the tip of his dick and engulfing his whole body in butterflies. Tingles shot along his spine and a garbled noise escaped him as he emptied himself down Finn's throat. Stumbling with unsteady legs and a dizzy head, he collapsed beside Finn and fell into a deep, sated sleep.

Most of the clattering and chattering drifting up from the lower levels of the house had quieted and Alannah observed the time on the red digital display beside her: 10PM. Luna had clambered down to the foot of the bed, making way for Neve, who dozed fitfully beside her dad, while Alannah sat up against the headboard, running her fingers through Brendan's soft tousled hair. 'Please, babe,'

she whispered. 'I need you to stay with me. I can't lose you again, especially not like this.' She could already feel her recently-mended heart and soul breaking, and if Brendan did not pull through, there was a high chance she would help the dragons burn down the world. *Then I'll burn the fucking dragons.*

Movement at the door caught her attention as Jacob popped his head in. 'Hey. Mind if I come in?'

'Please do,' she rasped with her dry throat.

'Yikes! Sounds like you could use a drink.' Jacob picked up the empty glass on her nightstand. 'Of water,' he added when she gave him an incredulous scowl. He disappeared into the bathroom, returning with a full glass, which he handed her.

'Thanks.' She gulped down the cool liquid.

Jacob perched on her side of the bed. 'How's he doing?'

'Much the same. I've been giving him regular doses of Ross' healing potion, but it's not enough. He needs concentrated healing magic. I don't understand why Ross, his own fucking father, won't get his arse back here to help,' she replied in a hushed yet angry voice.

Jacob sighed. 'You're right. There's definitely something off about the situation.' He rubbed her back soothingly for a few minutes. 'By the way, you have some interesting visitors downstairs. One of them looks like Brendan's twin.'

She gaped at him, hope sparking in her chest. 'Tyler?'

He shook his head. 'Danny, a warlock from Mount Gambier. He is clearly another doppelganger, though.'

Blowing out a breath through pursed lips, she recalled her battlefield conversation. 'Now that you mention it, Liam told me another doppelganger was heading this way. He said Danny had been gravely injured?'

Jacob nodded. 'Danny regained consciousness a couple of hours ago and he's keen to meet you… when you're ready.' He turned his gaze toward Brendan and a blanket of silence began to smother them.

A fresh batch of tears trickled down her face. 'What if… he doesn't recover?'

'I'm sure he will.' Jacob's voice trembled. 'Otherwise, I'll hold Liam down while you gut him like a fucking fish.' He made of show of extending his cat-like claws and slicing them through the air.

She laughed drily. 'Maybe you should do the gutting. You're better equipped.' It relieved her to hear someone else express murderous rage over the situation, to know she was not alone.

'Caleb wants to see him,' Jacob blurted. 'I told him what happened, and the guy is beside himself.'

She clenched her fists in her lap. 'I'm still seriously pissed with Caleb.'

'Figures,' agreed Jacob. 'He explained everything to me this afternoon. I was chatting to him about it when Liam....' His voice trailed off, filling the air with a thick cloud of ominous tension. 'I know he did you both wrong, but Thornsy still loves Brendan deeply. I think you should give him a few minutes at least.'

She sighed. 'Fine. I'll go meet Danny in the meantime.' Curiosity was getting the better of her anyway. 'Come get me if Brendan's condition changes… for better or worse.' She rose and left the room, joints cracking as she moved her legs and straightened her spine for the first time in hours.

Chapter Eleven

Alannah found two strange men talking softly with Amy and Connor in the family room. Her eyes grew wide the moment they landed on the tall blond guy and her breathing faltered. *Fuck!* Shimmering gold skin covered sculpted cheekbones and a chiselled jaw, yet his ears were not pointed like those of Seelie fae. Immense power radiated from his aura too. He was easily the most beautiful man she had ever seen.

Chuckling, Connor rose to greet her with a warm embrace. 'Hey, Alannah.' He whispered in her ear, 'You might want to wipe the drool from your chin.'

'Shut up, Foley.'

When they broke apart, he formally introduced her to Hugh Doran and Danny Erling, the latter man captivating her in his own doppelganger way. Her eyes locked with his and the rest of the room faded away.

Danny cleared his throat. 'Your friends tell me I look almost identical to your lover. This must be quite unnerving for you, especially given the circumstances.'

She snorted as she dropped into one of the armchairs. 'That's a huge fucking understatement. Did they also tell you about Tyler?'

Furrowing his brow, Danny shook his head.

'Tyler is a warlock from Broken Hill, although he lives in Sydney now. He also shares Brendan's face, among other… qualities.'

'He's the one you had an affair with, right?' Connor asked.

Amy's brows rocketed into space. 'The fuck? What's he talkin' about Alannah?'

'I sought comfort in Tyler's arms soon after Brendan ghosted me.'

'Wait, I'm confused,' interjected Danny. 'Isn't Brendan the man upstairs?'

She heaved a sigh and explained her complicated history with Brendan, Liam, and Tyler.

'D-a-m-n.' Danny simpered. 'So, you've boned two dudes who look just like me? Should I be worried about my virtue?'

She laughed. 'If you're anything like either of them, I'm sure you lost that decades ago.'

'Touché. Can you shed some light on this whole doppelganger thing?'

'Well, the resemblance is more than skin deep. We share a mystical connection that enhances our magic when working together.'

Four faces fixed her with bulging eyes and slack jaws.

'What?'

'You said "we,"' Danny pointed out. 'Do you have doppelgangers too?'

Biting her lip, she realised her mistake. After casting a quick soundproofing ward over the room, she narrowed her eyes on Amy and Connor. 'What I'm about to say does not leave these four walls.' She shifted her gaze to Hugh. 'Understood?'

After gaining the reassurance she needed, she took a deep breath and let it out: 'I am also one of Brendan's doppelgangers. In fact, the mystic link we share is even stronger than the one he has with Tyler.'

Hugh gasped. 'What are your attunements, Lady Winters?'

'I'm a conjurer by trade, but I have many attunements thanks to the Beltane Blessing. I also hold the seat of Aether on the local Mage Council. Why do you ask?'

'Aether,' mused Hugh below his breath. 'I wonder… is Brendan connected to the stygian element?'

Her heart pulsed like a rapid-fire machine gun. 'We both are.'

Hugh smiled. 'Danny, do you specialise with your elemental magic?'

Danny crept forward in his seat. 'Um, yeah. I wield fire like a boss, hence the ink on my back.'

Her nerves tingled when she imagined Danny without a shirt. *I would so love to see that tattoo.*

'Makes sense,' muttered Hugh as he turned his attention back to her. 'What about Tyler?'

'He's got an affinity for lightning attacks and air magic, from what I understand. Where are you going with this?'

'I believe you are the prophesied *In Circulo Elementa*.'

She gave him a sidelong glance. 'The what now?'

'*In Circulo Elementa*,' he repeated, as if the gibberish he spoke was self-explanatory. 'Doesn't anyone here know Latin? The Circle of Elements?'

'I figured that much,' she huffed. 'But I don't get the significance, nor do I know anything about a prophecy.'

Hugh frowned. 'I guess the Council kept this one quiet. Centuries ago, the Gods observed that while magic grants us the power to protect, it also gives the power to corrupt. They agreed that should the magic world fall into ruin because of itself, they would give us one last hope for redemption. The Elves recorded their sacred words.' He closed his eyes and recited the prophecy:

From the ashes six powerful mages will rise,
a coven stronger than any other; born of the
Gods and connected by spirit. An element to
each, they will stand upon each of the
watchtowers and close the circle. Alone they
are powerful, together unstoppable, and they
will cleanse the evil within.

She exhaled sharply. 'What makes you think this applies to us?'

'I can't recall the exact phrasing, but there was more to the text, and it spoke of three men who would look like brothers, and three women like sisters, yet none connected by blood. The timing of your appearance cannot be purely coincidental.'

Rubbing her temples, she tried to make sense of the cryptic words. 'You said there are six of us?

But there are only five watchtowers in a ritual circle.'

'Most mages practise magic with an incomplete circle,' Hugh explained. 'They reject the sixth element out of fear and ignorance.'

In that instant, Hugh gained her respect. *He's not just a pretty face.*

'I'm guessing you would take the apex with your attunement to Aether, while Brendan would sit across from you, wielding nether. As a polar pair, you balance each other and share a strong spiritual bond. The same would apply to Danny and Tyler's other halves.'

'What about the line, "Born of the Gods." Does that have anything to do with our Beltane Blessings?' asked Danny.

She cocked her brow at him. 'You're a Beltane baby too?'

'You betcha.' He winked at her, eliciting another shot of traitorous hormones.

Down girl! This is so-o not the time to be lusting after another man, even if he looks like Brendan.

'Possibly,' Hugh went on, oblivious to the simmering chemistry in the air. 'Are Brendan and Tyler blessed?'

Spluttering, she caught Danny's smirk and blushed. 'Um, not in the Beltane sense of the word.'

Amy sniggered. 'The rumours are true then? Figures a guy with his rep would have a massive schlong.'

Ignoring her foul-mouthed friend, Alannah focussed on the *important* issue at hand. 'Tyler told me the doppelganger gene comes from our ties to the Gods of magic rather than the creators. He traced his ancestry back to Egypt, theorising Isis had something to do with his bloodline. As for myself, I never knew my bio dad, but I guess he had similar origins, as would Danny's father. Brendan was born first, so he is the Original, no doppelganger gene needed. Wait! What's your date of birth Danny?'

'Fourteenth of August 2002.'

She nodded. 'Same as me and Tyler.'

Danny sucked in a deep breath. 'Say we are this *Circulon Elementus—*'

'*In Circulo Elementa,*' corrected Hugh.

'Yeah, that. How do we find the other two chicks?'

'We could hack into the Council's registration database to find other mages who share our birthday,' she suggested. 'Although it might be a moot point if Brendan doesn't recover from his injuries.'

Hugh shifted forward in his seat. 'His father said Brendan's condition had stabilised, that he just needed rest.'

'What the hell?' she screeched, jumping to her feet. 'Why would he lie about that? Brendan needs powerful healing magic, not just the pissy little potions Ross left me with.' Her gut twisted into knots and bile climbed her throat as she realised what was happening. 'Ross doesn't want Brendan to get better,' she whispered. 'He must be working with the enemy.'

Connor and Amy both turned a deathly shade of pale when her gaze met theirs.

'No,' Connor wheezed.

'I can heal him for you,' Hugh declared. 'I brought Danny back from the brink of death, so I'm sure I can help Brendan.'

'Oh my Gods!' She clapped her hands together and bounced on her toes. 'You'd do that for us?'

Hugh nodded. 'I'd do anything in my power to help The Circle.'

Embracing her trembling daughter, Alannah watched Hugh perform his magic. Jacob had escorted Caleb back to the attic as soon as she had entered with the enigmatic man. Unlike other abjurers she had seen, Hugh did not need to close his eyes and meditate while sending waves of healing energy through Brendan's body. Ultramarine light emanated from Hugh, providing vivid contrast to his golden skin. Had she not known better, she would have thought him an angel, but such entities did not exist. Spirits—the untethered souls of magical beings—were the closest thing and they did not possess the power to heal living creatures. 'So what's your deal, Hugh Doran?'

He glanced at Alannah with amber eyes. 'What do you mean?'

'You know, where are you from? What are your attunements? What do you like? That sort of thing.'

A warm smile graced his lips and Neve's breath hitched, prompting Alannah to chuckle. 'Well, my home is back in England,' replied Hugh.

'Yeah, I figured that much from your accent. What part?'

'Sussex originally, but I have been all over. I am attuned to the primordial, so I can channel all sources of mana, and I like lots of things. Can you be more specific?'

'Men or women?' squeaked Neve before she averted her eyes and blushed.

Hugh blinked a few times. 'Oh, you wish to know if I have a sexual preference. Honestly, I do not know. No one from either gender has caught my eye yet.'

This freakishly stunning man is a virgin? Good Gods! Alannah wondered how old he was. Without a hint of grey in his hair, or fine lines touching his perfect skin, he could not be a day over thirty. But his wise eyes and sophisticated manner implied a level of maturity well beyond a twenty-something.

Neve's shoulders slumped.

'I am sorry if I have offended you, little lady.'

She hid her face in Alannah's sleeve.

Alannah ran soothing strokes through her hair. 'Don't worry about it, Hugh. My daughter is only fifteen, far too young for you.'

'*Mum!*' Neve complained in a muffled voice.

Rolling her eyes, she moved onto a safer topic: 'Do you have any hobbies?'

'Certainly. I enjoy the great outdoors. Fishing, hiking, mountain climbing. The list goes on.'

'I guess that explains your impressive tan.'

'Thank you for the compliment, My Lady.' His intense gaze held hers and she felt the heat rise in her own cheeks as liquid lust pooled in her core.

Brendan's groaning drew her attention back to where it ought to have been. 'L-Lana?'

'I'm right here, babe.' She took his hand in hers and gave it a gentle squeeze.

Keeping his eyes closed, he gave her a lopsided grin. 'Please tell me I'm the reason for your state of arousal.'

'TMI!' Neve screeched and fled the room, startling Luna, who scurried to her usual hiding place under the bed.

Leaping at him, Alannah straddled Brendan and pressed her lips to his. His arms flew up to hug her close and he deepened the kiss. As the scent of his manly musk penetrated her senses, she forgot the rest of the world existed. Then a throat clearing brought her back to reality.

Breaking lip contact, but still holding her tight, Brendan glanced over her shoulder. 'The fuck? Who the hell are you?'

Mirth rumbled through her chest, and she rolled back to her side of the bed. 'Brendan, this is Hugh Doran from Sussex. He is the one who healed you… well mostly. Your dad started the process, but then Hugh came and kicked his arse at the whole abjuration thing. You should've seen the way he—' Realising she was rambling; she snapped her mouth shut.

Narrowing his eyes, Brendan studied her, and she wondered if he was reading her aura and possibly her mind.

She broadcast her thoughts to reassure him, *'Yeah, I think he's hot, but there is no real attraction there. I'm mostly just impressed by his magical abilities.'*

Brendan breathed a sigh of relief, smiling at Hugh as he extended his hand. 'It's good to meet you, bro. Thanks for the patch up, although I gotta admit, I'm hazy on the reason for needing medical attention.' After shaking Hugh's hand, he returned his attention to Alannah. 'What happened? One minute I'm… uh—' his eyes darted to Hugh and back to her '—pleasuring you, the next I'm waking up to the sound of this dude's voice.'

Thinking back to the incident, her mood soured. 'Liam walked in on us and shot you with a lightning bolt.' She paused to take a deep breath. 'Your heart stopped, and you nearly fucking died.' Choking on her grief, she swallowed against the lump in her throat and tasted the salt of her tears. 'You almost left me again.'

Embracing her, Brendan whispered soothingly, 'Hey, it's okay gorgeous. I'm right here and I promise it'll take a lot more than my douche canoe of a brother to remove me from this mortal coil. Where is that fucker anyway?' Sitting up, he winced and cursed under his breath.

'You should take it easy,' suggested Hugh. 'It is likely there is some residual damage. Your body needs time to mend.'

Brendan frowned. 'You sayin' I'm not ready to f—make love to my woman?'

'If it means strenuous activity, then I'd advise against it.'

'There's no *ifs* about it,' scoffed Brendan.

She sighed. 'To answer your question, I don't know where Liam is. I screamed at him to get out and he hasn't dared to show his face in here since. Have you seen him, Hugh?'

'No, not since we all arrived yesterday. He may have returned to the battlefield.'

Brendan pulled her against his side and draped his arm across her shoulders. 'Or he's brooding in a gym somewhere. Listen mate, I'm super grateful for what you've done, but would you mind giving me some time alone with Lana?'

'Certainly.'

As Hugh rose to leave, she halted him, 'Wait! I think we should introduce him to Danny. Would you mind bringing him up here?'

'Of course.' He was out the door before Brendan could protest.

221

Alannah braced herself.

'Seriously Lana? I just wanna snuggle with you.' His tone was mild, much less angsty than she had expected. Turning to face her front on, he ran his hands along her sides, brushing her breasts before gripping her hips. He leaned in to kiss her, but she withdrew, and he pouted.

'You heard the man. Nothing strenuous,' she reminded him. 'And kissing will likely tempt us to take things further.'

Brendan huffed. 'Fine. Who is this Danny fellow, anyway? Should I worry about *him* turning you on?'

She gaped at him, wondering if Liam had short-circuited something in Brendan's brain. 'What's with the sudden possessive alpha male attitude? You've never been jealous of me being with anyone other than Liam before.'

'I don't know. I guess I felt intimidated by that guy.' Wisps of hair tumbled around his face as he lowered his gaze and she noticed the first hints of grey dappling his otherwise jet-black hair. After the stress his body had just been through, such a sight did not surprise her.

Climbing into his lap, she ran her fingers through his salt and pepper locks, admiring his new, distinguished look. 'You have nothing to worry about with Hugh. I think he might be asexual for one thing. You're the man I love with my heart and soul.'

A moan slipped from his lips, and he claimed her mouth in a savage kiss. She should have scolded his reckless behaviour. She melted instead, succumbing to the smouldering heat, the embers of their love. Throwing fuel on the fire, she began to grind against his erection, cursing the layers of underwear between them.

'Is this a private party, or can I join too?' Danny's voice sizzled her nerves.

Ending the kiss, she sucked in a breath and almost creamed her panties when she thought about fucking them both at once. *Heck, why stop at two, when I could have all three?* She hid her blushing face against Brendan's shoulder the moment the idea occurred to her. She did not even know Danny, not really.

'Tyler?' Brendan queried in a bemused tone.

Laughing, she tickled Brendan's neck with her breath, loving the soft gasp that escaped his gulping throat.

'Nah man, I'm Danny, but you're like the tenth person who's called me Tyler and I'm beginning to see why.'

'Fuck! Lana, why didn't you tell me I had another doppelganger here?'

Regaining her composure, she sat up and looked Brendan in the eyes. 'I was about to, but then you… distracted me.'

As Danny's footfalls drew near, she attempted to move, but Brendan spun her around to face their visitor, keeping her arse firmly planted in his lap.

Hugh hovered in the doorway. 'I'll be downstairs if you need me.'

'Actually, can you stay?' she asked. 'You'll do a better job of explaining The Circle.'

Glancing warily at Brendan, then uncomfortably at Danny—who had already made himself at home on the end of the bed—Hugh heaved a sigh and nodded. 'Very well.' Sitting in the desk chair, he explained what he knew about doppelgangers and the *In Circulo Elementa*.

'Ah hell! You telling me there's another two Lanas out there? I've got my hands full with this one.' Brendan made a show of cupping her breasts.

Snorting, she elbowed him in the ribs.

'Oof! Careful gorgeous, I'm under strict orders to take it easy, remember?'

Tilting her head back to make eye contact, she popped her tongue out briefly, not giving him the opportunity to catch it when his teeth gnashed at her. 'Do you think this could be the real reason our enemy wanted to keep us apart? To prevent us completing The Circle?'

The humour left Brendan's expression. 'Possibly. If we do search for the other two, we will need to be extremely careful, although I'm honestly not sure what we hope to achieve by closing The Circle.'

Danny straightened as his brows arched. 'Dude! Did you miss the bit in the prophecy about unstoppable power?'

'Yeah, but to what end?' Brendan countered. 'Why does the prophecy exist? What's this unnamed evil we're supposed to cleanse? I don't get it.'

She gasped. 'This must be the ultimate secret Tara referred to, surely.'

Brendan's eyes widened. 'That's a fucking good point. Pity most of my research materials are in Sydney and there's a huge war going—oh shit! My books are probably a pile of ash! Not to mention my building.'

'We don't know that for sure. I could ask Tyler; I was thinking of checking in with him anyway.' Wriggling out of Brendan's lap, she rose and retrieved Brendan's work phone from the desk.

'Mind if I use this to call him? This conversation warrants a secure line.'

The left side of Brendan's lips quirked. 'On one condition.'

Alannah rolled her eyes. 'Brendan—I'm not having sex with you until you have finished healing from your near-death experience.'

He smirked. 'That's fine. I should be good in a few hours. That's not what I meant though. I want you to return to my lap while you talk to Tyler.'

Her mood brightened. 'You're too cute, babe.' She settled back into her warm seat against his firm body and dialled Tyler.

The phone rang six times before Tyler picked up. 'Hey man, what's up?' He sounded flustered and short of breath.

'Hi Ty, it's Lana. Have I caught you at a bad time?'

Tyler sucked in a breath. 'Hey, beautiful. There aren't exactly any good times to be had here these days, but I'm free to talk.'

'After my recent trip to the frontline, I can imagine the nightmares you guys are facing. Any injuries or fatalities I should know about?'

'Shane got badly burnt, but aside from that, we've escaped the brunt of it. How are things over there?'

'Kieran is keeping me in reserves and putting my conjuration skills to the test. Thankfully, I have Brendan here to help. Speaking of whom, mind if I put you on loudspeaker?'

'Go for it.'

Brendan nestled his jaw in the crook of her neck. 'Hey Quirke, how's my city holding up?'

Tyler huffed out a dry laugh. 'She's seen better days, but don't worry—your building is still standing. Must have some powerful wards because most of the neighbouring towers have collapsed.

'That's a relief,' Brendan exhaled.

'So,' Tyler started, 'have you and Lana kissed and made up?'

'Among other things,' replied Brendan with a Cheshire grin. 'Listen bro, there's a couple of other guys here I think you should meet.' He introduced Hugh and Danny as mages from Mount Gambier.

'There's something else you should know about Danny,' she added. 'He looks just like you and Brendan.'

Tyler whistled, short and shrill. 'Another doppelganger?'

'Yup,' Brendan answered. 'Plus, my theory about Lana is correct. She's a magic twin too. Hugh here believes we're all part of some powerful circle born of the Gods and written into prophecy. If this is true, Lana has a couple of doubles out there somewhere.'

'Have you ever heard of *In Circulo Elementa?*' Hugh asked.

'Can't say that I have,' replied Tyler. 'What's the significance of this circle?'

Hugh repeated everything he had told them to Tyler.

'Don't share this intel with anyone, Ty, not even Jaxon or Sam. We need to be careful,' she warned. 'I think this is the reason Bridey was trying to keep me and Brendan apart.'

Brendan filled Tyler in on the latest regarding the she-devil and the bombshell Caleb had dropped.

'I'm sorry, man. That's gotta sting. Don't worry, I won't put you guys at risk by blabbing. So, what's the plan? You wanna go find the other two ladies?'

'Yes,' she admitted. 'Once this war is over. I need you to stay safe until then, which is why I want to send you a special set of armour I have imbued. It's the only thing that will properly protect you from dragon fire.'

'That's swell, beautiful, but how do you intend to get it here? Hopping ley lines ain't exactly safe right now.'

'I'll send it via demon courier,' Brendan offered. 'It's not like Lana's going to dob me in for using dark magic.'

True that. If anyone else channelled the stygian element in her district, she would report it as a matter of course, but she knew Brendan used his attunement for good. 'I'm sorry I can't send more sets of armour for the rest of your team, but I'm flat out making enough for Kieran's army.'

Tyler sighed. 'I understand. Thanks for sparing one for *moi*; I should get going.'

They signed off just as her own phone buzzed with a message. She stared at the text, unable to believe the words on her screen.

'What's wrong?' Danny asked. 'You look a little pale.'

She looked up at him. 'High Magus Kieran just died.'

Chapter Twelve

'What?' Danny screeched, his brows shooting skywards. 'How?'

Alannah took a moment to compose herself from the initial shock of Monique's message. 'Kieran was meeting with the human army to coordinate our next ambush when the dragons attacked. They burned the human barracks to the ground, along with everyone inside.'

Hugh sighed. 'I'm sorry, Lady Winters. I did not know the High Magus very well, but he seemed like an honourable man.'

Tears pooled in her eyes as she nodded.

Brendan's arms tightened around her, and he kissed the crown of her head.

Her phone chimed again, and she gasped as she read the latest message from Monique. 'The Council has called an emergency meeting to vote in the new High Magus. We can't afford to go without a leader in the middle of a war.'

A deep, guttural sound rumbled in Brendan's chest. 'Where do you plan to meet? The Council chambers aren't exactly safe to use right now.'

'Good point,' she agreed. 'I'll invite them here. The formal dining room should suffice if I cast a sound ward.' She typed out a quick reply to Monique explaining the plan, then clambered to her feet. 'I need to get ready. This place will be crawling with Council reps in several hours.'

Sliding out of bed, Brendan stood before her. 'I'll make myself scarce in the attic, but first, I want to join you in the shower.'

The assembled councillors sitting around the jarrah dining table buzzed with nervous energy. When Monique entered with her husband Steve, an eerie hush washed over the room, and everyone rose as a sign of respect.

Embracing her, Alannah whispered condolences. 'Are you sure you're up for this? You could have sent a proxy.'

Monique nodded. 'I need to focus on this. There's no time to fall apart.'

After giving Alannah a brief hug, Steve glanced around the room. 'Where's Liam?'

'He left.' When Steve's eyes widened, she quickly added, 'We had a big fight and he stormed off in a huff. I assumed he went back to the Murray Bridge garrison.'

He shook his head and a pang of guilt gnawed at her gut. 'I'm sure he's fine,' Steve assured her.

'I'm not,' she croaked. 'It's not like him to refuse an official Council summons.'

'True. Maybe you should try a scrying spell after the meeting?'

'Okay.' She dropped into her chair as dread settled in her stomach. Despite their differences, and all the trouble Liam had caused her, she still cared for him, and she would never wish him dead. Not really.

Monique set up her laptop, connecting to the nine other South Australian districts via video conferencing. Except for Danny, the councillors from these districts had assembled in separate rooms at the garrison. 'As the returning officer, I officially open this special general meeting at 9:12AM,' Monique announced, placing a sealed envelope on the table. 'I have with me my late father's nomination for the new High Magus. Councillor Sheridan, please confirm the authenticity of this letter.'

Duncan Sheridan in the Seat of Matter took the envelope and studied the imbued wax seal that held it closed. 'I can confirm that this has been sealed by the late High Magus Kieran Lane.' The seal popped as he pried it free and retrieved a single sheet of paper. 'I can also confirm that this document has been signed by the late High Magus Kieran Lane.' He returned it to Monique.

Monique read the letter aloud: 'As the High Magus of South Australia, I Kieran Lane formally nominate Lady Alannah Winters to take my place in the event of my demise.'

Ross stamped his fist on the table. 'This is preposterous! He cannot be serious! Alchemist Lane, are you sure that is the latest letter, that there hasn't been a mistake?'

Monique glared at Ross. 'Quite certain, Abjurer Winters. Does anyone second my father's nomination?'

Raising her hand, Nora piped up. 'I second the nomination for Councillor Alannah Winters.'

Folding his arms, Ross harumphed as he slumped back into his chair.

'Very well.' Monique smiled at her, filling her chest with bubbles of hope and anticipation. 'Lady Alannah Winters is an official candidate in the running for High Magus.' Looking at the screen, she addressed the remote attendees, 'Are there any other nominations?'

The Council nominated two other valid candidates, each of whom spoke about their plans for winning the war.

Alannah took to the proverbial stand to give her campaign speech. 'My name is Councillor Alannah Winters, conjurer, and member for the Seat of Aether. As many of you would know, I am attuned to the primordial and efficient at channelling all twelve mana sources.' She took a deep breath before continuing. 'You have already heard what the other candidates intend to do about the war. What they fail to realise is that without ready access to the stygian element, we do not stand a chance against the dragons.' Murmurs stirred throughout the room, but she persisted. 'While many of you were bravely fighting, I was working under the express instructions of Kieran Lane, preparing your battle gear. He was the one who ordered me to imbue your weapons with spell breaking and your armour with spell resistance. Both abilities require a link to the stygian element.'

The crowd erupted in a heated argument.

'*Quiet!*' Steve boomed. 'Do not forget that Lady Alannah was found not guilty during her trial sixteen years ago. And it's not like she has kept her nether attunement a secret. Listen to what she has to say.'

'Thank you, Councillor Steve Maher. I assure you there is nothing inherently evil about the stygian element. As with other mana sources, the onus is on practitioners to use it appropriately. I ask you this: is there anything wrong with protecting the lives of our brave heroes, or equipping them with the necessary tools to defend our people?' She waited for the new wave of chatter to die down. 'If you vote for me, I promise to decriminalise the use of nether in this state. After that, we can provide our conjurers with the means to imbue weapons and armour that will win this war. Moving forward, I will also petition the global Council to legalise it so we can elect new members in every district who can properly monitor the use of this powerful magic. If you doubt I can succeed, let me remind you that I was the one who pushed for the global recognition of the true Beltane Blessing. Many of us came into this world with an innate affinity for the primordial, yet this truth was hidden from us by the Arch Mage. Vote for me because I stand for truth, transparency, and progress.' Tense silence filled the air as she returned to her chair.

Handing out imbued ballot papers to each councillor in the room, Monique explained how to vote. She called for complete silence as everyone fulfilled their democratic duty.

Even though it was a no-brainer, Alannah felt weird choosing herself. Still, she wasn't about to throw her vote away on the less competent options, so she wrote her name with mystic ink. Not only did her name appear on her ballot paper, but it automatically added to the tally on Monique's computer.

Once everyone present had cast their votes, Monique cleared her throat. 'We have a clear winner. Congratulations to High Magus Alannah Winters.'

Her supporters clapped and cheered for her and the councillors in the room congratulated her with hugs or handshakes. All except her own uncle. As Ross scowled his disapproval, she made a mental note to investigate his affiliation with the enemy.

'We now have an opening in the Seat of Aether,' Monique pointed out. 'High Magus Winters, whom do you nominate for this position?'

'If he is interested, I'd like to invite Hugh Doran to join our district Council. He is a very skilled mage with the Beltane Blessing.' She could not think of a better fit.

'I second that,' said Danny. 'The dude saved my life and healed me of fourth degree burns.'

'That's quite the recommendation,' Monique agreed. 'But since you are from a different district, we'll need someone else to second his nomination.'

Nora raised her hand again. 'I second the nomination of Hugh Doran. I have seen his work first-hand.'

Alannah turned to Danny and asked, 'Could you please summon Hugh for me?'

'Absolutely!' Danny strode out the room, returning with Hugh in tow.

'Hugh Doran, I invite you to apply for the Seat of Aether on the Fleurieu Peninsula district. Do you accept my nomination?'

Beaming, Hugh's face would have put the sun to shame. 'I would be honoured. Thank you, Lady Winters.'

'Actually, it's High Magus Winters now,' she proclaimed with a grin. 'Councillor Lane, please send word through official channels that any other pure blood mage in the district with an attunement to Aether has five business days to apply for this position.'

A bunch of Councillors had left, and the sound ward had dropped, so the meeting had clearly finished, but Brendan's soulmate had not yet emerged from the dining room. He peeked inside, spying Alannah hunched over a series of maps. Her aura spoke volumes: a black cloud surrounding her. Moving closer, he spotted a scattering of scrying crystals across the maps. 'What's wrong, gorgeous?'

'Brendan? What are you doing here?' Steve straightened in his chair, alerting Brendan to his presence for the first time. He was not the only other family member present either. Brendan's parents were still there.

'Oh hey, cuz, I've been staying here. It *is* my family home after all.'

'Yeah, but....' Steve's voice trailed off as he shot Alannah a concerned look.

'Brendan and I have resolved our differences,' she explained. 'We are officially back together.'

Steve's eyes bugged out. 'Is that what you and Liam fought about?'

Brendan snickered. 'Dude, it was more than just a fight. The dickwad almost killed me dead.'

'Yet here you are, looking perfectly healthy,' his dad deadpanned.

'No thanks to you,' Brendan scoffed. 'Thank the Gods for Hugh Doran. What's with all the scrying gear, Lana?'

'Liam's missing and we can't find him anywhere,' she replied.

Brendan shrugged. 'What's the big deal? He's probably laying low after knocking me flat on my amazing arse. I bet he thinks he committed murder, or some shit.'

'Of course!' Alannah sprang to her feet. 'He would have figured we'd scry for him, so he's hiding with someone who can conceal him from detection magic. Brendan, is Connor still here?'

'Yeah, he's making the most of his time with Amy before heading back to base with Mum and Dad.'

With a nod, she dashed out of the room and climbed the stairs two at a time.

He followed hot on her heels. 'You planning to tell me who our new High Magus is, or do I have to get the news from Mum?'

'I am.' She continued up the stairs as fast as her hot little legs would take her.

'Don't keep me in suspense. Who is he? Fuck I hope it's not Dad.'

'No, babe. It's me. I'm the new High Magus.'

He clamped a hand on her shoulder as they reached the upper landing, halting her advance. 'Wait up, why didn't you share this fantastic news with me before?'

'I'm sorry. Liam's disappearance overshadowed my good news.'

'Fuck Liam!' He winced. 'No, I take that back. Don't ever do it with that jerk again. Still, he doesn't deserve all this attention.'

She sighed. 'What if he's dead because of my outburst? I could never live with that guilt. Besides, I still care about him.'

When his heart surged up into his throat, he gaped at her.

'As a friend and cousin, not as a lover. You're it for me, Brendan. I promise.'

Shoving her up against a wall, he kissed her deep and rough, beyond caring about those so-called doctor's orders. He was done taking it easy. As she mewled into his mouth, he hoisted her up, wrapping her legs around his waist.

'Brendan!' she protested.

'I'm fine, Lana. The only part of me that hurts is my cock, and it aches to be inside you, gorgeous.'

'I need to speak to Connor,' she grumbled with a voice like gravel, but her hooded eyes betrayed her inner turmoil.

'Your sense of honour and duty are admirable, Lana. You'll make a great High Magus *after* I'm done fulfilling your more important needs.

Besides, I'm pretty sure Connor is busy right now. You can talk to him in the morning.' His teeth grazed her neck, eliciting a groan, followed by goosebumps in their wake. 'That cool with you?'

'Yes,' she rasped.

He carried her to their room, kicking the door shut behind him.

After fucking Alannah senseless, he watched her slip into a peaceful slumber. He had always loved watching her sleep, and old habits die hard. He admired the dainty diamond in her nose, the soft smile on her slightly parted lips, and the gentle rise and fall of her luscious breasts, only partially covered by the white cotton sheet. Mesmerised by her breathing, he drifted off to sleep.

Waking in a volcanic landscape, it took him a moment to gather his wits and assess the situation. Sulphurous fumes rose from bubbling pits of lava, swirling into a red hazy sky. As he took a step, the ground seared the soles of his feet. Glancing down, he wondered, *why am I wearing my dark mage robes and no damn shoes?* Braving the burn, he approached a cave, hoping it would provide shelter from the suffocating heat.

'It's so good of you to join me,' a deep voice echoed through the cavern as he stepped inside.

'Who's there?' he called out, slowing his pace.

A mage light sparked to life in the man's large palm.

No, not a man. Nor is that a normal mage light.

Hellfire flickered against the red flesh of the monstrous being who stood before him. 'I must say, for such a powerful dark mage, you are quite the disappointment. What would your Syndicate think of you if they knew how soft you were at heart?'

'Set? How did you—' he gulped. 'You dragged me to the Underworld?'

The evil God chuckled. 'I wish. This was just a convenient vision to spook you with. No, you and I are both inside your head.'

'I'm dreaming?'

'In a manner of speaking. You're not imagining me, though. I'm as real as the naked beauty sleeping beside you. Mm, what I'd give to ravish her. She would make a worthy mother of my spawn.'

He balled his hands into fists. 'Touch her and I'll kill you.'

Throwing back his head, Set laughed, the raucous sound piercing his eardrums. 'Don't be silly, boy. You can't kill a God. I'm a true immortal.

Why do you think the Celestials banished me to this hellish place?'

'What are you doing in my head, and how'd you even get here?' he asked in a seething tone.

'I attached part of my psyche to yours during that banishment ritual you betrayed me with. I've been riding around in your head for sixteen Earth years.'

He gasped. 'Those revenge dreams were your doing?'

Set grinned, showing a full snout of razor-sharp teeth. 'Indeed. The fact that you enjoyed them is the one redeemable quality you have left.'

Shaking his head, he tried to deny it, even knowing how futile it was. The demonic lord of chaos was deep inside his mind, which meant he was privy to every thought, even the most personal ones he had buried deep.

'It's time to enact your revenge,' Set insisted. 'The perfect opportunity has arisen.' When he furrowed his brow, Set explained, 'Liam is hiding with the merfolk. Strike now and your precious Lana will never know you took your brother's life.'

'No! I won't perform such a heinous crime.'

'Not even for the sake of your beloved?'

'I fail to see how committing murder benefits Lana, especially when she still cares for the douchebag.'

Set licked his chops. 'If you don't do it, I will claim your woman as my own.'

'Pfft.' He waved a dismissive hand. 'You're bluffing. I trapped you in hell. There's no way you'll be returning, not with your cult in ruins.'

'I may not be able to travel to your plane, but I can convince Alannah to come to mine. It only takes a short hop from your head to hers now that your soul link is mending itself. I can be quite persuasive when I want to be.'

'What?' This was news to him. He had figured it would take a repeat of the passionate ritual to repair their soulmate bond.

'I'll give you a week.' Pressing a finger to Brendan's forehead, Set pushed him backward.

Landing with a *thud*, he awoke with a start, sweat pouring down his face. The brand above his heart was throbbing and when he placed a hand over the cartouche, it felt hot. 'Fuck!' he hissed to himself.

Alannah stirred beside him, and her eyes fluttered open. 'What's wrong, babe?'

'I need to leave town for a couple of days to deal with my inner demons.'

She jack-knifed in bed. 'Why?'

'Remember how I told you about Set giving me this brand?' He pointed to the burning scar.

'Yeah,' she whispered.

'Turns out the arsehole used it to sort of possess me. He stowed away in the depths of my mind, riding me hard with his desires for revenge.'

'What do you mean?' she asked.

'Set wants me to take revenge on Liam for what he did to us. If I don't find a way to exorcise Set, I'm afraid he'll drive me to murder.'

Alannah's jaw dropped. 'You wouldn't—'

Scooping her into his lap, he peppered kisses all over her face. 'Not if I can help it. This is why I need to go on a road trip. I heard about an exiled Acolyte up north who should be able to help.'

'You can't travel safely right now. There's a war going on, or did you forget the dragons?'

He forced a smile, hating how much his heart hammered at the prospect of coming face to face with a dragon. 'Of course not. I promise I'll be careful. You don't become the successful leader of a criminal syndicate without learning how to move undetected through the shadows.'

'You better wear some of my imbued armour, to be safe.'

'Thanks, gorgeous. That'll definitely help. I ought to start getting ready.' Jumping out of bed, he packed a few basic supplies in a backpack. He washed off the residue of sex in the shower, taking advantage of the opportunity to give Alannah a long goodbye kiss. After getting dressed, he claimed her lips again, groaning as he pulled back with a growing erection. 'Gods, I'll miss you, Lana.'

'Me too,' she rasped.

'I'd better go.' Turning, he trudged across the floor, pausing at the doorway to feast his eyes on her. 'Oh, and Lana, Liam is hiding with the merfolk.' Turning away from the most beautiful woman in the world, he made his exit lest he lose his nerve.

Four stark walls closed in on Alannah as she sifted through the documents on Kieran's desk. *My desk now*, she reminded herself. War sure as hell produced a lot of paperwork and her mind was in no state to make sense of it. Not with her thoughts turning to Brendan every other second. *What if a dragon snatches him up during his travels? Or what if he can't break his connection to Set?*

The intercom buzzed, pulling her out of her downward spiral. 'Excuse me, Your Honour, there's a young Seelie man here to see you,' explained Melody, her receptionist.

She sighed. 'Who is he and what does he want?'

'His name is Erik, and he says this is important. It's about your daughter.'

'Thank you, Melody. Please send him up.'

The tall platinum-blond waltzed into her office with far too much swagger in his hips. 'Thank you for seeing me, Your Honour.' Like honey, his saccharine words oozed from his tongue.

'Have a seat.' She gestured at the chairs on the opposite side of the desk. 'What can I do for you, Prince Alvarsson?'

'I ask that you reconsider signing the betrothal contract.' In response to her indignant huff, he quickly added, 'I'm deeply in love with her, Your Honour, and if you ask her, I'm sure she'll admit to mutual feelings. I know you're worried about the virginity clauses in the contract, but I have found a way around that. I spoke with an orc healer who is willing to restore Neve's hymen and keep the procedure a secret from the Seelie Court. I'll cover the costs, but you would need to sign the consent form.' He placed the form in question on her desk, along with a pamphlet about the operation.

She skim-read the brochure. The orc was a registered practitioner and the procedure looked safe enough. Still, her concerns for Neve went far beyond the matter of her virginity. 'No,' she replied flatly.

Erik's countenance darkened. 'Please, Your Honour. I beg you to think this through. This betrothal is the only way to protect Neve from the dragons.'

She snorted out a dry laugh. 'She doesn't need Seelie shelter. I've upgraded the wards around my family estate to withstand dragon fire.'

'That may be so, but your nether ward won't stop the dragons crossing the barrier and launching a ground assault. Even if you're all wearing imbued armour, they can lay waste to your house and crush you with their jaws. The only way to guarantee her safety is to mark the place under Seelie protection. I'd be willing to do that for you if you sign the betrothal contract.'

Her heart thumped hard against her ribs. She had not considered the possibility Erik described. In theory she could shield the house itself, but imbuing each panel, pane, and sheet would take days, if not weeks, and her new role as High Magus already demanded too much of her time. Leaning back, she inhaled deeply. 'I'll sign on five conditions. First, I want you to protect the garrisons and all mage homes in the district, regardless of bloodline purity.'

'That's a huge ask, Your Honour.'

She arched her right brow.

'I will make it happen. What else?'

Schooling an expressionless mask, she gave herself a figurative high-five. She much preferred dealing with Erik than his father. 'You must also promise me that no member of the Seelie Court will harm Neve.'

'So long as she abides by all our laws, you have my word. I won't let anyone touch a hair on her precious head.'

She nodded. 'Good. When you are living with her, I also expect an open-door policy for myself and Brendan, Neve's real father. You can expect regular visits from your in-laws.'

Erik gulped. 'Yes, of course, Your Honour.'

'You must wait until she is eighteen to marry her—I want that in writing—along with an exit clause for Neve in the event she no longer loves you. You will not coerce my daughter into marriage—do you understand?'

'Yes, Your Honour.'

Picking up the hymen restoration pamphlet and form, she waved it at Erik. 'I'll take Neve to this healer tomorrow if you make the orc's house dragon-proof. You can cough up the money when I sign the betrothal contract *after* the procedure. As for Neve's living arrangements prior to your wedding, I think it best she stays with me. Dates and house visits are fine, but there will be no sleepovers. Understood?'

'Yes, Your Honour.' He ground out the response through gritted teeth.

Chapter Thirteen

'Fuck it's hot,' Brendan grumbled under his breath as he continuously waved flies away from his face. It would have easily been thirty-six degrees[6] in the shade, not that there was such a thing in this desert. The heavy leather armour Alannah had given him clung to his chafing flesh like a second skin and sweat poured from his forehead like torrential rain, stinging his eyes. Glancing at a hand-drawn map, he followed Jacob's directions to the dugout home. Good thing he still had those glamour piercing sunglasses too, else he would have missed the entrance flanked by recycled glass bottle windows. He knocked on the solid timber.

An old Aboriginal man opened the door and frowned. 'I have no business with your lot.'

Before he could shut him out, Brendan stuck his foot out to catch the door. 'Please, Your

---

[6] 36°C = 96.8°F

Holiness. I know you must think I'm here on behalf of the Council, but I broke my ties with them years ago.'

'I can tell by the dark patches in your aura. I know who you are, Mr. Winters. It's your affiliation with the Syndicate that bothers me.'

'Then you must know I mean you no harm. I just need your help and I promise to pay whatever it takes.'

The ancient acolyte scratched at his chin through a long, scruffy beard. 'With Syndicate resources at your disposal, what could ya possibly need from me?'

'I have an unwanted hitchhiker and I hear you specialise in their extraction.'

'Hmph. You'd betta come inside.'

Stepping into the underground house, he relished the instant relief from the sweltering sun. He glanced around the dimly lit living space, marvelling at the earthen walls. Amy would love it. 'Nice place, Acolyte Jeffries.'

'I don't go by that title anymore. Just call me Lloyd.' The holy man invited him to sit on an antique armchair covered with a patchwork quilt. 'What type of demon ya got?'

Smacking his leather clad chest, he asked, 'Mind if I strip out of this first? It's not the most comfortable travel gear, especially in these parts.'

Lloyd nodded. 'Looks official. You boost it from the mage armoury?'

He chuckled. 'Hardly. My woman gave it to me.' He unzipped the jacket and hung it on the back of the chair. When he turned back to his host, the old man gasped.

'W-what's that?' He pointed at the brand on the left side of Brendan's chest.

'It's what I'm hoping you can help me with. This is the sigil of Set, Egyptian Lord of Chaos and Revenge. He is my demon.'

Lloyd shook his head. 'How'd you manage to attract *his* attention?'

'It's a long story, one I don't have time to tell. Can you help me?'

'In theory, yes, but I'd need to channel the stygian element and I'm not willing to break the law again. I can't risk it, I'm sorry.'

He grinned. 'Not a problem, Lloyd. The new High Magus has decriminalised the use of nether. She understands the misconceptions about this mana source and won't punish people who use it for good causes.'

'She?' Lloyd asked with a furrowed brow.

'I guess you haven't heard yet. Kieran Lane died in a dragon attack and Alannah Winters—*my woman*—took his place.' He beamed.

'Stranger things have happened, I'm sure. You'll want to lie down for this, so you can use my bed.' Lloyd led him down a narrow passageway into a simple room with minimal furniture.

He made himself comfortable on top of the quilted bedspread, tucking his arms behind his head.

'I need to gather a few things. I'll be back in a jiffy.' Lloyd left him alone to study the intricate painting on the opposite wall.

Millions of dots formed an underwater paradise with a mermaid at the centre. He wondered if Liam gave up his legs in favour of a tail, or if he was just seeking temporary asylum. *Given the tryst Connor witnessed, it wouldn't surprise me if Liam chose the former.*

Lloyd returned with a colourful woven basket full of ritual tools and a steaming mug of something smelling like bitter herbs. He offered Brendan the concoction. 'Here, drink this.'

Sitting up, he took the cup, sniffing the brew and wrinkling his nose. 'What is it?'

'An infusion that will put ya body to sleep while opening your mind to me. The ritual will tax ya body and hurt too much if you're awake.'

He gulped the foul liquid down, stifling the urge to gag. As he settled back against the mattress, Lloyd began chanting in an unfamiliar language, likely his traditional dialect. The room began to fade around him, plunging him into darkness.

'*Can you hear me, Mr. Winters?*' Lloyd asked from inside his head.

Yes. This is weird. It's like I'm awake but I can't feel my body or see anything.

'*Good. The potion worked. I want ya to bring Set to the front of ya mind. Talk to him if you have ta.*'

He thought about his last conversation with the God. *Hey Set, I want to discuss your revenge task.*

A deep-bellied laugh rumbled in his head. '*You are a fool to think you can trap me again.*' Set replied in a voice that echoed all around him.

Dammit! He should have known Set would take evasive measures at the first sign of betrayal. He needed something to coax him out with. What could the devil possibly want? All he cares about is chaos, destruction, and…. A cunning idea sparked to life; a way to kill two birds with one stone. '*Tell you what, Set, I'll make you a deal. If you do me this favour, I'll let you have Bridey. You've been riding around in my head long enough to know how hot that piece of arse is.'*

'I'm listening.'

'Lloyd, rather than banish him, can you transfer Set to another host?'

'That's not a good idea, Mr —'

Can you, or not? he snapped.

'Yeah, I can, but the new host would need to be someone you share an intimate connection with.'

'Not a problem. I've been fucking her for sixteen years. Trust me when I say the evil bitch deserves it for the way she betrayed me and Alannah.'

Set moaned as though he had just eaten a delicious morsel.

'It's still wrong to inflict this upon another living soul,' Lloyd protested.

'Do this for me and I promise to get High Magus Winters to pardon you. I bet you'd love to return home to your family, wouldn't you Lloyd?'

'Very well.' Lloyd inhaled a deep breath. *'Focus your thoughts on this woman, willing your hitchhiker out of your mind and into hers.'*

He followed Lloyd's instructions. *'How about it Set? You ready to violate the woman who betrayed me more than Liam ever did?'*

The beast's face flashed before him, grinning. *'Absolutely. Farewell for now.'*

As Set faded from his conscious, he slipped into a peaceful oblivion.

After hopping miles upon miles of ley lines, Bridey collapsed against a red brick house nestled amongst a thicket of Mallees and Blue Gums. Beyond the trees, lines of vines coated the sweeping hills as far as the eye could see. Taking a deep breath, she pressed the buzzer beside the solid oak door.

Levi grinned as he opened the security screen wearing nothing but a pair of skinny jeans, his lean torso just begging for another round with her whip. 'You look a little flustered, Lady Violet.'

Brushing past him, she harumphed. 'It took ages to get here via your directions.' She let him take the hooded cape from her shoulders and watched as he hung it on an old-fashioned coat hook in the wide hallway.

'I couldn't very well have you running through the line of fire now, could I?' He led her along the corridor into a cosy living room full of purple velvet sofas and armchairs.

Her heart melted a little at the sight. 'Reminds me so much of home.'

'I thought you'd like it,' Levi beamed, hovering near the door.

Making herself comfortable on a two-seater, she glanced around the ornately decorated room, admiring the collection of antiques on display. 'How did you acquire such a good safehouse?'

'Our mutual benefactor, of course.'

She perked up a little at that. 'Have you met them?'

He maintained his rigid position by the door. 'Not personally, no. Can I get you anything to drink? Tea, coffee, something stronger perhaps?'

Slumping back into her seat, she forced a smile. 'Tea would be lovely, thank you.'

Levi returned a few minutes later, carrying a silver tray with two vintage teacups and a plate of sugar cookies. He set the lot down on a mahogany coffee table before handing her one of the steaming beverages.

Staring at the violets floating on the surface of her infusion, she breathed in their delicate aroma. 'Mm.'

Sitting beside her, Levi caught her eye and grinned. 'I haven't forgotten *any* of your preferences, My Lady.'

'You are too good to me.' She took a few sips and settled into the crook of his arm. 'This is exactly what I need after suffering so much heartbreak. Not only has Brendan betrayed me for that vile woman, but he has also stolen my beloved Caleb.'

His soft yet strong hand caressed her bare thigh, creeping beneath the hem of her short skirt. 'If it's any consolation, I'm always happy to give you an outlet for your sadistic streak or return the favour if you are in the mood for some pain.'

Gulping down the rest of her tea, she placed the cup on a side table and closed her eyes as the natural sedative took effect. Violets did not usually act so quick or to such an extent, but she had already worn herself out with grief and a long journey, so she put it down to compounding factors. She certainly did not have the energy for a full scene, regardless of which end of the flogger she chose. 'To be honest, right now, I'd rather be fucked into oblivion.'

A deep, primal sound rumbled in Levi's chest. 'It would be an absolute pleasure to oblige.' Reaching out a hand, he helped her to her feet and guided her droopy body to bed.

Their clothes disappeared in a haze and before she knew it, she found herself lying face up on a king-sized mattress and her wrists bound to the bedposts with silken rope. 'You know me too well,' she murmured.

Levi chuckled as he pushed a knee between her thighs. 'True that. There's no room for something as dull as vanilla sex in your life.'

She gasped as he plunged deep inside her without any foreplay to prepare her.

'Gods!' Levi hissed. 'It's been so long I'd forgotten how tight you are.' His hands wrapped gently around her throat. 'Fancy a little breath play?'

Liquid heat pooled in her core at the mere suggestion. 'Mm, yes please.' The pressure against her windpipe increased and he edged her with expert finesse. On her fifth climb, she begged in a quavering voice, 'Please go harder. I don't think I can take much more.'

With a sly grin, he squeezed her throat more. 'If you insist.'

She tried to tell him that was not what she meant, but only a wheezy squeak escaped. The moment one of his hands clamped around her nose, her eyes bugged out and she bucked against him.

Levi responded with a malicious smirk and pelvic thrust. 'You have greatly disappointed my master, Bridey Hawthorn.'

The sick fuck is killing me and getting off on it.

'You failed to keep the apex couple apart. Your death will be a warning and if they fail to heed it, I'll send your precious Caleb to an early grave.'

No! Please Gods no! She had never prayed so hard in her life.

'*They won't help a condemned soul like yours, but I can,*' a deep, masculine voice whispered in her mind. Set appeared within her subconscious in his tall, beastly form.

What the hell? Where did you come from?

Set grinned, although he looked more like a snarling dog. '*You're my parting gift from Brendan. I'll admit, I'd hoped to spend more time in this mortal realm, but I'm willing to acquiesce to this new situation. Submit to me now, promise to be mine for eternity and I'll make you my queen. Together we can rule the Underworld.*'

And if I refuse?

'*You'll join the rest of the lost, tortured souls in the Underworld.*'

She did not doubt for a second that she would be in for a rough ride when her black soul sank into the fiery pits. The dark Gods of hell would see to it that she suffered an eternity of torment for all her evil deeds. At least if she struck a deal with Set, she could escape the worst of it. *How bad could marriage to a God of Chaos really be? 'I submit to you, My Lord.'*

Hellfire glimmered in his eyes as he licked his chops. *'Excellent.'*

The left side of her chest began to sting, as if a flaming brand seared her skin. She shrieked a silent scream, one that only she could hear within her head because she could not draw air into her lungs. Then everything faded to black.

Sitting on her bed, Neve scrolled through her socials, missing all her friends. Most of them had posted about how bored they were, stuck inside without much to do. A few had shared sad news about the death or injury of loved ones. The bedroom door opened, and she glanced up at her mum.

'Hi hun. I have a surprise for you.'

Springing to her feet, she burst with excitement. 'Oh? What is it? Please tell me the war is over!'

Her mum sighed. 'I wish. No, this is a more personal matter. Get dressed because there's somewhere I'd like to take you.'

'What sort of place are we going to?'

'You do understand the meaning of the word surprise, right?' Alannah teased with a chuckle.

Rolling her eyes, she crossed the room to her wardrobe. 'I need to know how to dress appropriately.'

'Just wear something comfy for now. You can change again when we get back.'

Her brows jumped up her forehead. 'Colour me curious.' After throwing on a pair of trackpants and a singlet top, she followed her mum outside.

'Hold my hand. We're hopping the ley lines into town. It's not safe to travel by car.' Alannah reached out and gripped her hand firmly.

With a nod, she closed her eyes and focussed on the ley line route into town that her mum had shown her. While not the most direct path, it ensured minimal detection by human eyes.

'3, 2, 1, Go!' Alannah repeated the countdown at each stop along the way until they reached the Council Chambers. From there, they walked to an old cottage. Myriad flowers and herbs lined the cobblestone path leading up to the colonial house. She tapped the brass knocker and stood patiently beside Neve, who could not stop fidgeting.

Solid footsteps preceded the arrival of a large orc woman who opened the door. 'Ah, greetings, Your Honour.' She smiled at Neve. 'You, young lady, must be my patient.'

Trying to piece the puzzle together, she stared at her mum with a furrowed brow.

'Mòrag here is a healer and with your consent she can perform a delicate procedure for you.'

'Why do I need a….' Her jaw dropped as her mum's words slotted together and her cheeks burned hotter than dragon fire. 'Oh, um…'

'Don't worry, hun. Mòrag assures me this is a non-invasive procedure, and she will keep the matter quiet.'

Stifling the heat in her face with chilling thoughts of the Alvarsson twins conspiring to make Jasper steal her virginity, she grounded herself. 'Does it hurt?'

'Not much. It's more of a tickle,' Mòrag explained.

'Then I'd like a chance to restore what was taken from me.'

'Very good. Come on in.' Mòrag opened her door wider and gestured for her and Alannah to enter. 'Follow the hallway down to my ritual space in the basement.' The room looked much like the one in her home, only smaller. The orc instructed her to lie face-up on the thin mattress within the painted pentacle on the floor.

'Shouldn't I change into some ritual robes?' she asked.

'No, dear. You are the subject of this ritual. Only I need to wear the appropriate attire.' Mòrag swept a hand over her teal silk gown. 'Close your eyes and relax.'

Sitting back in the corner of the room, her mum offered her an encouraging smile and nod.

She shut her eyes and practised some mindfulness breathing while Mòrag cast the circle.

Kneeling beside her, the woman placed her hands on Neve's belly. 'The healing process will feel uncomfortable, but it shouldn't hurt. If you feel pain, please raise your hand, okay?'

'Kay,' she squeaked.

The room fell silent as Mòrag began her work.

Uncomfortable was an understatement. The sensation of tissue knitting itself back together in her most sensitive region tickled like a bitch, and it took all her self-control not to squirm away. *This better work.* Then just as she couldn't bear any more of the torture, Mòrag removed her hands from Neve's belly and drew her athame across the circle.

'It is done,' the orc assured them.

Her mum shook Mòrag's hand. 'Thank you. As per our arrangement, I will send your payment once an independent party has verified success of the operation.'

'Of course, Your Honour.' Mòrag, along with her mum, signed some paperwork.

Once they stepped out of the cottage, she cleared her throat. 'How do we prove the procedure worked?'

After scanning the street, her mum smiled. 'There's a human gynie nearby who will accept cash and the promise of shelter from the "apocalypse rain" as payment for a consult on the downlow. Come on, this won't take long.'

With her so-called virtue intact, Neve returned to Cailleach Estate to find Erik waiting on the doorstep with a briefcase in one hand. A tempest of mixed emotions rattled her as she stood before the faerie prince. 'What...why...you're here.'

His teeth sparkled as he smiled. 'Yes, my love. I'm here to win you back.'

They followed her mother into the sitting room where she glimpsed the paperwork in her mum's hand. 'Does he know about...?'

Her mum nodded. 'It was Erik's idea.'

She felt the walls closing in around her.

'I promised to protect you from the chastity tests. I love you, Neve.' He took her hand in his own, stroking her knuckles with his thumb.

Closing her eyes, she shook her head.

'Stop denying it,' Erik insisted. 'I know your feelings for me are still strong. You told me as much in your dreams.' His other hand came up to her chin and she opened her eyes to see the raw emotion swirling in his.

Her mum was retrieving a thick wad of paper from the briefcase that was now in her possession, and she began reading the document.

'What's that?' Neve asked with a shaky voice.

'That's a new betrothal contract,' Erik explained. 'My deceitful sister will play no part in our future happiness. She was the one who released your sex tape and I promise to make her pay for what she did to you, to us.'

She jerked her gaze back to Erik, the fog clearing from her mind. 'Elna betrayed us?'

His expression soured as he nodded. 'She never cared for you because she wanted someone else. Still, that was no excuse to sabotage *our* chances of happiness. Providing Jasper with drugs was also her idea and I'm so sorry I went along with her vile scheme. I never should have trusted her.' The fingers gripping her chin reached out and brushed over her lips, bringing pleasure-filled memories front of mind. 'Will you marry me, Neve Winters?'

She searched his soul for any trace of wicked deceit and found nothing but genuine love flowing from his exposed aura. 'Yes. So long as Mum is happy with the terms and conditions in the new contract.' Turning, she exchanged a look with her mother who nodded.

'Don't worry hun, I insisted on some new clauses in this contract that state you will not be marrying Erik until you are eighteen and only if you still love him. In the meantime, this arrangement will protect you and lots of other mages in our region from the dragons.'

'Then, yes, I will marry you, Erik.'

The moment her mother signed the contract, Erik pulled her into a savage kiss that sent her mind reeling and left her legs trembling when he made his exit. In a daze, she stumbled up to her room and collapsed on the bed. *What the fuck just happened?* Unlocking her phone, she tapped out a text to her dad: APPARENTLY I'M ENGAGED TO ERIK NOW.

Chapter Fourteen

Sitting at the head of the Murray Bridge garrison's war room table, Alannah tried to make sense of the Holo-Map. 'Explain to me again what each of the coloured dots mean.'

A rugged, middle-aged man stepped forward. 'Certainly, Your Honour.'

'Who are you, again?'

'Councillor Johnathan Ryan, Mayor of the Limestone Coast,' he replied with a formal salute. She should have guessed his clan by the ginger hair and freckles.

'At ease, Councillor. I'm too tired for formalities right now.' Understatement of the year. She could sleep for weeks and still feel exhausted. Instead, she gulped down more of her double-strength coffee. The other regional heads took that as their cue to sit while Ryan explained what each dot on the map represented. Her army clustered in the large red-brick building, awaiting orders, while the dragons circled the skies, spreading as far as the Barossa Valley, although most of them focussed their attacks on the CBD. The human population of Adelaide was screwed unless they had access to underground bunkers.

Her phone vibrated on the table, startling her, then she smiled as she recognised Nothing But Thieves singing 'Forever & Ever More.' *Brendan must have hacked into my phone and changed the main ringtone*. She answered the unknown caller, 'High Magus Winters speaking.'

'Hello, Your Honour. This is Erik. My father and I have fulfilled our end of the bargain.'

'I hope you understand that if any dragons attack those places, your contract is null and void.'

'Yes, of course. I assure you no such harm will come to anyone within your garrisons or any of the mage homes on the Fleurieu Peninsula. May I please continue wooing Neve?' No amount of arrogance could hide the desperation in his tone. Knowing how much the boy cared for her daughter filled her with hope.

'Very well. You may visit her at my family estate until she is comfortable returning to your house.' Hanging up, she breathed a sigh of relief and smiled at her fellow officials. 'I've secured a deal with the Seelie.' She explained the nature of the protection she had bought them.

'Just in time, it would seem.' Ryan pointed out the dragons who redirected their attention south of the city.

She exhaled with a whistle. 'Damn. This is going to make ley line travel more dangerous. I'll have to plot out a route that makes use of the mage properties between here and home.'

'Or you could stay here,' Ryan offered.

She shook her head. 'I have too much work to go on with. That is, if we still want an arsenal capable of taking these bastards down.' She noticed Hugh flinch from where he sat quietly in the corner of the room. *Curious. He may shrug off the advances of women, but I didn't take him for a complete prude who takes offence at minor cursing.* She turned her attention back to Council leaders. 'Besides, it's not like you can do much in the meantime.'

'Are you suggesting we sit on our backsides while the dragons lay waste to our state?' huffed one of the older councillors with grey hair.

'Would you rather send our people to certain death?' she snapped back. 'I made an election promise I intend to keep, but that takes time and resources. I will not march back into war without the proper equipment.'

'Is there anything we can do to prepare while we wait?' asked Ryan.

She thought about the nature of their battles with the dragons. 'This entire facility is under Seelie protection, which means our troops are safe to train here. I want them focussing on ranged weapons, especially archery. I imagine our healers already have their hands full, but if they can do everything in their power to restore our injured warlocks to full health, that would make a huge difference. The rest of our support personnel may as well rest up. They'll need all their energy for our next strike.'

Ryan nodded. 'Very well, Your Honour. Has there been any word on the whereabouts of Warlock Winters?'

She rubbed her temples as her head started to throb. 'He is with the mermages.'

Grey Haired Douche scowled. 'Your husband chose a miserable time to abandon us.'

'He didn't desert the army. Liam has good reason for his trip under the sea.' When several sets of eyes narrowed, she clarified, 'Council business.'

'Perhaps you should send word, letting him know we have urgent need for him back on the frontline,' Ryan suggested.

She nodded. 'I will do that. Thank you, Councillor.'

'I also recommend taking a tour of the facility to meet and greet your army. Rubbing palms with the new High Magus is sure to boost morale.'

'Of course. I was hoping to make an appearance anyway. Please lead the way.' Walking with Hugh to her right, she followed Ryan, letting the other officials trail behind her. They entered a massive mess hall where several televisions and couches lined the perimeter. A small games arcade sat to the right and a makeshift casino to the left of the dining space. The ambient buzz quietened as awareness of her presence spread and mages stood to honour their leader. Spotting a small podium, she waited there for all eyes to focus on her. 'Please be seated.'

Chairs screeched across wood laminate floors, and she let the din settle, using this time to search the crowd for familiar faces. Her friends sat at a table near the back. Catching Cara's eye, she offered a smile. The scowl she received in return tightened her chest, and she flicked her attention to Monique, who sat with her clique at another table. She forced a smile despite the grief she must be suffering over the loss of her father, and Alannah returned the kindness. Clearing her throat, she addressed the room: 'It is an honour to stand before you as your High Magus, yet I would not be standing here if it were not for the tragic loss of a great man. Let us not forget the years of sweat, blood, and tears Kieran Lane poured into our community, nor the sacrifice of our fallen allies. I call upon you to offer a minute of silence as we remember our fallen comrades.'

As everyone bowed their head, the seconds ticked by, and she thought about the lives lost in the name of this war. She may not have agreed with Kieran on everything over the years, but she recognised that he was a good man at heart and a fine leader. The South Australian magical community could have done much worse, that's for sure.

An instrumental rendition of 'Carrickfergus'[7] played through the sound system, marking the end of their minute, and she prayed to the Gods, asking them to guide Kieran's soul to a joyful afterlife. Glancing at her prompt card, she read the *Mages Ode*:

---

[7] Traditional Irish folk song commonly played at funerals.

Our beloved brethren shall no longer
weather the storms of our mortal realm
The wind shall not chill their bones
Fire shall not touch their flesh
Rain shall not soak their clothes
Nor the earth bruise them with its stones
Go in peace, beloved brethren
The Gods await your beautiful souls.

Wiping a few rogue tears from her cheeks, she watched in amazement as hundreds of battle-hardened soldiers did the same. 'I bring some tidings of hope in these dark times.' She explained the deal she had made with the Seelie, along with her plans to bring them weapons capable of defeating the dragons, breathing a sigh of relief when frowns lifted, and smiles touched some of their faces. 'Please carry on with your lunch while I mingle amongst you.'

Dust coated every surface of Brendan's travel-wearied body as he slumped onto his bed at the estate. He wanted nothing more than to curl up in bed and sleep for a week. Actually, he really needed a shower first, but then he had a bone to pick before he could afford the rest he so desperately craved.

Kicking off his boots, he peeled the leather armour from his skin and tossed it on the floor before heaving himself up and staggering into the bathroom. He scrubbed away days' worth of grime, finding a use for Alannah's nailbrush for the first time in his life. After towelling himself dry, he wrapped the terrycloth around his waist and returned to his room. A sense of déjà vu swept over him as he met Alannah's hungry stare.

'You're back,' she remarked in a gruff tone, eyes roaming over his bare flesh. 'Set's seal has vanished. Does that mean your mission was a success?'

'It was,' he replied flatly.

Her gaze snapped back to his and her eyes widened. 'Are you okay?'

A growl slipped from him as he advanced on her. 'No Lana, I'm not fucking okay.'

The pitch of her voice rose as she asked, 'What's wrong?'

'You betrayed our daughter, that's what. How could you sell her to that Seelie prick? Our own flesh and blood, the child we conceived under a blessed moon in a moment of true love. You traded her for what? Protection for a few douchebag mages?'

Her mouth gaped open. 'It wasn't like that. Yes, I made a deal with Erik, but only under several conditions that would ensure Neve's safety—'

'Her safety?' he roared. 'What about her free will? Or her heart? Don't Neve's feelings enter into this?'

'Of course, they do. Please calm down, Brendan.' She placed her hands on his chest, achieving the opposite effect.

He shoved her back, not caring when the towel fell from his waist. 'Don't you dare try to pacify me! I'm not one of your merry little soldiers.'

Stumbling back onto the bed, she glared at him. 'You might want to put some clothes on then. Your nudity doesn't exactly lend credence to your argument.'

'Fuck you! This is my room, so I'll dress how I like.'

Licking her lips, she grinned at his cock. 'Yes please.'

Rolling his eyes, he could not help but laugh drily at the irony of their role reversal. 'Looks like I've been rubbing off on you too much.'

'Not enough, more like.'

He sighed. 'Lana, this is serious.'

'I know, but you should put some clothes on. I can't concentrate with your gorgeous naked body standing before me like this.'

Reaching into his dresser with a huff, he felt the fight leaving him. *Damn she's good at conflict resolution.* After slipping into a pair of trackpants and an old t-shirt, he sat beside her.

'Now,' she started, 'let's talk this through like mature adults.'

Resisting the urge to respond sarcastically, he bit his tongue before asking, 'Why did you do it?'

'Erik explained that we weren't safe from the dragons, even with our enhanced wards, because the beasts could still fly through the barrier. Then I thought about my responsibility to the magical people of this state. To be honest, I kind of panicked. When he offered a solution to help Neve pass the chastity test, I jumped at the opportunity.'

He shook his head in disgust. 'I can't believe you would sell our daughter—to my mortal fucking enemy, no less.'

'Erik legitimately cares for Neve, and she agreed to this,' Alannah tried to assure him. 'He was so desperate to win her back that he altered the clauses of the betrothal contract at my behest.'

Alannah told him about the new conditions in detail.

'That's all well and good, Lana, but Erik is an enchanter. What if he coerces her to love him?'

'I don't think that will be necessary. From what I gather, she already does. I've been reading her aura for days now.' When he arched his pierced brow, she added, 'You can check for yourself if you don't believe me. Erik will visit her here tomorrow.'

Hunching over, he raked his fingers through his hair. 'I still don't like it. Those Seelie scum are up to something shady with their Rhapsody rip-off.'

Her hand slid up and down his spine. 'Does that mean I should stop loving you?'

Jerking upright, he stared at her with narrow eyes. 'Why…?'

'Brendan, not only do you traffic drugs, but you also run a branch of the Dark Syndicate. I hate to say it, but you have more blood and rape on your hands than the entire Seelie Court, even if you didn't kill people directly. Yet here you are, suggesting our daughter shouldn't marry a guy who plays a small part in a sabotage ring.'

His jaw dropped lower with each word spilling from her. 'Lana, I—'

She raised a hand to halt his rebuff. 'I understand your plans for the Syndicate and your reasons for staying in the Boss chair. Even though my new role in the Council puts us in a major conflict of interest, I'm not going to stop you, nor will I give up on our relationship. I'm merely pointing out the hypocrisy of your stance on Neve and Erik.'

'It's not just about the drugs. The Seelie Court and Syndicate are mortal enemies. They use underhanded methods to sabotage our operations.'

'Has it ever occurred to you; they might do so with good intentions? Rhapsody is a dangerous drug. What happened to Neve is proof of that. If you take it out of circulation entirely, the Seelie won't have reason to sell their crap.'

'That'll make me hell popular,' he scoffed. 'Taking our biggest revenue stream off the market will likely cost me my job. This war with the dragons is the only reason I'm not already facing backlash from the freeze on production.' Springing to his feet, he began pacing the room. He needed a long-term solution, but nothing came to his exhausted mind.

'What if…. Do you still have Tara's potion book?' Alannah asked.

'Yeah, why?'

'Kids these days are all about the latest craze. What if you give them a new designer potion? One that doesn't aid date rape. They'll lap it up and Rhapsody will become ancient history.'

Spinning around to face her, he grinned. 'Lana, you're the sexiest genius to walk this earth.'

Soft blue light filtered through Liam's lids as awareness returned, and a most welcome sight greeted him when he opened his eyes.

Saoirse's sweet face smiled back at him. 'You made it through the transformation.'

He groaned groggily as salty water ebbed and flowed through his gullet. 'How long was I unconscious?'

'Five cycles of the sun.'

His brows rose. 'Wow, okay. I lost a bit of time then.' Glancing downwards, he gaped at the lower half of his body. Iridescent scales in various shades of sky blue covered the tail that had replaced his legs. Pushing himself up with his arms, he perched his bare buttocks on the raised platform covered in sea grass that he had been sleeping on. He scanned the room, or what passed for one in the underwater enclosure, and stared at the mage lights lining the rocky reef walls. 'Are we in an underwater cave?'

'Yes. We shape them a little with our magic.' Leaving her bedside seat, she drifted closer to him, and her breasts brushed against his arm.

The sensation flooded him with a wave of lust, prompting him to grab Saoirse and pull her into his lap. He swallowed her gasp with a hungry kiss as their bodies grinded together. The scales protecting his manhood unfurled with the growing desire. Glancing down at his erection, he breathed a sigh of relief when he saw that it had not changed with the transmutation. Meeting her hooded gaze, he groaned. 'I want to make love to you, Saoirse.'

A faint blush touched her soft cheeks. 'I want that too,' she whispered. 'But not here. Anyone could swim in on us.' She threaded the fingers of her right hand through those of his left. 'I'll show you to my quarters.'

Picturing Brendan's smug grin, he pushed his immediate urges aside for the sake of decency and followed her out of the sea cave. He found swimming with his altered body shape challenging. He kept wanting to kick his legs out like scissors, briefly forgetting he no longer had them. *Is this what phantom limb syndrome feels like?*

Saoirse offered him a simpering smile before coiling her arm around his waist and propelling him forward. 'Here, let me help. It will take time to adjust to your new anatomy.'

Had she been anyone else, he would have pushed her away and refused the assistance. He hated showing weakness, let alone relying on others to compensate for his shortcomings. Yet the woman beaming at him made him forget his stubborn streak as she pressed her beautiful curves against his bare flesh. 'Yeah, okay,' he replied gruffly. Letting Saoirse guide them through the water, he took the opportunity to start honing the new muscles in his tail, flexing them as he flicked the limb back and forth.

Emerging from the cave entrance, he gaped at the life thriving around the seabed. A school of pink snapper rushed past him on their right, while a solitary yellowtail kingfish sauntered by on the left. Ahead, he spied a pair of long-snouted boar fish with their brown and white stripes clear despite the lack of sunlight. 'How can we see so well this deep?'

'Night vision and enhanced colour perception are some of the traits we weave into the transmutation spell. They are essential senses down here.'

Nodding, he startled when a shadowy patch of the floor shifted, and a massive spotted eagle ray with a wingspan over three metres[8] emerged. It studied them, assessing the threat, before swimming away and leaving a cloud of murky water in its wake. 'Why don't the larger predators attack us?'

'We have established an understanding of sorts. Rather than attack them, we protect them and their food sources. Plus, we calm them with magic if needed.'

Land mages could learn a lot from the merfolk, he thought. His eyes widened as they approached a coral-coloured castle carved into the side of a rocky reef. 'Is this your home?'

'It is. Do you want me to show you around now, or—'

'Later,' he insisted. 'We need some private time first.'

The teal flecks in her eyes sparkled as the pink of her cheeks brightened. 'Of course. I'll take us around the back, to avoid the crowds.'

They circled around a tall spire and navigated a labyrinth of tunnels. An orange octopus wrapped two forearms around a nearby rock wall, peeking at them before ducking back in its hiding spot. 'This place is incredible,' he marvelled.

---

[8] Over 10 feet

'I'm glad you like my home.' With a wave of her hand, she unlocked one of the castle doors, revealing a large bedroom. The chamber looked much like something you would see on land, with one exception—the ocean still surrounded them. Sitting on her bed, she patted a spot beside her, her long, brown hair, billowing in waves around her face.

Needing little encouragement, he sat and pulled her into his lap. Blood surged through his veins as he claimed another searing kiss. Trailing his lips along her neck, he spoke in her ear. 'You are the most beautiful creature in all the realms, Saoirse.'

Her hot breath tickled his neck as she gasped.

Gazing deep into her eyes, he licked his lips, enjoying the salty tang of the seawater flowing through them. 'Have you ever had sex before?'

The rouge of her cheeks resembled a lobster as she shook her head.

A primal noise rumbled up from his diaphragm as he thought about taking her virginity. 'It might hurt a little at first, but I'll be gentle and take it slow, okay?'

'Okay,' she squeaked.

'Just try to relax and tell me to stop if it hurts too much.' He kissed her senseless while preparing her with his fingers.

She bucked against his hand as her climax took hold, and the sweetest little moan slipped from her mouth.

'Are you ready?' he asked, searching her eyes for any hint of hesitation, and finding nothing but wanton desire.

'Yes,' she replied breathlessly.

He grinned. 'Hold on tight, then.'

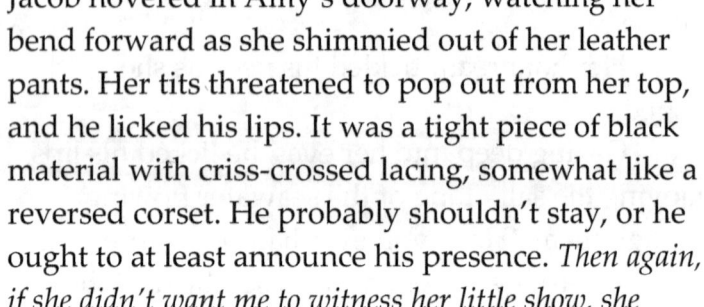

Jacob hovered in Amy's doorway, watching her bend forward as she shimmied out of her leather pants. Her tits threatened to pop out from her top, and he licked his lips. It was a tight piece of black material with criss-crossed lacing, somewhat like a reversed corset. He probably shouldn't stay, or he ought to at least announce his presence. *Then again, if she didn't want me to witness her little show, she wouldn't have left the door ajar.* Absolving himself of any guilt, he leaned against the timber frame, settling in to enjoy the spectacle.

Legs bare, she jerked upright, flicking a head full of coppery red locks back as she straightened.

He gaped at the runway patch on her mound: proof that she didn't bother with hair dye.

Fuck! Either she removed her underwear with her pants, or she'd gone commando. His eyes trailed up the path of exposed flesh that her top offered, feeling his dick grow harder with each intersection the laces made across her torso. When his gaze reached the plunging neckline, he watched her fingers unfasten the bow.

'Why are you standing there like a creeper, Bennett?'

He met her fierce eyes, and smirked. 'Why'd you leave the door open? Anyone could have walked past and copped an eyeful.'

'Very few of the people staying here would care.' Her hazel depths blazed, and he wondered if lust or anger had formed the kindling.

Scanning the room, he found it otherwise empty. 'I gather Connor has returned to Murray Bridge?'

She nodded. 'It's all healing hands on deck by the sounds of it. Alannah even wants to employ *my* expertise tomorrow.'

His bushy brows took flight. 'You dominating Alannah? That's a scene I'd pay my life's savings to see.'

With a deep, throaty chuckle, she shook her head. 'Smithing expertise, dumb arse. Sorry to disappoint, but Alannah's not exactly my type.'

'Who is your type?' he mused aloud.

Loosening the upper laces of her top, she shrugged out of it, and flung the thing across the room. 'Men with the balls to kneel at my feet.'

Reading the challenge in her eyes, he stalked forward, slamming the door shut behind him. Despite her nudity, she stood proud, every bit the predator waiting to pounce on him. That thought alone almost made him come, and his blue balls begged him to submit. But he wouldn't relinquish all his power. He enjoyed playing tug of war with her too much. For the first time in years, a fire raged in his soul, and Amy held the match. Peeling his shirt off, he tossed it aside, hearing her breath hitch at the sight of his taut muscles. Smug satisfaction warmed his insides, and he felt proud of the hours he had spent reshaping his pudgy body into a weapon for the Syndicate. Dropping to his knees, he lowered his gaze to hide the sly grin tugging at his lips.

The heel of her foot pressed into his back, pushing him onto all fours. 'You dare to presume I have any use for you?' she demanded.

Sniggering, he rose, letting her leg slide to the floor so that his teeth grazed her inner thighs on his ascent to her core. Her eyes bugged out as his hands grabbed her backside and his tongue flicked her clit. 'Let's get one thing straight, peaches: I'm no one's subbie. Sure, I'll take a flogging, but only for the fun of it. If we do this, we'll do it on equal footing.' To emphasise his point, he yanked her down to her knees.

Her gasp turned to a growl as she caught her balance. 'What makes you think I want to do *anything* with you,' she spat.

'Because…' he slipped his fingers between her slick folds and revelled in the way her vision clouded over. 'Unlike your annoying mouth, these lips don't lie.'

'You're such an arsehole,' she snapped. Yet despite her vocal lashing, she succumbed to his intimate touch, falling back on her heels, and spreading her legs wider.

He played the strings of her desire with deft fingers, bringing her to the edge several times, then easing the pressure to rob her of the climax she was chasing.

'Stop toying with me, Bennett,' she warned in a gruff voice.

'You want an orgasm, you'll have to *come* and get it,' he teased with an eyebrow waggle.

With a huff, she pushed him back on his arse and yanked at the zipper on his jeans, letting his erection spring free while leaving the rest of his clothes in place. 'You play a dangerous game.'

Lying back on the floor, he threaded his hands behind his head and chuckled. 'That's my favourite kind of game.'

She crawled across the floor and reached into one of her bedside drawers. Returning to his side, she held up a condom and a cock ring. 'Let's see how you like being edged.'

Another wave of desire surged through him at the mere suggestion. Biting his tongue, he chose to keep that morsel of truth to himself. *Let her think she has gained the upper hand for now.*

Making quick work of the foil packet, she slid the latex over his dick, followed by the silicon toy. Straddling him, she mounted his cock in one swift movement, crying out as he sank deep inside her. His mouth curled into a smug grin as he grabbed her hips and sank his claws into her flesh. Mewling, she ground her nub against the studded clitoral stimulator on the cock ring while her tits bounced up and down.

He watched her unravel, her hair swirling around her face like wildfire. *She's a sight of pure perfection.* As she continued to fuck him, keeping his own release at bay as promised, a terrifying thought crept through the cracks of his subconscious: *I'm already addicted to this woman.*

Chapter Fifteen

Waking to the sound of morning bird song, Neve groaned and stumbled out of bed. She peeked through a slit in the curtains and spied the orange glow of a new day emerging from the horizon. Shuffling across the floor, she stared into her wardrobe, wondering what outfit would be suitable for a meeting with her ex-now-betrothed. *Does this count as a date?*

A kookaburra laughed from the tree outside her window, mocking her ignorance. Chances were, the winged creature knew more about the ways of the fae folk than she did. Deciding on a simple summer dress with a pink floral pattern, she made her way to the ensuite to finish getting ready.

Her mum knocked on the bedroom door as she applied the last of her mascara. 'You look beautiful, hun.' Wearing black leather pants and a midnight blue corset, she closed the distance with confident strides. Standing behind Neve, their eyes met in the mirror, and she smiled. 'Pretty as the princess you'll be. How do you feel? You know, after….'

'Fine,' she replied with a blush, not wanting to discuss the particulars of her mystical cosmetic surgery. Honestly, she had not felt any different. Not physically, anyway. 'Is Erik here yet?'

'Yes. He is waiting for you in the sitting room and breakfast is being served as we speak. Your dad and I will be close at hand, so if that boy tries anything you don't like, just holler and we'll be there in a flash. You hear me?'

'Yes, Mum.' She followed her larger-than-life mother down the stairs, catching a glimpse of her aura. It had always shone bright, but in recent months, the halo of light surrounding her had grown bigger, oozing more power than Neve had ever seen. The woman was a natural fit for her new leadership role. Being the daughter of the world's first female High Magus filled her with pride.

Erik rose from the loveseat and bowed, peeking up at her through thick, lustrous lashes with a lascivious grin. He turned his attention back to Alannah. 'Thank you for this opportunity, Your Honour.'

Alannah narrowed her eyes on him. 'Don't try anything underhanded. Neve's father and I will be nearby, and we *will* know if you try to enchant her. Understand?'

Erik squirmed under the scrutiny, gulping as he nodded. 'Yes, Your Honour.'

'I will leave you to it,' Neve's mum explained, facing her. 'Don't forget what I said.'

She nodded, feeling the oxygen exit the room with her mother.

Drawing near, Erik gripped her shoulders and murmured in her ear, 'You know I can't enchant you when I visit your dreams. Fae need to be physically close to manipulate people's emotions, same as mages. What you feel for me is real.' His right hand cupped her face as he drew back an inch to peer into her eyes.

Willing her nerves into submission, she glanced away. 'What if this doesn't work out for us? Teenage love rarely lasts.'

Tugging at her chin, he redirected her gaze, locking it with his own emerald orbs. 'I could never tire of this pretty face.' He stroked her cheek for effect. 'And if your mother is anything to go by, I imagine you'll stay beautiful forever.'

She felt her cheeks heat in the furnace of his stare. 'But—'

He hushed her with a finger to her lips. 'Don't overthink it, my love. Let's just take each day

as it comes. You don't have to go through with this
if our feelings diminish by your eighteenth
birthday.'

'Okay,' she whispered.

Erik grinned a moment before crashing his
lips against hers.

Hunched over the breakfast bar, Brendan looked up
as Alannah entered the kitchen. Every part of his
body ached with fatigue after a restless night. He
had insisted on separate beds, still feeling salty
about the deal she'd struck with Erik. Between
worrying about his daughter's wellbeing, the pain
of Caleb's betrayal, and keeping his role in the
Syndicate, too many dark thoughts had plagued his
mind. But his soul did not like sleeping apart from
her and the separation anxiety added to his shitty
night.

'Are you ready?' she asked.

Nodding, he followed her to the front porch
where they could spy on Erik and Neve through a
crack in the curtains. The moment he caught sight
of Erik's filthy paws on her shoulders, he tensed,
and a red haze clouded his vision.

Alannah placed a hand over his clenched fist.
'Look at Neve's aura. Read her.'

After taking a deep breath, he let the magic flow freely through his conduits and focussed on the colourful glow around his daughter. Love and lust pulsed bright like a candy-coloured disco. Not only that, but when he paid attention to Erik's emotions and thoughts, he detected nothing but honest intentions and mutual affections. 'Well, I'll be damned. The kid's genuine. Still, I don't trust the rest of his family. How are we supposed to protect her from those arseholes when she marries into the Seelie Court?'

'We have years to work on that, babe,' she replied as she circled her arms around him from behind. 'Now that I am High Magus, I have the power and resources to police them more closely. And you have your spy network. We can do a lot of good together, Brendan.'

With a sigh, he tucked her into his side and kissed the top of her head. 'Yeah, we can. We just have to survive this war and a bunch of invisible threats from some unknown enemy.' The moment things escalated between Neve and Erik, he led Alannah inside, not keen to witness a pair of horny teenagers making out, especially not when one was his own flesh and blood.

Alannah perched her sexy arse on a stool at the breakfast bar and patted the one beside her. 'Can you help me stop the dragons?'

Taking the offered seat, he scooted closer, wrapping an arm around her, and his soul purred at their proximity. *Or is that the cat?* He glanced around the room, failing to spot Luna. *Huh.* 'I can try, but I don't know if there's much I can do. I'm a lover, not a fighter.'

She snorted in her adorable way. 'This coming from the Boss of the Dark Syndicate. I seem to recall you holding your own in a bunch of sword fights back in the day. Don't tell me you let those skills slip.'

He smiled warmly, remembering how much she used to love watching him spar with Liam. She may have verbally cheered for the other brother, but he had always sensed her eyes drilling into his shirtless torso, probably imagining all the ways she could enjoy his naked body. His dick twitched at the thought, despite the protests from the rest of his body. 'Don't worry, gorgeous, I still know how to handle my sword.'

She laughed, then her eyes darkened with lust. 'Oh, I know you do. You proved as much the other night.'

A burst of adrenaline shot through him, and he burst out of his chair. In one fluid motion, he scooped her into his arms and shoved her up against the pantry. He sank his teeth into the curve of her neck, knowing how much she loved being bitten.

She mewled and writhed against him. 'The way you go from zero to scorching amazes me.'

'Everything about you amazes me, Lana,' he growled as he hoisted her legs up around his waist. Walking across the room, he propped her up on the breakfast bar and turned his attention to the laces holding her blue corset together. With a single tug of the right strand, the bow unravelled, and he pried the brocade panels apart until they fell to the floor.

'Oh Gods, Brendan!' she cried as he drew one of her stiff peaks into his mouth and clamped onto it with his teeth.

His greedy lips moved to her other nipple, and he sucked it until she moaned, then released it with a *pop!* When he began unzipping her tight leather pants, she cursed.

'Are you seriously about to fuck me here? This bench is meant for food.'

Grinning up at her lidded gaze, he licked his lips. 'And I intend to eat from it. Now raise your hips so I can remove these sexy-arse pants.' She complied, letting him peel away her second skin, followed by her boots, revealing her bare core. Dipping his fingers between her lips, he found her dripping with desire. Blood surged through his already hard cock. 'Hot damn, Lana. I love how wet you get for me.' He practically growled the words, his more primal side taking the reins. Sitting in one of the stools, he adjusted the height down to bring his face between her legs. He traced her slit with his tongue, smiling when she shivered. Sliding two fingers into her channel, he pumped them while his tongue toyed with her bundle of nerves.

'You're fucking killing me, Brendan. Make me come already.'

Chuckling into her throbbing sex, he quickened the pace with his hand and sucked on her clit. Her muscles clenched his fingers, and she unravelled in his mouth. He drank her in, relishing her sweet musk. When he added two more fingers, she hissed. He looked up at her face to check if the noise was from pleasure or pain, but he found her eyes focused on something behind him. Whipping his head around, he spotted Jacob slouched against the door frame, his red hair still ruffled from bed. 'The fuck, Red?'

'Please don't stop on my account. You know I love a good show.' Jacob winked at Alannah.

Brendan turned back to find her biting her lip, her cheeks flushed as she held Jacob's gaze. 'Tell me what you want, Lana.' He had no qualms about fucking her in front of a full stadium crowd, but exhibitionism was his kink, not hers.

'Let him watch,' she replied huskily.

Wasting no time, he thrust his hands inside, working her up to another orgasm. Leaping to his feet, he undressed manically, clothes flying every which way. Assessing the height of the bench, he cussed under his breath. *If only I were a few inches taller*. He eased Alannah down. Wrapping her legs around his waist, they returned to the pantry door. 'Hold on tight, gorgeous.'

Nodding, she clamped on with her vice-like thighs and grabbed his shoulders with a death grip. Her nails dug into his skin, sending a jolt of pleasure down his back and straight to his dick.

Lining up at her entrance, he found her looking over his shoulder. 'What's Jacob doing right now?'

'He's just standing there, like before.'

'Tell him what you want him to do.'

She sucked in a breath. 'Let me see how turned on you are.'

'As you wish, Your Honour,' Jacob rasped.

Brendan slid the crown of his cock into her hungry pussy. 'Tell me what he's doing now.'

'He just untied his trackpants; now he is dropping them to his ankles.'

'Is he aroused?'

'Very.'

'Good.' He slammed into her, holding his position as she stretched around his girth.

'Can I touch myself?' Jacob asked.

'Please do,' Alannah insisted in a breathy tone.

Brendan pounded her into the timber with relentless force, each thrust bringing all of them higher as they chased their climaxes. He could easily picture Jacob's hand hard at work and the image fed his perverse imagination. Pressing a thumb to her clit, he commanded, 'Come for me, gorgeous.'

She shattered, triggering his own release, and collapsed into his arms.

'Now fuck off, Red.' It was one thing to let others witness them having sex, but no one else was welcome during the intimacy that followed. Sensing their audience disappear down the hall, he hugged Alannah close to his chest. 'I love you, Lana.'

'I love you too, Brendan.'

Seconds seeped into minutes as Alannah held onto Brendan and time ceased to mean anything in her euphoric state. If just about anyone else had intruded on their sexy times, she would have blasted them to the pits of the Underworld. Jacob had always been there for her, even when Brendan ran off. Not to mention that one time they slept together. It was different to the time she had caught Caleb spying. Back then, she wanted Brendan's other lover to join them, not just watch. This time, in the heat of the moment, she just wanted to share the experience with their most trusted friend.

'You okay, gorgeous?'

'Ah huh. Everything's perfect.'

'So, no regrets?'

'None.' She slid down his front, stumbling at first as he helped her find her footing. Tilting up on tippy toes, she pressed her lips to his, and devoured his mouth, tasting the tang of her own juices. Her phone ringing from the nearby kitchen counter cut their kiss short and she dropped back on her feet with a sigh. 'Would you mind checking on Neve while I get that?'

'Sure thing.' His lips pecked her on the forehead before he turned, gathering his clothes from the floor as he left the room.

Glancing at the lit-up screen, she read Tyler's name on the caller ID. Not wanting to give any of their other house guests a fright, she took the call and her naked body upstairs and into the bedroom as she answered. 'Hey, stranger. How's everything going over there?'

'Hey, beautiful. Much as you'd expect for a warzone,' Tyler replied with a rugged voice. 'I hear congratulations are in order. First female High Magus. I'm so fucking proud of you.'

'Thanks, Ty. I almost can't believe it myself.'

'What's it like in the big chair? I hope you aren't letting all that power go to your head,' he jibed.

She chuckled. 'Fear not. There's plenty of guys here who are keeping me grounded. Honestly, it's a little overwhelming. Politics was never my forte. I'd rather be on the frontline.'

'I hear ya. Thanks for that armour, by the way. It saved my life, and Jaxon's.'

'You're welcome. What happened? How did it save Jaxon?'

Tyler's resigned sigh coiled around her heart and cinched. 'There was a dragon air strike yesterday. Wiped out most of our squad. I launched myself at Jaxon, pushing him to the ground so I could cover him.'

'Shit! I'm sorry, Ty.' Tears welled in her eyes as she thought of the devastation her friends had suffered. Then another niggling matter made her pulse pump louder in her ears. 'Fuck! What about Walshy? Is he okay?'

He let out a short sardonic laugh. 'As much as one can be with third degree burns. But yeah, he was still recovering in the medic's tent, so he was fortunate to escape this attack.'

She exhaled, letting the panic dissipate. 'He probably doesn't think so right now, but he is lucky. I'm sure he will heal up just fine. Have you heard from Samantha recently?'

'Yeah, I spoke to her this morning. Filled her in on the latest here. She's getting a little stir crazy in her safehouse but is otherwise okay. Sends her regards, congrats, and all that.'

'Good, I'm glad she's safe. Gods, I miss you guys.'

His laugh warmed her to the core. 'Aren't my doppelgangers doing it for you?'

'Ha! What makes you think I've slept with Danny?'

'Well, if past form is anything to go by….'

'But I have Brendan now!' she protested.

'So? As if you haven't fantasised about all three of us at once?'

'Threesomes with you and Brendan, sure, but Danny too? Although now you mention it…' His suggestion filled her mind with a porno reel as she imagined all the ways they could fuck her.

'Hehe. You're picturing it now, aren't you?'

'Ah huh.' A rush of desire shot between her legs. *Dear Gods, I'm gonna need to beckon Brendan to bed the second this call ends.* 'Just don't tell the other guys.'

'Somehow, I doubt Brendan will mind.'

'True, but he might tell Danny, and I don't want to scare the poor guy away because he thinks we're a bunch of deviants.'

Tyler burst out laughing.

'What's so funny?'

'It's cute that you think such a thing would bother Danny. If he's anything like the rest of us, he *is* a deviant. Man, I can't wait to find your doubles. Just think of all the orgies we'll have.'

'Tyler! Please.'

He sighed. 'Fine. If you're worried, I'll keep my mouth shut.'

'Thank you.'

An uncomfortable silence brewed between them for a few seconds, then he cleared his throat. 'Listen, I have a favour to ask.'

'Go on,' she prompted.

'Do you think you could persuade High Magus O'Grady to decriminalise the use of nether in New South Wales so that we can better equip our army?'

'I can try. It wasn't easy passing the change here.'

'I know, but you did, and now you've set a precedent. You truly are amazing, Lana.'

She blushed at his praise. It meant a lot coming from the people she cared most about. 'I appreciate your faith in me. No promises, but I will do my best.'

'That's all I ask, beautiful.'

After signing off, she lay on the bed, planning her approach with O'Grady.

The door creaked open, and Brendan entered, a lascivious grin tugging at his lips. 'Hot damn, Lana! Please tell me you're thinking about me ravishing that gorgeous body of yours.' His gaze trailed up her naked figure, lingering on her breasts before meeting her eyes.

'I *was* thinking about politics.'

Laughing, he sat on the mattress beside her. 'I didn't know that was one of your kinks.'

She slapped his arm playfully. 'Do you ever *not* think about sex?' His pierced brow arched, and she rolled her eyes. 'Stupid question.'

'I'm guessing that phone call was Council business?'

'Sort of. That was Tyler.' She filled him in on Tyler's news and the request he had made.

'Yeah, O'Grady's a tough nut to crack, but he has a soft spot for Jaxon's team, so you could always play that card.'

'That's actually pretty useful intel. Thanks, babe.'

'Anything for you, my love.'

Chapter Sixteen

After memorising an email, Jacob tapped DELETE on his phone screen. In his line of work, he preferred relying on biological rather than digital memory. Should anyone he didn't trust get hold of his phone, he had rigged it to blow, but removing the incriminating evidence was an added layer of protection. As he opened the next message, the floorboards above the living area started creaking, then Alannah's moaning followed. 'Fuck's sake, are they seriously at it again? When are they going to take a break?' He glanced at Caleb across the room, curious to gauge his reaction, but the guy maintained his poker face.

Amy chuckled from her side of the couch, her feet in his lap rubbing against his growing arousal. 'With everything Alannah is dealing with, I'm not surprised she needs to blow off some steam right now.'

'That's all well and good, but they could have spared us by putting up a sound ward. I can't easily concentrate on work when my dick is painfully hard.'

Leaning back into his recliner with a clink of his chains, Caleb grinned. 'We could always give 'em a taste of their own medicine.'

Amy huffed. 'Seriously guys? I've got enough FOMO[9] thanks to those two.' She tilted her head up toward Brendan's room.

Dropping his phone, Jacob grabbed Amy's feet and pressed his thumbs into their soles. 'Why don't you join us then?' The moan that escaped her plump lips sent a wave of desire through his veins.

She sucked in a breath as he increased the pressure. 'Fuck me, why does that feel so good?'

'Oh, I very much intend to fuck you. Although, it won't feel much like a noise battle if we take this to the attic.'

'You could dispel the sound wards,' Caleb suggested.

A short laugh escaped him. 'You are such a spiteful little beyach, but I love your thinking.' Rising from the couch, he offered Amy a hand. She took it and together they led Caleb up to the attic.

---

[9] Fear of Missing Out

After securing the bolt across the door, he used the day's pent up sexual frustration to channel his connection to the nether. As the power flowed, he focussed on the wards directly protecting them. It took a hot minute to unravel the sound protection from the lattice of magic surrounding the hidden room. 'Gods, it would be easier to use Amy's room.'

'Where's your sense of petty retribution?' Caleb prompted. 'This way, they'll know we're doing it to get back at them.'

Shaking his head, Jacob refocussed on the sound barrier. He visualised his stygian power manifesting as a flame that burned through the fabric preventing the attic from being audible. As soon as the barrier had dissipated, he doused the mystical fire with his keen sense of control, lest it go wild and destroy all the wards around the place. *Alannah would most definitely kill me then.* 'It's done.'

Caleb slouched against one of the beams, giving them a good view of his bare chest. 'So, Amy, how do you want to do this? Who gets to be piggy in the middle?'

She met the challenge in Caleb's dark eyes. 'Me of course. And don't think for one second that I'm letting you out of those chains.'

Caleb's lips curled into a sly grin. 'Suits me fine.'

Grabbing his chains, she shoved Caleb toward the bed. 'You ought to shut that bratty mouth of yours before I gag it.'

Watching her manhandle Caleb sent another rush of blood straight to Jacob's dick. Logically, he knew punishing the backstabbing bastard would only satisfy the guy's masochistic desires, but it still felt like he was serving a dose of justice on Brendo's behalf. Strangely, that thought alone turned him on more than the sadistic thrill or rush of power that also coursed through him. Withdrawing a bit gag from his drawer, he tossed it on the side of the bed. 'I think we should gag him anyway. This thing looks fucking hot between the jerk's lips.'

With a snicker, Amy retrieved the gag and straddled Caleb as she shoved it in his mouth and tightened the straps. 'For once we agree on something, Bennett. Since you can't use any verbal safe words,' she instructed Caleb, 'blink twice to make us slow down, or three times to stop the scene.' A muffled laugh slipped from Caleb's lips, and she gave Jacob a questioning look.

'He's used to edge play with Brendan and Bridey. They never bother with safe words.'

She shook her head. 'Crazy fools.' As she shuffled down the bed, she removed the lounge pants from Caleb's scrawny legs, releasing eight inches of his hard, throbbing flesh. She licked her lips at the sight before grinning up at Jacob. 'Should we give him a show?'

'What did you have in mind?'

'I want you to undress me.' Slipping off the bed, she stood in front of him while facing Caleb.

'You're full of good ideas today, shorty.' Drawing close to her muscular body, he whispered in her ear, 'Traffic lights okay with you?' The moment she consented to his proposed safe word system with a nod, he wrapped his arms around her waist and sank his teeth into the side of her neck.

Mewling, she bucked against his aching cock.

He slid his hands up under her silky camisole, tugging it over her head. Caleb's eyes widened as Jacob revealed the black bra and harness combo beneath. A sense of smug satisfaction crept in as he considered the probability that she was wearing this sexy-as-sin fetwear for his benefit. *Not like Connor's here to enjoy it.* He ran his fingers down her chest and dipped them into her bra cups. 'Your tits are so damn perfect.' Her breath hitched as he twisted her pebbled nipples. 'I'm not sure Caleb deserves to see them.'

'He can look, but it's not like he can touch them,' she pointed out in a gravelly voice.

312

'The ultimate tease,' he agreed. Dropping to his knees, he peeled her leather pants from her milky thighs, pausing at her knees so that he could hook his fingers in the straps of her G-string and remove it, along with the pants. Rising to his feet, he unclasped her studded bra and let it fall to the floor with a thud. The harness remained, giving her sumptuous breasts some extra lift. 'This can stay,' he told her gruffly as he tugged at it.

Throwing her head back against his chest, she peered up at him through lidded eyes. 'Lose the clothes, Bennett.'

He cupped her chin, brushing a thumb over her bottom lip. 'Always so demanding. Maybe I should gag you too.'

Her eyes narrowed. 'Don't you fucking dare.'

'Relax, peaches, I was only joking. Besides, that would defeat the point of our vengeance scheme. Caleb and I need to make you scream this house down.' He omitted the fact that he was growing to love her smart mouth and bossy attitude. Grabbing two foil packets from his drawer, he sauntered over to the bed. 'And trust me, sweet cheeks, you are going to *scream*.'

'Oh fuck!'

Caleb stirred at the sound of Jacob's cussing and shuffled about in the bed until he could gaze up at the man who'd spent the previous night destroying him in the most delicious ways.

Jacob was sitting up in the bed, reading something on his phone. He glanced at Caleb with a pained expression.

A sudden wave of nausea surged through his gut as his blood turned to needles. 'What happened?'

'She… I…,' Jacob stammered.

'Just spit it the fuck out, Red,' he snapped. It didn't take a mind reader to know the news involved Bridey, and where his beloved sister was concerned, his protective hackles rose. If his hands weren't bound in chains, he would have grabbed the phone, fail-safes be damned.

'I'm sorry, dude. She's dead.'

His heart skipped a beat, then the tears pooled in his eyes as he shook his head. 'No. No, she can't be. Your informant is either lying or mistaken.'

Jacob turned the phone to show him a photo. 'Hard to read this wrong.'

The image of her severed head propped an inch above her naked body, which was sprawled out over a bed of purple satin sheets, turned the contents of his stomach. He barely rolled over in time before emptying it all over the timber floor.

Jacob rubbed his back gently with one hand while holding his hair back with the other. Once the worst of it settled, Jacob helped him sit up. 'We need to tell Brendo about this.'

He nodded, unable to project his voice past the lump in his throat. As they rose, he searched the attic for Amy.

'She went back to her own room in the wee hours to get some sleep,' Jacob explained.

He showed his mute understanding again as Jacob helped him into a pair of clean trackpants. The stairs leading down from the attic posed a challenge in his reduced capacity and he stumbled a few times. Good thing Jacob possessed enough coordination and balance for them both. When they reached Brendan's room, Jacob hammered his fists against the door until their smoldering Boss threw the door open and glared at them both.

'The war better be at our fucking doorstep to justify this interruption,' he growled, every bit as intimidating without a scrap of clothing on his body. Under better circumstances, Caleb would have dropped to his knees and begged for punishment, but grief had a terrible way of killing all desires.

'Bridey's dead,' Jacob deadpanned.

'The fuck?' Brendan's face paled.

'Ding dong!' Alannah called from where she sat up in the bed, shamelessly exposing her tits.

Brendan turned and gaped at her.

Alannah shrugged. 'What? You know how I feel about that woman.'

Shaking his head, Brendan ushered them both into his room and shut the door. 'What happened?'

Caleb shuffled over to the bed and plonked himself down at the foot of it. He still hadn't heard the full story, and knew he'd need to brace himself for the rest.

'Levi happened,' Jacob explained, making himself comfortable in the leather armchair by the window. 'He sent me a photo of her mutilated corpse, along with a note that I haven't read yet because… well, it's addressed to the pair of you.' He gestured to Brendan and Alannah.

Oh fuck! Caleb already knew where this was going.

'We're both here, so read it,' insisted Brendan as he commenced pacing across the Persian rug.

Jacob glanced at Caleb, who nodded for him to continue. 'Very well.' He cleared his throat and began:

Brendan and Alannah,

*You were warned, so now the consequences
of your insubordination will rain blood upon
the Earth. Each month, as you continue to
live and work together, I will kill another of
your loved ones, and I'll take pleasure in
doing so. I've never…*

Jacob's voice faltered as his eyes scanned
ahead. 'That sick fuck!'
Brendan snatched the phone from his hands
and continued:

*I've never come so hard in my life as I did
while wrapping my hands around Bridey's
throat and watching the life fade from her
eyes. She was a fool to trust me.*

*I expect you'll do the right thing, but just in
case, I'll be watching.*

Levi.

'Gods fucking damn it!' Brendan tossed the
phone at Jacob, who caught it mid-air. 'Doesn't that
prick care that we're in the middle of fighting the
dragons? We can't handle multiple fronts. We

should be working together against the bigger threat.'

Unable to bear it any longer, Caleb's flood gates broke, and tears crashed down upon his cheeks. 'This would never have happened if I'd stayed with her.'

Brendan stopped pacing and stared at him. 'Ah shit! Thornsy, I'm sorry.' Kneeling before him, he released the shackles binding Caleb's wrists. 'You're wrong, though. If you were with her, he would have killed you both. At least this way, I don't lose you as well.' Taking a seat on the bed, Brendan pulled him into his lap for a hug.

The others fell silent as they watched him weep in his estranged lover's arms. Yet, he didn't just feel anguish over losing Bridey at that moment. Something warm burned in his chest, like the blackened wick of an old candle coming to life again. As the violent sobs gave way to whimpers, he snuggled against the crook of Brendan's neck and whispered, 'I love you.'

'I love you too.' Brendan kissed his forehead and squeezed him tight around the waist. 'We need to recover her body, so that we can pay our respects and say goodbye properly.'

He returned the strong embrace and kissed Brendan's cheek to show his gratitude.

'I'll see what I can do.' Jacob tapped his phone a few times before lifting it to his ear. 'Yes, I got your message. ... They know. ... The Boss wants her remains. ... Good, you do that.' He lowered the phone as the call ended. 'Levi will text me directions to a safe meeting place.'

Alannah rose from the bed and strode across the room to the wardrobe, not the least bit ashamed of her nudity in present company. 'I'm coming with you.'

Brendan's arms, still holding him close, tensed. 'Are you insane, Lana? Or just deaf? How do think he'll react to seeing us together so soon after sending that message?'

'That's half the point. We have a month before he kills anyone else. So long as we don't exceed that amount of time, we'll be fine. I'm also not about to let the jerk whisk you away from me again. He was, after all, the master of Bridey's puppet strings.' She slipped into a matching black lace set before donning her midnight blue mage robes.

'But—'

'Don't argue with me, babe. You know I can hold my own in a fight and with the pair of us working together, there's no way he'll stand a chance. Besides, I intend to show him what happens when he messes with the new High Magus.' To emphasise her point, she grabbed her sword and rammed it into its hilt on her belt.

Brendan cussed under his breath and Caleb felt the man's desire growing beneath him. 'At least let me extract some information from him before you start slicing and dicing.' Caressing Caleb's back, Brendan pressed his lips to the shell of his ear. 'Will you be okay here, while I go retrieve Bridey's body?'

'I want to come with you,' he asserted as best he could in his pitiful state.

'No, that's a really bad idea. You're beside yourself with grief, and at the risk of sounding cold, your presence will only hinder us. I can't have that arsehole using you against me. Please tell me you understand,' Brendan pleaded.

With a sigh, he conceded Brendan's point. 'I understand.'

Twigs snapped under Alannah's boots as she stomped along the dirt path that wound through the old rural graveyard. The rugged sandstone chapel they passed on the way suggested these grounds dated back to the mid-to-late eighteen hundreds. It also happened to be all that remained of the otherwise burnt-out township. 'I never would have guessed that the dragons respect the dead.'

'They strike me as honourable, even if they are a misguided bunch of zealots,' Brendan mused. 'Levi on the other hand…,' his voice trailed off as they rounded a bend, and a grand Romanesque mausoleum came into view. The building might have drawn the eye more if it weren't for the grotesque distraction in front of it. Bridey's head stood atop a spike, marking the location of her remains. '…always had a flair for the dramatic. I hope the rest of her body is intact, otherwise Caleb will be spitting chips.'

She shuddered as she stared into Bridey's cold, dead eyes. Even in death, the woman glared at her with contempt. 'Let's get this over with so I can go back to fighting dragons.' Her heels clicked against marble floors as she crossed the threshold. *This building is so out-of-place in such a backwater.*

'Well, well, well. Alannah Winters in the flesh. Today must be my lucky day.' A tall, slim man slouched against one of the columns on the far wall. A few rays of light filtered through a stained-glass window, illuminating his chiselled features in an otherwise gloomy space.

'Geez, Levi. You're really embracing the vampire vibes these days: hanging out in a tomb, with a black leather cloak on your corpse-like figure. Is there something you'd like to tell us?'

Pushing off from the wall, Levi chuckled, his long denim-clad legs stalking toward them. 'You're just jealous that I look better in skinny jeans.'

She huffed. 'Puh-lease. No one's arse looks better in tight pants than Brendan's.'

'Except for yours, gorgeous.' Brendan winked at her.

'Naw, you two make the cutest couple,' scoffed Levi. 'Pity it can't last. Oh, and believe, me, sweetheart, I know how good Brendan's arse looks.'

She shivered despite the warm weather. Shooting a questioning look at Brendan, she breathed a sigh of relief when he shook his head. The thought of this creep violating her man would have haunted her nightmares otherwise.

Levi drew close to her and traced a finger along her jaw. 'Now I finally get to see what all the fuss is about. No wonder Brendan and Liam fought over you. Perhaps I'll take you for myself. That'll be one way to keep my master happy.'

Brendan shifted behind her. 'Get your filthy hands off her, you degenerate arsehole.'

Projecting her thoughts into Brendan's mind, she warned him to stay back. '*This jerk knows our weaknesses; don't let him use them against us. Our plan is working.*' Refusing to shy away from Levi's touch, she licked her lips and smiled. 'Where's the body?'

The pulse in Levi's hand quickened as he gripped her chin. 'In the coffin near the door.'

Moving into action, Brendan checked and confirmed, 'That's definitely Bridey.'

She hated how confident he sounded identifying the naked woman by her body alone, but she pushed her envy and hatred aside to focus on the issue at hand. Stepping forward, she pressed Levi against a crypt, their bodies close enough for her to feel his arousal. 'Tell me, Levi, what do you have against my relationship with Brendan?'

'Me personally? Nothing. My master is the one who wants to keep you apart.'

'And who is your master?'

He snickered. 'You're kidding, right? As if I'd give away his identity that easily.'

She slipped her hand between his legs, stroking the massive bulge in his jeans. 'I promise to make it worth your while.'

Fast as lightning, he flipped their positions and pinned her against the stone structure that probably encased a dead body. 'Nice try, sweetheart, but I'd never betray him over a piece of arse, not even one as sweet as yours. But I'll still take you up on the offer, your side of it anyway.'

A sly grin tugged at her lips. 'There's no time like the present.' She pushed her backside up onto the crypt, opened her robes, and spread her legs.

With wide eyes, he took in the sight of her near-nude figure. 'Are you serious?' he asked on a hopeful whisper. When she nodded, he glanced over his shoulder at Brendan, who stood stock still with the meanest glower fixed on his face. 'What about him? I doubt your boyfriend is so keen on the idea,' Levi asked.

'My body, my choice.'

His mouth crashed to hers, devouring her with a ravenous kiss. Sliding a hand beneath her panties, he shoved four fingers deep inside her. 'I hope you like it rough,' he rasped.

She bucked against his hand then sprawled out over the stone slab. 'Is there any other way to fuck?'

In a flash, he dropped his jeans and climbed on top of her. 'I still can't believe I'm doing this.' After tearing her lace panties to shreds, he buried himself inside her.

Grinning, she entwined her fingers with his. 'I can.' Then she gave Brendan the telepathic signal he needed, '*Now*.'

Levi's weight shifted as Brendan slammed into his back and grabbed his throat with a garotte wire. She tightened her grip of Levi's hands to prevent his escape.

'How does it feel to wear the shoe on the other foot, you perverted maggot?' Brendan seethed, his face as red as the blood dripping down Levi's throat.

Levi laughed. 'Considering I'm the one with my dick inside your woman, I'd say I feel pretty good right now.'

Digging her nails into the backs of his hands, she sneered at him. 'I guess your depravity knows no limits. You'd better make the most of my sweet pussy, because it's the last you'll ever get, unless you tell us who your master is.'

A lightbulb flicked on inside Levi's head, his eyes widening. 'The pair of you enchanted me. That's why I couldn't resist my lust for you.'

'If you and Bridey taught me anything, Levi, it's that sex can be the deadliest weapon.' Brendan tightened the garrotte. 'Makes this whole situation quite poetic, don't you think? Now spill it before I sever your carotid arteries.'

'I'd sooner die than betray him.'

'Careful what you wish for,' Brendan threatened. 'You can't carry out your master's will if you're dead.'

'My death would be but a mild inconvenience to my master, as there are many who serve him.'

'Then I guess, *they'll* have to continue his dirty work without you.' Brendan tugged the wire with considerable force, spraying her with Levi's blood.

She snapped her eyes shut to keep out the spatter and gasped in a lung full of air when the dead man's weight lifted from her.

As she peeled her eyes open, Brendan appeared above her, grinning victoriously. 'Do you have any idea how hot you look soaked in the blood of our enemies?'

'No, but I have a feeling you're about to show me.' Her soul hummed and muscles quivered as she welcomed him inside, letting him cleanse away the memory of Levi's foul touch.

As they left the mausoleum, Brendan cradling Bridey's remains, Alannah's phone lit up with a call from Connor. 'Hey, Foley, what's up?'

'Um, hi, Your Honour. We have a situation.'

Gods it feels strange receiving such a formal greeting from one of my closest friends. 'Go on,' she prompted.

'The dragons have wiped out the greater Adelaide region and they're heading south. Oh, and a few of them have surrounded the Murray Bridge garrison at ground level. They might not be able to get us in here with the Seelie protections, but the moment we leave, we're screwed.'

'Dammit!' *Think, think, think... bingo!* She channelled her Aether connection and prayed to Kieran's spirit for guidance. The answer entered her mind, and she relayed the message: 'There are secret tunnels running beneath the building that you can access from beneath the map table.'

'Really?' Connor queried. 'How the hell did you know that? You've only been there once.'

'Kieran told me.'

'How—never mind. I'll get the troops out of here, but what do we do about our home?'

'The Seelie have protected all the mage estates in our region, so the army will be safe here while we regroup. Listen, Connor, if we are to have any hope of winning this war, we need Liam back on our side. Apparently, he has taken up residence among the merfolk. Do you think you could contact him for me and deliver a message?'

'Yeah, okay. What should I tell him?'

'Tell him… Brendan survived, that he's fine. Tell him… I'm sorry and that I forgive him. Obviously tell him about Kieran.'

'Yes, of course.'

'Oh, and tell him… I need him.'

Chapter Seventeen

Waiting restlessly in the front row of the Town Hall with her fellow officials, Alannah thought about Brendan and Caleb. While she was paying her respects to their former High Magus in a very formal setting, her soulmate was laying Bridey to rest out in the wilderness according to the old Unseelie customs. She did not ask what that meant. The less she knew about Brendan's private moments with Bridey, the better. Still, she felt for him and for Caleb; they had both lost someone dear to them.

A gut-wrenching wail pulled her out of her head, and she looked down the row to see Monique bawling her heart out in Steve's arms. Alannah exchanged a sorrowful glance with him before turning her attention to the whispered conversation around her, catching snippets of despair.

'What are we supposed to do about the dragons now....'

'Did you hear about Sydney?'

'They say the Arch Mage doesn't even give a damn…'

'Hey, look….'

The whispers died down as several heads turned. She followed their gazes and gasped as Liam strode down the aisle in his black suit, his eyes fixed on her. Reaching the front row, he patiently waited for her neighbours to make room for him at her side. He was still her husband, technically. 'I'm sorry, Lana. I—'

'Can we talk about the personal stuff later, please? My nerves are shot, and I still have a eulogy to read.'

He nodded. 'I guess I missed the wake, huh?'

'I only managed a flying visit myself,' she admitted. 'Things have been a bit crazy at home. I've invited the Lanes and the Mahers back to Cailleach Estate for drinks after this.'

'Good, that'll give me a chance to talk with them all properly. So, why are you reading? That usually falls to family and….' His eyes widened as the situation dawned on him.

'Connor didn't tell you that bit?'

'I guess congratulations are in order, Your Honour.'

'Please don't be so formal with me, Liam. Even with everything that's happened, we're still family.'

He sighed as the procession started. Six pallbearers carried the coffin toward the front of the hall to the lilting melody of a live Celtic harp.

Acolyte Foley addressed the crowd, speaking of love and loss, of finding peace in a better place.

She hadn't thought about it until now, but she assumed Kieran would be in the Celestial Realm. *Does that mean I'll meet you again in the afterlife? I know we had our differences, but you were a good man and a great leader. I'd like an opportunity to express my gratitude for everything you did for me.* Her thoughts drifted to all the times he pushed her to improve herself. Lost in her reverie, it took a nudge from Liam to bring her back to reality.

'You okay?' he asked softly.

Nodding, she glanced at the Acolyte, who smiled and gestured for her to take his place at the lectern. She rose, withdrawing a sheet of paper from her pocket as she adjusted the microphone. 'Kieran Lane has been a pillar of this community for much of his life. A sporting captain and head prefect in school days, then member of the Council straight after. At the age of twenty, he broke the record for the youngest Mayor ever sworn into the role in

Australia. If my maths is correct, that was before Monique was even a twinkle in his eye, but only just. It was in his capacity as Mayor that I first remember him from my own childhood, an ever-present role model at festivals and fairs. Of course, this was before I knew everything I know today. Following my induction into the world of politics, I looked up to Kieran as a great leader. He inspired me to strive for self-improvement, and to protect the innocent. His sense of justice was always strong, something that put us at odds at a darker time in my life.' Glancing across the sea of faces, she did not detect a single look of contempt or scorn, then her eyes connected with Danny's, and he gave her an encouraging smile.

'But Kieran was also a man of reason who learned to accept the greater truths that others seek to hide from us. We certainly did not see eye-to-eye on everything and I'm sure my fellow Councillors recall many heated debates.' A few chuckles echoed through the room. 'Yet Kieran also encouraged me to break that glass ceiling and I wouldn't be standing where I am today if it were not for his support. So, blessed be, Kieran Lane.

'If you are able, please rise and join me in song:

Of all the money that e'er I had
I have spent it in good company
Oh and all the harm I've ever done
Alas, it was to none but me

And all I've done for want of wit
To memory now I can't recall
So fill to me the parting glass
Good night and joy be to you all....'

—'The Parting Glass,' Traditional Folk
Song

As the formalities concluded, dozens of
mages approached to introduce themselves with
words of condolences and congratulations. One
familiar face took her a moment to place.

The blonde woman smiled warmly as she
extended her hand. 'I always knew there was
something magical about you, but I never would
have placed you for a pure blood.'

She shook the offered hand. 'Linda Maguire?
My Gods, I could say the same for you, although I
didn't even know magic existed back in my
Melbourne days. How are you?' Linda had been
one of the mean girls in high school—much like
Monique—but Alannah came to realise much of

that came down to their upbringing. When society gives you a superiority complex, it can be hard to put it aside and act humble.

'In a similar boat to you guys as far as the dragons are concerned. Nice eulogy, by the way. Very… diplomatic.'

She laughed. 'Thanks. I just hope I was subtle enough as far as any reference to magic goes. Becoming a public figure and straddling the two worlds is a challenge. Kieran always made it look easier than it is.'

'It was perfect,' Linda assured her. 'Listen, I wanted to touch base and make myself known to you because I'd like to bring our communities together, to form an alliance if you will. The different states have been working alone for far too long, but if we have any hope of beating the dragons, I think we need to come together.'

'You know, I've been thinking along the same lines.'

'I also think you're the High Magus to make it happen,' Linda suggested.

'I appreciate the vote of confidence and I'll certainly give it a red-hot go.'

Alannah stroked the adorable fluffball in her lap, thankful for the comfort Luna offered. Grieving a friend while staying in the political spotlight was fucking exhausting. Not to mention the inevitable conversation she needed to have with a certain ex who was still technically married to her. Liam was hovering nearby and every time he caught her eye, she felt like millions of pins were piercing her nerves. *I really hope he doesn't want to make a go of our marriage anymore.*

'Here, I made you an Irish coffee—should help you relax a little.' Brendan grinned as he held out the glass mug so that she could take it by the handle. 'I promise I went easy on the whiskey in yours.'

'Thanks. Also, are you crazy, making an appearance with so many people here?' Her eyes skimmed the crowd of mourners in her living room for any suspicious spectators, but most were immersed in their own conversations. Only Liam watched them like a hawk getting ready to dive on its prey.

Brendan sat next to her and tickled Luna behind the ears before taking a sip of his own cocktail. 'Don't worry about it. I've worked something out.'

Her brows lifted as she queried him, 'You gonna let me in on your plan?'

'Nah.' He shrugged. 'You'll work it out soon enough.' He leaned in and whispered in her ear, 'Just try and hold back on the PDA.'

Monique approached them a moment later, giving Brendan the once-over. 'Danny, right?' She held out a hand for Brendan to shake.

'Yessum. And you must be the lovely Monique. Please accept my condolences for your loss.' Rather than shaking Monique's hand, he turned it over and kissed the back of it, bringing a blush to her pale cheeks.

Alannah tried hard to stop her jaw from dropping, to play along with the act. *Genius, really, using the doppelganger thing to mask his identity.*

'Thank you.' Monique shook her head as she sat in a nearby chair. 'It's uncanny how much you look like Brendan.'

'So everyone says,' he replied on a laugh.

Leaning in, she lowered her voice to a conspiratorial whisper, 'Watch out for this one,' Monique gestured toward her. 'You're exactly her type.' She followed it up with a wink.

A deep, gravelly chuckle bubbled up his throat. 'Oh, I'm not worried at all. I hear Brendan likes to share.'

This time she turned bright red. *So much for keeping that fantasy from Brendan.*

Meanwhile, Monique sprayed her drink across the coffee table and quickly grabbed some tissues to mop up the mess. 'Geez, woman, how do you always get all the fun?'

'Just lucky, I guess.'

'Does that mean the rumours are true? Are you back with Brendan?' Monique asked in a hushed voice.

She nodded. 'But please don't confirm the rumours with anyone. The conflict of interest won't look good for either of our careers. Plus, we are also up against another enemy who is lurking in the shadows.'

Monique's wide-eyed reaction assured her that it was safe to confide in her friend.

'Promise to keep a huge secret?'

'Pinkie swear.' Monique offered her the ultimate promise and their little fingers shook on it.

She explained a little of the plot to keep her and Brendan apart and the threats made on the lives of their loved ones, but she left out the details about The Circle.

'Holy crap!' Monique exclaimed. 'I always hated that endarkened bitch for what she did to you and Brendan. I'm glad she got what was coming to her.'

Glancing at Brendan's hands, she noticed his fists tensing in an effort to school his expression.

'I never knew her, but don't you think it's a little harsh to wish ill of the dead?' Brendan countered in his best attempt to maintain the ruse.

Monique sighed. 'I suppose you're right. There are probably people out there thinking the same of my father, although most of them would be scumbags he put behind bars. Still, it's easy to make enemies in politics and the justice system.'

'Your father was a great man, Monique. May his soul rest in peace.' Brendan surprised her with his genuine sentiment. Then again, you don't become a successful Syndicate Boss without picking up some good acting skills along the way.

'Thank you, Danny. Now if you'll both excuse me, I have more people to speak with.'

'Of course,' Alannah simpered. 'Please take care.'

'I should take my leave too.' Brendan sculled the last of his drink. 'It's time to give the real Slim Shady a chance to stand up. I'll catch you when this is all over.'

'Okay, babe. Thanks again for the drink, it's really good.'

He grinned. 'You want another before I go?'

'Yes, please.' She watched his backside as he sauntered off to the kitchen.

Liam swooped in the moment his brother vacated the room. 'Ready for that talk?'

'No, but we should get it over with,' she conceded.

'You and Brendan looked pretty cosy just now.'

She gaped at him. 'But that was—'

'That was my brother doing a decent job of disguising himself, but I know him too well. No amount of glamour will pull the wool over my eyes.'

Thinking about it, she had also known who he was from the get-go. 'Of course. I imagine it's the same deal with your parents. And yes, things have been cosy with Brendan. Not that we want the world to know, but we are officially a couple again.'

Staring off into space, Liam gritted his teeth and nodded. 'Good, I'm happy for you. So, why do you need me?'

She grabbed his hands and turned his attention back to her. 'Before I get to that, I want you to know that I still love you as a friend and cousin, Liam. We've been through hell together and I don't want things to end on bad terms. I appreciate everything you've done for me and for

Neve. And for what it's worth, I'm sorry things couldn't work out on the romance front.'

He caressed the back of her hands with his thumbs. 'Thank you, Lana. I needed to hear that. And I meant it when I said I'm happy for you. I know how much Brendan means to you and when I was watching the two of you together today, I could see how much brighter your soul beams with him in your life. I just hope you know what you are doing with the risk this poses to your political career.'

'We are taking precautions, hence the disguise.' She glanced across the room and spotted Brendan by the kitchen door, eyeing them warily with two Irish coffees in his hand. Smiling, she ushered him over.

A few long strides closed the distance, and he handed one of the drinks to her. 'Sorry. I was hesitant to interrupt what looked like a private moment between husband and wife.'

'Cut the crap, Brendan,' Liam hissed. 'You know this marriage is over. Just don't do something stupid and break Lana's heart again because I won't be around to pick up the pieces.'

Brendan stood there gobsmacked.

'What do you mean, you won't be around?' she asked.

Liam's expression softened as he focussed on her. 'After I do whatever it is you need me to do, I'll be retiring back to the ocean and my new home with Saoirse.'

'I see. I guess that means I have another seat to fill on the Council.'

'I'm sure you'll manage. There are plenty of young warlocks who would jump at the chance.'

'They'll have some big shoes to fill. You're a natural born leader and strategist, Liam, which brings me to my request.'

Brendan cleared his throat. 'If ya'll are gonna talk war and politics, I'll leave you to it.' He sauntered toward the front hall, and she watched him walk away. About halfway across the room, he spoke in her mind, '*Stop staring at my arse, gorgeous. People might get suspicious*.'

Laughing, she turned back to Liam.

'Did I miss something funny?' Liam asked.

'No, Brendan just said something to me telepathically.'

'I probably don't want to know. So, what do you need?'

The humour vanished from her disposition. 'The war is on our doorstep, and I need your help to win it. The troops are lost without you. Kieran may have been a great High Magus, but you were their army leader.'

'I don't know, Lana. It all seems pretty hopeless to me. Nothing we tried worked against them.'

'Except for stygian magic,' she reminded him. 'And I just passed a bill to decriminalise the channelling of nether in our state.'

He gawped at her. 'You never cease to amaze me.'

'I hope you mean that in a good way.'

'Mostly,' he teased. 'Won't they think I'm a deserter? I've been AWOL for what… a week now?'

'I'll tell them Kieran sent you on a secret mission, or some bullshit.'

He shook his head. 'Won't work. Connor knows the truth, so chances are, half the bloody army knows.'

She gave the situation some thought for a moment. 'I'll have a word with Connor, but I doubt he would have spread anything about Brendan and me, which means we can work the merfolk angle better. I've already planted the seed, suggesting you were there on Council business. What if you were trying to convince them to help us?'

'Seems plausible, I guess. Okay, I'll do it. If you organise all the gear we need, I'll lead us to victory. Just do me a favour, will you?'

'What's that?'

'Keep Brendan out of my hair. I still can't stand the guy.'

'Why? I thought you were happy for me.' She tilted her head and studied his sour expression.

'I'm happy that you're happy, Lana. My rivalry with Brendan goes way back and it wasn't always about you.'

'Don't take this the wrong way, but I can understand his gripes. You were and still are your father's favourite. How can you hold that against him?'

He laughed drily. 'Because Brendan was and still is Mum's favourite, despite everything he's done.'

Chapter Eighteen

Alannah's fingers flew across the keyboard as she typed email after email to other influential mages around Australia. Much of the content was copy and paste, but to be effective, she knew she needed to personalise each and every one of them.

> Hi Linda,
> It was great catching up with you the other day, even if the circumstances of our meeting were less than fortunate. I'd love to grab a drink with you sometime to hear all the goss from the old school days. Whatever became of Zac? Anyway, I digress....

> Hi Fergus,
> Thank you so much for paying your respects at High Magus Kieran's funeral and for taking the time to introduce yourself. I'm sorry to hear about the devastation in Perth,

yet thankful that your beautiful family are safe. I hope you'll send me more baby photos soon.

I'm writing to you now because I'd like to form an allegiance that crosses borders, one that will help us win this war against the dragons. I recently passed a bill in my own state to decriminalise the channelling of nether for non-nefarious purposes. Previous legal cases here have set the precedent to show that this magical practice can be both safe and moral. I have also proven the effectiveness of stygian magic on military gear in my own army. Thus far, this is the only form of magic that gives us a chance against the dragons. I urge you to rally with the other councillors and mages in your state to petition your High Magus to pass this same bill....

After a light tap on the door, Brendan entered wearing nothing but a pair of grey trackpants. 'Any progress with the dragons?'

Taking in the view, she licked her lips. 'The what now?'

He chuckled. 'Dragons—you know, those gargantuan flying lizards that breathe fire?'

She snapped her fingers. 'Oh right, those things. Sorry, I'm a little distracted at the moment.'

Perching his perfect backside on her desk, he grinned at her. 'And why would that be, hmm?'

'Oh, I don't know. Maybe because the world's sexiest man is sitting on my desk and he's practically naked.'

'Sorry, not sorry. I can't seem to help myself after the world's sexiest woman blew my… mind with the most amazing good morning kiss.'

Her thoughts wandered back a few hours to that glorious moment when she was choking on his cock and the wonderful look in his eyes when he woke up. 'You're welcome. Not that I don't love your company, but don't you have an empire to run?'

He shrugged. 'They're all in hiding. Hard to do business with a bunch of ghosts.'

'So when you told them to go underground….'

'They took it literally. The Unseelie keep their safe houses secret from everyone. On the plus side, I'm one hundred percent yours. Just tell me how I can help.'

'Unless you can magic a dragon-fighting army out of thin air—' Her laptop pinged with an urgent message, summoning the global leaders to a video conference. 'Sorry, babe. I need to attend an online meeting with my boss. You should probably make yourself scarce.'

'Your boss? Holy fuck! Does that mean you're meeting with the Arch Mage? The top wanker himself?'

She rolled her eyes and pointed to the door.

'What? It's true. As if that old crony is still getting laid, so he'd—'

'Out!' she hollered. *Gods almighty! It's hard to imagine someone so juvenile actually runs the biggest crime syndicate in the southern hemisphere.*

Raising his hands in surrender, he gave her a huge panty-dropping grin and slowly backed out of her office, pausing at the doorway to blow her a kiss.

As soon as the door shut, she logged on to the call. Arch Mage Gréagóir[10] Callaghan was an older man who appeared to be in his forties but considering how long he had been in this role; he couldn't be younger than sixty and no one knew his real age. Some joked that he had found the fountain of youth and kept its secrets to himself. She didn't put much stock in the rumours, even if they were mostly in jest, but she had to admit that he looked

---

[10] Irish form of Gregory

good for his age. Traces of black still peppered his short, cropped silver hair, and while it was thinning a little on top, he was far from bald. The severe angles of his face and penetrating stare gave him a powerful, dominant edge, one that she found sexy if she was being honest with herself. She wondered what the man got up to behind closed doors.

He sat silently as he waited for the stragglers. There were already thousands of mages on the call, all with their microphones muted. This was to be a one-way conference. As time ticked by, an eerie, prickly sensation washed over her, and she couldn't help but think that his dark brown eyes were focussing on her. *Should I feel flattered or scared, because right now I'm feeling both?* As if reading her mind, one side of his mouth curled into a sly grin, and he began stroking the stubble on his chin. *Shit!* Her panties were drenched. *This is not cool! Nothing good can come from crushing on my boss, especially not when he is the Arch Fucking Mage.* Then it occurred to her that she probably stood out as the only female High Magus on the call. *Makes sense that he would pick me out from the crowd. But what's going through his mind?*

She didn't have long to contemplate the possibilities before he cleared his throat. 'Let's get started, shall we? Thank you all for attending at such short notice. I know this is no easy thing right now since most of you are busy leading the war efforts in your own regions. For this reason, I'll cut to the chase. I've decided our only hope against the dragons is to seek aid from the human military powers of the world.'

What the fuck? There's no way that will end well.

A swarm of shocked emojis littered the screen followed by a torrent of negative comments.

'I know many of you are horrified at the mere suggestion, but there is nothing to be afraid of here. The human race has grown much more tolerant as a whole, so I don't see a need to hide the magic world from them anymore. I have spoken at length with my advisors on the matter and preparations are underway to lift the veil. I will keep you all posted with significant updates. Thank you. That is all.'

The screen went blank, and she gaped at it. *What the actual fuck?*

Like one of Saoirse's siren sisters, the sea called to Liam the longer he spent away from it. His soul had always yearned for the ocean to some extent, but ever since the transformation, his body physically ached for it too. The moment he dived in, his legs transmuted into a scaly tail and his windpipe closed, allowing his gills to suck the oxygen he needed from the water. His new physiology was miraculous, really.

He found Saoirse standing guard by one of the riptides that served as a highway bypassing their home. *Huh! This place already feels like home to me.*

She grinned. 'Oh good, you're back!'

'Only briefly, I'm afraid. The mage army need my help.'

Her brow furrowed. 'I thought you put all that behind you? You promised to stay with me.'

'And I will, once I deal with these damn dragons. People are counting on me to help them, to save their lives and their loved ones' lives.'

She shook her head. 'Please don't go, I beg you. You don't owe those people anything, so why risk yourself for them?'

Pulling her into his arms, he wrapped his tail around her. 'Saoirse please, I need you to understand that I grew up with these people. Many of them are my friends and family, all of whom I still care for. I'll be fighting to protect them and their way of life. Even if it is no longer how I choose to live, I must respect their choices and do what I can to help.'

Pressing her forehead against his, she stared deeply into his eyes. 'You are too noble for your own good, my love. Please promise me you'll take every precaution with your own safety.'

'I promise,' he whispered against her lips before kissing them passionately. She whimpered as he pulled away, sending a jolt of desire through his body. 'If you weren't on duty, I'd ravish you here and now.'

Her cheeks turned the colour of coral and she pouted. 'How long before you return to make love to me?'

'Honestly? I have no idea. It could be weeks, it could be months.'

'Then please don't make me wait a second more than necessary.'

Reading the wanton lust in her eyes, he conceded. He took her hands, wrapping her arms around him, and fell into the slip stream, letting it take them wherever because anywhere was better than straight across from the old aunt's place. She squealed with delight as they rushed by the familiar sights of home at lightning speed. The tide dumped them in a dark cavern about twenty kilometres[11]

---

[11] 20 km = 12.43 miles

from any merfolk territory. 'Now to give you a proper goodbye.'

After seeing Saoirse back home, Liam swam to shore where he endured the painful transformation back to a landwalker. He did so within the privacy of an old boatshed where he had left a change of clothes and a set of stygian-enchanted battle armour. Alannah had assured him that he would find ample weapons at the new garrison. Once his legs felt steady enough to stand on, he dressed himself, taking care to cover the gills on his neck. That would take some explaining otherwise. Then he geared up for battle. Ley line travel had become even more treacherous.

Four jumps into his journey, an almighty roar sounded above. He ducked for cover beneath a manhole, but not before a fireball whacked him in the backside. It would have burnt him to a crisp if not for the armour. That was still too close for comfort, so he negotiated the rest of his journey using nexus stops within the sewer system.

Arriving at the newly populated garrison, near the shifted frontline, he sensed the powerful magic warding the property as he passed the barrier. *That's some strong mojo the Seelie put on this place.* A few warlocks saluted him as he strode on by, but most stopped and stared, giving him a queasy feeling in his belly. *What did Lana tell them? Did they believe her?*

The sun was setting, so unsurprisingly he found most of the troops milling about in the mess hall. He spotted Alannah's friends crowded around a pool table and as he approached, they glanced up from their game of eight ball and glared at him. 'Not the warmest welcome I've ever received,' he jested, trying to defuse the situation.

Connor stepped forward, pointing a pool cue at Liam's chest. 'Most of these idiots may have bought Alannah's story about seeking aid from the merfolk, but we know what really went down, so you can save your breath.'

'There ain't much water round here, so he'll need it,' Bailey jibed.

He heaved a huge sigh. 'Come on guys, can we please put all this antagonistic tripe aside and try working together? Lana wants me to lead this army to victory, but I can't do that without your cooperation. So, what do you say?'

Their silence grew deafening.

'Fuck off, Liam!' Cara spat. 'We don't need deserters like you to beat those damn dragons.'

'You better scurry back under your reef or I'll kick your scaly arse,' Bailey threatened.

Liam decided not to remind them how much stronger than them he was, that his transformation to mermage had not lessened his magic in any way. The time would come soon enough when he would get a chance to demonstrate his powers on the battlefield. 'Too bad I'm not going anywhere until I win this war for you all.' Shoving Bailey aside, he stormed off to find his real friends.

Chapter Nineteen

As Alannah opened the wardrobe, Luna scurried out from the shelf where she had made a nest of Brendan's socks. 'Silly kitty, did you go and get yourself trapped again?'

'Meow.' Luna wove between her legs, brushing up against bare calves.

Giggles slipped from her mouth. 'That tickles. Come on you.' She picked up the cat and carried her to the door where Luna scrambled free and dashed down the hallway, almost tripping Brendan over as he approached the bedroom.

'Damn cat,' he chuckled as he caught his balance on the wall.

She dropped to the floor in a fit of laughter, a much-needed stress reliever after the shit she had been dealing with. Three days had passed since the Council laid Kieran to rest, two since Arch Mage Gréagóir had announced his idiotic plan and Liam had reassumed his post on the frontline, which now stood on their doorstep. According to the latest footage, Noarlunga resembled hell on Earth.

'Geez woman, you're a mess.' Brendan bundled her up in his arms and carried her back into their room, kicking the door shut behind him. He deposited her gently onto the bed and gazed at her with a fire in his eyes. 'You okay?' he asked with a gravelly voice.

'Depends on your definition of okay,' she rasped.

'I think someone needs to fuck your brains out, don't you?'

She nodded eagerly, beyond caring how desperate she appeared.

'Why don't you slip into something *less* comfortable while I go shower?' He kissed the crown of her head before disappearing into the bathroom.

Gods, I love that man. She made her way back to the wardrobe and considered her choice carefully. The style of lingerie she chose would set the tone for her evening. Soft satin and lace would lead to a night of love making, for example. But that was not what she needed. At the other end of the scale, she could wear nothing but her collar and hair up in a ponytail. While she was in the mood for kinky, she was not up for hardcore BDSM. So, she settled on a full-body harness and covered it with a silk robe.

Brendan appeared amidst a cloud of steam with a black towel around his waist, water dripping from his jet locks. 'Keeping me in suspense, I see.'

With a grin, she made her way over to the bed and perched on the end of the mattress. 'I know about your nightly sexcapades, when you vanish to visit Caleb.'

His Adam's apple bobbed. 'I—'

Raising a hand, she halted his words. 'It's okay. Caleb needs your love as much as I do, if not more right now. But I was thinking, we should invite him to our bed from now on.'

His eyes widened. 'Is this something you really want? Not just for me, but for yourself?'

'Yes, it is.'

Sucking in a deep breath, he marched across the room and grabbed his phone from the desk. 'Hey Red, is Thornsy with you? … Put him on, would you? … Hey man, get your pretty little arse down to my room on the double. … Only if you want to be.' He disconnected the call and dropped the phone where he found it. 'Caleb's on his way. Just to be clear, is there anything you don't want to explore in this situation? Any hard limits?'

She shook her head. 'None beyond the usual.'

He stared at her intently and she could only begin to imagine all the perverse possibilities filling his mind in that moment. A knock at the door broke their eye contact and he checked who it was before ushering Caleb into the room.

The endarkened man took three strides before skidding to a stop and gaping dumbfounded at her as she rose from the bed and dropped her robe.

'Hi Caleb,' she greeted him with a sultry voice.

He gulped, but remained frozen in place, his eyes the only part of him moving as they roamed across her figure. His own body was half bare, with only a pair of black jeans covering his soft, silver skin.

Brendan embraced him from behind and pressed his lips to Caleb's ear. 'Don't be rude now, Thornsy. Say hi to Lana.'

'Hi.' The word came out as a breathless whisper.

'Isn't she the most stunning creature you've ever seen?' Brendan asked.

'Yes,' Caleb replied without hesitation. This coming from the two men who had recently laid their beloved Bridey to rest. Her chest swelled with pride.

'I think we should show her how much you appreciate her beauty.' Brendan's hands lowered to Caleb's waistband, where he made quick work of unfastening the button and zipper before stripping him bare. When Brendan's hand wrapped around Caleb's arousal, a small moan slipped from her throat, and she dropped back to the bed. 'My filthy Lana likes to watch. Let's give her a real show.' He spun Caleb around and pushed him to his knees. 'You know what to do.'

'Yes, Sir.' Caleb unwrapped the towel around Brendan's waist and tossed it aside before taking his lover's cock between his lips.

The moment he entered Caleb's mouth, Brendan grabbed a fistful of the man's hair and fucked his face like his life depended upon it. 'Pleasure yourself, Lana. I want to hear you come when I empty myself down Thornsy's throat.'

Her hand was already halfway there, so she did not need to be told twice. Slipping her fingers between her soft folds, she delighted in the shockwave of pleasure that rippled through her core. The harder Brendan pushed himself down Caleb's throat, the more intense her body throbbed, until she was screaming out her climax.

With a grunt, Brendan released Caleb, letting him drop to the floor as beads of cum dripped in trails from Caleb's lips to the tip of Brendan's dick. 'On your feet, Thornsy. I want to see you fuck Lana's sweet mouth just like I did to you.'

'Yes, Sir.' Caleb closed the distance between them, pausing only briefly to admire the sight of her with a hooded gaze before grabbing her hair and ramming his cock down her throat. The force of it pushed straight past her gag reflex and flooded her with desire. After the treatment Brendan had given him, Caleb did not last long before shooting hot streams of salty goodness down her throat—and she savoured, every, last, drop.

'Now return the favour, Thornsy,' Brendan ordered.

'Yes, Sir,' Caleb replied in a gruff voice as he knelt before her.

She shuffled forward and spread herself wide, giving him better access as she met Brendan's eyes across the room. He looked like a God slouched against the door with his arms crossed against his muscular chest. Caleb's hands on her thighs drew her attention back to him and she caught a scent of cinnamon and cloves as he peppered kisses along her tender flesh.

'How wet is she, Thornsy?' Brendan asked.

Caleb thrust two long fingers inside her, aiming straight for her G-spot and she cried out. 'Absolutely drenched,' he confirmed.

'And how does she taste?'

Caleb's tongue trailed along her quivering lips before joining his fingers. Her eyes closed and she spasmed with pleasure as his tongue curled inside her.

'Look at him, Lana,' Brendan ordered, and her eyes snapped open. 'Look at the beautiful man who is eating you out.'

She obeyed, meeting Caleb's intense gaze, his onyx orbs burning into her soul with heated passion to rival dragon flame. A moment later, he withdrew his tongue and clamped his teeth down on her clit.

'Holy fuck!' she cried aloud as the climax crashed through her.

'She's delicious,' Caleb announced as he licked his lips.

Brendan appeared behind Caleb, tugging him to his feet by his long, obsidian locks. 'I want to taste her too.' He claimed Caleb's lips in a savage kiss.

The way their mouths made love with such raw brutality prompted her fingers to return to her aching core. They broke apart at the sound of her cresting another wave, both breathless and staring at her with ferocious hunger in their gazes. Her eyes darted between them, both men turning her on in their own way, taking her to new heights of arousal.

Brendan whispered a simple order in Caleb's ear: 'Fuck her.'

'Yes, Sir.' And like a good subbie, Caleb sprang into action, motioning for her to climb further up the bed. 'What position, Sir?'

'Lana on her back, you on top. I have plans for that delectable arse of yours,' Brendan promised in a deep voice that oozed with dark desire.

Hovering above her, Caleb traced the straps of her harness with his fingers before finding her breasts. He pinched one hard bud, then the other, squeezing them until she screamed out in a frenzied mix of pleasure and pain. One of his hands dipped between her legs, testing the waters as he clamped down on her nipple again. He grinned as she came all over his hand.

'Hot damn, Thornsy,' Brendan groaned. 'I'll make a Dom of you yet.'

Caleb grabbed her legs and raised them above his shoulders. He took a second to line himself up before sinking deep inside with a hiss. 'How are you so effin tight?'

'Because she's perfect,' Brendan growled in his ear before lifting his hands and bringing his palms down on Caleb's backside in an almighty *smack*! The impact jolted him deeper inside her and she cried out as her walls tried adjusting to his girth. 'Does that feel good, Lana?'

'Hell yes!' Especially the way Caleb's cock twitched inside her in the aftermath of Brendan's assault.

'Brace yourself, gorgeous, because you ain't felt nothing yet.' Brendan positioned himself behind Caleb, pulling him back slightly before ramming himself inside the man's tight hole. The chain reaction felt instantaneous as Caleb plunged deeper inside her and their screams rang out in a discordant chorus.

'Jesus fuck, Brendan!' she chided him. 'I can't believe you did that without prepping him. Are you okay, Caleb?'

'Ah huh,' he looked at her with glazed, unfocussed eyes.

She cast a wary glance at Brendan over Caleb's shoulders, which still supported her legs.

'He's in subspace, Lana, and he's fine. He fucking digs this shit. The rougher, the better. Don't worry about him, just focus on your own pleasure… and pain. You remember your safeword?'

'Yes,' she assured him.

'Good girl. Now run your fingernails along his back.'

Caleb's body trembled as she carried out Brendan's orders moments before the chain reaction started all over again. The intensity grew with each thrust, and she soon spiralled into her own trance-like state of euphoria. She lost count of how many orgasms hurtled through her body. There was no place for abstract concepts like time or numbers in her state of mind. All she knew was bliss. All she registered was the sensation of Caleb filling her up with his own ecstasy, until the three of them detonated in the mother of all climaxes.

They collapsed in a pile of sweaty limbs, taking a full minute to untangle themselves before settling into a spooning chain. From his position in the middle, Caleb wrapped his long arms around her. She sighed with contentment and drifted off to sleep.

Startling awake in Caleb's lead-weight arms, Alannah took a moment to register the sound that woke her. Her phone buzzed and sang from the nightstand, and she shimmied her way out of his grip. Sitting up, she gazed down upon the two men spooning beside her and smiled.

Brendan stirred and his eyes inched open. 'You want me to get that?'

'No, it's fine. Let him sleep, he looks so peaceful. Sorry if I woke you.'

'Don't be. I'm a light sleeper. Comes with the territory.' He returned her smile and closed his eyes.

Reaching for her phone, she frowned when Liam's name flashed on her screen, and a pang of dread settled deep in her gut like a heavy dose of bad prawns. 'Hey, Liam, what's going on?'

Brendan's lids flicked open, and he watched her intently.

'She's dead, Lana,' Liam sobbed down the line. 'I can't believe (sniff) she's dead.'

Every muscle in her body tensed. 'Who's dead, Liam?'

'Mum! The fucking dragons killed her,' he hollered, turning her blood to ice.

'What? How?' She gaped at Brendan, tears streaming down her face.

Brendan's brow furrowed and he sat bolt upright. 'Who died?'

She covered the voice receiver with her hand and whispered, 'Nora.'

All the colour drained from his face as he mouthed a big, '*No.*'

'You still there, Lana?' Liam asked in a choked-up voice.

'Yeah, I'm here. Sorry, I was just conveying the message to Brendan.'

The man in question snatched the phone from her and shouted, 'What the fuck happened to Mum?'

'Brendan!' she protested, grabbing her phone back and putting it on loudspeaker. *No hope of letting Caleb sleep now, anyway.*

The third member of their threesome rolled onto his back and groaned. 'What's with all the shouting, guys?'

'Who's that?' Liam asked through the speaker.

'That's Thornsy,' Brendan replied. 'Listen, dickwad, are you gonna tell me what happened, or do I need to beat it out of you?'

'Piss off, you twat. Lana, would you mind telling me why Caleb's joined the call?'

'I just put you on speaker to pacify Brendan as best I could. You kind of um… woke the three of us up.'

'Oh, dear Gods! So what, now that Bridey's gone, you're just gonna fill her spot in their twisted little menage? I thought you respected yourself more than that?'

Furnaces blazed in her cheeks. *The nerve!* 'What I do with my personal life is no longer any business or concern of yours, Liam. Now tell us what happened to Aunt Nora.'

'Dragons happened, Lana. They burnt her to a crisp, complete with free cremation.' The rage in his voice subsided into another wave of grief as sobs wracked through him.

'But how do you know... how did it happen?' she queried in a softer tone.

'I don't. Fucking. Know,' Liam spat. 'Dad saw it happen, but he's gone into catatonic shock, so we can't get any more details from him. All we know is—' he broke off in another sob. 'Mum's ashes have scattered with the wind.'

'No, she can't be dead!' Brendan screamed at the phone then stormed out of the room, slamming the door behind him.

'Shit! I need to go deal with him before he does something reckless. Stay close to your dad and look after each other, okay?'

'Yeah, okay,' Liam sighed. 'Tell him I'm sorry.'

She blinked twice as the line went dead, then raced to the door.

'Lana!' Caleb called from the bed.

Halting, she turned and stared at him. 'What did you just call me?'

He shrugged. 'After last night, I kinda figured... Am I wrong? Did I get my wires crossed?'

She shook her head. 'No, it's fine. I'm just surprised is all. What is it, Caleb?'

'You might want to cover up before leaving the bedroom, and maybe take a pair of pants for Brendan,' he suggested.

Glancing down at her near-naked body, she cursed under her breath and marched over to the wardrobe. She slipped into a nightgown and robe before grabbing a pair of Brendan's trackpants. Then she bolted out of the room, following the trail of plaster debris from where he had punched the wall several times along the way. *Fuck that must have hurt, given how solid these old walls are.* She couldn't recall ever seeing him this unhinged and it worried her.

Neve stuck her head out of her room as she passed. 'What's going on, Mum? Why did Dad just do a nudie run down the corridor like a raving lunatic?'

'Hey honey. Now's not a good time to explain. I need to mediate your dad's mood before he does something we'll all regret.'

Glaring, she stood tall with her hands on her hips. 'You're not breaking up with him, are you?'

'What? No!' She sighed. 'Someone special to your dad just passed away and he is struggling with his grief, okay?'

Neve's eyes bugged out. 'Grandma! Was it grandma?'

'How?' she gaped at her daughter.

'I saw it happen, in my dreams earlier. I thought it was a nightmare.' An edge of panic filtered through Neve's voice.

'I'm sorry, baby, but I really need to tend to your dad right now. Why don't you go up to the attic and hang out with Jacob and Amy? Just make sure you knock on the door first, okay?'

Neve rolled her eyes. 'I'm not stupid. I've heard what they get up to in there. So much for soundproofing.'

She cringed, feeling like the worst mother on Earth. She had meant to question Jacob on that matter, but it slipped her mind, and she stopped caring, figuring it was just petty revenge from when she'd forgotten to erect her own sound wards with Brendan. But all this time, her poor daughter had been subjected to every filthy sound. 'Remind me to fix that tomorrow, will you?'

'Whatever,' Neve huffed as she pushed past and headed towards the attic.

Alannah found Brendan on the bench swing that hung from the Moreton Bay Fig. He sat in a daze, just staring off into space with glazed eyes. She held the trackpants out to him like a peace offering. 'Thought your arse might get splinters on that old thing.'

He took her offering and balled them up in his lap. 'You know, this was where it happened?' His voice sounded cold and distant.

'Where what happened?'

'The last time my world fell apart, you were sitting right here.'

'Brendan—'

'Only, I didn't really lose you, did I? I just thought I did. And it's not like you died.' He glanced at her with eyes misting over.

Her heart broke. Sitting next to him, she placed a comforting hand on his shoulder and waited for him to continue. But he didn't speak; he just curled up in her lap and cried his heart out. She didn't try to shush him like a child, nor did she console him with meaningless platitudes. She just wrapped her arms around him and let him grieve.

He sniffled, wiping his nose on the pants that were meant to provide a modicum of modesty. 'I can't remember the last time I told her I love her. I was such a shitty son.'

'Do you recall what your mum did when you first returned here after all those years?' she asked. When he stared at her blankly, she continued, 'Nora welcomed you back with open arms and told you how much she missed you. Remember?'

He nodded, tears pooling in his eyes.

'And you hugged her back with all the love words simply couldn't convey. She knows.'

'Still, I must have been quite the disappointment. I can't imagine her proudly boasting about her boy becoming the Boss of the Dark Syndicate,' he spat bitterly.

'I doubt that mattered to her. Nora was a smart woman. She likely surmised you had your reasons, just as I did. Liam told me something interesting the other day,' she began.

'First time for everything,' he huffed.

She fought the urge to roll her eyes. 'He pointed out that while he knew he was always Ross' golden boy, you were your mum's favourite. The more I thought about it, the more I tended to agree. Nora loved you unconditionally with all her heart and she had every faith in you, even when no one else did.'

He collapsed into her arms and turned into a blubbering mess again. This time, she stroked his hair until he fell silent. 'I probably can't attend the funeral, huh?'

'Not unless you pull off that glamour trick with Danny again,' she agreed.

'It won't fool dad though.'

'I don't think Ross will fault you for attending your own mum's funeral. You might just need to keep your distance, is all.'

'Nah, I think it's safer if I avoid the limelight. I can still grieve her at the wake, right? Shit!' He sat up in a panic. 'How are we supposed to do a proper wake without her remains?'

That had not even occurred to her yet. 'I'm sure we'll find a way,' she assured him.

Chapter Twenty

The pumping bass of Dance Heart Cult rang out from Neve's phone, interrupting her spiral of depression. She pounced on the device and answered Erik's call with a little too much enthusiasm. 'Hi, where are you?' She had been expecting him for their date ten minutes ago.

'At your front door, but I'm afraid to ring the bell. I'm sensing some seriously dark vibes in your place right now. It feels like a thick smog is about to swallow me up. Are you okay in there?'

'Honestly? No,' she squeaked, trying her hardest not to crack under the weight of her own grief. 'My grandmother passed away.'

'Oh Gods, I'm sorry, sweetheart. If you let me, I'd like to comfort you. May I come inside?'

'Yes, of course! I'll be right down.' Hanging up, she checked her reflection in the mirror and touched up her makeup before sprinting downstairs. She swung the door open and flew into his arms. Squeezing her tight, he kissed the crown of her head and she melted. After a full minute, she took his hand and led him upstairs.

He glanced at all the closed doors along the corridor. 'I guess your parents are too absorbed in their own grief to concern themselves with supervising our date.'

Reaching her bedroom, she turned her back to the door and peered into his eyes. 'Or maybe they trust you now.'

He laughed. 'About as far as they can throw me, I'm sure.' He gripped his chin between his thumb and finger, feigning serious thought. 'Although come to think of it, that would be pretty far if they employed magic.'

She giggled at the thought of her mother drop-kicking Erik across the peninsula.

His expression turned serious. 'I appreciate the vote of confidence, sweetheart, but it would take a miracle for your folks to trust any Seelie — especially your old man.'

'Well, I don't see them trying to stop you from entering my room,' she huffed, opening the door and ushering him inside for effect.

He arched a brow before accepting her invitation. 'Defiance is a sexy look on you, Neve — so long as you're not disobeying me that is.'

She gaped at him. 'What makes you think you're the boss of me?'

Kicking his shoes off, he made himself comfortable on her bed and propped himself up on his elbows. 'Our betrothal contract, for one; and when you marry me, I'll own you, heart, body, and soul.'

'That doesn't mean I have to obey you without question.'

'You can question me, sure, but at the end of the day, my word is final. Now get your pretty, little butt over here so I can hold you.'

Her feet carried her to the bed despite herself and she crumpled in his arms. 'And what if I defy you when we're married?'

'Then I'll bend you over my knee and turn your arse cheeks red.'

Jolting her head upright, she gawped at him. 'Are you for real?'

'Absolutely.' He traced a finger along the crook of her neck, bringing goosebumps to the surface. 'Who knows, maybe you'll enjoy it.'

She shivered, unable to fathom how she could take pleasure from such a humiliating punishment.

He tucked her under his chin, holding her close to his chest where she could feel his heart thumping strong. 'You have much to learn, sweetheart, but don't worry about any of that now. We have years to prepare for our future. How are you feeling?'

'Like a dragon plucked me up in its claws and dropped me from a great height. Have you ever lost a beloved family member?'

'By lost, I presume you mean to death?'

She nodded.

'No, fortunately. About the closest I've come is Elna turning her back on us.'

'I'm sorry I came between you,' she mumbled against his shirt, a crisp white button down. 'She's your twin, so I imagine her betrayal must sting like a bitch.'

'It does,' he sighed. 'But don't be sorry, my sweet pea. Your love means the world to me. Besides, today is about *you* and making *you* feel better.'

'And how do you hope to do that?' she grumbled.

Cradling her chin, he gave her a sly grin. 'I have a few tricks up my sleeve. Would you like to see?'

She nodded.

He held his wrists out for her. 'Go on then.'

'I didn't think you meant that literally,' she replied on a laugh.

Waggling his brows, he extended his arms further under her nose.

Taking the hint, she unbuttoned his cuffs and peeked under his sleeves, finding nothing but the shimmering gold of his faerie skin.

His forehead creased. 'Hmm, I must have put them inside my collar. Better check in there.'

Undoing the top two buttons, she peeked inside, still coming up blank.

'Damn, they seem to have slipped down.'

Waking up to his game, she bit her bottom lip and gazed into his twinkling eyes. Button by button, she unfastened his shirt, exposing the toned muscles on his chest. 'Nothing here; maybe they fell into your pants.'

The glimmer in his eyes burned brighter. 'You're welcome to check.'

Sucking in a breath, she unbuckled his belt and unclasped his chinos, his arousal already straining for release. One leg, then the other, she slid his pants free and returned her attention to his bulging Y-fronts. 'Perhaps they're in here?'

He chuckled, deep and throaty, then in a flash, he flipped her onto her back, drawing a squeal from her. 'I just remembered that I left them here.' He pushed his palm against her apex and desire flooded her core. 'Should I check?'

She nodded.

'What was that sweetness, I didn't hear you?'

'Yes, please,' she pleaded breathlessly.

Pulling her leggings down, he tossed them aside. Pausing, his gaze travelled up and down her body, then he tugged at her tunic. 'I'd better remove this too, just to be safe.'

Raising her arms, she let him strip her down to her white lace panties.

'Virginal white looks good on you,' he observed with a throat full of gravel.

She gulped, wondering if her newly restored virtue would be safe when they were so hot for each other.

Hovering above her, he whispered against her ear, 'Don't worry, my love, I would never do anything to jeopardise our future happiness.'

'I'm not sure I trust myself, though. I want you so bad right now.'

A wide grin filled his face. 'There are other ways to make love without compromising your hymen. Would you like me to show you?'

'Yes please.'

As Brendan rolled over in bed, his stomach grumbled, and he sighed. 'I suppose I'd better feed the damn thing.'

Alannah planted a chaste kiss on his lips. 'You two stay here. I'll go make us some breakfast.'

When the door clicked in place, Caleb slipped an arm around Brendan's waist and pressed up against his back. 'Did you manage any sleep at all?'

He entwined his fingers with Caleb's. 'Not really, but I'm sure you can relate.'

Caleb's fingers combed through Brendan's hair. 'Very different circumstances, though.'

'Grief is grief. We might all process it differently and the relationships we lose may be vastly different, but that doesn't make what any of us feel less valid.'

'That sounds like psychobabble from your counselling days,' Caleb scoffed.

'Would you believe there was wisdom to be found in that stuff? I guess what I'm trying to say is that I know you're still hurting over Bridey and that's okay.' He turned onto his back and pulled Caleb against his chest.

'Would you listen to yourself, Winters? You just lost your mum and you're still trying to be the strong one here. Why don't you let me comfort you for a change?'

'What do you think this is, Thornsy? Just having you in my arms is comfort. Looking after you brings peace to my soul.' He chose not to mention all the ways Alannah had eased his pain; it did not seem like the time to bring her into the conversation.

'What about Lana?' Caleb asked, as if reading his mind. 'You didn't hesitate to take the comfort she offered you.'

No avoiding the topic now. 'The dynamics of my relationship with Lana are very different and… complicated because of who and what we are.'

'Because you are soulmates,' Caleb suggested.

Sinking his hand into Caleb's scalp, he threaded his fingers between his locks and gently tugged, knowing how much the gentle hair pulling would relax him.

Caleb yielded with a groan.

'It's true that Lana is my soulmate,' he explained. 'But there's more to it than that.'

'What are your long-term plans with her, if you don't mind me asking?'

He understood the thinly veiled meaning in Caleb's question. 'I don't know. There are too many forces at play. The only thing I know for certain is that I want you to stay in my bed and my heart for as long as we both live.'

Caleb sucked in a breath and sat up, peering down at him. 'Do you really mean that?'

'Of course. Having Lana back in my life doesn't lessen my love for you.'

'Even after everything I did to you both?' The smoky cloud of grief in Caleb's aura darkened, showing the guilt he felt for his part in the plot to keep Brendan and Alannah apart.

'Come here.' He summoned Caleb back into his arms and waited for him to settle before continuing. 'I know you did it out of love and I forgive you for that, so please let it go.'

Caleb's body trembled with silent sobs.

'I can't help but wonder,' he mused, 'if I'd listened to you and Bridey, if I'd maintained my distance from Lana, would Mum still be alive?'

'What?' Caleb gaped at him with tears welling in his eyes. 'Are you crazy? The dragons killed her. Liam said as much.'

'You heard the man: he was iffy on the details.'

Caleb shook his head. 'Levi's dead; besides which, he gave you a month. That gives you time to come up with a plan.'

'Exactly, Levi's dead. Chances are we are dealing with another agent of my enemy, and he probably has different rules. I can't keep risking people's lives for my own selfish desires.'

'Stop blaming yourself for Bridey's death. The only people responsible are the arseholes who killed her. Don't let this cowardly enemy of yours keep you and Lana apart anymore. You belong together.'

'That's easier said than done. What if they take Neve next?' They fell silent and his thoughts wandered into some dark places. 'Have you ever killed someone, Thornsy?'

'I've squashed plenty of insects in my time, but not people. Why?'

'I think that's what defines true innocence. Not if, or when you've had sex, but if you've sent someone's soul to the eternal hereafter. Even if you justify the reason, killing another person changes you: it hardens your heart and darkens your soul.'

Caleb shifted to look into his eyes. 'Is this about Levi? You never did tell me what happened there, and Lana only gave me the CliffsNotes.'

'I've fought in a few battles over the years, so his wasn't the first life I'd taken, but it was the first time I've truly enjoyed killing. First there was the thrill of snuffing his wretched life from his filthy body, then came the euphoric satisfaction of knowing I had succeeded in my revenge plot. Does that make me a bad person? Has Set permanently tainted me?'

'You're no worse than me,' Alannah proclaimed as the door swung open. She entered carrying a silver serving tray piled high with steaming food. 'We took that man's life together and I enjoyed it as much as you did if the sex that followed was anything to go by. So no, I don't think it had anything to do with Set.' She placed the tray on the desk and offered him a plate. 'I prepared a full Irish breakfast for you and a vegetarian one for Caleb. Come and eat.'

After chowing down on her own Irish breakfast, Alannah excused herself. 'I wish I could stay in bed all day with you both, but there's still a war going on and my High Magus duties never end.'

'Way to make me feel like a useless sloth, Lana,' Brendan jibed.

'I'm not—' just as she started trying to explain her meaning, Brendan's lips curled up and she glared at him. 'You're the worst. Truly despicable.'

'But no worse than you, apparently.'

Rolling her eyes, she strode out of the bedroom and headed for the office. *At least Brendan is in good humour again, even if he is using it as a defence mechanism.* She paused outside Neve's room and peeked inside. Her heart melted at the sight before her: Neve and Erik holding each other beneath the quilt, snoring faintly, and to top it all off, Luna curled up at the foot of the bed. 'Too cute.'

Neve stirred. 'Mum?'

'Shh, it's okay hun, go back to sleep.'

'Kay.' Neve inhaled a deep breath and snuggled closer to Erik.

Closing the door gently, she continued down the stairs. After firing up her laptop, she opened her inbox and found an email from her boss marked as IMPORTANT.

> *Attention Mage Leaders of the World,*
> *Preparations have been made to lift the veil hiding the magic world from humans. In ten days, I will be meeting with one of the humans' most powerful military leaders to begin negotiations. Please prepare your forces for the possibility of working alongside human soldiers.*
> *Regards,*
> *Arch Mage Gréagóir Callaghan*

A knot formed in her gut as she thought about how the human world would react. *I need to do something and fast.* Glancing at the headset on her desk, she grabbed it and set up a video conference, inviting all the Council leaders on her contact list who she trusted.

'There has to be something we can do to stop him,' she insisted. 'Not only do we risk the witch trials all over again, but there's also the very real danger of a nuclear holocaust.'

'We could motion a vote to veto his decision,' suggested one of the mages from the UK. 'But I don't fancy the backlash from presenting the results to him.'

'I'll do it. I'm not afraid of Callaghan,' she lied. Truth was, the man terrified her, but she refused to let fear get in her way.

Several gasps crackled over the line and one of the Irish men chuckled. 'It's your funeral, new blood.'

'It might be everyone's funeral if no one acts!' she fumed. 'Isn't it ironic that the only woman among the lot of you has the biggest balls here.' They all fell silent. *Bunch of cowards, the lot of them.*

'We'll vote in favour of keeping the veil in place if you assume responsibility for the motion,

Councillor Winters.' This from the UK mage who suggested it in the first place.

'Fine, send me the administration details I need, and I'll set it up.' She disconnected the conference call by slamming her fist on the keyboard and throwing her headset down in disgust. 'The world is doomed.'

'That sounds like a defeatist attitude,' Brendan remarked as he barged into the office.

She jumped, cussing under her breath. 'You can't just waltz in here while I'm working. What if I was still in a video chat?'

'Please give me some credit, Lana. I waited for the conference call to finish.' He perched his backside on the edge of her desk.

Her eyes narrowed on him. 'You were eavesdropping on Council business?'

He shrugged. 'Old habits die hard, I guess. When were you gonna tell me about the Arch Wanker's plans to lift the veil?'

'When I tell everyone else. Our sleeping together doesn't grant you early access to privileged information.'

'Maybe not, but don't you think becoming partners for life trumps all that?'

Rising to her feet, she stood before him, her eyes darting across his face. 'Is that what we are now?'

Dropping to his feet, his hands gripped her shoulders. 'Are you telling me you don't feel it? The soul link, I mean?'

Sucking in a lungful of air, she tried to steady her breathing while focussing on her soul, on what she felt deep within herself.

'I didn't come here with intent to spy on you, Lana.' His right hand moved up to cup her chin. 'Your anguish beckoned me, drove me to seek you out and comfort you.'

'But how?' she whispered.

'I don't know how this ancient magic works, but I'd guess it has something to do with all the time we've spent together lately. Does the how really matter though? Fact of the matter is, our souls have reunited.'

He spoke the truth. She felt that deep sense of companionship she had lost all those years ago when Bridey had severed their connection. She felt emotions that she couldn't reconcile with her own mood. To test his theory, she pinched him and felt the sting in her own arm.

'Ow, what d'you do that for?' he complained.

She smiled. 'You're right. Our soul link is complete.'

'Of course I'm right,' he huffed. 'You didn't have to go and prove my point by abusing me.'

She slapped him playfully, relishing in the echo on her own flesh. 'Don't be such a wimp.' Her smile turned into a full-fledged grin, and she leaped on him. 'This is amazing news. Do you know how happy this makes me?'

His arms flew up to support her as her legs clamped onto his waist. 'Ah, yup,' he laughed. 'Soul link, remember?'

She kissed him deeply, then pulled away when she registered his anxiety. 'What's wrong?'

Placing her carefully on the desk, he clamped his hands on her shoulders. 'I love you more than life itself, Lana, but this soul link could complicate things.'

'What? Why?' her own nerves began to jitter.

He dropped his forehead to hers. 'Levi may be dead, but we shouldn't take his threats lightly. Not to mention the meteor-sized conflict of interest we face in our professional lives.'

She jerked back and stared at him with wide eyes. 'Are you saying you want to leave me?'

'No, absolutely not! But what I want and what is right find themselves at odds yet again. Say for argument's sake, we stay together and our enemy picks off our friends one by one. What then? Do we continue living together, pretending that our selfish choices aren't killing the people we love? What happens when he targets Neve?'

Large salty tears dropped from her eyes and splashed on her cheeks. 'There has to be a way around this. I can't live without you in my life again, Brendan. I just can't do it.'

'Ah fuck! I'm sorry, gorgeous. I came in here to comfort you and only made you feel worse.' He wrapped her in his arms and peppered kisses along the top of her head. 'I guess I felt like I needed to voice the turmoil plaguing my thoughts before you read it on my mind anyway.'

'There must be a way to hide our relationship. Surely your Syndicate has ways and means. Can't they make anyone disappear?'

His pierced brow arched. 'You know that normally means killing people, right?'

She sighed. 'I mean the way the Unseelie are good at vanishing, even from each other. Ghosts, remember?'

'Right, of course. I'll see what I can arrange.' He forced a smile that did not reach his eyes. 'I'm sorry for letting you doubt me. My head's been a mess lately. Kinda hard to think straight.'

'I get it, Brendan. There's been too much death and destruction in our lives. We will work this shit out together, okay? Please just promise you won't go AWOL on me again.'

'Promise.' He sealed the deal with a deep kiss.

Chapter Twenty-One

Liam followed his father, who carried a small blue and orange ceramic urn close to his chest that held his mum's remains within. Fortunately, his dad had managed to scoop up some of her ashes before all of them scattered in the wind. Liam's own hands were full of white lilies which he carried into Cailleach Estate. Brendan greeted them from his seat beside their mum's bed with a silent nod. The wide antique dresser already looked like a beautiful shrine thanks to the fragrant red blooms and framed photo of Nora's smiling face. Her wake[12] had officially started.

As Ross placed the urn on the dresser, he regarded the vase of flowers with a sour expression. 'What are these doing here?'

---

[12] This period of grieving lasts for three days prior to the funeral, during which time close friends and family visit to pay their respects.

'Brendan put them there,' Liam explained.

'They're gardenias, Mum's favourite,' Brendan reminded him.

'Get rid of them!' Ross demanded.

Brendan gaped at him. 'But—'

'I said, get rid of them. Now!'

Liam put his own massive floral arrangement beside the urn. 'What's the big deal, Dad? It's not like they'll clash with the lilies and there's plenty of room—' The menacing look in Ross' eyes hushed him, so he gathered up the bunch of gardenias. 'Brendan, can I speak with you outside?' Once Brendan joined him in the hall, Liam closed the door. 'Here, you may as well put these in your room. No point letting them go to waste.' He handed the flowers to Brendan. 'Dad seems especially touchy right now and I don't think your presence is helping. You should probably keep your distance from him.'

Brendan glared ice-cold daggers. 'Are you seriously kicking me out of my own mother's wake?'

'No, Brendan,' Liam let out an exasperated sigh. 'I just think you should give Dad a little space is all.' Last thing any of them needed was a full-blown row.

'And how am I supposed to do that while still paying my respects to Mum? You know what? Never mind. I'll go drown my sorrows with people who give a shit. It's not like I need a few lumps of ash to mourn the woman who gave us life.' Brendan shoulder-checked him on the way past.

'You don't have to be a dick about it,' he called after Brendan. 'Just give Dad some time, then I'll let you know when the room is clear.'

Halting a metre down the hall, Brendan spun on his heels and scowled at him. 'Who are you calling a dick? If anyone deserves that title, it's Dad. You know, I'm glad I got to be Mum's favourite because it means you're stuck with the arsehole parent.' He stormed off down the corridor until he reached his room and predictably, slammed the door.

Welcome home, Mum! Returning to the wake room, Liam sat beside their father and placed a comforting arm over his shoulder. 'I'm sorry about Brendan.'

'Why?' His dad asked. 'Not like it's your fault he's a devil child.'

He shook his head, unable to fathom the extent of his dad's hatred for Brendan. The guy had been a royal pain in the arse, sure, but he was still family.

Brendan placed his mother's favourite flowers on the dressing table in his room.

Alannah hugged him from behind, filling his nose with her sweet strawberries and musk fragrance. 'I thought you got these flowers for your mum.'

He grunted. 'I did, but Dad freaked out when he saw them and demanded that I get rid of them.'

'Curious.'

Turning in her embrace, he wrapped his own arms around her. 'I know it's weird. Dad's being especially asstastic at the moment.'

She shook her head. 'No, I mean his issue with the gardenias in particular is strange, because they…. No, I'm sure you're right. Ross is probably just having a hard time processing his grief and he's taking it out on you.'

He studied her for a moment until the doorbell rang. 'Now the wake officially begins, I guess.'

'You want me to get that?' she asked.

'Yeah, but I'll join you. I want a drink.' He followed her downstairs and briefly watched her greet Cara and the others who had returned from the garrison before making his way to the kitchen.

He reached for a top shelf whiskey, only to watch it disappear from his clutches as Ross confiscated it.

'I was saving that for a special occasion,' His father griped as he put the bottle aside on the breakfast bar.

'Don't you think celebrating Mum's life counts as special?' He yanked the bottle back across the bench.

'Of course I do, but I'll be the one drinking this.' Ross slid the bottle back to his side. 'You've stolen enough from me over the years.'

It sounded as though someone hit the mute button on the din in the front hall and he sensed several sets of eyes watching him. Not that he cared. 'It's not like you *gave* me anything, least of all your love.' Snatching the whiskey, he clutched it close to his chest.

Ross rose to his full height, towering over him by a few inches. 'That's it! I want you out of this house. Better yet, I want you out of this town.'

'Well, that's too bad, 'cause I ain't leaving, not without Lana.' He shuffled around the breakfast bar, putting it between them and spotting Liam at the other side of the kitchen.

'Alannah doesn't even belong to you!' His father's face turned red as he slammed his fist on the bench. 'She's married to Liam.'

'Only on paper,' he retorted. 'They don't want each other anymore. Liam's even found himself a new love—isn't that right bro?' He looked to his brother, goading him for an intervention.

Liam sighed. 'It's true, Dad. I've fallen in love with Saoirse.'

Ross gaped at Liam. 'Who on Earth is Saoirse?'

'Actually, she's more like under the Earth, or below sea level anyway,' Brendan mused.

Liam glared at him. 'Do you mind letting me explain?'

This should be fun. 'Go right ahead, I'll grab the popcorn.'

Liam turned back to their father. 'Saoirse is a mermage.'

Ross' brow furrowed. 'Don't be ridiculous, son. There's no future to be had with a mermaid.'

'Mermage,' Liam corrected. 'And I've already undergone the transformation. Once this war is over, I intend to retire to a life in the ocean.'

That red face turned purple. 'You cannot be serious!'

'Oh, I'm deadly serious,' Liam deadpanned.

'So you're just going to abandon your family and shirk your Council responsibilities?' Ross asked incredulously.

Brendan sniggered. 'This is too good. The Golden Boy falls from grace. Now that I think about it, that would make an awesome movie title.'

'Shut it!' Ross ordered.

'Fuck off, Brendan!' added Liam.

'Fine. I'm done with this bullshit excuse for a family anyway.' Marching out of the kitchen, he grabbed Alannah with his spare hand and dragged her toward the back door. 'Come on, let's use the guest house.'

Cara cornered him on the way out and he halted before barrelling into the fiery redhead. 'It's good to have you back, Brendo.'

'Don't mess with me right now, Hughes. I'm really not in the mood.'

'I honest to Gods mean it. Bring it in, big boy.' She opened her arms wide.

His brows skyrocketed from his face. 'I thought I represented everything you despise?' *Her words, according to Jacob.*

'That was before I knew the truth. Now where's my hug?' She invited him with beckoning hand gestures.

He shot a questioning glance to Alannah, who gave him an encouraging nod, so he accepted Cara's embrace.

'I'm sorry about your mum,' Cara whispered. 'That woman was a saint. She didn't deserve an early grave, but at least she died honourably.'

'Thanks, Cars,' he choked out, drowning in another wave of emotion. Pulling free of her grip, he surveyed the group rallying around him. The only living people missing from his old clique were Caleb and Jacob. Even Nick, Ben, and Bianca had shown up to pay their respects. Retrieving his phone from the pocket of his jeans, he flicked his spymaster a quick text: COME JOIN US FOR A DRINK IN THE GUEST HOUSE. BRING THORNSY AND NEVE.

His friends made themselves at home in the cosy living area, Cara taking one of the couches with her lovers, who included Ben at this point. Amy sat in an armchair with Connor on a beanbag at her feet. Bianca gave Brendan a hug before settling into her own beanbag, leaving the sofa bed for him and Alannah.

When Caleb entered, he paused to take in the scene. 'Well fuck! I didn't know we were due a high school reunion.'

Brendan shrugged. 'Apparently, they don't hate us anymore. Now get your arse over here.' He patted the spot next to him and Caleb snuggled into his side.

Jacob beelined for Amy, squeezing his backside into her chair and throwing an arm over the backrest. Connor did not so much as bat an eye.

Finally, Neve appeared with the cat in her arms. 'Luna loved Grandma too. I didn't think she'd want to miss this.'

'Good thinking, honey,' Alannah agreed. 'Come join me.'

As Neve curled up in Alannah's lap, Luna scurried under the entertainment unit, hiding such that only her bright blue orbs were visible.

Looking around the room, a few tears pooled in Brendan's eyes. 'Ah shucks, I'm feeling warm fuzzies and shit.'

Alannah squeezed his leg in a show of support before casting a sound ward over the building. 'I thought it might be nice if we all shared a memory of Nora.'

'And drink to her memory,' he added, waving the stolen bottle of whiskey. *No, not stolen. I won this fair and square.*

'Would you like to start?' Alannah asked him.

'Probably best, before I turn into a blubbering mess.' He cast his mind back to all the times his mum patched him up after he got into a fight, usually with Liam. Memories of her laughing and chatting with him as she prepared meals came flooding back. But one moment stood out above them all. 'I'll never forget my initiation. Mum beamed with so much pride that day. She looked stunning in her velvet gown—Winters blue rather than Maher orange—bringing out the colour in her eyes. As the ritual drew to a close, she knelt in front of me and said, "You are destined for greatness, my little prince. There will come a time when your magic saves the world, and you will go down in history as one of the best mages of all time." I knew she was just saying what any proud mother would at their kid's initiation, but it warmed my chest and filled my heart with love.' Holding up the bottle he added, 'Cheers to Mum!' He took a long swig of the whiskey, savouring the burn in his throat, before handing it to Alannah.

'It's hard to pick just one memory. Aunt Nora's cooking and decorating prowess could have rivalled Martha Stewart. I guess one moment that has stuck with me is the time she discovered the soul link Brendan and I had just formed. I'd never seen her so happy. That was also the day we

adopted Luna from her clinic. Cheers to Nora!'
Alannah drank a large mouthful before handing the
whiskey to Neve.

Their daughter blinked twice at Alannah,
then at the bottle. 'I think I might have the coolest
mum ever.'

'Don't get used to it, princess,' he affirmed.
'And we're not about to let you get lit.'

She gave him a melodramatic pout before
sharing her own memory.

The stories continued well into the afternoon,
even after they finished the first bottle and started
on a second. Alannah conjured a bunch of snacks at
one point, to soak up all the alcohol, most of which
she resisted after her first swig. When he returned
to the sofa with the third bottle, she leaned in and
whispered in his ear, 'We should tell them about the
threats, while we have them all here.'

'Can you trust them all?' he asked.

She nodded. 'With my life, although it's
theirs at risk.'

'Then go for it.'

She reinforced the sound wards and cleared
her throat. 'Excuse me guys, there's something
important Brendan and I need to share with you.'
They all looked at her expectantly.

'This better be good news,' Cara implored. 'We could use a little merriment to give us a break from all the doom and gloom.'

'It's mixed news, I'm afraid,' Alannah replied with a simper. 'Before I say any more, I need you all to swear to secrecy as if your lives depend on it, because it very well could.'

With wide eyes, they all promised to keep their mouths shut.

'What's going on, Mum?' Neve asked in a frightened voice.

'Someone is trying to split your dad and me apart again, and he's threatening to hurt the people we love.' Alannah explained the whole situation, starting with Caleb and Bridey's part in their initial separation and how Levi manipulated them. She touched briefly on Bridey's death, sparing them from the grisly details, then mentioned how Levi got what was coming to him. 'We don't know who our real enemy is, or what his beef with us is, although we have our suspicions. I can't tell you too much about that and the less you all know, the better, for your own safety.' Pausing for breath, she searched his eyes for the reassurance she needed.

He took her hand and finished the explanation for her: 'Lana and I have mended our soul link and we do not intend to separate ever again. That said, we don't want to put any of you at risk, so we are devising a strategy to hide our relationship from the world. We can't guarantee it will work and much of our plan will rely on you to maintain the façade for us. If the prospect of dying from your association with us freaks you out too much, then I recommend getting the hell out of Dodge right now. We won't hold it against you.'

The room fell silent and a few of them fidgeted. Cara rose a moment later. 'We just got you back, dickwad. Don't think for a second that you're getting rid of us that easily.'

Jacob stood next. 'I've always got your back, Boss.'

'Ditto,' added Caleb with a sly grin as he slid a hand under Brendan's backside to cop a feel.

Amy stood beside Jacob. 'You guys have offered me refuge; I'm not about to turn my back on you now.'

'I second that,' Connor added as he stumbled to his feet. The half mage had drunk just as much as Brendan with half the constitution for it. It amazed him that Connor could stay upright at all.

Nick strode across the room and pulled Brendan into a bear hug. 'Anything for you guys. It's good to have you back, bro.'

'I ain't going anywhere.' Bailey hiccupped. 'And not just 'cause I can't get up.'

Caleb snickered. 'Good thing Cara has Nick and Ben to service her.'

Nick smacked the back of Caleb's head. 'Watch it, you.'

'Careful,' Brendan warned, observing the pink flicker in Caleb's aura. 'Thornsy's already half hard for you.'

'Mm, now there's some M/M action I'd love to see,' Bianca drawled from where she draped herself across a beanbag. When all eyes turned to her, she laughed. 'Hey, you know me, Brendo: I'm down for anything, even if it means risking my life.'

He nodded, thinking it would be fun to invite Bianca over for a foursome sometime, then chuckled when Alannah's thoughts replied with a *'Yes please.'* The wood nymph was skilled enough in the art of seduction to turn even the straightest women gay.

Glancing at Ben, he waited for the last of his friends to join the cheer squad.

'I'll keep your secrets so long as they don't pose a threat to my pack,' Ben conceded.

'That's fair,' he agreed. 'Now who's up for another drink?'

In the wee hours of the morning, Alannah
navigated the maze of sleeping bodies on the floor
of the guest house. It put her in mind of the parties
they used to host back before life threw her a curve
ball. Once inside the main house, she snuck through
the hall and quietly made herself a cup of tea to
avoid waking anyone with the coffee machine.
Armed with a steaming mug of caffeine, she
entered the Winters' family library. She had rarely
used the space, finding most of the magical tomes
she needed in the cellar. As for the fiction books,
they were not exactly to her taste. Not a single title
from the last hundred years sat on the dusty
shelves, so there was no chance of finding anything
by Anne Rice, Charlaine Harris, or L.J. Smith. Even
the classics like *Dracula* were bound in hard cover,
making them far too uncomfortable to curl up with.
But none of that mattered to her in this moment.
She was on a mission to unravel the mysteries of the
prophecy and hoped to learn some more family
history along the way.

Browsing the spines of the old paper
volumes, she stopped as one caught her attention.
The Hidden Meanings of Flowers. Thinking back to
Ross' violent reaction to Nora's favourite blooms,
she snatched the book and flicked through the
pages until she found a section on gardenias. She

skimmed through the introduction that focussed more on the white variety and gasped when she reached the paragraph on the red ones:

The red gardenia symbolises secret love. It can be gifted to a secret lover to assure them of one's affections. Alternatively, a secret admirer might use them to proclaim the extent of their feelings.

She snapped the book shut and returned it to the shelf, losing herself in thought. *Does that mean Nora had a secret admirer, or did she perhaps have an affair?* Her head reeled with the possibilities, and she briefly considered summoning Nora's spirit to ask outright before dismissing the absurdity of it. *Conjecture over the woman's love life is hardly grounds for a séance.* Instead, she focussed her attention on searching for the information she was seeking.

Hours later, when the words started blurring together and the frustration was wearing her thin, Brendan found her slumped over the reading table. He slid his hands over her shoulders and started massaging them. 'Come on, gorgeous, it's time to eat. I've cooked breakfast.'

Chapter Twenty-Two

Cailleach Estate was already swarming with people who had trailed Neve's family back from Nora's funeral, which followed the three-day wake. Erik took her hand and squeezed it as they entered the living area. He looked scrumptious in his black suit. Returning the gesture, she smiled at him. 'Thank you for going with me today.'

'No problem at all, my love. Besides, someone needs to look after you since your parents are otherwise pre-occupied.' He spoke with a bitter edge to his voice.

'It's not like they've completely neglected me. Mum has a lot going on and Dad... well he couldn't risk being seen in public.'

He shook his head. 'Doesn't matter. Parents should always put their children's needs first.'

'You sound a little salty there. Sure you're not projecting your own daddy issues?'

'This has nothing to do with my parents.' He pulled her closer and spoke in her ear. 'I promise that you will always be my number one.'

Warmth flooded her chest and she felt herself falling further for her faerie prince. 'Unless we have kids, right?'

One side of his mouth lifted, and his voice turned to gravel, 'Are you saying you want my babies, sweetheart?'

Gasping, she slapped his arm lightly while trying to ignore the fire between her legs. 'Must you always think about sex?'

'Hard not to with you on my arm,' he rasped.

Biting her lip, she considered stealing him away to her room, but at the same time, she didn't want to appear rude by skipping out on her grandma's funeral reception. 'Excuse me a moment, I need to freshen up in the bathroom.' *And take a cold shower*.

He nodded, a knowing glint in his emerald eyes.

After taking a moment to centre herself, she touched up her makeup and returned to the gathering. Even more bodies filled the space, and it took a second to spot Erik by the bar across the room. She started sifting through the crowd toward him, halting half-way when her mum's blue-haired friend sought him out. Bianca was a Seelie enchantress, like Erik, although her complexion was that of a woodland nymph: tanned skin with iridescent green leafy vine markings weaving across her arms and legs. Unlike Erik, she did not hide her aura and there was no mistaking the shades of lust that encompassed her. Curious to know how Erik would react, Neve hid behind a curtain and channelled senses mana to eavesdrop on their conversation.

'Well, hi there, handsome. I don't believe I've seen you around these parts before.' Bianca's voice sounded deeper than usual.

His gaze roamed over her scantily dressed body. 'No, I don't believe I've had the pleasure, nymph.'

Bianca's fingers trailed up his arm. 'Perhaps we should do something about that.'

Ick! Talk about a cougar! Neve needed to exercise every scrap of willpower to stay rooted in place and not give in to the temptation to rip the hair from Bianca's head.

'As a Seelie Prince, I could offer you a position as a concubine at court. You'd need to audition first, of course.'

Bianca licked her lips. 'Of course.'

That's it! She began to jostle her way closer, pausing only when she sighted her saviour. Hugh entered from the nearby kitchen and offered her a comforting smile. If he were any more radiant, they wouldn't need electric lights. If she didn't know better, she'd think him a distant cousin to Erik. *He'll make the perfect distraction.* Returning his smile, she linked arms with him. 'Hugh! It's so good to see you.'

'Likewise, Neve. Please accept my deepest sympathies for your loss.' His deep, British accent certainly went some way to ease the ache in her chest.

'Come with me.' She started dragging him across the room. 'There's someone I'd like you to meet.'

'Certainly. Any friend of yours is a friend of mine.'

Damn, he's smooth. If she were any older, Erik might have some real competition. Reaching the guy in question, she maintained her grip of Hugh's arm and stroked his muscular bicep with her spare hand. 'Hi sweetie. I'd like you to meet Hugh Doran.' She gave herself a figurative pat on the back when Erik's gaze homed in on her hands and his jaw clenched. 'Hugh's a bona fide hero for saving my dad's life.'

'You give me too much credit,' Hugh protested. 'I merely used my magic to heal him.'

'Don't be so humble,' she insisted with a flirtatious giggle. 'Your healing magic achieved what even my grandpa's could not. Anyway Hugh, this is my boyfriend, Erik.' She released her grasp to facilitate their handshake.

'Wow, that's quite a grip you have there, young sir,' Hugh observed as their hands released.

She glanced at Bianca, finding the woman staring in awe at Neve's angel. *Bingo!* 'Oh, and Hugh, this is Mum's *old* friend, Bianca.'

The moment Hugh's eyes met Bianca's; they lit up brighter than dragon fire. 'A nymph, if I am not mistaken?'

Erik tugged Neve into a possessive hold and growled in her ear, 'What do you think you're playing at?'

Batting her lashes, she gave him a demure smile. 'Nothing.' Then she turned her attention back to Hugh, who was kissing the back of Bianca's hand.

'From what I understand,' Hugh went on, 'a nymph's beauty only grows with age, so that must make you a lady of considerable years.'

Bianca laughed. 'Oh, you are quite the charmer.'

'Come with me, *now*!' Erik demanded in a low, threatening tone as he pulled Neve away from Hugh. Once they had crossed the room, he stopped and glared into her eyes. 'Don't you ever dare flirt with another man again, especially not in front of me.'

'I was only giving you a taste of your own medicine,' she countered.

His eyes opened as wide as suns, then he chuckled. 'I see how it is. My girl is jealous.'

'Don't laugh at me! You were blatantly flirting with that blue-haired hussy. How else do expect me to feel?'

Grinning, he embraced her and whispered in her ear, 'Don't worry, my love. Nymphs are good for one thing and one thing only.'

'Is that supposed to make me feel better?' she muttered against his stupidly hard chest. 'The thought of you hooking up with that old skank makes me sick to the stomach.'

'That's a shame because I kind of fancied the idea of watching her make you come.'

Spluttering, she choked on her own disbelief. 'Bianca is old enough to be my mother—possibly yours too.'

'Which makes her young for a nymph,' he explained.

She gaped at him.

'What? We Seelie folk live long lives. You know what your envy tells me?'

'What?' she snapped.

'It tells me that your feelings for me are very strong. If I'm honest, I find it a little sexy.' His hand drifted down her spine and cupped her backside. 'Is it too early to leave the party?'

Heat pooled in her core as a wave of desire surged through her nerves. 'Probably,' she rasped. 'But let's go anyway.'

The morning after Nora's funeral, Alannah found Liam packing a suitcase in his room. 'We need to talk.'

'Sounds ominous,' Liam replied, glancing up from his folding. 'What's up?'

'A few things. Can we meet in my office?'

'Fine.' He followed her downstairs and took a chair opposite her desk. 'This seems rather official, Your Honour.'

She collapsed into her own seat with a sigh. 'There is some Council business to discuss, but first I have a personal matter I wanted to address.'

Leaning forward, he planted his elbows on the desk. 'Go on.'

'As soon as this war is over, I want a divorce.'

Jolting back into his chair, he snarled at her. 'Pete's sake, Lana. I only just laid my mother to rest, so to speak. Do you think this conversation could have waited?'

She shook her head. 'There's never a good time for a conversation like this, Liam. I need to know that we're on the same page. Separation is one thing, but divorce is another.'

'At this rate you'll be a widow anyway, so it's unlikely you'll even need to file for divorce,' he scoffed. 'How much longer are you going to hide away with your politician friends? We could really use your help on the frontline.'

'Actually, that brings me to my next matter of business.' Leaning back, she steepled her fingers beneath her chin. 'I have every intent on joining the frontline once I clear up a political issue that has the mage community up in arms.' She explained the Arch Mage's plans to lift the veil, and the veto vote she had called for.

His eyes grew wider with each syllable. 'Damn, that's heavy stuff. I'm sorry, Lana. I had no idea you were dealing with such a shitshow.'

'That's one way of putting it. I had no idea the Council was full of so many spineless twats.

Callaghan instructed us to prepare our forces for working with the human military. I'm hoping the vote will prevent the need for this, but just in case, I want you to break the news to the troops, so it doesn't come as a shock if the army rocks up on our doorstep.'

'Yeah, okay. Let's pray it doesn't come to that.'

'Do you think the Gods can help us with this one?'

He shrugged. 'They tend to stay out of our wars and politics. That said, lifting the veil on the magic world is a pretty big deal. It might raise a few Celestial eyebrows.'

'Fair point,' she mused, staring off into space as she considered how to get the Gods on side.

'I'll do it.'

'Hmm, what?' she asked, breaking free of her trance.

'If we both survive this war, I'll file for a divorce with you. I was planning on returning to the sea anyway, so I may as well cut the last of the tethers holding me to this place.'

Breathing deeply, she practically tasted the winds of change drifting between them. 'Thank you, Liam.'

'Does this mean you intend to marry Brendan?'

Her heart swelled at the thought. 'We haven't talked about it yet, but it's not impossible to imagine. We have mended our soul link.'

He nodded. 'I figured it was only a matter of time. I still promise to rip that man a new one if he breaks your heart again.'

She shook her head. 'I wish you guys would put your differences aside and just be brothers for once.'

'I don't think we know any other way to relate. The resentment and rivalry are rooted too deep in our souls. When we weren't competing for our parents' attention, we were fighting over you. I'm ashamed to admit that I sensed your deep connection with him at an early age and it fed the green-eyed monster deep inside me, so I made it my mission to steal you away from him. When you returned to Gaeilge Shores, I even made him believe he wasn't good enough for you, which wasn't hard considering the self-destructive path he was already on.'

His confession knocked the air from her lungs. 'Does that mean you never really loved me? Was I just a pawn in your twisted game?'

Shooting forward, he grabbed her hands. 'No! It wasn't like that. I've always loved you, Lana. What I meant to say is that I'm sorry for keeping you and Brendan apart for so long. If I wasn't so driven by hatred and jealousy, I would have left you both to your own devices, to let your souls find each other despite my own feelings for you.'

'Sounds familiar,' she mumbled under her breath. *Was Liam just a cog in the enemy's machinations?*

'What did you say?' he asked.

'Nothing. Look, I appreciate the apology, and your honesty for that matter, but I think it would be best if we put the past behind us. I can't deal with all the what ifs right now, not while I'm trying to stop a global catastrophe and win a war.'

'Suits me,' Liam conceded. 'Just tell me how I can help.'

The dying rays of dusk filtered through the sheer curtains behind Amy's bed, bathing her in golden light that softened her hard edges. The copper highlights in her hair glowed with a radiance that almost rivalled the fire in her hazel eyes as she stared upon her intruder. Jacob slouched against the doorframe, crossing his arms over his chest as his eyes feasted on her beauty. She had stripped down to her underwear by this point and was about to unclasp her bra when he invited himself into her room. 'Please, don't stop on my account, although I'd prefer if you took the show to the attic. My bed feels cold and empty without you.'

She sighed and dropped her hands to her sides. 'We can't keep doing this, Bennett. The more we fuck each other, the harder it will be to stop when I return to Connor.'

He stalked toward her. 'Who said we have to stop?'

'It wouldn't be fair to him. I love Connor deeply and I won't do anything to sabotage our relationship.'

Something cinched in his chest as he closed the distance between them. Twisting his fingers through strands of her fiery locks, he tugged her head back, lifting her gaze to his. 'Your Bunny appeared perfectly happy when I had my hands all over you the other night. Seems to me like he might have a cuckold fetish. Have you ever considered that possibility?'

'Yes, but I—'

'Stop making excuses, shorty. And stop fighting what you feel. I for one am sick of denying my feelings for you.'

Emotion swirled in her eyes. Rather than give her a chance to back down from the truth, he kissed her smart mouth with the full force of his love. In the short time they had spent together at Cailleach Estate, he had grown more certain that his heart wanted her, and not because of her resemblance to Cara. Amy Smith set fire to his soul in a way that no one else had. He burned for her and if she asked, he'd set the world aflame for her. He tried to convey all this and more as his lips melded with hers. She moaned, granting his tongue access to her minty mouth and he rewarded her with languid strokes. Desire surged south and he dropped to the bed, pulling her into his lap and groaning as she ground herself against his arousal. 'Tell me how much you want me,' he demanded.

Grabbing his hand, she slipped it inside her panties. 'Feel for yourself,' she replied in a voice as gruff as his.

He slid his fingers through her slick folds and hummed. 'As much as I love how wet you feel, I want to *hear* how much you want *me*. Not just my dick, but all of me.'

'Fuck!' she hissed as his thumb found her clit. 'You expect me to string fucking words together when… Oh Gods… when you do this to me.'

Easing his fingers back, he peered deep into her eyes. 'There's really only one word I need to hear from you, and it starts with L.' She gasped, her lips parting slightly, and he took the opportunity to stroke her bottom lip with his thumb, the one coated in her own desire. 'Don't be afraid to say it, shorty, because I feel it too.'

'You better not be messing with me,' she warned.

'Did that kiss feel like a joke to you?' Pushing her, he slammed her back into the mattress and straddled her. 'Now tell me.'

Biting her lip, she shook her head.

The pain in his chest amplified, so he tugged her bra cups down, exposing her nipples, and clamped one of them between his teeth.

'Oh fuck!' she screamed, her flood of arousal soaking through his own pants.

Diving between her legs, he ripped her panties away and fed on her sweet juices. He brought her close to the edge, then stopped. 'Tell me,' he growled. When she refused to admit her feelings, he worked her up towards a climax only to rob her of it again.

'Stop edging me, arsehole,' she shrieked.

'Then tell me how you really feel about me,' he countered.

She glared at him, her breathing frantic and shallow. 'Why do I have to say it aloud?'

'Voicing it makes it real, Amy.' He traced his fingers along her clenched jaw. 'It will mean tearing down the last of your emotional wards and letting me in. I know it seems like the scariest thing in the world right now, but I promise you can trust me.' Grinning, he added, 'And when you do say it, I'll make you come harder than ever before.'

'Fine!' she spat. 'I love you and your stupid fucking arse! Happy now?'

'Ecstatic,' he beamed. 'Because I love you too, short stuff.' He then delivered on his promise.

Chapter Twenty-Three

Smug satisfaction emanated across the barrier to Alannah's office and Brendan grinned. *That's my girl.* After tapping lightly on the door, he let himself in.

She beamed up at him. 'All votes are in, and the majority voted to veto the Arch Mage.'

'I never doubted you could pull this off. Have you sent the results to Arch Wanker yet?' He perched his backside on her desk, a hair's breadth from the mouse mat.

'I have now,' she replied after one click of her mouse. Then her expression sobered. 'With that out of the way, I'm ready for the frontline.'

'Not before a good long ride on my cock, you're not.' He doubted he would feel ready to say goodbye ever again. The pain of separation would likely kill him, and he wasn't the one who would need to concentrate to save their own life.

Eyes misting over, her hands slid up his thighs. 'I'll miss the hell out of you, Brendan, but please don't worry about me. I can handle myself out there and as for the soul link separation issue, I mentioned that to Hugh, and he has a painkiller for us.'

'Huh, an analgesic for the soul. Sounds like a song by the Eels.'

She snorted. 'Don't ever lose your sense of humour, babe.'

'No chance.' He flashed her a toothy grin that turned heated the moment she leaned forward, her t-shirt gaping and revealing her cleavage. The view combined with the pressure of her grip on his upper thighs unravelled his train of thought, sending it way off course. He slid his hand along the polished timber of the desk before knocking it. *Feels as hard as me.* 'You ever done it on here before?' he asked, waggling his brows. 'You know what, don't answer that. I really don't need to think about all the places my brother fucked you.'

She rolled her eyes. 'I assure you this wasn't one of them.' Her fingers walked toward the fly of his jeans and slid the zip down, all while holding his gaze.

It took considerable effort to block out her thoughts. Foreplay was more fun when she kept him guessing. The moment her hand touched his dick, he hissed and threw his head back. Even through the silk of his boxer shorts, her fingers teased his sensitive flesh. Unfastening the buttons, she freed his arousal and took it in her firm grip, pulling a groan from his diaphragm.

'Does that feel good?' she asked in a gruff voice with her lips against his ear.

'Uh huh,' he rasped. Peeling his eyes open, he peered into the green flames blazing in hers.

'Looks tasty.' She dropped to her knees and licked the bead of precum from his tip.

'Fuck!' His head swam and he needed to grab her hair with both hands to steady himself. The scent of strawberries wafted through the air, driving him that little bit closer to divine madness. Her velvet tongue circled his crown, the gentle friction sending waves of desire through his nerves. Then she flicked his piercing and pleasure jolted him like an electric shock. 'Dammit, Lana. You're killing me here.'

'I'm sorry.' She batted her lashes. 'Would you like to take control?'

'By the Gods, I love you, woman.'

She grinned. 'I love you too, Sir.' Her mouth lowered onto his cock, taking him deep into her throat.

Unable to resist her invitation, he tightened his grip of her locks and fucked the prettiest face to ever walk the Earth. Consumed by a frenzy, he catapulted toward his climax, exploding into millions of stars that scattered across the galaxy of his own universe. Blinking, the real world came into focus and he gazed upon her smile. 'Holy fuck, Lana. You better get your sexy arse up here so I can return the favour.'

Shaking her head, she returned to her chair. 'I want to hear what you were planning to tell me before you got too sexed-up to think.'

He chuckled. 'Right, of course. Jacob found an underground safe house for us. The only way to access the place is via stygian portal magic.'

'Really? That sounds perfect.' She leaped into his arms and kissed him passionately.

'There's a catch though,' he explained on a sigh. 'To ensure security, the portals require blood magic. My soul's already damned, so it doesn't bother me, but I don't want to condemn you to an afterlife of eternal torment.'

'Better that than an eternity without you. Our souls are linked, babe. Do you honestly think they're going their separate ways when we leave this mortal realm?'

Searching her eyes, he read the truth they conveyed even without reading her mind. 'I guess I never thought of it that way.'

'Who knows, maybe blood magic is like channelling nether.' At his blank look, she added, 'Not innately evil. It's the way you use the magic that marks your soul.'

'Perhaps. Unlike stygian magic, however, it is still illegal,' he pointed out.

'Then I'll just have to bribe my organic mana councillors to keep their mouths shut,' she suggested with a sly grin.

'I love the way you think, gorgeous.' Sliding off the desk, he lowered himself to the floor and spread her legs wide. Her skirt rode up her thighs, revealing her black lace panties. 'Now shuffle forward and let me rock your corrupt world.'

Approaching the garrison with Hugh at her side, Alannah surveyed her army hard at work in the training grounds.

Danny walked out from a shed, greeting them with a wave before jogging across the lawn to join them. 'Hey, Ya Honour.' He leaned in and kissed her on the cheek before presenting his hand to Hugh. 'Sup, Councillor.'

'Hello, Danny.' Hugh shook his hand formally, earning a disappointed sigh.

'We need to work on your fist bumps, bro. Come on guys, I'll show you round.' Danny led them back to the shed. 'This is the armoury.' Shelves upon shelves filled the space, each covered in weapons and armour, all imbued with stygian magic. A door at the other end of the shed opened into the main building and they followed the corridor until he revealed a vacant bedroom. 'Your lodgings, milady. You can dump your luggage here unless you want to bunk with me.' He winked.

She snorted. 'I think Brendan's been rubbing off on you.'

'Nah, this is just me, doll. You'll get used to it.' He gave her a moment to drop her suitcase beside the wardrobe before taking them to the adjacent room. 'These are your digs, Doran.' Slapping the timber frame for effect, he waited for Hugh to disappear within before whispering in her ear, 'You can find me across the hall if you get lonely.'

A leggy blonde sashayed up to them. 'Hey Danny Boy, we still on for tonight?' Glancing at Alannah, she did a double take. 'Oh hi, Your Honour. Sorry for the intrusion. Please excuse me.'

She hurried away, drawing Danny's eye until she vanished around a corner.

'Looks like you'll already have company,' observed Alannah.

He shrugged. 'The more the merrier.'

'We are here to prepare for battle, Erling.' Liam appeared from his own room, chiding Danny. 'We're not here to participate in orgies. And I doubt High Magus Winters appreciates the unsolicited flirting. She's not one of your floozies.'

Standing to attention, Danny saluted Liam. 'Yes, sir. Apologies Your Honour.'

She gaped at Liam.

'You're dismissed, Erling. I'll finish giving Alannah the tour.' He gestured for her to follow him.

'You needn't be such a wet blanket, Liam.'

'This is war, Lana. The troops need discipline to maintain order and work as a cohesive unit. We can't win if everyone does their own thing.'

'And what about morale?'

'That comes from success,' he replied. 'Something we're severely lacking at the moment.'

Her brows rose to accommodate her wide eyes. 'Even with the stygian gear?'

'Even with the gear. The troops are lacking direction, going off all half-cocked.'

'That's what I sent you here for. You were supposed to lead us to victory.'

'That's what I need to discuss with you. In here.' He opened a door to a large boardroom. 'This is the war room.'

Stepping inside, she surveyed the maps lining the walls, a far cry from the technology at the old garrison. Then she recalled hearing how the dragons had destroyed most of the mystic cameras that streamed to the Holo-Map. At the sound of a lock clicking into place, she turned back to Liam. 'What's going on?'

'They're not buying your story about me seeking help from the merfolk. As soon as someone discovered my gills, they labelled me a deserter.'

'But Danny—'

'Put on a show for you. You still have their respect, Lana. They will follow *you*, which is why we need *you* on the frontline.'

'I've only ever fought in small scuffles before. I have no idea what to do on a large battlefield.'

'That's where I can help.' Flicking off the lights, he turned on a projector that illuminated the far wall.

'What's all this?'

'A lesson in combat tactics. Grab a seat.' He pointed toward a chair.

Spotting a whiskey decanter, she allowed herself one nip and settled in for the lecture. By the end of his presentation, her head throbbed, and she was massaging her temples to ease the pain. 'I'm never going to remember all that out on the field.'

'Then I guess you'll just have to keep me close. If we share a tent, we can talk strategy between skirmishes.'

Glaring at him, a dry laugh escaped. 'You devious bastard. I see what you did there.'

'Trust me, Lana. It's safer if we maintain the ruse. We're still married in the public eye. As for those who know the truth, they're not going to question your reasons for keeping up appearances.'

'Brendan will throw a fit when he finds out.'

'Or he'll thank me for keeping you safe from a mob of horny soldiers who want a piece of the world's first female High Magus.'

She shook her head. 'Unlikely. He's more jealous of you than every other man on this planet combined.'

'We're just sharing sleeping quarters, Lana. It's not like we'll have sex.'

'You better not try anything,' she warned.

'You have nothing to worry about. I wouldn't betray Saoirse.' Switching off the projector, he rose and turned the lights back on.

Raising a hand to her eyes, she shielded them from the fluorescence. 'Can I think about it?'

He heaved out a sigh. 'You have until tonight.' Storming over to the door, he paused and glanced at her over his shoulder. 'Oh, and Lana? Don't make the mistake of falling into Danny Erling's bed. If you do that, you'll *lose* everyone's respect and then we're all fucked.'

She shot up from her chair. 'What the hell, Liam? Do you have so little faith in me?'

'Yeah, actually, I do. We were legit married when you screwed around with one of Brendan's doppelgangers because you missed the real thing. What's to stop you doing that again?'

'How about the fact that "the real thing," as you put it, is waiting for me at home?'

Turning on the spot, he crossed his arms and scowled at her. 'Spare me your incredulity. I know Brendan doesn't subscribe to monogamy and neither do most of your friends. You've also made no efforts to hide your ongoing sexual relations with Caleb, so sue me if I have reason to believe your promiscuous behaviour will continue here.'

'I don't expect you to understand the lifestyle, Liam, so I'll explain something to you. Being sex positive is all about choice. I do *not* open my legs to everyone.' She stood tall before him.

'And let me make something else clear. I am your boss, and you *will* treat me with the respect I deserve.'

He held her gaze for a long, torturous moment before grinning. 'See, now you get it, Your Honour.'

Opening the email from High Magus Winters, he read her beautifully constructed words and smiled:

> *Arch Mage Gréagóir Callaghan,*
> *In light of your breach of protocol, we have taken it upon ourselves to vote on your proposal to lift the veil and seek military aid from the humans. I have attached the detailed results for your reference, but to summarise: an 80% majority of The Council has voted to veto your decision. Please heed these results carefully because failure to do so will lead to a vote of no confidence in accordance with Section 8.3 of the Magical Constitution.*
> *Kind Regards,*
> *High Magus Alannah Winters*

Excitement simmered in his blood as he read and reread her message. *I simply cannot wait to become personally acquainted with you, Lady Winters.*

He recalled the video conference when he caught her lustful gaze and lascivious thoughts. *If Gréagóir Callaghan impressed you then, my lady, you will love what you see in the flesh when we finally meet.* Pushing his own libidinous musings aside, he closed the email and dialled his newest political ally.

'Mr. Callaghan! How are you?'

Cringing, he let the lack of social graces slide, reminding himself that humans did not *yet* understand protocol in his world. 'Greetings Mr. President. I am well, thank you.'

'Ah, that's great to hear. How's the weather over in Ireland?'

'A little too warm for March, thanks to the dragons.'

The President nodded. 'Sounds familiar. I assume you have news on that front?'

'Indeed. Everything is ready on my end. Have you organised my meeting with the United Nations?'

'Sure have. I've even taken the liberty to arrange a live broadcast of the whole thing. That ought to get your message across.'

He grinned, imagining the look on Lady Winters' face as she watched the whole thing unfold. 'Perfect. I will see you tomorrow in New York City.'

'See you then.'

With business taken care of, he let his mind return to more pleasurable thoughts, like visions of Alannah Winters on her knees before him.

Chapter Twenty-Four

Rows upon rows of houses stood abandoned, nothing more than burnt-out husks, ghosts of their former selves. Bricks crumbled away from timber and steel frames like flesh rotting from skeletons. The decaying structures betrayed echoes of their former glory, giving glimpses of happy families running through their halls and lounging in living areas. Luckily, Alannah had not seen any human remains as she sifted through the ashes of these suburban ruins. More than likely, the former residents had evacuated before the dragons decimated their homes. The advancing mage army used the broken buildings as partial cover while approaching the great beasts circling the skies. 'Where do you suppose they all went?' she asked as she pushed a door aside, watching it split away from its hinges and fall to the floor.

'The humans?' Liam tested the integrity of the floorboards before easing his way into the room.

'A bunch of them probably ran as far south as they could get, knowing that the apocalyptic rains, as they are calling them, have not yet struck there. Others would have gone underground if they had access to bunkers or out to sea if they owned boats, while others, the less fortunate folk, would have died in the fires.'

An almighty roar boomed through the ruins and the ground shook beneath their feet. Glass crunched under her boots as she dashed across the room and looked out through an empty window frame. A green dragon approached from the north. 'I think we caught their attention!' she hollered to the troops behind her. 'Ready your weapons and fire on my command!'

Liam dropped beside her and loaded his bow with a spell-breaking arrow. 'One, two, three.'

'Fire!' She watched hundreds of tiny missiles sail into the air, a few striking the dragon's shield. 'Reload and fire damage-based projectiles at will!' The volley that followed struck the beast in several places, but they all bounced off its scales.

'We need to wait until it comes close enough to aim for vulnerable spots,' Liam explained.

'Tell me when.' She held her breath, waiting as the dragon flew closer, unable to hear much beyond the blood pulsing in her ears.

'In one, two, three.'

'Fire!' This time several arrows struck the belly of the beast and it plummeted to the ground. 'Swordsmen!' she commanded, pulling her own blade from its sheath, and watching in horror as the injured dragon crashed through houses like a wrecking ball, heading straight for them.

She charged the creature, taking a flying leap for its throat. Anticipating its mind tricks, she veered left when it feigned an evasive manoeuvre to her right and struck her target dead centre.

Cries of victory sounded for a moment before a gust of wind knocked several soldiers on their arses as another, larger dragon with silver scales trampled the lot of them.

'Oh shit! Where the fuck did he come from?' she screamed. 'Take down that bastard's shield *now*!' More arrows whizzed through the air, destroying Silver's forcefield. Unfazed, it stomped toward her, sending tremors through the ground as it opened its mouth and lobbed a ball of primordial flame. 'Down!' They all hit the floor and let the fire sweep over them. *Thank the Gods for stygian armour!* Another fireball, then another blazed over their backs and she wondered how much fuel these damn dragons had in their guts.

'We can't stay here,' Liam warned, shouting directly in her ear. It was the only way she would be able to hear over the firestorm. 'These floorboards will catch alight any minute, and that dragon will be in melee range soon after that.'

'Agreed. Magiport retreat!' She jumped the ley lines back to the nearest nexus and waited for the troops to regroup in an empty field. A cloud of smoke on the horizon pinpointed Silver's location and that cloud was hot on their heels. 'Formations!' she yelled with faux confidence. 'What the hell do we do now?' she asked Liam in a whisper.

'Without access to its belly, we need to aim for the eyes. That means getting a sniper up high.'

She swept her arm around the wide-open space. 'Right, because there are so many sniper nests to choose from.'

He shook his head. 'If I'm careful, I can sneak into those buildings to the west of him.'

'Are you crazy; I'm not sending you on a suicide mission.'

His mouth quirked. 'Good to know you still care.'

'Of course I still care about you, Liam. You're family. Now who's our best sniper?' When his brow arched, she corrected herself, 'Second best sniper?'

'Harvey,' he replied, pointing to one of their archers.

She beckoned Harvey over with a wave, but just as he reached them, Danny intercepted. 'We've got more incoming, Your Honour.' He pointed to the shadows approaching from the east.

'Harvey—speak to Liam while I prepare everyone else for the next wave!' She barked orders left, right, and centre, making herself dizzy as she spun about amidst the sea of soldiers. *Or maybe that sulphurous stench is making me queasy. Wait, why can I smell*—whipping around to the west, she spied a humanoid army with red glowing eyes marching toward them. *Demons?* A grin crept across her face when she thought of their most likely source. *Thanks for the assist, Brendan.* She watched with fascination as hellfire poured from their hands, burning their foe to a crisp.

'Yikes! Talk about fighting fire with fire,' Liam mused.

Yet no sooner had she rolled her eyes, than another surprise thundered over the hill. Someone or something lead a battalion of tanks toward them.

A man in green camouflage jumped out of one of the armoured vehicles and approached her. A human, she could tell by his muted aura: far less intense than any magic wielder. 'Excuse me miss.

Can you please direct me to the mage in charge here?'

Her heart stopped for one microsecond before kicking back into full throttle. 'You're looking at her. Who are you? And better still, how do you know about mages?'

'You must be High Magus Winters. It's a pleasure to meet you. I'm Major Frank Fitzwilliam.' He bowed as though she were royalty.

'Ah….' Words failed her.

'We are here to offer any assistance we can against the dragons,' Fitzwilliam explained like it was the most natural thing in the world.

The penny dropped. *The fucking nerve of that arsehole.* 'Conventional modern weapons are no good against a magical threat. You should just focus on getting your own people to safety.'

'Them nukes in the US worked just fine.'

She gaped at him. 'You know what? Have at 'em. We'll leave you to it.' Turning on her heels, she strode toward her troops. 'Mages, retreat to base!'

'What?' Liam snapped at her. 'You can't just l—'

'Shut it, Liam!'

'He's right, Your Honour. You can't just leave,' Fitzwilliam echoed.

'I can and will,' she countered.

'The Arch Mage won't be pleased with your desertion,' Fitzwilliam pointed out.

'The Arch Mage can suck my massive lady balls!' She stormed away and followed her troops back to base.

As soon as Liam appeared on the lawn in front of the garrison, he marched up to her. 'What the hell are you doing, Lana? Those humans have no idea what they're up against. We can't just leave them to fend for themselves.'

'Did you fail to hear what Major Idiot said about the US having deployed nuclear weapons? We are heading for a global disaster and I for one don't fancy being at ground zero when the humans start bombing our state.' Searing hot rage burned in her blood as she strode into the building.

Appearing out of nowhere, Hugh halted her in the hall. 'Excuse me, Your Honour. We have a situation—'

'Damn straight we do,' she cut in.

'Please, may we talk in private?'

Sighing, she led him to the war room.

As Liam entered, Hugh's brow furrowed. 'Apologies, Councillor, but if you don't mind—'

'Liam stays,' she asserted.

Hugh eyed Liam warily as he sat next to her. 'I am sure you will appreciate my concern after what he did to Brendan.'

Liam growled. 'Forgive me for getting a little protective of my *wife*.'

'I understand that is a mere technicality these days,' Hugh retorted.

'It wasn't back then,' Liam pointed out. 'Even now, we are still *family*.' He did not need to verbalise the underlying threat in his tone.

'Liam will only retaliate if someone physically attacks me. You are safe, Hugh.'

'Very well. I wanted to discuss the situation with the humans using weapons of mass destruction.' Hugh hovered by the shuttered window.

'Go on,' she prompted.

'As you are likely aware, such measures pose a huge threat to the environment and this is something my kindred will not tolerate.'

Hairs prickled the back of her neck. 'Your kindred?'

'I am not what I led you to believe I am.' Hugh's eyes flickered, and the slits narrowed to a more reptilian shape.

A chair crashed to the floor as Liam leaped to action, prompting her to hold out an arm to stop his advance. 'You're a spy?' Liam asked in a menacing voice, reminding her of the years he had devoted to the Council as a warlock.

'Not exactly.' Hugh stood straight, towering above them, and she could have sworn he grew six inches taller. 'When I first encountered Danny Erling, I glimpsed a spark of promise, one suggesting that mage kind are not as corrupt and selfish as we first suspected. That is why I transformed and rescued him from my line of fire.'

She gasped. 'You're the dragon from Mount Schank.'

'Yes, I am,' Hugh affirmed. 'I apologise for the deception, but it was the only way to gain your trust and learn what I needed to know.'

'What, like our weaknesses?' Liam huffed.

She glared at Liam a moment before returning her attention to Hugh.

Hugh shook his head. 'I learnt that Lady Winters and Brendan are the key to restoring balance to the magic world, to fulfilling an ancient prophecy. This gives me hope enough to grant amnesty to your kind.'

Liam's jaw dropped. 'Lana, I can see, but Brendan? The only prophecies I see him fulfilling are his own destructive ones. That guy—'

'Zip it, Liam!' She scowled at him. 'And don't you dare speak a word of this to anyone, especially not your father.' Once he slumped back into his seat, the tension in a few of her muscles eased. 'What do we do about the humans?' It felt strange to think of them as such a distinct race from her own when only twenty-one years ago she identified as human.

'On behalf of my kindred, I offer a peace treaty to mages and humans alike.'

Her chest began to flutter. 'Are you in a position to speak for the other dragons?'

'Yes. We are in constant telepathic communication. I assure you the others are on board with this proposal. There will be… conditions, of course.'

She nodded. 'Of course. I can hardly expect you lot to renounce the cause you've been fighting for.'

Hugh's lips curved into a slight smile that did not reach his spooky eyes. 'I am glad we are, as you say, on the same page.'

Finally, an end to this madness appears possible. Alannah exhaled a massive breath of relief as Liam led Hugh out of the room, leaving her alone to make the necessary call. Opening her laptop, she connected to the secure conferencing app and dialled the Arch Mage.

Callaghan's arrogant smirk appeared on the screen before her. 'Morning, Lady Winters; or should I say, evening?'

'Evening, Your Grace.'

'My sources tell me you have withdrawn your forces from the war. First your husband, and now your entire army deserts.' Shaking his head, he clicked his tongue.

'You have some nerve,' she fumed. 'If you hadn't violated the constitution, we wouldn't need to prepare for a nuclear holocaust.'

He laughed. *The arsehole actually laughed.* 'Needs must, Lady Winters. And before you threaten me again with a vote of no confidence, you can save your breath. I intend to retire once this war is over.'

She gaped at him. 'You're unbelievable, Callaghan.'

'More than you know, Lana.'

Her brow furrowed at his gall. *How dare he address me so informally!*

'I could say the same for you,' he retorted on a grin.

She stared at him with wide eyes, in awe of his ability to read her mind from the other side of the world. 'Stay out of my head!'

'Oh, but it is such a marvellous place to venture.' His eyes glimmered and his smile turned crooked. 'Are you going to tell me your good news, or do I need to fish it out myself?'

After erecting the most powerful mind shield possible, a horrific memory wormed its way into her mind. *He read my thoughts when I was lusting after him.* 'A dragon has contacted me, proposing a peace treaty with us and the humans. I wish to discuss the terms with you and the UN.'

His eyes lit up brighter than dragon flame. 'I knew you could pull this off, Lady Winters. You will make an excellent Arch Mage one day.'

Her jaw hit the floor. 'You're kidding, right?'

'Not at all. Why do you think I paved the way for your election to High Magus? Your little lobby group stirred waves, my dear. Waves too big for me to ignore. I did my research and discovered that the world's most powerful mage is currently a woman.'

'A female High Magus is one thing, but Arch Mage? Don't you have to stay single and avoid tying yourself to commitments like children? The magic world will never allow women to give up our roles as mothers for the solitary life you lead.'

'Change is afoot. You are already more powerful than the current pool of candidates for my seat, all of whom have lived like monks… and to what end? You have proven that dedicating your life to magic alone does not achieve the results we had assumed it would,' he explained. 'But I digress. We can discuss your future promotion once this nasty business with the dragons draws to a close. I am currently in New York City, and I would be delighted to make your acquaintance at the UN headquarters. I'll arrange a portal for you at once.'

'But portal magic is forbidden,' she gasped.

Leaning forward, he lowered his voice. 'Only to plebs who cannot be trusted with such power.' He tapped his nose and winked at her. 'I think you will find there are very few limits to the magic you can use when sitting on top of the world.' His words sent a shiver down her spine. 'I look forward to sharing what I know when you join the Arch Mage Academy.'

'What makes you think I'll—'

'Oh, I know you can't resist an opportunity like this.' He gave her a knowing smile.

Alannah had never *seen* a portal, let alone travelled through one before. Some of the arcane texts she had read mentioned them and their forbidden nature, but none of these books described the experience. Brendan likely possessed more detailed accounts within his Syndicate library since the Unseelie were the only people she knew of who used them. This was due to the use of nether, a mana source that until recently had been outlawed completely. Even after she decriminalised stygian magic in her own state, the Arch Mage had restricted its use to conjuration and combat. Apparently, portals were too dangerous.

Standing before the glimmering tunnel of hellfire, she was beginning to understand why. To teleport across time zones, she needed to traverse the Underworld, a realm where space and time operated differently. She wished Brendan were there to see it, but then she supposed he would get a chance once they moved into their new home together.

'Are you sure this thing is safe?' Liam asked from beside her.

'Hell, no!'

'Ha! Nice pun.' He gave her a cheesy grin and she rolled her eyes.

'I will protect Lady Winters from any unforeseen threats in the Underworld,' Hugh assured them. 'I am no stranger to the realm.'

'Plus, if anyone attacks me, you can go full dragon on their arse, right?'

Hugh nodded. 'Right.'

Liam pulled her into a hug, whispering in her ear, 'Please take care. I don't want Brendan sending me to an early grave for getting you killed or kidnapped.'

She chuckled. 'There was a time when he feared you. How the tables have turned.'

Liam's brow creased. 'I'm not afraid of him, I just appreciate how much stronger and more powerful he has grown since taking over the Syndicate.'

'Uh huh. Anyway, I promise to be careful.' She stepped back from his embrace and glanced at Hugh. 'You ready?'

'Yes, Your Honour. I will take the lead, to assess the situation and defend you against any threats.' Hugh entered the portal, his silhouette shimmering like the heat distortion on a summer's day.

She followed him through a passage lined with flickering light beyond which she glimpsed a volcanic landscape. 'What is this stuff?' she asked, reaching out to touch the speckles.

'Don't breach the forcefield,' Hugh warned. 'It might break the portal and we could get lost trying to find our way back out.'

She jerked her hand back and hurried after him. Given the horrendous state she had found Caleb in when she rescued him from the Volcanic Pits sixteen years ago with a summoning ritual, she did not fancy spending more time in this realm than necessary. About a hundred metres later, they reached the other side, stepping out into another form of hell. The city she had only ever seen in movies or television shows had fallen. The once majestic metropolis was nothing more than smoking ruins. All that remained of the United Nations headquarters was a burned-out husk. Tears welled in her eyes. 'Are we too late?'

'Fortunately, these humans had the foresight to build underground,' Arch Mage Callaghan explained as he stepped out from the shadows.

She took a moment to marvel at his powerful aura before straightening. 'Greetings, Your Grace.'

Taking the hand she extended, he turned it over and kissed her knuckles while maintaining lascivious eye contact. 'It is a pleasure, Lady Winters.'

The intimate contact heated her cheeks, and she suppressed the urge to sink to her knees and beg him for a spanking. Clearing her throat, she gestured to Hugh. 'This is Sir Doran, Golden Custodian of Mount Schank.'

After revealing his true identity and proposing the peace treaty, Hugh had spent some time explaining dragon society, including their proper forms of address.

Callaghan looked him up and down. 'Quite the effective glamour you have there. You look like a mage to me.'

'It is not a glamour,' Hugh explained. 'I physically transformed my shape, much like one of your shamans.'

With a nod, Callaghan led them toward a manhole. 'This is the best way to access the bunker.' After walking through a short stretch of the sewer system, they came across a large, round, metallic door. He tapped a sequence that could have been morse code for all she knew, then he stepped back to allow it to swing open a second later.

A security guard greeted them with a nod before escorting them through an airlock followed by several security checkpoints, which felt like a joke considering who he was dealing with. *If the humans really want to protect themselves from magic, they will need to learn a thing or two.*

Callaghan, who remained close by her side, whispered in her ear, 'This entire facility is lined with cold iron.' When she gave him a wide-eyed look, he shrugged. 'They must have unwittingly consulted a mage when designing it.'

Explains why the air feels so heavy in here. At first, she had put it down to the subterranean atmosphere.

As they entered a large boardroom, an elegant Mediterranean woman in a pantsuit greeted them. 'I am the secretary-general, Paraskevi Spyros. It is a pleasure to meet you all.' Following their own formal introductions, she explained, 'I will review the terms of this treaty with you all first before presenting it to the General Assembly. Please, take a seat.' She ushered them towards the oval table.

Hugh explained the goal of the treaty was to ensure a global improvement in the way humans treat the environment and talked through each clause in detail. 'We are more than happy to provide technical knowledge and financial aid wherever it is needed to ensure a mutually beneficial arrangement.'

Unlike in the movies, there was no grand introduction to the human world's most powerful politicians. Instead, the secretary-general left them waiting a couple of hours as the assembly debated the pros and cons of accepting the dragons' terms. When Spyros returned, her countenance had lightened. 'They majority voted in favour of accepting your treaty. I hope your treasuries are overflowing because there will be plenty of nations calling on your promised aid.'

'It is to be expected,' Hugh agreed as he shook her hand.

Watching the ink dry on the treaty, Alannah felt a weight lift from her shoulders and a smile reach her eyes. As her gaze lifted, she caught Callaghan staring at her and the air evacuated her lungs. Her expression sobered and she fidgeted under his scrutiny. It had been a long time since a man unnerved her the way he did, and she could not decide if she welcomed his interest. A ruckus outside the door drew their attention.

'The media are keen for a piece of you,' explained the secretary-general. 'I can send my guards to escort you out if you don't want to talk to them.'

'I think we can manage,' Callaghan assured them. 'Take my arm, Lady Winters,' he insisted as they rose from the conference table. 'To show a united front; and let me field the questions.'

After a moment's hesitation, she linked her arm with his and he led them out through the swarming journalists and their flickering camera flashes. The vultures descended, firing rapid-shot questions.

'What prompted the dragons to bring peace to the table?'

'Why did you keep the magic world hidden from us for so long?'

'Is it true that Lady Winters is the first female High Magus?'

'Why did you lift the veil when you did?'

Callaghan stopped for that one. 'I lifted the veil because I knew it would bring this peaceful resolution that we so desperately needed.' Just as more questions fired at him, he raised his hand to hush them. 'To answer a previous question, yes, Lady Winters here is the first female High Magus and I hope that one day she will become the first female Arch Mage, with me as her tutor.' He winked at her, and the crowd went wild.

Oh shit! Now the world will expect me to step up and fill his shoes at some stage.

'Lady Winters—how does it feel to receive such a glowing recommendation from the current Arch Mage?'

She looked at Callaghan and took his nod as permission to speak. 'It is a great honour. I will give it some serious consideration once my daughter grows up and leaves the nest.'

'Tell us about your daughter. Is it true that she's a Beltane baby?'

'Is there any truth to the rumours that you arranged her marriage to a faerie prince?'

Dear Gods! Where do they get all this intel?

Callaghan raised his hand to shield them off. 'No more questions, thank you.' He signalled to Hugh, who flanked her from the left and they hurried along the underground tunnel to another sealed door. 'I do believe this is cause for celebration, Lady Winters. Will you and Sir Doran join me for a drink?' Callaghan inquired.

She glanced at Hugh, hoping he would save her from an awkward situation.

'Certainly, if that is what Lady Winters desires.' Hugh's response did not help one bit.

Grinning, Callaghan leaned in close, his voice turning to gravel as he asked, 'And what *does* Lady Winters desire?'

'I really ought to be getting back.'

'Surely you can manage one drink?' Callaghan's voice entered her mind to add, '*There's no need to act so virtuous. I know your marriage is over.*'

The hairs on her neck bristled and something told her mentioning her other lovers was a bad idea, even if she did not drop any names. 'Thank you for the offer, but I must be getting home to my *daughter*,' she reminded him before taking Hugh's arm. 'Would you do me the honours, Sir Doran? I'd love to be the first female High Magus to fly on a dragon.'

'Certainly, Your Honour.'

Chapter Twenty-Five

Alannah gaped at the lush green landscape Hugh landed in, illuminated by a full moon and a twinkling blanket of stars. While she knew the Fleurieu Peninsula served as home to some spectacular spots, none of them could have equalled the rugged beauty of this foreign location. Instinctively, she knew where they were. Even if she had not seen images, the way her mana conduits resonated with the magic in the air told her she had returned home. Not the home she had grown up in or where she had bought her house, but her ancestral home. Alighting from Hugh's back, she slid from his golden scales, her boots hitting the ground with a thump. She whistled her awe and turned to him just in time to watch his glorious transformation. 'Not that I'm complaining, but why did you bring me to Ireland?'

'Because I asked him to,' Brendan's voice called from behind.

Turning, she ran into his arms. 'Gods, I missed you.'

'It feels so fucking good to hold you again, gorgeous.' He squeezed her in the tightest embrace.

Sensing another presence, she looked up and spied Caleb hovering behind Brendan. He gave her a sly grin. 'Hey, Lana.'

'Get your arse in here, Caleb.' She beckoned him into a group hug. As the three of them held each other, her heart swelled, and a contented sigh escaped her lungs. Her gaze lifted and she shifted her attention to the glimmering air in the distance. About a mile away, and up on a hill, stood a large structure that shimmered into focus as she pierced the glamour that had disguised it. 'Is that… a castle?'

'Yup,' Brendan replied with a massive grin. 'Welcome to Cailleach Castle, original home to the Winters Clan.'

She began wandering toward the building that housed centuries of family history, but Brendan grabbed her hand and tugged her back. 'We'll get to that. There's something else I want to show you first.' He led her along a trail that wound up towards a cliff. Caleb joined them, although Hugh remained in the field where they had landed. 'We wanted some time alone with you before your official welcome home and the spectacle that is sure to follow,' Brendan explained. 'I hope you realise that you're a big fucking hero all over the world now. Cara was going apeshit when she saw you on the news.'

'Sounds about right,' she replied with a laugh as they reached a small ring of standing stones overlooking the ocean. Waves crashed against the cliff face in a wild display of nature's fury. 'Wow! This place is spectacular. Thank you for—' Glancing over her shoulder, she lost her words when she spotted Brendan and Caleb both on the other side of a standing stone with a large hole through the middle, about a metre across. They both reached their hands through the hole, inviting her to join them with heated stares. Sucking in a breath, she stepped closer. 'Does this mean what I think it does?' Tears brimmed her eyes and her chest felt about ready to burst.

Brendan nodded. 'We both want you, Lana, in our bed and in our hearts. Forever.' He took Caleb's right hand with his left, and they both extended their spare hands toward her.

'I know you have your soul link, but that isn't something I can share,' Caleb added without the slightest hint of resentment. 'And I understand its importance with regards to the prophecy. This, however,' he raised Brendan's hand, 'is a way for the three of us to commit to one another. By joining hands here tonight, we propose to live a lifetime of love together, and if after a year and a day, we all still want this, we can confirm our commitment with a handfasting.'

This was far from how she had imagined her life with Brendan turning out, yet somehow it felt better. Caleb bought something to their relationship she never knew they were missing. 'Fuck! You guys are the absolute best. I love you both so much.' Reaching into the hole in the stone, she took both their hands. Energy sizzled around them as she closed her grip and sparks flowed between their bodies.

Brendan hissed. 'I am going to fuck you both so hard tonight.' He glanced at the ground in the centre of the standing stones and shook his head. 'We should get back to the castle before I desecrate this holy site.' Linking arms, the three of them half skipped, half stumbled toward the castle.

A woman with amber hair and a bright orange dress greeted them at the entrance. 'It is so good to meet you at last, my child. Welcome home.'

'Great Aunt Dana?' she queried with wide eyes.

'In the flesh. Please come inside. We have much catching up to do.'

Unable to rest after all the excitement, Alannah tossed and turned beside her two sleeping lovers. Dana had told them much about how she came to hold her mantle as Queen of the Cursed while also guiding Brendan to his seat at the head of the Syndicate. This gave the Winters Clan the advantage they needed against the Enemy. When Alannah had questioned her more on the identity and nature of this enemy, Dana had dismissed her line of inquiry with a warning. 'When you know who and what he is, he will come for you. When that happens, you must be ready for him. That means closing The Circle.'

Giving up on sleep entirely, she sat up and threw her legs over the edge of the enormous canopy bed. The delicious ache in her muscles reminded her of all the ways her men had violated her. Yet even having them fuck her senseless had not chased away her underlying anxiety. *Perhaps it has something to do with the hordes of cursed who also roam these halls.* She did not exactly have a great track record with vampires and such. Dana had assured her that none of them would harm her or her party. Even so, she could not help but shiver at the thought of so many blood-sucking fiends in close proximity.

Donning a fluffy robe and slippers, she traipsed down the hall. Halting, she gasped as a white shimmering figure appeared before her. As her eyes adjusted to the light, she focused on the face of her mother's smiling spirit.

'I am so, so proud of you, my child.'

'Mum?' A single tear slid down her cheek. 'What brings you to this realm?' Normally she needed to summon spirits through her Aether channel. 'And how?'

'I am a Winters, and this is our ancestral home. My soul is connected to it.'

'I bet you love what Aunt Dana's done with the place,' she scoffed.

Her mother shook her head. 'Since your grandmother joined me in the Celestial plane, I have come to understand why they did what they did. Come, there is something you must see.' Aileen Winters led her along a corridor of ancient stone until they reached a grand library.

'Holy shit! *Beauty and the Beast* eat your heart out.'

Aileen smiled. 'That was always your favourite movie as a kid.' She floated over to a shelf and gestured for her to inspect the contents. 'Nora

462

and I were both avid with our journaling back in the day. I think you will learn a lot from these.'

She retrieved two diaries, one blue and the other orange, each engraved with the Winters and Maher clan crests respectively. Dusting them off, she opened the blue one first and read the inscription:

> *Dearest Alannah,*
> *If you are reading this, it means I failed to hide you from the world of magic, but there is also a good chance you have grown into the powerful mage I know you are destined to become. Now is the time for you to learn about the identity of your real father, along with the story of how you came to exist.*
> *Love you always,*
> *Mum.*

She grinned up at her mother. 'I love you too. Fuck, I wish I could hug you right now.'

'I promise we will have a chance one day. Take care, my sweet girl.' Her mother vanished as quickly as she had appeared.

Sliding Aileen's diary behind the other, she opened the orange book and read Nora's neat cursive:

Dearest Brendan,

*If you are reading this, it means you have
found your way back to Alannah as I knew
you would. I understand why you left. You
needed to find the path to your destiny, and I
never doubted that you would become a
powerful mage. Now it is time for you to
learn about the identity of your real father,
along with the story of how you came to exist.
After everything you've been through, I trust
you won't judge me as harshly as Ross did.*

Love you always,
Mum.

'I knew it!'

'Doing a little late-night research?' Brendan
asked in a gravelly voice when he appeared in the
doorway.

Snapping Nora's journal shut, she peered
across the room and lost her train of thought as her
eyes drank in the sight of Brendan's naked body.
'Geez, babe, you'll catch a chill like that.'

'I'm plenty warm with you on my mind.' He
waggled his brows. 'You should come back to bed. I
know a great way to kill time if you can't sleep.'

'Actually, I think you should read this.' She handed him the orange volume.

'What is it?' His brows rose as he glanced at the familiar crest, then he gave her a questioning look.

'Your mother's diary.'

Brendan's hand jolted back, as if he had burnt himself on the journal. 'Why would I want to read Mum's diary? It probably contains personal shit I don't care to know about.' He stepped back, to avoid contact with it. Hell for all he knew, it might be like Pandora's box. Mages stowed secrets away in various locations for all sorts of reasons and diaries were one such place.

'Actually, she wants you to read it. There's even a note addressed to you at the front.' Alannah shoved the book in his face with the front page open.

With a sigh, he took it from her and read the note from his mum. A smile crept over his face at mention of Alannah, but it vanished the moment he realised he held an account of his mother's extramarital affair with another man. 'Holy fucking shit balls! Do you realise what this means, Lana?'

'That Ross isn't your father?' she suggested.

'Right, which means I'm not really a Winters. Well, probably not. We are yet to learn who my bio dad is. Fuck! I hope we don't have the same old man. That'd be real messed up.'

She chuckled. 'Could explain why we look so alike.'

He glared at her. 'Don't even joke about that.'

'We made a kid together, babe, and she turned out fine. I don't think there's anything to worry about.' Taking his arm, she led him to a plush chaise longue in a reading nook. 'May as well get comfy, right? I've got my own mum's diary here to read.'

Sitting down, he pulled her into his lap. 'She better not detail any sexcapades in here, else I might have to wash my eyes out with bleach.'

'You could just skim read those bits if you find any.'

He kissed her cheek and nodded. 'Right. That would be better than blinding myself because then I wouldn't be able to see your sexy arse.'

'Shit! How would you cope? You'd have to *feel* your way around.' She emphasised the word feel by grinding her backside into his groin.

He hissed as a wave of desire washed through him, building between his legs. 'Fuck, Lana. You're really not making this easy for me.'

'Well, I do love making things *hard* for you,' she retorted in a gruff voice that oozed sex.

'Right, that does it.' He bent her over the edge of the sofa. Lifting her robe, he revealed her bare core, dripping with lust. Smacking her arse cheek hard, he left a handprint and marvelled at the way her pussy flooded with need. Leaning in so that he could press his lips against her ear, he rasped, 'Fuck now, read later.' He buried himself inside her, holding for a moment before going brutally hard and without letting up. Within seconds she was clenching around his cock and her orgasms did not stop until he found his release.

They collapsed back onto the seat, and he snuggled into her.

'I love it when you take me quick and dirty like that,' she mused.

'I could tell by your vice grip on my dick. Now let's see what our mothers have to say about our real fathers.' He picked up the diaries that had fallen to the floor in their moment of passion and handed the blue one to Alannah. He soon lost himself in his mum's immersive storytelling. Nora's description of her lover both intrigued and unsettled him:

> *I told him that he ought to seek medical attention from a doctor or abjurer. As a vet and shaman, I was better equipped to help animals.*
>
> *'What if I told you I am a bit of an animal?' He winked and I couldn't help but laugh at his obvious flirting.*
>
> *'Not the sort of animal I mean,' I replied with a blush.*
>
> *'I love that your mind went there, darling, but I'm serious.' Grinning, he flashed a few sharp teeth and revealed a hefty tail, letting it swish about behind him. Then horns began protruding from his forehead.*
>
> *Gasping, I asked, 'What are you?'*
>
> *'I think you mean who? I've been known by many names. The Christians called me Satan. In the middle east, I'm known as Ahriman.'*
>
> *'You're a God?' I asked on a whisper.*
>
> *'That is how your kind refer to us, yes.'*

'Well shit! No wonder I'm such a badass.' He could hardly believe what he was reading, but deep down he felt the truth in his gut.

Alannah glanced up from her own book. 'Why's that?'

'My dad is the Lord of Darkness and Chaos. He's essentially the fucking Devil, Lana.'

Her jaw dropped. 'Like an actual God?'

He nodded. 'Wait! You don't suppose that line in the prophecy about being born of the Gods is meant to be taken literally?'

'Given the way Mum is describing my father, I wouldn't be surprised. Listen to this….' Raising the blue journal, she recited Aileen's words:

> *He stepped out of the smoky haze as if appearing from nowhere. Not a sound or shadow hinted at his approach. In the light of the fire, I drank in the sight of his symmetrical face and flawless body. Not even a sculptor could have carved such perfection. His beauty took my breath away and I barely registered the floral coronet on my head before he spoke.*
>
> *"As much as I appreciate your ogling, you still need to complete the ritual as a sign of your consent."'*

'Did I mention that I met him when I was in the lock-up?'

He cringed, recalling the circumstances that led to her family reunion in the Celestial Realm. 'Ah, yeah. You mentioned it in a conversation we had with Tara. Would you say your mother's description is accurate?'

'From what I remember, yes. Not that I saw him naked, thankfully. Let me keep studying this to see if I can learn his name.' Resting her head against his chest, she resumed reading.

After combing his fingers through her hair for a few minutes, he attempted to finish his own mother's diary, but his thoughts kept straying. *What does it mean to be direct descendants of Gods? Does that make us a new race? Or are we just uber mages? And what does it all mean for Neve?* The questions kept coming even as he skimmed the remaining pages.

'Here it is!' Alannah cried with excitement as she sat upright and read from the journal:

> *He introduced himself as Ruad before explaining that the child I carried was destined to become a powerful mage according to prophecy. Then he handed me an ancient book. 'She will lead the* In Circulo Elementa—*the world's most powerful coven—but only if you protect her identity from those who will seek to harm her.*

Unfortunately, she will have many enemies, even before her role in the prophecy comes to light.'

When I asked why, he replied, 'Many will see her sheer power as a threat.'

'How do you know all this? What makes you sure that our daughter will be this prophesied leader?'

'Because I wrote the prophecy. Take care of our dear child, Aileen. I will watch and guide her as much as possible, but there are limits to how much I can interfere with your realm.' He vanished before my eyes, leaving me gobsmacked.

Not wasting a second more, I settled into an armchair and read the old book he gave me. It was in Gaelic, so there were times I needed to reference a translation guide, yet I persisted until I understood every word and its significance. Learning that a God had chosen me as the mother of such an important figure blew my mind. I did a little extra research on the side, after discovering his full name was Ruad Rofhessa, and almost lost my mind when finding that he was more commonly known as The Dagda, the great father, king,

and druid, also the lord of great knowledge
among other epithets.'

He grinned at her. 'Explains why you're such a kickass mage and leader to boot. That passage also answers my question about whether or not we are still mages.'

'Huh. I never considered the possibility that we weren't. Makes sense though, that you would question it, I mean. If our fathers aren't creation Gods, how can we still be mages?'

'Hmm, maybe it has more to do with our mothers being bloodline mages. Plus, there's the whole doppelganger thing. I'd love to know what that has to do with the prophecy.'

'Fair point.' She rose to her feet, and her robe fell open, revealing her luscious curves. 'Let's see if we can find that old book on these shelves.'

'Okay, fine. Once we do, though, I'm taking you back to bed and fucking you senseless. Gotta get my Lana fix before we head back to Gaeilge Shores.'

Humour twinkled in her eyes. 'Are you saying I'm like a drug?'

'Yup. And I have no intention to ever get over you.'

Chapter Twenty-Six

6 Months Later

The only thing more horrifying than gathering all of Neve's acquaintances and family together in one place was adding her boyfriend's lot to the mix. Unfortunately, there was no escaping it on occasions such as these. Waiting in the wings, she watched her guests assemble in the Cailleach Estate ballroom. Gritting her teeth, she tried to focus on the positive side. *Today is the day I become officially engaged.*

Drawing up behind her, Erik gripped her shoulders. 'You feel tense. You're not having second thoughts, are you?'

'Not at all. It's all the people. Can we just elope when it comes time for the wedding?'

His deep chuckle rumbled in her ears and tickled her hot spots. 'Afraid not, sweetheart. You need to get used to crowds like this. When we marry, we will move to the Seelie Court and that place is like a party every night.'

'Yeah but at least they are *different* people. I can't wait to get out of this town, to move out of my mother's shadow.'

'And I can't wait to make you mine.' His hands drifted down her sides and crept inwards once they reached her pelvis, fingers curling into her chiffon dress.

Her skin turned hot all over. Date nights over the last six months had grown increasingly frustrating. She'd had a taste of what sex with Erik could be like and maintaining her restored virtue was driving her slowly mad. 'I don't know how I'll survive the next two years,' she rasped.

'I know exactly how you feel.' He nibbled at her neck, and she almost shattered in his arms.

'Ah, there you are!' Alannah pulled the curtain aside, revealing their hiding spot. She grinned at them. 'You make the cutest couple. Come and greet your guests.'

Stifling a groan, she had no choice but follow as her mum had grabbed her hand. 'Have you invited the whole town?'

'Just about,' her mum admitted. 'Events like this are a great morale boost during a time of rebuilding and healing after the war.'

'*Will Dad be here?*' she asked telepathically.

'*Yes, but he will glamour himself as Danny Erling.*'

She nodded her understanding, knowing the risk he took showing up at all. At least he would be there to support her.

As if his ears were burning, her dad waltzed through the door in full disguise. Glancing her way, he smiled and spoke in her mind as he approached: '*It's good to see you happy, princess, even if it's with my mortal enemy.*' When he reached them, he extended his hand to shake Erik's. 'Hey man, I'm Danny. Congrats on the engagement.'

'Thanks.' Erik cast his gaze over Brendan's glamoured form. 'It's creepy how much you look like Neve's father.'

Her dad laughed. 'Yeah, I get that a lot.'

A ruckus of dolphin squeaking near the door alerted her to another arrival.

'Oh look, it's Aquatic Man!' Bailey shouted with a snigger.

Liam strode past the welcoming committee, ignoring their jests and beelining for Neve.

'Uncle Liam? I wasn't expecting you.'

'As if I'd miss my girl's engagement party.' He pulled her into a hug. 'I'm super proud of you.'

'Um, thanks,' she replied, plucking a strand of seaweed from the hair that he had let grow long, and dropping it in a nearby bin.

'If we knew you were coming, we would have hired a fish tank,' her dad jibed.

She had to bite her tongue to hold back the laughter.

'It's probably *betta* that you didn't,' Liam retorted.

The group that had mustered around them fell silent and she blinked a few times.

'Really? Has no-one here even heard of a betta fish? I continue to be entirely wasted on the lot of you.' Liam shook his head.

She cleared her throat. 'So anyway, I'm glad you could make it.'

After an hour of welcoming people, she was about ready to retire for the evening even though it had barely started and that was before the Maher family arrived with Caitlin in tow.

Her ex best-friend surveyed her with a cold indifference before stepping forward with a stunning young lady on her arm; enlightened if the golden glow of her complexion was anything to go by. 'This is my girlfriend, Taneisha. She'll be starting at our school next term.'

'It is lovely to meet you, Neve,' Taneisha spoke in a haughty tone before glancing at Erik and nodding. 'Cousin.'

Her eyes widened as the significance of Caitlin's date sank in. She watched the couple sashay over to the bar, wondering if a betrothal was on the cards.

'Taneisha will make fierce competition for the crown, especially if Caitlin becomes her bride,' Erik whispered in her ear. 'When it comes to bitchiness, that girl makes Elna look like a saint.'

'Joy. Sounds like my last two years of high school will be a nightmare. I wish you were there for some emotional support.'

He gave her a wide grin that showed off his pearlescent teeth. 'I will be. I'm repeating my last two senior years.'

She gaped at him. 'Really? I thought you were doing with your schoolwork?'

'I am. I'll be doing different subjects for the hell of it. I figured it's the best way to maximise my time with you.'

'That's so sweet! Thank you, my love.' Rising up on tippy toes, she smacked a loud, sloppy kiss on his lips. Before she could move away, he sank his fingers into her hair and deepened the kiss. Losing herself in the moment, she barely registered the cheers and whistles from their audience. *This right here is perfection.* Grabbing a champagne flute from a nearby waiter, she called for a toast. 'Here's to a happily ever after with my faerie prince!'

Erik clinked his glass with hers, the crowd echoing his response. 'Cheers to that.'

6 Months Later

Glancing at her reflection in the dressing room mirror, Alannah cringed. She studied the elaborate blue embroidery on her white gown and felt the beginnings of a nervous breakdown set in. 'This is too much.'

'It's perfect,' Cara assured her. 'A dress fit for a queen—or the world's most powerful mage in your case. Your guys are gonna lose their minds.'

'I think they already have,' she replied with a laugh. 'Why else would they tie themselves to a Council official?'

'Because they're kinky fuckers?' Cara suggested.

She rolled her eyes. 'You know what I mean. We aren't going to get a lot of opportunities to spend time together in future.'

'That will just make your time together so much sweeter,' Cara replied with a wink. 'Come on, Your Honour. It's time to tie those knots.'

She followed her best friend through the corridors of her ancestral home—the hidden Cailleach Castle—until they reached a large room full of their nearest and dearest in raked seating with a wide aisle down the centre. The din in the room hushed as if the building itself drew a breath at the sight of her. She locked eyes with Brendan, who stood beside Caleb, both in jet black tuxedos with silver ties. Her heart skipped a beat when peering into his emerald orbs and she felt his rush of desire through their soul link. Shifting her gaze to Caleb, his beauty stole her breath. His silver skin shone with an iridescence to rival the moon and his sleek ebony mane caressed his broad shoulders. When she met his eyes, she read the promise of passion within their dark depths.

A delicate melody started on a Celtic harp and her desire for her two lovers carried her feet down the aisle. When she reached them, she took their hands in the same way as she had through the ringed stone one year and one day prior.

Brendan's voice entered her mind, '*Your dress is gorgeous, Lana. I can't wait to tear it off you later.*'

'*It's a good thing I don't plan to wear it again,*' she replied.

Tanya, Jaxon's wife, addressed the congregation, introducing herself as their celebrant. After the war, she had retired to the life of an acolyte. She had seen enough bloodshed to last a lifetime. 'Tonight, we assemble to secretly witness the lifetime commitment that Alannah Winters, Brendan Maher, and Caleb Hawthorn make to each other….'

It sounded strange to hear someone address Brendan formally since his recent name change. She understood why he did it, of course. With no blood ties to Ross, he felt free to cut all legal ties too.

'Do each of you promise to love one another, to respect each other's boundaries, and nurture the relationships you have built with honesty and compassion?'

The three of them replied, 'We do.'

'Now we come to the handfasting,' Tanya continued. She held a black ribbon above their hands. 'This thread binds the three of you together in a pure love. Together you are stronger for the gifts that each of you bring to this union.' She wrapped it around their wrists before producing a dark blue ribbon. 'This thread binds the three of you together in fidelity. Stay true to one another and your relationship will thrive.' The blue ribbon joined the black one, then she added the silver one. 'This thread binds the three of you together in protection of each other and your family unit. May the fervour of your love endure the challenges life throws your way. Alannah, Brendan, and Caleb — the three of you have made your commitment to each other before your friends and family and now you are bound to one another in love. May the Gods smile upon your union and fill your lives with happiness. Blessed be.'

'Blessed be.'

'Each of you may seal your union with a kiss,' Tanya finished with a knowing smile.

Alannah let Brendan and Caleb kiss first and she slipped into her voyeuristic headspace, enjoying the sight of her two lovers ravishing each other. Whistles and cheers reminded her of their audience just as Caleb came up for air and grabbed her. His eyes were wild with carnal need and his soft lips claimed hers with a finesse that reminded her of his skills elsewhere. A slight moan escaped her, granting access to Caleb's tongue. Imagining what else that tongue could do, she almost melted in a pile of goo. Brendan sucked in a breath, his own arousal flooding through her veins. Then he took Caleb's place, kissing her with such raw savagery that the contrast from Caleb's gentle touch sent her head spinning and her core gushing.

'*Fuck!*' Brendan spoke in her mind. '*I'm so damn hard, I could fuck you both right here and now.*'

She grinned against his lips. '*If there weren't kids present, I'd let you.*'

'Hot damn, woman!' he gasped as their mouths drew apart.

When they reached the dining hall for their reception, Monique gifted her with a lucky charm, embracing her as she whispered, 'Congrats, hun. I'm a little jealous of all the fun you'll be having later.' Stepping back, she fanned herself. 'That was way hotter than any wedding kiss I've seen before.'

Brendan snaked his arm around Alannah's shoulders. 'Of course it was; with me in the mix this time.'

Monique chuckled. 'Maybe Caleb was the missing ingredient.'

'You got a thing for Thornsy now? I'm sad that your crush on me has waned, Mon.' He gave her a melodramatic pout and Alannah joined her friend's laughter.

Steve shook Brendan's hand. 'Hey Cuz, it's good to see you settling down at last. Aunt Nora would be proud of you.'

'Cheers, bud.' Brendan's wave of grief resonated through Alannah's soul and cinched at her heart. 'Thanks for coming. I think you'll enjoy the meal. We sourced the best steak and salmon in Ireland.'

Silver chimed against crystal, and they all looked to where Dana stood at the end of the banquet table. 'If you could all charge your glasses and find your seats, I have a few words before we begin eating.'

Brendan helped Alannah into an ornately carved chair that would have looked at home in a medieval museum.

'Thank you all for coming,' Dana continued, 'to celebrate the union of my great niece and her two handsome men. Of course, I mean great in just about every sense of the word. I think you will all agree that Alannah has exceeded everyone's expectations as a powerful mage and an excellent leader. I have a feeling we've seen just the tip of the iceberg. I'd also like to thank all of you for putting your fears and preconceptions of the cursed and the Syndicate aside. The fact that we can all feast here together fills me with hope. Please raise your glasses; I'd like to propose a toast for a future full of love and harmony.'

Lifting her glass, Alannah joined the chorus, 'To the future.'

Squeezing her leg, Brendan asked telepathically, '*You gonna tell them*?'

Nodding, she cleared her throat and clinked a spoon against her glass. Once all eyes focussed on her and the murmurs hushed, she smiled. 'Thank you, Aunt Dana, for those lovely words. I'd also like to commend you all for your compassion and understanding. Having you all here to support us warms my heart. I have some news I wish to share.' She took a deep breath. 'In a few years, once my beautiful daughter has settled down with Erik, I will be leaving Australia.' She let the gasps settle before continuing, 'When this time comes, I will be resigning as High Magus and putting forth my recommendation for Monique Lane to step up.'

Monique's eyes bugged out. 'I'm honoured, but why are you leaving?'

'Because....' Alannah sipped some water to ease her dry throat. 'I will be attending the Arch Mage Academy.'

The room fell silent as they all gaped at her a moment before erupting with applause. An excited buzz filled the air as their meals came out and an evening of merriment followed. After hours of dancing, she returned to her seat to rest her aching feet and enjoy another glass of bubbly. Brendan and Caleb soon joined her, taking their places either side of her.

Leaning in close, Brendan rasped in her ear, 'Just say the word, gorgeous, and we'll retire to the bedroom.'

She could not stifle the grin as she imagined the sweet mix of pleasure and pain she would soon experience. 'In a bit. I just want to take in the scene first.' Surveying the party, she registered every smiling face and the reasons for their joy. Neve and Erik looked as happy as ever, reassuring her of the deal she had struck when signing their betrothal contract. Caitlin and Taneisha made a great couple, and she suspected another engagement party was on the horizon. Jacob made the perfect addition to Amy and Connor's relationship.

'Looks like your Melbourne friends are getting lucky tonight,' Caleb observed.

He was not wrong. Melissa was getting mighty cosy with Shane and Emma could not keep her hands off Danny. At least they knew not to expect anything long-term from Danny. He had his own date with destiny. 'Have you guys noticed the sparks flying between Hugh and Bianca?' she asked.

'Yup,' Brendan replied. 'I'm curious to know how that turns out. Bianca's a flighty little nymph.'

She shrugged. 'I reckon Hugh's determined enough to make it work.'

Tyler and Samantha approached them with their hands linked. 'Awesome shindig,' Tyler remarked. 'We're gonna go make use of the wicked digs, if you catch my drift.' He emphasised his point with a brow waggle.

'Good thinking.' She slid her hands along her lovers' thighs. 'We won't be far behind you.'

'Have fun,' added Sam. 'Oh, and Lana? If your guys flake early, you know where to find us.' With a wink, she turned and left the room, Tyler smacking her backside on the way out.

'You know she's dreaming right?' Brendan's gruff voice stoked the flames of arousal in her core. 'There's no way any of us are getting any sleep tonight. You can expect a repeat of Beltane, only with the addition of Thornsy's sexy arse.'

'What are we waiting for, then?' Rising to her feet, she let Brendan lead her back to their room where he and Caleb fulfilled every dark promise their heated gazes had made throughout the evening.

3 Years Later

Scalding water blistered Ross's skin as he scrubbed away the filth. Yet no matter how hard he tried; he could not wipe away the feeling clawing his heart. Getting the love of his life killed may have come close, but this topped the list of messed up shit he had done in the name of duty. At least Nora's death did not end with her literal blood on his hands. *There was no blood*, he reminded himself. His phone started ringing, startling him, and he cursed under his breath when the boss's name appeared on the screen.

'Is it done yet?' his master demanded.

'Yes, sir. Although, I need to know why her? Why such a young innocent?' Never mind the blood ties he shared with the baby: that meant nothing to such a brutal man.

'That child was born a seer and given her parentage; she would have come into her magic well before adolescence without needing initiation. I could not risk her revealing the other coven members to Alannah. Remember, The Circle must not be completed.'

'Or we're all doomed. I know,' he replied with a sigh. 'I just wished there was another way.'

'You better not be getting soft on me now, Winters. The time may come when you'll have to kill the boy you raised as your own.'

'Honestly, I would have preferred that to infanticide. Why *is* Brendan still living and breathing?'

'Because like the other Circle members, I have greater use for him alive than dead. They are all powerful mages in their own right. So long as they don't all come together, I can use their magic. Killing Brendan will only ever be a last resort.'

To be continued

What's Next?

Thank you for reading **Winter's Mother 2**. I would be most grateful if you could show your support by leaving a rating or even a review.

If you are game to read about Neve's disastrous marriage, check out *Winter's Bride*. Release date TBA.

Trigger Warning *Winter's Bride* is a dark paranormal romance with depictions of domestic abuse. It also includes graphic sexual content, incest scenes, and dark themes. Feel free to skip ahead to *Winter's Crone 1*, the next main entry in the series, if such matters are likely to offend or be a psychological trigger.

Alannah and Brendan's story will continue in *Winter's Crone 1*, release date TBA.

Bonus Content

Would you like to read a cute little deleted scene in Luna the cat's perspective? Subscribe to my newsletter and grab a copy from the Freebies page at www.starlaarts.com.

Acknowledgements

Firstly, I would like to thank you, my beautiful readers, for your patience. I know this has been a tortuous wait after the cliff-hanger I left you with in the previous book. My writing pace has slowed down considerably now that I have returned to full-time work in the corporate world. On the plus side, I love my new job and welcome some of my colleagues into my readership. You guys are awesome!

I am also excited about my very first Kickstarter campaign. Within 10 days of launching the hard-cover omnibus special edition of *Winter's Maiden*, the Season 1 collection, I was 100% funded. This is great news for my fans because it means I will be returning to this crowd-funding platform with a follow-up special edition of the second season. That's right, Winter's Mother 1, 2 and Bride, will all appear in one big collector's volume with a bunch of exclusive content, so please keep an eye

ACKNOWLEDGEMENTS

out on my social media for this in future. And if you missed grabbing Season 1, you'll get another chance when this campaign goes live.

My thanks goes out to the usual suspects: Jana Hoffmann (www.janahoffmann.com) who continues to deliver beautiful illustrations for covers of this series, Felix Staica for his excellent editing efforts, and Priyanka Mukherjee for her amazing work as my personal/virtual assistant.

I have a couple of beta readers to thank: Joshua Wake, who suffered through my drip-feeding of chapters, and Elli Morgan who was an absolute champ about cramming this in at the last minute.

And a big shout out to my street team! Your reviews make a huge difference to the success of my books.

The Winter's Magic Series

A modern fantasy and paranormal romance about secrets, mysticism, empowerment, and the complexities of love.

Winter's Maiden 1
Winter's Maiden 2
Winter's Thrall
Winter's Mother 1
Winter's Mother 2
Winter's Bride (TBA)
Winter's Crone 1 (TBA)
Winter's Crone 2 (TBA)

Winter's Bride

If your faerie prince seems too good to be true, he is.

To the casual observer, Neve Winters had it made: all the money she could want, a place in the Seelie Court, and the love of a gorgeous man. Yet in a world full of magic and glamour, looks are always deceiving.

Claimed by Erik Alvarsson at the tender age of fifteen, Neve was too young to understand the ramifications of her fatal attraction. Even on her wedding day, three years later, she was blind to her husband's rotten core and his coercive ways.

It takes an unlikely friend to shed some light on Erik's abuse. When the curtains are pulled back on her marriage, Neve has an opportunity to escape. But will she have the courage to leave him? And will she give an old flame a second chance?

Note: This spin-off in the *Winter's Magic* series tells Neve's story following the events of *Winter's Mother 2*.

Warning: This book contains coarse language and explicit scenes, including depictions of graphic sex scenes, incest, and domestic abuse that may upset or offend some readers.

Winter's Crone 1

Knowledge brings power, but too much of either can be deadly.

In her attempts to find the final members of the world's most powerful coven, Alannah stumbles upon the secrets that her grandmother had warned her about. But she is not ready to face the ultimate truth; none of them are.

Armed with this knowledge, Alannah's search becomes urgent, and the need to hide her covert operation more critical. But how will she gather her forces in time when she can no longer trust her closest friends, let alone her family?

Note: This is the fifth of six main books in the *Winter's Magic* series. It is advisable to start with *Winter's Maiden 1*.

Warning: This book contains coarse language and explicit scenes that may upset or offend some readers. It also ends on a cliff-hanger.

Also By L. Starla

The Phoebe Braddock Books
(Taboo Romance & Forbidden Love)

I Heart Mr. Collins
From Prying Eyes
Crystal's Crucible
Undeniably Wrong
Book #5 to be Announced

Serial Fiction Boxsets

Well I'll Be Damned Season 1
The Dark Matter Between Our Hearts Season 1

About the Author

L. Starla is an Australian author who often raided her mother's shelves for any form of fiction she could get her hands on. Her first love was the horror genre, but she owes her love affair with the romance novel to her high-school English teacher, who started her on the classics. Given her earlier reading, magical realism and paranormal romance were a natural progression. Along with steamy romance, these are the genres she writes.

Starla also loves spending her spare time playing tabletop and video games, paper crafting, singing, dancing, and watching anime.

Access Exclusive Content

Join my newsletter to access free stuff like short stories, deleted scenes, and invitations to special events.

Newsletter: www.starlaarts.com>freebies
Facebook Group: groups/l.starlareadersgroup

Follow me Online:
Website & Blog: www.starlaarts.com
Goodreads: L. Starla
BookBub: www.bookbub.com/profile/l-starla
Amazon Author Profile: author/l.starla
Instagram: L. Starla Author
Facebook: L.Starla
Kickstarter: Laelia Starla

www.ingramcontent.com/pod-product-compliance
Lightning Source LLC
Chambersburg PA
CBHW070150120726
47909CB00001B/54